Nick Ashton-Jones is a farmer, an environmentalist, a writer who cannot help himself, a psycho geographer and historian. He has spent most of his working life in the tropics: in the South Pacific and in Southeast Asia, but mostly in Nigeria which is his second home, if not his first. Nick was born in Sheffield, has a son who is Swiss, and is based in Derby. He thinks the best bit of Britain is the Isle of Arran, and he shares his life with his partner, David, an artist and illustrator.

Dedicated to Susi Arnott, with love.

Nick Ashton-Jones

BOOKS PEOPLE DISCARD

Copyright © Nick Ashton-Jones

The right of Nick Ashton-Jones to be identified as author of this work has been asserted by him in accordance with section 77 and 78 of the Copyright, Designs and Patents Act 1988.

All rights reserved. No part of this publication may be reproduced, stored in a retrieval system, or transmitted in any form or by any means, electronic, mechanical, photocopying, recording, or otherwise, without the prior permission of the publishers.

Any person who commits any unauthorized act in relation to this publication may be liable to criminal prosecution and civil claims for damages.

A CIP catalogue record for this title is available from the British Library.

ISBN 978 184963 426 7

www.austinmacauley.com

First Published (2014)
Austin Macauley Publishers Ltd.
25 Canada Square
Canary Wharf
London
E14 5LB

Printed and bound in Great Britain

Contents

PART ONE

1	But It is not what It seems	**13**
2	David and Sally Leave England	**16**
3	David and Sally Meet Harry	**23**
4	Delightful Intercourse	**36**
5	Another Music	**45**
6	A Tangled Web Woven	**57**
7	Sleep Now, Sleep	**71**
8	Falling Over a Precipice	**84**
9	Where We Exterminate Each Other	**96**
10	The Suppliant Hand	**114**

PART TWO

11	The London Books	**123**
12	The Londoners	**136**
13	At a Hotel	**142**
14	A Great Wave	**169**
15	A Well Kept Lawn	**180**
16	The Start of a Family	**190**
17	And the End of Another	**200**
18	Via the Hotel	**206**

PART THREE

19	To the Beach	**220**
20	Mac (with respect to John Dos Pasos)	**225**
21	Steppenwolf	**240**
22	Sally Finds Her Man	**256**
23	Mother of Exiles	**263**
24	Groping After It	**281**
25	The Voice of Kindness	**288**
26	But There is no Need to Hand it On	**297**
27	I Dreamed I was Dancing (David)	**309**
28	Wanei, and, at any rate, Sons	**314**
29	Sally	**320**
30	Alice	**331**
31	And Sonia	**335**

PART ONE

1   But It is not what It seems

"You can take those," she shouted, as if the idea had only just occurred to her. "I was going to give them to the club."

She had made up the box especially for him, selecting the books she wanted him to think she read. She had read them, a lot of them, some of them, most were David's. Hers were the historical novels, the Hollywood memoirs, the things she had bought at airports and from the newsagents in town which didn't know any better. I'm not ashamed of what I read. You have to read something. David always seemed to have a solid nineteenth-century novel with him: a Penguin Classic of some sort. I read what was going, in those days.

The Somerset Maugham short stories had been going in Hong Kong, where they were stuck for six hours waiting for the connection to Port Markham. She read through the lot, almost without a break, annoyed when David pushed the book up into her face to see what was keeping her so uninterested in him. Oh, those things, he said. She ignored him.

The idea was that I'd read it again on the way back to England. Somerset Maugham keeps me sane. She had said it at the club as a thing she had wanted to say. But somehow it got into the box for Harry instead of into my travelling bag. I mustn't forget it. She had forgotten it, so it was the first thing Harry saw as he carried the box away.

Oh, those things, he thought, shouting over his shoulder. "You can keep these," and he dropped the book onto the lawn.

It was supposed to be a joke but it lay discarded, inoffensively enough, open at a page stayed by a few drops of rain, a passing cloud. Clara picked it up later. She read a few sentences but decided she would take it to the man who sold second-hand books outside the supermarket, laying them out flat on a piece of plastic: *This is My Testament*, *O Level Geography*, *The Picture of Dorian Gray*. He might give her something for it.

Prynne was the manager of the rubber estate up the river and now and then they spent the night with him. Sometimes when he wanted a change he came down to dinner and slept at the DO's bungalow. They both liked him. He was a man of five-and-thirty, with a red face, with deep furrows in it, and very black hair. He was quite uneducated, but cheerful and easy, and being the only Englishman within two days' journey they could not but be friendly with him. He had been a little shy at first.

The Door of Opportunity, by W Somerset Maugham.

Harry had come to say goodbye. She knew he would, so when she saw him ambling up the garden path in his clumsy way, brushing the hibiscus hedge, she rushed into the bedroom, shouting to him, standing, she imagined, awkward, on the veranda.

"Wait a minute, Harry, I'll be with you," pretending she was busy. "Sit down Darling," as she wiped a little of the sweat and dust from her face.

She called to Clara, "Please give Mr Harry his coffee." She said it in a way that suggested Clara was a darling too because it was how she treated the house staff who adored her, despite her making them use the back door. They had their own lavatory as well: a pit latrine hidden in the shrubbery behind the kitchen.

She decided she would be young, happy and adorable. A bit silly, ready to give him the greatest and most precious thing she had to give: a little of her time. There he would be, large and gawky in the rattan armchair which was too small for his sprawling limbs. She would rush at him, breathless, catching him off guard so he'd stammer a little in that sweet way he had and then be speechless for a moment, forcing him to look at her, flushed and a bit untidy, so he would remember her that way, forever. The memory would brighten the routine of his days for the rest of his life. He would realise he was not really good enough for her but that knowing her, knowing them both, had made him better all the same and he would be grateful. She would sit opposite him, leaning forward towards him, her hands on her knees so that he might, if he wanted, take them in his long, brown, bony hands, with the golden hairs on the back. If he did she would just look into his eyes for three or four seconds, squeeze a little and say.

"David ... " So that it was clear she was a loyal wife.

They would both let go at this point and she would talk sensibly but with a tiny catch in her voice. She would tell him that he was one of the family and wouldn't it be lovely for him to be godfather to their first child, if God ... etc., etc., etc. Only that was the problem, God had done whatever it was He had wanted to do and it was all a bit embarrassing. Better for Harry not to know at all. What would he think of her? What would he think of Wanei? She could deal with David. She had dealt with him already but Harry might have laughed.

"Are these books for me?" He called from the veranda.

"Yes."

"Thanks."

She went out but he had gone.

"You're welcome," she said to the thin air.

2 David and Sally Leave England

Ever since Sally could remember, they had taken in student lodgers. A father in the household, there had never been. Just Mummy and herself. And the ever-changing cast of students.

The two women were more like sisters really, sharing the back bedroom with the view over the little garden, the recreation ground, the poplar trees and the endless fens beyond. Often, as a child, Sally had stared at that view, kneeling on her bed, elbows on the window sill, face pressed against the glass. The Fens were the world, stretching out to the sky and beyond. Sometimes, she could not resist the idea of a shadow passing over, like a large, dark, swooping bird from which she would want to duck. She would cover her head with her arms as if to protect herself while knowing it did not exist and wanting to look at it at the same time. She was more fascinated than afraid.

The big front bedroom with the bay window was taken by two students. Another occupied the little room above the front door. The three of them shared the front living room where they were served a hearty English breakfast and a frugal but well-prepared dinner at half past seven sharp. Men were supposed to be out during the day, otherwise tolerated only if they were very quiet. The house was run as a quiet house.

There was no shortage of takers for the rooms in the university town. Sally's mother could afford to be selective. She was. Quiet, studious types were preferred. Nice boys.

Definitely not girls. Girls would forever want to do bits of washing and would even want to invade the kitchen. It had been tried: it had failed. The two girls in question – brainy types from the North – wanted to be intimate and chummy with the mother and daughter. They had wanted to recruit them into the world of women freed from men. Worse, they had wanted to know the mother and the daughter; they had asked questions. They went.

Anyway, Sally and her mother liked men. It was men against whom they defined themselves. It was only men whom they could serve day after day because in exchange they were treated as ladies. Sally's mother demanded a sort of medieval chivalry from the men who were her lodgers. They gave it willingly because in return she treated them like the sort of men to whom women seem to defer. And, she provided very comfortable lodgings. She became well known for it. Mrs Grant is a lady, you are lucky to have rooms there.

Sally's mother was the type of woman who could fill the house just by having a headache, or, as easily, disappear into a corner. In those days she was still young and, like her daughter, attractive in a slightly dishevelled way that hid the smudged features and eyes that were often focused elsewhere. She could give the impression of being intensely interested in you while her mind was actually miles away. It was quite clever. She had a neat and active figure that distracted some men.

The general impression of the house was that it was run in an anarchic manner by a gentlewoman who, by force of unhappy circumstance, had fallen on hard times. Sally's mother would hint at – and there were things around that suggested – an unfortunate young widow forced out of her country home by ruinous death duties and the debts of the dashing, much-loved but irresponsibly spend-thrift deceased partner. No questions were to be asked; it was too painful but life must go on; one must remain cheerful. After all, other people were in worse positions and this was rather a lark.

Nonetheless, despite the apparent anarchy and slightly aristocratic indifference of the matriarch, the house was decorated tastefully in pastel colours to set off chintz and nineteenth-century watercolours. Vases of flowers and 'intelligent' books lay around. Sheets were changed, rooms cleaned and windows polished to rainbow brilliance regularly. The bathroom was never less than spotless and the food never less than well cooked and predictably English.

'Better than my mother's, Mrs Grant'.

'Thank you, Mr Whoever-you-are, and so it ought to be unless your mother is the Queen of England'.

All this, it was given to believe, was the natural result of 900 years of good breeding.

In fact, the house was run along the lines of a good West End theatre. The front room, reminiscent of an English country house drawing room, might well have been the setting of one of Somerset Maugham's or Noël Coward's plays. It was. The purposefully neglected back garden, with its apple trees, a corner of the Cherry Orchard, before it was cut down. The tiny front garden was packed with roses of which the Queen Mother would have been proud, and the sit-up-and-beg Ford Popular, straight out of... an Ealing comedy.

Sally never questioned the setup. Not born to it exactly but too young to comprehensively remember the move from the smelly room above the butcher's shop in North London. It was her life, she enjoyed it and she fell in with her mother because she was happy. She was as much a born actress after all. She took what life brought and made the best of it. She liked the view of the fens but she did not want to go there. Not yet, at any rate, and there was always the fascinating idea of the dark swooping bird.

Early on, when Mrs Grant was still casting around for the right plot, there had been a non-student lodger who was respectfully known by the little girl Sally as Mr Prynne. He was a large, silent, black-haired and healthy outdoor man who managed a market garden nearby. He was younger than Mrs Grant but he seemed old to Sally who, as a nine or ten year old, would sit on the kitchen floor – cool, mottled-blue linoleum – in order to watch Mr Prynne put on his boots in the morning and take them off in the evening. She did not know it was rude to stare: she was fascinated by the spectacle of his large hairy hands working his large woolly socked feet. The naturally ruddy nature of Mr Prynne's face would burn. He was a shy, good-natured man so he said nothing. Sally was drawn to him; her mother noticed.

Mr Prynne went, the rudeness of staring was explained, the economic necessity of providing nice accommodation for nice, well-spoken people – unlike Mr Prynne who spoke with a broad Fenland accent – was impressed upon the young Sally, and the household became more the English upper-ish middle-class setting that we know. Mrs Grant was good with Sally: she was not the imposing mother but much rather the conniving sister. Us two against the world and all that. It was a good idea, it worked and Sally fell in with it. Nonetheless, the bird swooped from time to time. It swooped about the time Sally began to realise she could be attractive to men. This was when a beautiful dark-skinned Indian was in residence for a couple of terms. Sally regretted his departure but then David Pryce-Williams appeared, about the time Sally left school and was wondering what to do with two 'A' levels. The idea of an independent existence of some sort did not cross her mind.

David believed Mrs Grant's setup as he would have believed the theatre. Not because he was completely taken in but because he saw it as the setting he wanted for his life. The difference was, he wanted it for real and he knew he was clever enough to get it. He was a bit better off than the usual student. Enough to take the whole front bedroom for himself, which he tactfully and subtly remoulded to give the impression of a gentleman's study. He wore a smoking jacket in the evening and he occasionally smoked a cigar in the garden after dinner. It ought to have seemed pretentious in one so young but he carried it off well because he believed in it. He had a forceful nature which impressed the two women.

David Pryce-Williams was a handsome, fair young man, square and well built, with a voice that barked commands even when it used the conventionally polite terms. 'Be so kind as to do this or that for me'. 'Thank you ever so much', stressing the *ever* as if he would never forget you or the deed all his life. He was the type that played rugby in the winter and tennis in the summer. Not because he liked it much but because it kept him fit. He liked the male camaraderie; the opportunity to push and shove with men; to drink with them in the bar; to say silly things and look them in the eye.

David compared well with the other lodger, the one who had the little room. A doctor's son and a medical student, he was studious and shy, subject to long hair, spots and no idea how to dress. Nonetheless, he had good manners and was no trouble, his father paying a term's rent in advance directly into Mrs Grant's account. He would sit at the dining table in awe of David. He would clear the table in the evenings while David wandered into the garden for a cigar. He did David's shopping for him when he did his own. Like the two women, he fell for David's healthy good looks, and as a result found David's commanding nature equally attractive. His brief part in the play was to make David look good. He'd have got good reviews.

[][][]

What surprised Sally as she set about her part of being David's wife, was that she felt no regret upon leaving the house in which she had spent the past fifteen years or so.

As they drove down to London she tried to think of her mother. She could not even picture her face. She did remember that at the wedding her mother had worn a nice light, waisted coat and matching yellow turban-like sort of hat. She had looked a bit like Anna Neagle: well maintained but no doubt about her age.

"As soon as you've settled, Darling, I'll come down. We can meet for lunch and do some shopping. Such fun!"

"Yes Mummy".

She hadn't and they didn't. In the end, neither cared a jot about the other. It was a relief.

David and Sally had barely got into the tiny flat in the Earls Court end of South Kensington before David's company sent him out to New Sudan in the South Pacific. It was a large trading and plantation company. Not what it had been before the war, but illustrious all the same and David was proud to have got a job with it. He worked in the Estates Department, his degree in Oriental History and Languages deemed appropriate for some reason. He quickly grasped that his job was purely administrative: something to be done, organised, and then passed on to someone else. A local man could do the job more cheaply, he had explained to one of the London directors who was making a tour of inspection. What had eluded everyone else was obvious to David. He was promoted to Estates Manager.

This meant he had to administer all the company's New Sudan estates from the capital, Port Markham. Markham was a port at the head of the highway that led into the interior. It was a pleasant place in those days, exuberantly green with spectacular coastal scenery. As he explained to Sally.

"We're lucky to be here."

The job was routine but the way of life which went with it was attractive to people of David's and Sally's type. They lived in a romantic old bungalow in a large tropical garden in a tree-lined street. They had a driver, a garden-boy and a house-girl.

The 'girl' was over forty with half a dozen children already. She disliked her new charges but she could act as well as Sally, playing the faithful old retainer, Clara, superbly. She knew how to do everything perfectly but deliberately spotted Sally's clothes with bleach and disarranged David's shaving things every morning. She could serve at dinner parties as well as the next person but dropped things, brought them in cold and forgot to clear away properly with such smiling charm that she was never asked to do it again. She sincerely approved when Sally stopped playing the formal hostess and moved on to curry buffets and help-yourself drinks like everyone else. Then, she was happy to wash up and put away properly. It was her gift to Sally.

The job involved a great deal of travel around the interesting country. Sally was allowed to accompany David on the less arduous trips. Although left on her own she was quite happy to spend her days with the other ladies of leisure around swimming pools, or on verandas, discussing the shortcomings of the servants. She was the ideal company wife. She was attractive, entertaining, intelligent, but not too clever. Well bred, or, at any rate, able to act it; jolly to have around but not silly; and she seemed to have not one single original idea in her head.

Mr and Mrs David Pryce-Williams enjoyed playing the old colonial life and they enjoyed acting at being grown-up. They found the planet upon which they had landed easy and entertaining. Life would go on in much the same pleasant way for ever. The scenery would change, of course: first, a tiny house in a good part of London, when David was promoted to the Board; then, when children came along, something large and comfortable – probably Victorian – in one of the better suburbs from which David would catch the train into town each day. Good boarding schools for the children and a country cottage for the weekends, perhaps in France. The latter would become the retirement home. People would envy the Pryce-Williamses: such a nice family.

3   David and Sally Meet Harry

Harry was a planter. Not working for the same company as David but for a much rougher outfit. One which did not have an Estates Manager or a very impressive structure at all. Instead, it had a cynical old accountant, Mac, who had – it was his answer to everything – seen it all. He kept the books in Markham, organised the sales and was the contact with the Board in Sydney, which felt it had somehow been lumbered with something it did not want.

Harry's company – Mac really – got its expatriate plantation managers in New Sudan: there were plenty of men who did not want to go home for some reason. So long as they could do the job and proved honest enough in their dealings with the company, they would do.

Harry was about average in terms of humanity as a whole but a little above it in terms of the company. He had an agricultural degree and he was an honest, competent and even, on rare occasions, imaginative manager. He found the copra and cocoa plantation – with some grubby, hump-backed Brahmin cattle on the rougher ground – easy to run and the salary sufficient for his needs. He liked the life. He liked being on his own; he liked working with his men; he liked the quiet of the nights and the long walks under the moon; he liked the worn-out, hot, lazy feel of the plantation in the sun-bleached middays; he loved the roaring rains of the wet season when a wall of black water swept the country, isolating him in the old bungalow. But above all, he loved the lack of contact with other Europeans. His monthly trips to town were the only times he had any contact with them; most times, the only white man he talked to was Mac, the only one, apparently, who understood him.

Harry's plantation was about twenty miles down the coast. Access was via a rough road that Harry himself maintained.

Sometimes the beach became the road. It was impassable at the height of the wet season.

When Harry met David and Sally, he was 32. He was 33 when David was transferred back to London. So he was always a bit older than them.

They met at the Port Markham Club. Not what it had been: anyone could join these days, so long as you could pay the fees. Thus the more undesirable elements were kept out. Some of the companies paid for their senior staff, David's amongst them. Harry paid his own fees. It was a convenient place for him to stay in Markham because it had a few simple bedrooms and you could get something to eat.

The club had been rebuilt after the Japanese occupation but it maintained an atmosphere of old colonial leisure, with wide verandas, humming fans and lots of servants dressed in spotless lap-laps and white shirts. Situated at the head of the golf course, there was a stunning view out to sea towards a mountainous headland and the distant volcanoes of the Van islands. It impressed David and Sally, indeed anyone who had not seen that sort of thing before. Harry took it for granted; he could remember when the golf course had been the airstrip. He liked the seediness of the place.

[][][]

Even hardened and determined bachelors, tough, antisocial types such as Harry and Mac, have to eat somewhere, and Mac reckoned that Nosh Nite at the club, on a Friday evening, was the best investment in nutritional and calorific intake there was around. The women members, mostly expatriates – and by some sort of rotation in groups, which no one fully understood – cooked a big buffet meal for everyone else. Plenty of servants to do the washing up. For this great big feed and no effort, you paid about two dollars. That is, the same as the daily wage for one of the servants who did the washing up. It had been started by some interfering woman, tired of her husband's Friday night beer binges, with the idea that the massive weekend intake of alcohol would somehow be reduced by the food. The idea had caught on and become a holy club tradition amongst the expatriate population of Port Markham. Indeed, those expatriates who did not attend were considered rather beyond the pale, if not traitors to their race. Generally, the men stayed around the bar, the women hung around the food and then the lounge area, the children made a noise on the veranda and, in the school holidays, the adolescents sulked on the golf course or otherwise worked on their carnal knowledge where ever they could. Alcohol intake by both males and females had never been higher, enhanced by the introduction of a pre-Nosh Happy Hour about the time David and Sally arrived.

Nosh Nite at the Port Markham Club then. Mac and Harry sitting at a small table, apparently silently disgusted by the domestic dramas going on all around but eating a good meal all the same. Beer stubbies and elbows on a red and white chequered cloth.

Sally and David enter: fixed smiles. As if, as if absolutely at ease, they weave their way around groups of humanity. They are evidently spoilt by the demanding choice of upon whom to bestow the favour of their convivial presence. Usual balancing act of plate – macaroni cheese, baked beans, sausage roll and mashed potato – gin and tonic in tumbler, knife and fork, red paper napkin. Find themselves in zone of local members – oh, so difficult to know what to do – see Mac and Harry, white males, zoom in, sit. 'Mind if we join you? Favour you old ruffians with our educated, cosmopolitan and cultured presence?' Harry smiles; seems to suggest it's a pleasure to be visited by two such exalted and heavenly personages. Mac shuffles to one side recognising, just in time, that their (fucking?) right to exist more or less equals his own. David satisfactorily establishes to himself that they have landed on inferior planet where natives friendly but may become embarrassingly deferential. These little green men will, he knows, benefit from our, at any rate, my, educated presence. Sally follows lead. For all she is a superior being beneath whose feet we are barely worthy of being trodden, she is a delightfully chatty sweetie really and they must not bow down on bended knee; or if they do, it must not be too embarrassingly obvious.

Thinks David, 'She is getting quite good at this enhancement of my towering personality.' Looks at her for five seconds – anyway, three. Gratitude beats in English breast – Port Talbot way, 'Thank God I found her: every appearance of the upper-ish middle classes and cheap at the price'. Gratitude spreads to himself.

He looks at Harry. Then he looks at Mac in relation to Harry, and he dismisses Mac as a broken-down old drunk; as detritus that the receding tide of colonialism, he says to himself, has forgotten upon the abandoned beach of empire. This is because the Macs of the world frighten David. They are, apparently, independent types, also isolated, like himself, but isolated by choice – some choice, at any rate – rather than by emotional deficiency. Someone like Mac, David suspects, might not even notice his existence, let alone make the conscious decision to dismiss him.

So, anyway, with Mac conveniently dismissed, David turns back to Harry. He looks at him and tries to work him out. He doesn't fail but he backs away from his immediate, disturbing reaction. He starts again, according to a tried formula: too young to be a Mac; too old, by a decade at least, to be one of the volunteer aid workers whom he could easily patronise. Not in work clothes but nonetheless untidy and uncared for. Hair needs cutting; shirt needs ironing. Wonder what sort of shoes he's wearing? I have on my old English country brogues. His table manners are inoffensive but not English and the man will scoop up his food with his fork, elbow on table. He might have removed that elbow with the entrance of My Wife, but he hadn't.

All the same, all the same, for all his apparent casualness, David notes, consciously – and Sally unconsciously because in a way she expects it – that this good-looking man with a big mouth has welcomed them. When they had arrived at the table – having lost their dazzling retinue along the way – he had welcomed them with a smile of such warmth on his whole face that he might have been madly wagging his tail. And, as it happened, it was true: despite his usual taciturnity, Harry was pleased by the appearance of this obviously insecure couple who so badly wanted him to adopt them. He would adopt them. Sally and David appeared in Harry's vision just at a point in time when he felt well fed, relaxed and secure inside himself; not, as was usually the case, wanting to rush back to the plantation with a sort of panic-driven desperation. He was happy, for this evening at any rate, to give these two people whatever it was that they might want of him.

David might have indeed dismissed Harry as an ill-educated, ignorant type – and in a small way he did – but, and against what he would have described as his own better judgement, he didn't want to. He was attracted. Harry reminded him a little of the doctor's son. As he said to Sally later, while he undressed.

"Odd fellow that Harry Whatishisname. Don't know what to make of him."

Harry, also, was interested in David Pryce-Williams. Later, Mac said that Harry was only interested in them as a pair, as a couple, as a social specimen or, even, as a phenomenon. But he was only partly right because Harry was also interested in each of them as an individual component of the phenomenon.

So that is how it all started: as a not very serious dilettante-ish interest on all their parts. But, it was always a bit lopsided. There was David and Sally, the single animal recognised by Mac, on the one side, and there was Harry on the other. In the end it would be the animal, the beast more like, going off, leaving Harry behind. All the same, Harry was not at a disadvantage because, as Mac had noted, it was Harry who was the manipulator, playing on the inexperience and the emotional dishonesty of David and Sally. To start with, there was a lot of social posturing, especially on the part of David and Sally. They could say – to each other – that they loved Harry, but they did not. Their use of the word love was general. The words 'love' and 'nice' more or less covered everything they liked. And because they were dishonest, they did not know themselves, or rather, they were afraid to know themselves, and therefore they buried their social responses under the construction of ... of the public beast that enabled them to survive each day under the public gaze. It was the relationship with Harry which changed all that.

Sally and David and Harry, therefore, at the same table in the club. The outcome of the possible, the potential, the potential social dynamics is, they are terrific. On our little spinning planet, these three meet, stay together for a while and work themselves out upon one another. They suffer as a result. But is it not suffering that makes life significant?

And Mac? He detached himself, and watched. It would be interesting to see what happened because the essential Harry was, as Mac well knew, a loner. He was not the type to mess around with these social types. These *bon viveurs*. Something interesting was bound to happen.

[][][]

A tropical night of thick and heavy darkness, damaged, like the flaws in a black diamond, by a maddening random array of conflicting and discordant disturbances that appear and are gone without sense: yellow light, hot body parts, fabrics, human sounds and fragments of emotion.

But David focuses.

"Busy isn't it?" He barks at Harry to be sure he is heard.

Mac watches.

Harry smiles upwards from his plate.

"Yes it's the food I suppose. Friday night and all that." He returns to the plate.

David cannot place the accent, which disorientates him. There is an Australian drag in the intonation but also a more rounded pronunciation that suggests English upper-ish middle class to David's practised ear.

It seems as if while the two roughnecks, one of whom is not so rough after all, are happy to share their table, they expect the newcomers to entertain themselves. David – unusually – does not feel put down: the man, this particular man, who interests him, does not appear to be deliberately ill mannered, merely uneducated. He ignores his wife who is smiling blankly at the entire company, for all the word as if she is dead drunk. He shouts at Harry.

"I'm David Pryce-Williams by the way," shoving his meaty hand at Harry's face, "I work for Haldan and Cruikshank. You?"

David's hand hangs in space until Harry takes it, holding the weight of it rather than shaking it as if testing its validity. Testing his own, more like. He retains his fork in the other hand.

"Harry Williams," he says, "maybe we're related." He smiles back at David, eyebrows raised in mock astonishment, as if one of them, at least, would find the idea astonishing.

Mac watches as the two men hold hands above the food. He has seen this before. He goes to the bar.

It is for David to disentangle his hand. Nonetheless, he holds Harry's awhile as if thereby more able to categorise the Harry-ness of it. He tries but again backs away from the idea. When he finally lets go he begins to eat Harry-style, scooping up the food with his fork. It is not the usual David way of eating, which is to hold his knife and fork like pencils, close to his body, tight as if his eating is a very private – English – affair. Wow! Not this Harry-style at all, elbow sticking out into Sally. What's up? Does he want to point something out to her? Or perhaps he wants to push her away? Whatever it is, she notices nothing.

Now they are all eating.

Is it an awkward silence?

It is not.

Harry is happy: meals are for eating, not for conversation.

David is happy: he knows not why and he does not associate his contentment with this man, Harry.

Sally is happy that they are not alone and that they are sitting with someone who appears to be an established member of the club. When Mac returns with more drinks she waves at him as an old friend. Such a character and, for her, he will be a character if that is what she wants, the stupid woman. He will get drunk enough to fall down the steps later if she wants.

In the noisy heat of the club they establish a sort of relationship. Like cartoon characters on a desert islet, they sit with their backs to the one bent palm tree in the middle. They look towards the distant horizon beyond which anything might lie. They make polite conversation but they hear little of what is said. It is their own prejudices ... No, preconditioning is a better word: it is their own preconditioning which builds up ideas about the others. What else can you do in a few hours of drinking? Which, if nothing better, enables you to get through the evening; enables you to believe you have made social contact, which may – or may not – prove to be significant; enables you to fend off the thought of those encircling sharks that might attack should you test the sea, out there.

They part company in the car park. Mac does not fall down the steps although he stumbles, grabbing Sally in the process. But it is Harry who catches him this time. So Sally thinks Harry is sweet.

"You must come over sometime," she says.

"Yes, that would be nice, Sally." But he does not look at her, and David breaks in:

"Goodnight Harry."

"Goodnight David."

[][][]

"They seem OK, Mac. Why don't you like them?"

"Did I say I didn't like 'em?"

"Not in words."

"So, there you are. Goodnight Harry."

"Goodnight Mac."

[][][]

"Odd? I thought he was rather sweet. We must ask him over. I'm sure he's lonely." She meant it for the moment but it would not have gone any further had David not reminded her.

They lie in bed, back to back. David sees that chap Harry in his mind's eye. He tries to catch the essence of him beyond what is his habit to construct, but fails. Harry slips away.

▢▢▢

"I wonder what's happened to that Harry fellow?" David glances at the table where they had sat the preceding week. He had expected to see Harry sitting there as before but it is occupied by some other people who are ... who are not Harry.

"Who?" Drunken stare and fixed smile as if she is miles away but she is desperate to see someone to whom she can wave. There is no one.

"The chap we met last week." David is cross with his wife because Harry is not there: "Planter fellow," he snaps at her. He is cross with Harry for not being there: "Odd man; not quite. ... You know." He snaps at Harry but Sally gets the mark. He looks around the room as if the act of looking will produce Harry, about whom he has thought all week.

Sally interprets this as David being sweet, because his bad temper is usually aimed at waiters and the like for her sake – so it seems – producing results like a bottle on the house. It is sweet because she can act getting him out of it without having to actually get close to him because it is a predetermined thing that he will be got out of it by the adoring little wife. It is a thing he does and is all part of playing at being married. The Pryce-Williamses, so sweet with each other, they imagine people saying about them; people who mostly do not say it because they are playing the same game themselves.

But, this time, this time although Sally does not notice the difference, David really is a bit cross. Not deeply cross because already the resentment of Harry for not being there is working on him so that the cheap little poser is not worth My Crossness. Why would someone of my stature condescend to, to consort with a cheap little tick like him who is, after all, only a second-rate planter? Again, David thinks of the long-haired doctor's son. But, all the same, David's crossness is, for once, real; it is not enacted as a cover for establishing his superiority. It is indeed outrageous that an uneducated hobbledehoy like that should stand us, the Pryce-Williamses, up like this. It is an insult to My Wife.

Sally takes her cue, focusing on Her Husband to mollify him as the wifely thing to do. She takes hold of his arm and nuzzles close, the sweet Pryce-Williamses, so much in love they don't care what is going on around them.

"But Darling, he told us."

"Told us what?" What outrageous thing did he tell us?

"He said he only came into Markham once a fortnight. To get the wages and things for his men." She squeezes his arm as she looks out into the room. "Don't be such a crosspatch."

"He said that to you?" David also looks out into the room, feeling a stab of jealousy. "It's not his own plantation. He's just a bum manager." It satisfies David to be able to denigrate Harry in front of Sally. He is eager for her reaction.

But there is no reaction.

"Oh look there're the Bittams. Hello, Margery," she calls, leaving David to wave at one of her morning coffee/bridge/tennis/swimming/sitting and complaining about the servants friends. She is waved back at, they join the Bittams – they're OK although Bob's not quite, you know, he's only red brick – others come and go, and really it's much more fun than hanging around with thingamajig and his friend last week, we did rather get stuck with them.

David's booming voice dominates the evening. He organises everyone around tables and things and orders most of the drinks and therefore pays the most money, but it's alright because he earns more than they do. I'm not stuck here, I'm just learning the ropes and we'll be back in London in a few years' time. Yes, he's marked for the Board, he's one of their Oxbridge men and frightfully clever at languages although that's not much use here, I just shout very loud. They seem to understand ha ha ha. The Pryce-Williamses, such a sweet couple and so in love they adore each other.

"You're in a Brown Study, old chap. What you thinking about?"

"Oh nothing, Bob. Have another drink? Whisky was it?"

"Thanks David. You need cheering up. Your wife's a gem. One in a million."

"Yes."

"Let's have that chap over next week."

"Who's that, Darling?" She stretches her body inside the satiny pink nightdress but it doesn't seem to have any effect. He's drunk too much. Just like a man. And that idea satisfies her a little. He was so bossy in the club he made the other men look like shadows. She was glad she was Mrs Pryce-Williams and she wondered if they could get her mother out for a few weeks. She vaguely imagined her mother in the club, proud and a little above everyone else but charming and chatty without being boring. People grateful to be noticed by her. Mummy, you must meet the Bittams. Mrs Grant, Sally's mother, mum, so sweet. Really? The old trout. Who does she think she is?

"The planter chappy, Harry Whatshisname."

She didn't know what to say. There was no reason why he should not come over but no obvious reason why he should. She couldn't even remember what he looked like.

But David insisted.

"You asked him."

"Did I, Darling?"

"You said he must come over sometime."

"Alright then, but how will I tell him?"

"Write a note and give it to the old drunk, Mac. He'll pass it on somehow."

"Was he there tonight? I didn't see him."

"He was propping up the bar."

"He might have come over to say hello."

There was no answer to this so David gave none. He had briefly chatted to Mac each time he went to the bar, watching him get more and more drunk. He was afraid the old man might say what he thought.

"You could've given him a note then," said Sally, touching his toe with hers but getting no response.

"I didn't think." Cross again. "He can come here and we'll go to the club together next Friday. Then he can come back and stay on until Sunday. Or Monday morning if he likes. Switch off the light."

They lay side by side on their backs in the moonlight that flooded the room. A slight breeze rattled the palm fronds outside. Black, jagged shadows broke them up into pieces under a white sheet.

"So what will we do with him? David? Are you awake?"

"Yes." Cross.

No need to act the fond little wife here, in private. She would have made love to him if she thought he expected it. Once they got going she quite liked it. Playing with his body as something quite detached from him. She liked to suck him but in the process she would have all sorts of ideas not associated with David. She would have sucked any good-looking man. But they didn't get going so that was alright.

She thought of their first time. David had been so nice and gentle. She had imagined it would be quite violent but it was just like having a bath really. She had enjoyed his handling of her in his impersonal, efficient way. When it was over she felt she had taken a step forward in her life. The view of the Fen sky from her childhood came into mind. It looked just the same but no black bird swooped.

"What will we do with him?"

"Do?" He asked incredulously as if she was stupid. "Look after him." Then, sounding happier: "I bet he lives a sparse sort of bachelor life down there. We can give him some decent food. Talk. We'll have a late breakfast on Saturday. Bit of a walk, siesta, we'll go to the club and watch the film in the evening. Maybe some tennis on Sunday morning and you can make a really nice lunch."

"Alright." But there was a question in her voice because it was unlike David to bother about someone who, after all, did not matter much. Although – she checked her own thoughts – Harry whatever-he-was-called had been quite nice at the club, and it would make a change.

"I know, I know he's not quite our type. And not very well educated. But we mustn't embarrass him and he's probably lonely. I should think he needs looking after."

"Oh David," she moved a little closer.
"What?"
"You are sweet."

4   Delightful Intercourse

David is an intelligent man. His parents gave him confidence and a good education. They thought about his schooling so that getting into a proper university was not difficult. They got on with their life and were content to have the well-behaved boy come along with them. He's a credit to you, old man. What more could have been asked of them?

As an only child growing up in a comfortable house where his parents, who were both teachers, read and listened to classical music, David went to the university with the intellectual capacity to appreciate the mainstream culture of the place. He felt secure and confident in his ideas so that he was not adventurous and he avoided the sort of people who, who might have taken him on adventures of body and mind.

David listens to what he thinks he ought to listen to. But while he prefers a symphony to a string quartet, a concerto to a piano recital, his response to music is a genuine emotion. In fact it is the most genuine thing about the arrogant young idiot: he is stirred by the *Emperor Concerto* and the great choruses of Verdi. It is his idea to have a set of the Dvorak symphonies for the car cassette player so that the magnificent music enhances the magnificent scenery through which they often drive. At one time, Sunday mornings were generally accompanied by the Schumann symphonies, until he noted that they seemed to make Sally unsettled and bad tempered. Otherwise all good outside music, as it were, to which David listens with pleasure, allowing it to knock me about. And there's nothing wrong with that. He is a young man with no need to reflect just yet. Time for that later, and indeed, a consideration of the inside would require an element of honesty that might – at this important point in David's career – cost too much.

[][][]

The most honest thing about both the Pryce-Williamses is their living room. This is because, like their lives, they have done little more to it than dump themselves and some of their things in it. Nonetheless, every time Sally enters the room she thinks of how other people might see it, and therefore of how they might think about David and herself. She wants people like the Bittams to see it as a reflection of the Pryce-Williamses but: a) she doesn't know what it is that ought to reflect them and b) even if she did, she would not know how to go about setting it up. Eventually she will start from where her mother left off, even inheriting some of the props. David will egg her on because he has always approved of Mrs Grant's style. He will think he can put Sally right if she goes wrong. But in the end, he is the one who will go wrong. She will go in her own direction, regardless of him.

Sally's mother's way of setting things up, as we know, is based on a stage set. Her way does not pretend to reflect the way she lives. She sets out her rooms to give an idea – the popular idea – of an upper-class English house that is easily recognised as such by anyone who has watched BBC, Hollywood or Ealing dramas about the subject. Sally's mother knows exactly what she is doing and she is under no illusions, which is why she enjoys her life and is generally happier than the average Mrs Grant. Mrs Grant is not unlike Mac: she observes and sees a lot more than most of us.

For the time being, however, Sally herself does not know what she is doing. That is, beyond having a vague idea about what she thinks she ought to do. This is why she is not yet her mother and why she does not yet dominate the Pryce-Williams' relationship. David does that. Later, it will change.

For now, the interior setting of their lives is rather depressing: the room is painted a useful beige with brown – mission brown – trimmings; there is the usual cheap modern rattan furniture imported from the Philippines; there is what is called a room-divider of veneer and sliding glass doors that divides the room for some reason; and there are a couple of strip lights to give ... to give light, other than the stuff that comes in through the window, that is. To this, the landlord's shell, have been added some colourful curtains made of the local trade cloth with cushions and tablecloths to match because that's what everyone does. Also some lamps and potted plants. It looks OK. There are no pictures on the walls, and the floor is naked, mud-coloured vinyl tiles because decent rugs cannot be found in Port Markham. Western culture is worshipped at a small book cabinet half filled with the few books brought from England and a growing library from the book club. David has left his records at home but he has invested in a collection of about thirty cassette tapes, just coming in at the time. Two big, expensive speakers sit at either end of the top of the cabinet.

When they return from their first leave, they will know what to bring back. They assume. Their life, with any luck, having gained some depth, or at any rate, some interior decoration.

[][][]

Two o'clock Saturday morning. They have been to Nosh Nite. David and Harry are sitting under the rushing fan that pushes out the roaring night. David had wanted whisky but since Harry insisted on keeping to beer that is what they are drinking. Sally has gone to bed, slightly drunk. She had pulled David with her, assuming he would follow – showing him off, showing off their sweet devoted Pryce-Williams thing to Harry – but his hand had easily slipped out of hers. She had kept going, on her own.

David and Harry are not drunk but rather in that state of unreality where anything might be said, and can be forgotten later. So far they have said nothing to each other all evening beyond the bare requirements of civility. It is not easy to talk in the club, there are distractions. Each time David had tried to talk to Harry he felt rebuffed: Harry would politely answer and then turn away to observe something else going on, for all the world as if they were at a play and David's conversation was embarrassingly out of place. In the end David had given up. But the three of them had hung together, all the same.

Now, in the Pryce-Williams' living room, David has Harry at ... At his mercy? Hardly! But he has him to himself.

"I'll put on some music," he says. What else can he say?

"OK." Harry is easy going, sprawled across one of the rattan armchairs which is too small for his gangling frame. He knows he is the centre of attention, and has been all evening. He lets David dance around him.

Big orchestral sound fills the room.

David sits down opposite Harry, swinging a leg over the arm of the chair. He smiles at Harry. In return he receives a bland expression of what seems to be satisfied pleasure. On what it is based, he is not sure. Harry looks towards him but his eyes are focused elsewhere.

"I love it. Don't you?" Demands David.

Harry closes his eyes.

"Yeah. It's the sea."

They listen to the music but David thinks only of Harry. He wants to make a connection. There is nothing in Harry he thinks will be of use to him, yet maddeningly, he wants to put Harry into his power. It had been so easy before, but this, this Harry resists him. David is not cross but he wants to do something violent. He is surprised by his feelings. Here, at last, he barely dares to admit to himself, is something I want. The drink, the music, the weekend, make it easier to think about: he is separate from his life as Estates Manager, Haldane and Cruikshank.

Harry seems to have fallen asleep, damn him. Can't he hear the music? Is it not wonderful? He really is a hobbledehoy. I'll wake him up thinks David. He shouts at Harry above the music.

"Stark, isn't it? Isn't it?"

Harry frowns, opens one eye, and says nothing. But he smiles.

"You know it?" Insists David. Connect with me, blast you.

"Hmmmmmm." Harry's eyes are closed now but the smile remains.

Like a cat thinks David, only cats don't smile. He gulps his beer angrily, gets up, looks down at Harry, still sprawled awkwardly on the chair as if he owns the place, fuck him. He sits down on the arm of the chair. The music crashes all around them but Harry makes not a move. He must prompt him into some sort of reaction if anything is going to happen. He'd like to smash his fist down on the top of his head, just where the hair is beginning to thin out.

"You like Sibelius?" He says. "Harry?"

"I like this one," he murmurs. "The Fifth, isn't it? Last movement?"

And this knowledge which Harry has annoys David. It alters his view of the whole world. So the Poles are not going to repulse us with the cavalry after all, they do have tanks and, therefore, we have not the advantage we thought we had. This is going to alter the whole course of the war. But perhaps, David reasons, drawing into himself and therefore away from Harry, he had to study it at school in some sort of music appreciation class. He considers starting a discussion about Sibelius to test him but he doesn't. He doesn't want Harry to have heard the other Sibelius symphonies. He wants to subdue Harry with his superior knowledge. This abstracted Harry, lost in the music, is a sham which he wants to smash. He wants to break Harry in order to tame him as his own man.

Harry, as it happens, is taken by the music. His apparent distance from David is the result of exhaustion. He has had a hectic week, he had driven into town to pick up the wages, returned to the plantation to pay them, and then come back into town as a result of Sally's invitation. He has been up and active for about twenty hours and now he just wants to go to bed.

But David sees what he wants to see and, and with drunken bravado, decides to make a move. His body is touching Harry's yet Harry seems entirely unaware of it. Or he is playing games, and if that's what he wants he can have it. But as David moves his hand towards the head he has been studying for so long the music crashes to its famous ending. With the last thump Harry jumps up as if he has – and he has – been waiting for it. He takes David by surprise, who falls back a little, slopping beer onto the floor.

Harry looks down at him, grinning.

"Time to sleep I think. You must go to your little wife and I'll go to my empty bed."

With that he stumbles off to the guest room, which is, in the usual fashion, on the opposite side of the house from the family bedrooms. David is left standing in the middle of nowhere watching him go, frozen as if waiting for the film to start running again. Legs wide apart, glass in one hand, the other stretched out.

The lights dim.

[][][]

David goes to his wife. He is drunk and, as we say, he gropes her a bit because it is the thing to do. She shrugs him off gently but definitely. No need to act here. They fall asleep.

In the guest room, unaware of what he has just read, Harry sleeps the sleep of the, at any rate, of the exhausted, and perhaps of the sanctimonious, or even of the calculating. He is unaware also – and serves him right – that he has a part to play in Sally's little scheme, you could call it, although she is barely aware of what she is doing. It has something to do with a short story she once read.

[][][]

Up late, Saturday. About ten o'clock. Sally cooks a brunch for Clara to wash up. They eat it on the veranda chatting the way people do who are beginning to feel easier with one another. Trusting, you might say. At least to the extent of knowing what the other is likely to say or, what you think they might say. Is it easy? Considering what David and Harry might have been up to in the living room the night before while Sally slept? It is, because: 1) we were a bit drunk; 2) Harry can tell himself he did not notice what was going on; and 3) David and Sally are happily acting out Mr and Mrs Pryce-Williams entertaining the boorish Harry Williams, who is, after all, only one of those bum planters.

So the weekend passes. Siesta and a bit of reading after the brunch; tea on the veranda; let's walk to the club for the exercise and play a very gentle set of tennis we'll find a fourth, fine; drinks at the club – what on earth is he doing with them? – and a meal at home, goodnight, it's been a pleasant day, they mean it, they are relaxed. Late up, again, Sunday, and Harry says he must get back to the plantation. They do not press him to stay but do have some tea before you go and you must see the garden Sally's been working on it with the boy. Harry gives advice and promises some things from his own.

David sits on the veranda – some other time, perhaps – watching the other two; watching Harry. They get on, those two. He is pleased. He is pleased with David Pryce-Williams. David Pryce-Williams sitting on his veranda, looking across what is considered to be, thanks to Mrs Pryce-Williams, one of the best small gardens in town. David Pryce-Williams is the Estates Manager for H and C. He'll go far. He'll be on the Board before you know it.

Goodbye. We must do it again.

"You and Harry seem to get on very well," he says, flippant but with a hint of accusation.

"Do we?" She stoops to investigate a plant while he stands above her, hands behind his back, as if he couldn't care a hoot. "It looked like it. All that laughing and giggling as if you'd known him all your life." But I don't care, do I?

She gets up, looking up into his face that stares beyond the top of her head, his stern look on his face, hands behind his back.

Now she must act her part.

"Are you jealous?" She laughs. Do I not only have eyes for you my beautiful brute of a crosspatch husband?

They play the game and it satisfies them and it puts things back in their place like straightening the cushions on the sofa.

By holding his hands behind his back she has her arms around him, pressing up close. She pushes her head into his chest and he pushes his chin down onto the top of her head, thinking, for a second, of Harry. But he is David Pryce-Williams, Estates Manager for Haldan and Cruikshank, married to the sweet and well-bred Sally. Such a charming couple, don't you think and he's going to go a long way. He'll be on the Board before long. Watch him!

The rest of the day they enjoy playing house. Making the dinner but asking Clara to be awfully sweet and do the washing-up again. Aren't we awful old colonials but of course Clara adores us and will do anything for us but she's awfully careless with the china.

[][][]

A good thing David was/is David. As David Pryce-Williams, Estates Manager for Haldan and Cruikshank in New Sudan etc., etc., he enacts his job superbly and he is a credit etc., etc., not only to himself but also, but also, but also ...

The ol' book, the ol' Harry book is put back on the shelf along with the Sibelius 5th (the American orchestras can be rather good at it in a brassy sort of way. The Pittsburgh isn't it? Or Cleveland? Fritz Whatshisname. Gave them what they wanted, or thought they wanted). A credit to his wife, Mrs Pryce-Williams, Sally, also. Don't forget her. That little well-bound volume is brought out and dusted. Nice feel; small and easily held in the hand. Nice sort of weight in the hand. It smells new despite the appearance of age. So tastefully bound as a sort of Folio Soc book of the month. Read it? Oh yes, I will sometime. When I have the time. Sort of embossed/impressed pattern of leaves in neat vertical rows. Gold on blue with a little weighty feel to it; as I said. Should I break the spine a little? Make it look as if I've read it? I have glanced at it. Period illustrations I notice. Nice touch, that.

She then read the first sentence aloud, which comprised the information of their having just resolved to follow their brother to town directly, and their meaning to dine that day in Grosvenor Street, where Mr. Hurst had a house. The next was in these words. 'I do not pretend to regret any thing I shall leave in Hertfordshire, except your society, my dearest friend; but we will hope at some future period, to enjoy many returns of the delightful intercourse we have known, and in the meanwhile may lessen the pain of separation by a very frequent and most unreserved correspondence. I depend on you for that.' To these high flown expressions, Elizabeth listened with all the insensibility of distrust; and though the suddenness of their removal surprised her, she saw nothing in it really to lament; it was not to be supposed that their absence from

Netherfield would prevent Mr. Bingley's being there; and as to the loss of their society, she was persuaded that Jane must soon cease to regard it, in the enjoyment of his.
Pride and Prejudice, by Jane Austen.

David reads a little but really it's girl's stuff. What did she know about the industrial revolution? Mill girls in Preston; little children crawling beneath the looms. All for Bingley's £5000 a year or whatever it was. Damn the bitch!

So it was with mixed feelings that David received the news of Harry's return to town. How would he greet the man, as surely he must at some function or other which they were both bound to attend? He felt a little nervous and was angry with himself for feeling it. Undoubtedly, he realised with an unbecoming blush, he desired Harry's good opinion. Nonetheless, a really well-bred man would have stayed on the plantation for a while. He would not have come into town. But, of course, he had as much right to be in Port Markham, as himself. After all, he, David, had made the advance. He, and only he, was responsible for the position in which he now found himself. Really it was too vexing. Put her head in the guillotine and chop it off.

Damn the bitch! One might say. But, after all, I never met her and she was dead at 41. Buried in Winchester Cathedral. Burial place of the Wessex kings.

Forget the man and focus on this new volume. The Pryce-Williams, volume II. Time for a baby; or two. Better concentrate on that for a while. Some of their friends have babies. Get Sally into the broody mood first. They say it improves the chances of fertilisation. Better while we're young. Don't want anything funny. I've still got nice clean sperms. I'll save them up for a good spurt. Supposed to improve the chances of a boy. What public school should it be? Mr and Mrs Pryce-Williams on Founder's Day. Sally'll do that one well. Such condescension! Those pervy teachers'll think she's wonderful. Damn the bitch!

5   Another Music

Friday afternoon. David goes home early. He fancies a shower, a nap and then on to the club with Mrs Pryce-Williams, his wife, Sally, later. As has become the habit, he sends the car ahead so he can walk. He enjoys the exercise; it is pleasant to walk the tree-lined streets of affluent houses in lush gardens on the hot afternoon, knowing he has not far to go. The only others around, the servants – *apinun sah* – are a respectful part of the picture; the cows chewing the cud in the Victorian watercolour in Mrs Grant's little house in England. The lazy, humid air is intoxicating. He dreams: the paddling pool on the front lawn, Clara sitting patiently, dry towel on lap, while the two Pryce-Williams children, naked, play their game. Such amazing children, so advanced and clever for their age. A credit to their parents. The little girl looks like her mother. Pretty little thing. Father's brains, luckily.

Somewhere on the dark, shaded veranda of his mind, Sally sits, watching. She has done her bit.

Approaching the house he hears his wife's voice. She is talking to someone. Showing him the garden. The chatter stops for a second or two of intimate silence. Harry's voice replies, telling her what she should do, as if familiar with what she wants. They might be Mr and Mrs Harry Williams. David stops to listen. A spy, an interloper behind the hedge like an old Punch cartoon, listening out for some comment to give him a line. He is an animal in the bush, waiting, sniffing, sensing. Are they friend or foe? Should he run or show himself? A small animal. A small adrenaline rush. Is he jealous? No! Possessive perhaps, but only of the idea of Mr and Mrs Pryce-Williams. Pleased a little also, although he recognises not the pleasure, the excitement almost, of knowing that Harry has come to them.

In at them then. No surprise, as it happens, because behind Harry's old utility truck is David's own four-wheeler, left by the driver. They are, therefore, waiting for him, excited like children with a secret. They might well have spent the afternoon in bed together.

Rush then of excited explanations. From Sally mainly.

"Harry has to go back to pay his men. We're going with him." Harry stands back like a public benefactor. "We met in town. He came for lunch. I fed him. He needed it." Arch glance of familiarity. I fed the hungry bad boy. "We talked. He knows so much about the garden. Come on, slow coach! No time for a shower. I've packed the car. Lots of food! We don't want to starve or live off biscuits. Come on Darling." She takes hold of David's arm with both of hers and nuzzles close, hoping Harry is watching the sweet Pryce-Williamses.

"Alright." Fond sigh, for public benefit. Lazy feeling gone with adrenaline rush. Yes, he is excited also. "Really, I am, it'll make a nice change," and anything for little wifey. "Really, I mean it."

"Of course, the road's OK. It's dry. Just follow me. It's not far. A bit rough, that's all." Arch look of familiarity. Would you not do anything for your little wifey?

Anything. All the same, David finds that the passenger seat in the Pryce-Williams' nice big white four-wheel drive, contains not Sally but a cardboard box full of the things needed for a meal she is going to cook. It includes a couple of bottles of red wine and a blue and white striped apron. Good ol' Sally. My wife, the wonderful Mrs Pryce-Williams daughter of Evelyn Grant of the County of Suffolk or Cambridge or Huntingdon or Woolwich (Plumstead to be precise), is an accomplished woman. It comes from generations of good breeding because statistically she is as equally descended from William the Conqueror as the bloody Queen of bloody England. And her father, a passing Polish army officer, stranded in England en route to somewhere, was undoubtedly, he said, a Razoumovsky, or something like that in addition to being a survivor of Katyn, he said. In fact it was Birkinau, for which he was, for some reason, deeply ashamed.

Sally goes with Harry. They are laughing like school kids. If that man has fucked her, would I mind? Some men find it easy to fuck around. Funny ol' world. I wouldn't mind him. New Sudan isn't England, you feel differently here.

They leave in another rush. Clara will sleep on the veranda as security. After all, she is not an expensive Labrador dog, which they would have taken with them. Wouldn't want him chopped up by the burglar's panga knife. Not on your life!

[][][]

Another evening another room. Harry's room. Shabby. Tidy. Dead. Floorboards move. Insects come in. Door open. Small, but too big for the one man who inhabits it. Some of the time. He sits on the veranda most evenings. When he sits.

The tropical night roars. They sit around the table, bleached with what might be age but is actually the tropical climate and the occasional sloppy scrub from Wanei. Wanei, the house-boy. Boy! He is a man. Same age as Harry, himself. Himself! Themselves more like. They are close, those two. Bum buddies it has been said. But there is nothing remarkable about that. Some men find it easy to fuck around. Is Harry one of those? Wanei? Sally? David? Perhaps.

Sally and Harry chatted nineteen to the dozen the whole way. Heads bobbing around, hands gesticulating. You could see the act through the back window. But as they approached the plantation house, bumping through the dusky emptiness beneath coconut palms, Harry fell silent, drifting away from Sally. A rickety looking veranda of peeling white paint and warped boards sat, it seemed in the warm darkness, temporarily, on the ground. A single lantern light held by the dark became Wanei, the man. An unusually black man. Harry's man. It looked friendly but as Sally climbed out of the car, and the man saw her, his expression changed swiftly to one of suspicion and then contempt. This, with his one eye, made him look threatening. Harry noticed and laughed in a hostile way, inviting the man to laugh at her with him. Sally was alone in a hostile world where she was not wanted.

"Don't look so worried Wanei, I didn't buy her in town, she's not staying long."

It sounded like a threat. Sally looked up over the rusty tin roof which disappeared into the night. Then, thank God, David: normality restored; all was fun and games and Harry so sweet he obviously adored her. He obviously adored them both, the Sweet. So nice to have them, the wonderful Pryce-Williamses, to brighten up his dreary life.

Harry is laughing. He takes her hand in such a nice way. Like an older brother.

"Sorry, Sally, I was miles away, thinking plantation things."

David stands back and watches.

The black man, Wanei, smiles at her. She decides she is going to like him, his one-eyed face making him look cheeky and funny like the pixies in her childhood books.

Harry puts Sally's hand into Wanei's hand.

"Sally, this is Wanei, who will look after you, show you to your room, give you some coffee and generally be your devoted slave. Won't you Wanei?"

"Yesah!" Wanei almost stands to attention. They're all in on the game now, whatever it is. He takes Sally through the veranda into the house. She looks back for Harry but he is gone to David. They fetch the things, appearing to ignore each other, Harry taking the lead because it is, after all, his place, and he's done it before.

Wanei leaves Sally in her room, where she stands alone, in the dark. A minute or two later, the generator splutters into life challenging the roaring night, bringing light. A light unto, unto something.

The two men utter not a word as they work but every so often Harry looks at David until David returns his glance. Then he smiles and gets on with the job. In this way, David does not feel awkward. As soon as he can, he seats himself in a comfortable chair on the veranda where Harry serves him with a drink. David therefore establishes his right to be the man, the man to whom they will all defer throughout the weekend. After all, he has put himself out for them. Has he not? He is happy in the place he sets himself, and the others are happy to go along with it. At this point in the game, he needs a bit of comfort. Wanei watches him with his one eye.

Later, around the table, they are eating the meal Wanei has cooked: masses of sweet potatoes and a hot stewey thing of unrecognisable vegetable matter and fish. They drink Harry's beer. They are saving Sally's cosmopolitan concoction for tomorrow. The light comes from the veranda to keep the insects out so the atmosphere is intimate; you might say shadowy. Are the expressions on their faces a trick of the light? Wanei watches from the shadows.

Harry has explained how the plantation works. He will walk them around tomorrow, siesta and swim; Sally will cook dinner. David maintains the conversation by asking intelligent questions about plantation economy and the socio-cultural implications of mainly male plantation workers living together in the compound. It is all frightfully intelligent and grown-up. The eye flashes in the dark. When he has had enough of this, Wanei brings in the coffee. The conversation stops abruptly. Wanei takes out some of the dishes leaving a mess of stuff around Harry's place. David coughs

"Do you have some classical music we can hear? I forgot to bring something. Chopin Nocturnes would be nice."

"Yes," replies Harry. "What do you like? Sally?"

"You choose."

David imagines something banal and loud he can recognise and disparage. But it is a string quartet he does not recognise. He cannot place the composer.

Wistful and sad, but in a youthful way. Precocity nonetheless recognising the limitations of life so recently assumed to be limitless. A sort of afternoon feel about it.

They listen.

Sally closes her eyes. She wonders if Harry will get hold of the fish he has promised for the dinner she is to make tomorrow.

Wanei watches. He knows this music. What they want it for? He looks at Harry.

End of first movement.

What is it? Dvorak? Dvorak, then. David chances it. Got to know these things.

"Dvorak?"

"Brahms," Harry answers. He might have added. "But I can see what you mean." Only he didn't.

David remembers a Prom concert once. Lying on the gallery floor listening to the big piano concerto. Wonderful it was: made him sweat. What things there were in life. He is honest now because the music has made a contact. He likes the stuff and blurts out, incredulously.

"Is it?"

"The Second Quartet."

"Oh yes." David is lying but this is more threatening than the idea of the man sleeping with his wife. He owns his wife and knows he can hang on to her. This knowledge, this Harry's knowledge, is more difficult to handle. The books, too, he had looked at before dinner: not the usual batch of airport rubbish but Dostoyevsky and Patrick White. Books on tropical agriculture, Australian agriculture. Books about architecture, for God's sake! Lewis Mumford. How did he get here? He says:

"You like music?"

"Yes. Sometimes. Not too much."

"You can't buy a Brahms quartet in New Sudan."

"A friend sends things up from time to time."

But David wants to get him.

"What d'you like?"

"Most things."

"Rachmaninov?"

"Yes."

"Beethoven?"

"Oh yes."

"Mozart?"

"Of course."

"Bach?"

Harry laughs.

"When he's not holding it in."

"Holding in what?" This is getting bad.

"His emotion. He can be a bit academic. When he forgets God he's as dry as old clothes."

David doesn't want to think about God. He pushes on with his recital.

"You like Brahms, I suppose? The second concerto when I was a student ..."

"Yes Brahms is good in its way but it's mad music."

"Why?" David is honestly surprised.

"It's the music of repression. The man releases it in his music. It's a substitute for his life. That's why it's frightening at times. Listen to the second movement of that concerto of yours. It's a man in agony. Mental anguish." He turns off the music.

David watches him cross the room: long gangly sort of man. Too big for the space.

Harry smiles back at Sally.

"You got things sorted out in your room, Sally?" But before she can answer he shouts into the thick noisy night.

"Wanei."

"Yesah!" Comes back the immediate reply from somewhere close.

Sally jumps, thinking of the fish and seeing the one eye in the dark.

Only when the generator stops do they notice the noise it had made. Then, they hear the roaring tropical night. Millions of insects and the beating of the waves upon the beach beyond. One roaring animal: another music.

Harry leads them onto the veranda, carrying the coffee pot. The veranda is the stage, the two or three tiny rooms behind, nothing.

[][][]

Harry sits silently hunched in his chair. A moody boy, thinks Sally, sitting between the two men. She is engaged, this Sally, with the two men. She wants them both. The music meant nothing. She would like someone to watch David make love to her. Then, she feels, she would respond properly.

She looks at Harry watching the sea somewhere beyond the palm trees. The light seems to come from the phosphorescence of the frothing waves that beat the shore. He ignores them but he is with them and they feel it. The mysterious night holds them in a fragile embrace. And Wanei, in the dark house, is connected with them also as if it is he who is the night. He would eat them if he could. Big white teeth grin below the eye and snap shut.

"What do you mean about Brahms?"

"What about him?"

"What you said about repression."

"I've no idea." And Harry laughs, dismissing them along with Brahms. "What you need, David, is bed. If you don't, of course, it's hell to lie there, but if you fall asleep, it's what you need in this heat. Lay the body out to recover and all that." And before David can think about his body being laid out, Harry jumps up and takes them to their bedroom. They follow obediently.

The bedroom is a wooden box without a ceiling. Clothes hang on a sort of washing line. They lie under a mosquito net that seems to draw in what little night light there is to them.

Whispering intimacy because Harry, they assume, is on the other side of the partition, in his own box. They nonetheless feel physically alone despite the fact that Harry, and all the things associated with him – Wanei, the insect symphony, the crashing waves, the solidity of the tropical night – make them feel they are but part of one single something or other beyond their experience. It is, in fact, an irresistible sexual energy which burns so intensely they are confused, and not able, as Harry may have suggested they ought, to fall asleep. They are both thinking of Harry as a manifestation of the sexual energy they feel, but do not recognise. They want to talk about him to each other. He encircles them, as it were, but there is more: there is the incomprehensible darkness beyond, which throbs with energy and which they feel is taking account of them personally, wanting to violate them in some way.

And the fact is, Sally and David do not know what to do, despite their having never felt so physically close; never so close as this. Hands are held, tight and loose like a beating heart. Toes touch with the desire to stretch and release like a satisfied cat. Then, unable to bear the tension any longer, Sally hisses.

"He's gay."

"What?"

"Sssh," but she laughs. "He told me in the car. It makes me like him, more." Which was not what she had felt at the time. She had wanted to discount the idea altogether.

"You sure?" David seems to gasp.

Sally squeezes his hand and rubs his foot with hers. She moves her hand to his cock, which is hard. So hard, it is a thing apart from him. The idea of Wanei comes into her head. This, she does not want to discount. It makes her feel strong but she does not know why.

To David's astonishment he comes fast and groans. He thinks not of Harry, but of the student back home, the long-haired doctor's son.

They giggle like children and fall asleep.

[][][]

The sun blasts them awake. Unaccountably, he thinks, David feels cross. Cross, grumpy, crosspatch. Sally is pulling on T-shirt and shorts. Legs too white which makes him more cross. It is the easiest thing to be: he can sit with his coffee and be cross and they will humour him. He feels better when Harry is around but nonetheless feels a little impatient with Sally, his wife, Mrs Pryce-Williams. Her legs look too white, a tiny bit flabby and really, not attractive. Vulgar; a bit. She ought to have a wrapper: it's more the thing that his wife ought to wear. He'll buy her one – nice silk one – and she'll wear it to please Mr Pryce-Williams. Her bum is even whiter; he knows that. What does the black Wanei, what does the one eye, think of all the white flesh? Is it driven crazy? David imagines black hand on white leg. Then what? He would like to see what would happen.

Harry passes by, walking down to the beach. A smile, a glance. A wink? David looks up like an expectant boy, grumpy. Harry, visibly smaller, then lost between the casual-looking palms. Bigger in David's head: Harry's legs are brown with crinkly blond hair. Skinny and strong below baggy old khaki shorts. Long bare feet press warm, wiry grass. David looks at his own white muscles. Strong, muscular and smooth. He is proud of them in his white, pressed, tennis shorts not too short because he has good calves. Peasant's feet he has been told; broad but damaged now by generations of confining shoes. Looks at his own white muscles. His pride! Yet he feels – within the idea of Harry walking to the sea – embarrassed and sort of small beside Harry. As if in front of Harry, naked, he is found wanting. He groans. For God's sake, what's he missed that Harry's got? The Brahms. He'll get it sent out from England. He'll listen to it again. What's it about?

Harry returning, emerging as a reality from amongst the thin, grey stems of the palms. Fronds rustling in the morning breeze. Warm. The hot sun will burn you. Bigger as David sees him, feels him before he is anywhere near. A small Harry figure treading the hot grass with his long brown feet. A big Harry idea, all the same. So he's gay is he? That makes a difference. Does it? Does it mean he fucks Wanei in the arse?

David sits on the veranda grumpy, holding the coffee cup Wanei has given him with careful deference to his grumpiness. He does not know what to do. He might have followed Harry like a little dog. But David does not know how to follow. David Price-Williams is a leader of Men!

Harry comes up the steps. He carries a fish for Sally. He has bought it from his men who fish on pay Saturdays having nothing else to do. Later he will pay them their wages so they can get drunk in the evening and make a noise and fall asleep. The bar is halfway between the plantation and Port Markham so it is a good walk. They will sleep in the warm bush; it is the end of the dry season. Those who do not drink will watch the white people swimming in the afternoon. They know Harry; or rather they know enough of him for their purposes and if there is a problem they talk to Wanei who sorts it out. They will wonder at the white woman who exposes her nakedness. They will wonder at the white man who allows it. To whom does she belong?

Harry smiles at David. David looks up into blue eyes under bushy blond eyebrows. The eyes look into him. He feels embarrassed for God's sake. He smiles a confident David Pryce-Williams smile. This is David Pryce-Williams MA, you little poofter. Did the fellow wink?

[ ] [ ] [ ]

Harry has gone anyway, nice brown legs and all. He is in the house with Sally who flirts with him, putting her arms around him. It's alright now he is gay and David knows. It's OK for Mrs Pryce-Williams, wife of the Estates Manager, Haldan and Cruikshank, to do this. To be on familiar – but condescending – terms with one of Those Planters. She has been helping Wanei with breakfast: porridge oats, healthy from Australia, fried sweet potato slices and eggs, lots of stale coffee with milk powder and white sugar. We'll get some coconuts for lunch. Wanei! Coconuts for lunch. Yesah! Oh they're so sweet, I love them both. Wanei smells of coconuts and she wants to rub her hand into his tight, woolly, black hair and smell it. His hair is also thinning on top. The deep empty eye socket fascinates her; she wants to touch it with one finger. She wants to rub her white leg against his shiny, black leg; his tight white shorts express bum and bump. He bumps her in the little room – hole more like – at the back where food is prepared – cooking in a little hut outside – electric bum to bum.

They sit inside to eat. Harry rushes his food. I have to pay the men.

"See you later. Wanei, look after them." Them! Them. These two tiresome thingamajigs from Markham who want to play games but we'll go along with them and give them a good time won't we Wanei? Is that it?

Harry gone, Wanei is watchful. Goes to the little hole to mess around with pots and pans, making clatter. No more bumping. Get out of the house. Harry's house. What you doing sitting at his table, eating his food?

They eat in the silence. David is no longer playing grumpy but there is nothing to say. Wants to talk about Harry. Sally wants to talk about ... She is not sure she wants to talk at all but she is thinking of David, Wanei and Harry all at once. David starts to talk but she waves him away impatiently. She is not playing cross, she is cross. She does not know why. She cannot work it out because she is Mrs Pryce-Williams, daughter of Mrs Grant. Picks at the cold fried slice of sweet potato.

"More coffee please, Wanei," she begs.

No response. They feel awkward; embarrassed with each other. This place gets to you: so close one minute; so far apart the next. Coffee is put out on the veranda. Get out there. Lots of noise from inside the house. Wanei comes out to sweep the veranda. Lots of dust and noise and energy. Ignores them. Pushes them out. Go for a walk or something. Lots of beach to see. White people like the hot beach. Oh how lovely. Oh. Oh, how loverly.

I need my hat and my sunglasses and my sun lotion. Me too. They return like naughty children. Wanei in their room making the bed, rolling up the mosquito net. What you doing here? Glares at them. They tiptoe, tippy-toe, tippy-toe carefully around the smouldering volcano. So sweet. Who does he think he is? Are our things safe? Of course they are, silly. Bump, bump? No bump. Tight white shorts all the same. Very nice.

It's a nice beach too. Lovely. Harry is so, so lucky. Goes on and on. Reef beyond upon which breakers ... break. Boys fishing. Boys? Harry's men. No shade though. It's tiring. Walk through the shallow waves. Even the sea is hot. So exhausting.

"Harry has dumped us, the bastard."

"But he's got work to do, don't forget. It's such fun."

"Call this fun?"

"To see how he lives."

"I don't call this much fun."

"But look at the view, Darling. So lovely." Little wifey act and takes his arm even though no one's looking. Maybe some of Harry's boys.

He looks out to the breakers ... breaking.

6   A Tangled Web Woven[1]

A white ball, hanging high in an exhausted white sky. The sea, a sideshow down there, sighs. Depressed, hot, sticky and tired, on the veranda, they are. Lunch, the breakfast leftovers and the coconuts, opened for drinking, dumped by Wanei for them to find. The flies have got there first. Harry has sent Wanei off for some 'Free Time'. He may be a 'Paid Servant' but he is not a 'Slave'. He challenges Sally as if she had suggested he was. She had not said a word except to offer help that was rejected as interference in 'Delicate Domestic Arrangements'.

David and Sally are helpless against Harry's rage. They watch his useless activity they know is aimed at them although we don't deserve it. A coconut is hurled at the palm trees, dribbling milk as it lobs through the solid air. It lands with an ineffectual thump on the grass where it will sit for weeks as evidence.

Where's the garden he'd talked about? No such thing. There's cow dung right up to the house, thinks David, apparently impassive. He gazes out to where the sea might be. His attention is focused on Harry. If it were not for damn Sally, he'd do something and damn the consequences. He'd fight the man. Wrestle him or something; get him on the ground.

---

[1]

O, what a tangled web we weave,
When first we practise to deceive!
A Palmer too! – No wonder why
I felt rebuked beneath his eye:
I might have known there was but one,
Whose look could quell Lord Marmion.

Marmion: A Tale of Flodden Field, Walter Scott.

Sally wants to smooth things over, partly because she thinks she ought to, and partly because she thinks David expects her to. She does not know that he would rather she walked out to sea and not stop. She stands up and sits down again, damn her, almost, it seems, wringing her hands.

"I'm doing dinner," she says brightly, "don't forget." She undoes her hands, suddenly confident in the face of the baby boys' bad tempers. It's Mrs Grant and they'll jolly well do what they're told.

"Wanei'll help you then," replies Harry crossly.

"No. I'll do it."

"You can't. You don't know how things work. He will be there." As a Slave, he has no choice in the matter.

He is right: Wanei will make it all work. He'll clean the fish for a start.

Mrs Grant would not have given in so easily. But what would she have done? What does David expect, now, here? Go and drown yourself for Christ's sake. Well, Harry's had a busy morning, the Sweet, I'll sit down, be quiet and see what happens. The sudden flush of confidence has gone down the plughole.

Nothing happens. She frowns. Her mother would have had them all working for her by now, and quite happy to do it in a resentful sort of way. Keep them busy Sally, men with time on their hands are dangerous. Don't stand it for one minute. David is no help. Pre-occupied, he looks, must have some worry at work. What I'd really like, thinks Sally, is a warm shower and a lie-down in an air-conditioned bedroom. Here, the water has to be laboriously pumped up by hand when the power is off, so that it can fall again over my body. But no Wanei to do the pumping. No Slave. I'd do it myself only Harry won't let me. He'd rather do it himself and then make a great fuss about doing it by sighing and stamping and being martyred to my feminine whims.

David makes himself detached. Did I want to come to this damned place at the end of the road? No I did not. It was their idea and they bullied me into it. I mustn't let myself be pushed around like this. The Estates Manager for Haldan and

Cruikshank. He gets up, pushes his chair back noisily and then sits down again. The others take no notice.

They sit at lunch but they might as well sit for ever for all the eating they do. Harry's aggression is almost palpable. Visible it is, as a fixed, jaw-clenched expression that makes him look – the common word comes into Sally's mind – mental. David thinks it's these queers; they're funny that way; emotionally unbalanced. He should know.

Having made it clear he cannot bear their company a minute longer, Harry suddenly jumps up and says crossly.

"I'm sorry, I'm a bad host." He sits down again.

David looks out to wherever it is he looks. Sally inspects her hands on her lap.

Harry sits down again. He puts on a sane, contrite, sad sort of expression. The doggy, cocking its head and drooping its ears. Spoilt boy wants spoiling and he will get it. Say it's alright.

"Forgive me."

He looks at them.

David smiles, looks at Sally, his wife, the wonderful Mrs Pryce-Williams. Sally smiles back at David, her husband. He really is a good man; I am so lucky. Sees them with their children in large garden behind large red brick and lots of white painted woodwork Victorian house in Southwest London or summer English countryside, doves cooing. The wonderful Mr Pryce-Williams. Or perhaps stone, in the Cotswolds, with dogs.

Harry does not notice the soap opera. He seems to sleep now, having been let off.

"All the same," says David pompously, "one must do something. What do you normally do on Saturday afternoon?"

Harry seems to sleep.

After all, is it normally so hot?

What can one do in this weather?

Harry seems to sleep.

"Harry!" David booms. Be so good as to answer my wife, the wonderful Mrs Pryce-Williams, the worthy decoration of her husband, the Estates Manager for Haldan and Cruikshank.

"I sleep. It's all you can do. It's only these few weeks at the end of the dry season. The rains'll come soon."

"Let's sleep then." It's what I need. It's what my worthy wife needs. It's what you need, my boy.

So they go to their rooms, to their wooden boxes, the uneaten lunch left for the Slave to clear away. Harry opens all the doors and window shutters to allow the little breeze that will come to blow through the house. But each lies down separately to dream private dreams.

[][][]

Nothing like a siesta in the tropics. It comes naturally. Obey instinct. Rests the body, but better, organises the brain. Makes sense of things. Some sense. Some things. Soothes the troubled brow and all that. Harry, Sally, David sleep. Wanei? He sleeps also.

It's hot so you tend to sleep on your back. So the body is open, exposed, as it were. The light activates the brain. Deep sleep contrasts with near waking. You dream of waking but you are asleep. The light insists but the body resists; the body needs its sleep.

A four o'clock breeze, and the loneliness of waking in the tropical afternoon is intense. There is a desperate need for someone to be close. The idea, the feeling of anguish, does not last long but it is real and memorable all the same. Harry awakes and thinks of his Wanei. Wanei awakes, wherever it is that he sleeps. He makes his way to the house. Time to check the generator. If you cannot feel, you do something.

Sally awakes. No idea where she is. For a few seconds. A little girl. Fixes, focuses and, relieved, looks to David at her side. The very solidity and there-ness of him reassures her that she is alright. He is a solid, white chunk of muscle she wants to touch, undress and kiss. She wants to devour his youth before it is too late. Is it instinct that suggests later she will not want him? Not want him when he is heavy and less clean and new. Must be. Must now be the time to have babies. Ironic, at that moment of waking, of feeling lonely and then immediately secure with him there beside her and wanting him; ironic that she is as fertile and as able to conceive as she will ever be in her life. It is perhaps the definite moment when Sally passes from girlhood to womanhood. And it passes without her knowing, wasted by ... Wasted by David who shrugs her off the moment she touches him.

So she gets up, barely realising what has happened. Somehow she will have a wash and she will have her way. She doesn't care sixpence for any of them. Where's the Slave?

[][][]

He groaned. He actually groaned as if in pain – despair more like – as she touched him. Rolls away from her. From where she had been. His loneliness in the moment of waking is intense. Wow, he wants Harry and awake does not know what it was he wanted in his dream. He feels, nonetheless, the void that needs to be filled. One might say poor man if only we knew how he suffered.

He hears his wife demanding her bath and insisting she will cook supper. Wanei, she says, will help her. No, she does not want to swim, Sunday morning will do. You boys can go off on your own.

He shuts his eyes pretending to be asleep. Pretending he does not feel Harry sit on his bed. The weight of Harry on his bed. Blimey O'Reilly, he thinks, he ought to think, the weight of Harry's Harry on the bed.

Harry does not touch him but he bounces jauntily up and down until David is awake and must grin at the grinning Harry who says.

"Come on, we're going swimming. Sally's told us to get out while she cooks dinner with Wanei."

David cannot stop grinning now. He wants to get out with Harry and never come back.

"Has she?"

"She has. Bossy woman, your wife."

And off they go.

Wanei does most of the work but it is Sally's ideas that carry them along. This will be a Mrs Grant meal which will amaze them. She can do miracles can my wonderful wife and useful decoration. She can make dinner out of nothing. You should have seen what she did down there at Harry Williams' place. He lives like a savage. But that Wanei is wonderful too. Yes, he's also a savage. Whoops, bumping about in the little black hole of a kitchen, my wonderful wife and that wonderful man. Whoops don't be too wonderful, Wanei. He is such a sweet, though. Don't you think? Bump, bump as he acts the adoring little fuzzy-wuzzy, grinning boy. Ooooh, the bad boy, he's done that one before. Knows what he's up to does Wanei. He'll get his revenge, see if he don't.

Well, yes, now she came to think of it, Harry was so sweet that time. He had wanted to help her himself but she had shooed him off. Told him to take David swimming. He had seemed even a little hurt. Really? Indeed, he frowned as if they had, or he thought they had, a well-understood arrangement that couldn't be discussed too publicly. But then suddenly he had brightened up and had been the sweet ol' Harry again. Good idea, he'd said and then he'd shouted for Wanei who had come rushing in grinning. He had literally held Wanei and passed him over to her as a gift, like a parcel, telling them that Wanei was to be her Slave and he was to do exactly what she told him. And Wanei had said Yesah, two or three times, as if it had been a great joke.

He left them to it in that little back room, the sort of lean-to that passed as a kitchen. It was a hot little hole and she could smell Wanei and the fish together. She told him to cook the fish outside; and the rice. On the little smoky fire he had made. She told him she was going to make a sort of kedgeree with spices and any edible green things he could find for her. What with the red wine, that would have to be it. She wanted to make a cake, she told him, only she hadn't brought the right things in the rush to come. Anyway, there was no oven. Only the kero stove.

Really, that was it! Nothing more, bump-bump, Wanei!

Yes, of course Harry was in love with her. And she felt very close to him. They had talked and talked hadn't they on the way down? Oh, about everything and anything; she couldn't remember exactly. She had told him how marvellous her mother was, and how marvellous David was. He had told her he was gay. Just like that. She had no idea why. The little flirt. Anyway, it showed how much he trusted her and liked her. Yes, she was flattered he should tell her of all people. It broke the ice so there was nothing else to be said although of course they kept on talking. But being gay didn't make any difference. It made her like him all the more. She didn't think for a moment he didn't want to sleep with her. All gay men were like that – except the effeminate ones of course, and he wasn't one of those. All gay men were like that; just over sexed really or plain shy. The boarding school thing. She could put him at his ease and make a man of him. Don't be silly, any really good womanly woman, pretty good-looking, intelligent enough to talk intelligently can get a man. They're all the same really. But of course I wouldn't have dreamt of it. There's David, I adore him.

That was how it was, she reckoned. Later. She had her pick.

Bump, bump, bump. She watched Wanei prepare the fish. Watched him cook the rice in the big billycan thing on the fire behind the house, the water bubbling and hissing into the flames. Far too much but he must have his share too. And why not? A plate piled high. She saw him eating it with his fingers like a savage. She saw him squatting beside the fire. Tight white shorts and a red T-shirt stretched over the slim, strong back. Black legs shiny and the woolly head sort of vulnerable but powerful also. In her mind's eye it was the one eye and big teeth. She wanted to touch him down there.

[][][]

Ummm, that was it. The breeze and the descending sun bring a bit of colour back and the promise of ... Of what? It doesn't matter. At least the depression of the afternoon has gone. It's David who suggests skinny dipping in a bossy, quick, no-nonsense sort of way so Harry can't say no. He wants to see Harry, no doubt about that. Therefore Harry suggests: 's'OK at this time of day anywhere; we'll walk a bit to where the creek comes into the sea; the water is cool and clear there; we can wade up to the lagoon which is sheltered. At least, this is the gist of what he says. David follows. Impatient silence plus a hurried casualness. Walking along the beach, the two men.

A burning orb sets the velvet sky aflame. Coconut palms leaning every which way, too slender for their load, are thrown back, in long weary lines, to the veranda. Here, dark in dark, one eye watches, shiny black legs burn in the last bit of sunlight. Two elongated shadows move away until lost together in the new night. No moon yet. Wanei then, taking in his fill, snaps his teeth and returns to the back of the house and Missus Sally. He has things to do before dinner is ready to eat.

They leave the thrashing, fluorescent beach under cover of the moonless night. Idyllic, thinks David and banishes Sally from his mind. Mangrove on the one hand and a little rocky shore on the other with overhanging trees. Clean baby beach where they leave their clothes. It's not the moon but there is light no doubt: it comes from the silent, cool water; it comes from the very nakedness of their bodies; it comes from, from the idea itself. The idea of two young men, free of the other world for a while and, in an odd way, forever. David stretches naked before he dives in. Shows himself and knows he looks good. Like Sally, he is at that moment at the very peak of his youthful prime. All man but only just. Harry sits and watches approvingly. Smiles at David who pretends not to notice although he is acutely aware. David all white and clean and solid like, like an alabaster effigy; only his face, which would be a little sun red, is hidden in shadow. His hair thick and blond. Harry, older and more weathered, ancient somehow. Wiry body, curved as he sits on the rock to watch. White torso and buttocks contrast with sun-bronzed limbs. Hair too long, hides his face. He is wild Briton against David's polished Roman. He stands and stretches also, as if in a cocky copy of David but he does not dive; he walks into the water. They swim around, each as if ignoring the other. Harry will wait; it's his nature. He will wait for David to pounce and then, apparently taken off his guard, watch the other's embarrassment rise before he takes the reassuring initiative. Harry is a bit of a bastard. No less David in his way; the doctor's son and all that despite a great deal of willingness.

Thus, they are primed. A view of bare buttocks as Harry swims primly around David. David thinks he'll duck him so they can mess around. Touching more and more until it holds. And then what? What, for Christ's sake?

Do it. He's a decent bloke anyway. Whatever happens it would be between ourselves. And so it was; so it is. Urgent and very, very hungry. Fast; there is no time to linger in the water. It's a struggling of the bodies, splashing and again thrashing in the water. Hugging so tight: never let me go. Eating the other and feeling, feeling, feeling; hands rapidly exploring in eager discovery of the new, already storing the memories for later stale remembrance. Wow! And they come more or less together as a hugging, heaving, impatient organism that is conceived, grows and reaches maturity already thinking of death in an instant. Mmmm, it's great in the water and Harry laughs in satisfaction as David thinks of the consequences.

Holding together as if an afterthought until the water threatens to drown, they drift apart.

[][][]

By the time they are back at the bungalow they are dry. Perfectly presented. Dressed up as their old selves and amazingly, says David to himself, as if looking himself in the eye, it is so easy to detach part of oneself and put it aside. Shut the book and put it back on the shelf. It really is amazing, he thinks throughout the subsequent evening – and into the night – how easy it is to be David Pryce-Williams and all that again. Stupid berk! Why should it not be for God's sake? Why should it be so difficult to return to acting the part, playing that particular game? He'd done it for long enough hadn't he? But, nonetheless, and indeed recognising this particular stupidity, part of him was amazed: the part which might take up the Sally book again with an amusement warmed by the idea – he deluded himself – that he had Harry also. Amazed he was – looking himself in the eye in a very deliberate David Pryce-Williams sort of way – by what he had done; amazed by his matter-of-fact reaction to what he had done, what he had done as a married man, as David Pryce-Williams, as husband of Mrs P-W. Amazed also – and somewhat relieved – that he did not feel bad about it or angry with Sally as if he had to justify what he had done by defining some deficiency in her. Quite the opposite, in fact. It is, after all, an interesting book.

Amused also – the silly innocent – when he looked – and looked and looked – at Harry, that Harry also – the older and, no doubt about it, more corrupted man – played along so well during the evening, bossing Wanei in a possessive sort of way and flirting with Sally as if she was the most important person in the world. Which was a turn up for the books! He had never ever thought about her like that.

But Harry was not playing that particular game. He was being Harry who would be, if it amused him, David's Harry for David. And, Wow, he fancied David as much as David fancied the idea of himself. The difference was that this particular game was new to David insomuch as David was not controlling things as much as he thought he was.

Sally's dinner went down well because they were all hungry, and Wanei – watching – had not, after all, cooked too much rice. They were satisfied. Good grub, Sally. Mmmm, jolly good feed, Darling. She was pleased to hear it as she kept quiet, looking quite happy and warm-like, as if, as if she too had a secret.

Two bottles of heavy, red Australian wine between the three was (minus a couple of swigs for Wanei), with all that food, just enough to make them feel contented and pleasantly relaxed. How nice to have Wanei to do the washing up. All those, all those, those indiscretions really outside the main story line. It did not, it does not matter and life will go on. Of course it will! It's hardly likely to stop; you've still got to clean your teeth and change the sheets. This is what being grown-up's all about. Thinking, taking decisions, taking risks and acting according to one's desires, one's needs; one's principles, damn it. It's what being human is all about, for God's sake. Being alive. Is it not?

So civilised really and that was what being grown-up was all about, as well. Surely?

Dinner finished they move out onto the veranda. The two men so, so manly and quiet and polite to Sally. Contented it seems. Contented in fact, David driving the conversation but not so insistently as usual. Harry, essentially quiet. Nice and helpful though, this time around, and seeming so there, there in the dark, smiling. Sally – ever so democratic, it seems, it seems, for Harry – helps Wanei clear the things away and makes as at a camp-fire, the coffee in Harry's old tin mugs that give the stuff a salty flavour it seems, but just as nice, the coffee spreading the contentment towards sleep. Sally brings the coffee herself to the two men – so nice in the warm, still night, the waves crashing down there forever – and pops back for her own, leaving Wanei to do the washing up in the cold water under the moon. They hear the billycan thrown across the grass at the back; the hens will peck it clean in the morning.

The moon, the moon is up and it's like the old Bounty advert. Rippled silver-grey clouds across night sky on an old LP cover, Harry Belafonte's Beach Party, Sally remembers. Harry says it means the weather is changing.

[][][]

A deep unworried sleep. The sleep of the just or of the innocent or something like that. Unworried, each alone, waking to a stiff breeze and a bracing ionic atmosphere that makes them feel glad to be alive. Must swim before breakfast together but each alone. On the public beach as it were, under the public gaze. And they know it. They are adults playing hard at being kids, perhaps recognising their childhood as it slips from their grasp. Wanei watches. He looks at his Harry, and knowing he has him slips back to the house to strip off the sheets. He likes to hang them in the rain after washing. It will rain, soon. They will not stay another night.

They do not, although David suggests they might.

"We could set off at four tomorrow morning, so I can be in the office on time." He'd like another swim with Harry but Sally is determined. As determined to leave as she had been to come.

"That's silly: you'll be too tired Darling." He frowns at her to shut up as Harry points to gathering clouds.

"It's going to rain. Heavy. Quite soon and these early rains can wash out the road, just like that," he suggests. The liar. "You'd better get moving. Wanei," he roars, "we'll have a brunch. What have we got? Anything?" As if they might have nothing. The liar. "Wanei, fix some food," he says as if it's an order. But it's not.

Harry busies himself with Wanei ignoring the anguished David as Sally goes to pack noticing the naked bed. She looks at it, recognising that point in time where, if nothing else happened, she ceased to be a girl, even if she does not now feel like a woman. She sighs, smiles and stuffs things into the holdall. In the middle of this hurried activity she stops. She is Mrs Price-Williams, daughter of Mrs Grant. She pulls the things out and begins to fold them, placing each garment carefully back into the bag. Except for her long skirt (ample, dark, almost royal blue, light material. Silk?), from which she ineffectually tries to wipe out creases. Anyway, it will have to do. She steps out of her shorts and into the skirt. What on earth will Clara do with shorts like that? But that's beside the point. You could use them to wash the floor.

David must suffer now. Better go now before the rain comes. But he is not cross as they eat a good meal of fried eggs, more rice, coffee with tinned milk and lots of white sugar; a bony burnt fish that Wanei finishes later, gnawing the bones and crunching the skull between his jaws. David is not cross because he does not feel like it. Empty is what he feels. They are packed off before he knows what is happening. He is not used to being bullied and cannot resist. Harry and Sally connive – sniggering it seems – as Wanei throws the things into the back of the vehicle. Then David and Sally are put together and sent away. Harry follows in his truck and will see them as far as the stony, dry riverbed across which they must pass: even more treacherous if the rains beat us to it. The liar! Wanei watches them go. He waves at the dust; then goes off to sleep. He will wash before Harry returns.

Harry dumps them on their side of the river. See you he says and is off back to wherever it is he wants to return or, more like, from whatever it is he wants to escape. Phew, is his likely response now he can get on with, with being on his own, the Wanei book there when required.

Harry behind them now, David takes charge, puffing himself up as Mr P-W, Estates Manager and all that. He talks to Sally on the way back. Mrs P-W is not listening although he does not notice. He does not mention Harry, even to denigrate him. He feels he would like to tell her exactly what happened. Not as an explanation of his extraordinary conduct. Blimey! Not likely. What he really wants to do is to discuss Harry with Sally as a very private specimen, which belongs exclusively to them both. Yes, I did such and such with him. Next time it's your turn and we'll compare notes. When we've finished, we could … We could do something else. But she sleeps despite the bumpy road. He does not care. He might have said it outright for all she knew.

[][][]

Crumbs, one might say, what a tangled web was woven that weekend. The clouds gathered offshore, dropping the rain into the sea. What was left fell on the mountains behind, having passed over the plain upon which mankind has made its mess of plantation, scrubby farmland and European town. A trail of dust marks the road. It is David's vehicle with Sally inside beside him; we see it enter the town so that the dust stops and we see it disappear into the greenery of the posh suburb in which they live on the golf course side of the town; we see it emerge again in the neat square garden with its big trees that partly obscure the glinting tin roof of the house and the dark lawn. It stops beside the house. Tiny insect people get out of the toy car, towards whom another figure moves from the house. Together they scurry back and forth between the little tin box and the big tin box. Then they are gone. A brilliant fire behind but we see only the lengthening shadows until darkness shuts us out, specks of yellow light marking where the town might be, insignificant in the universe.

Inside the house, David notices Sally is detached and lethargic. She seems to be pre-occupied with something that is not him. Odd, he thinks. Or is it he who is detached from her? Not sure but better keep mum. Perhaps it's the wrong time of the month. They go through the familiar motions and on Monday morning are settling back into being Mr and Mrs Pryce-Williams again. He finds it even easier once he is in the office, bossing the department and doing what has to be done. A series of meetings, annual estimates for next year to be co-ordinated and all that. The other book gathers dust.

7   Sleep Now, Sleep

The idea of Friday Nosh Nite looms large. They will have to go unless they make an effort not to. It is what one does on a Friday night. You go as much to stake your claim as a bona fide member of the expat community as to reassure yourself that you belong to some sort of community of ... of common interest. Or something like that. One could avoid the club but it is difficult to avoid Nosh Nite without making a statement: you been on leave? They will ask. We haven't seen you for a while. Don't forget us, we'll think you don't like us.

Associated with Nosh Nite is Harry and everything to do with Harry.

Neither of them wanted to go. Had one of them, for fuck's sake, been able to say it, then they would have been saved. David, I was thinking, let's stay home tonight, I'll cook us something. Or, listen Sally, I'm fed up with the club. That would have done it. Instead they did the usual things and therefore flagellated themselves until the blood began to flow.

Look, it was no big thing; it was not like the shadow of some monstrous bird hovering above them, ready to swoop. It was just something that nagged a bit because they wanted to push it to the back of their minds. Had he said anything, David would have said 'It's a bore'. Not because it was boring but because it's what people say. And really, it's David who thinks about things more than Sally. After all, what had Sally got to think about? On a conscious level anyway. And even David could just about have borne it. He was a grown man after all. There was no need to act like an over-sexed schoolboy.

At the club, they act their parts well. The Pryce-Williams, such a devoted couple. He'll go far. And all that shit.

"You're in a Brown Study, old chap. What you thinking about?"

"Oh nothing, Bob. Have another drink? Whisky was it?"

"Thanks David. You need cheering up. Your wife's a gem. One in a million."

"Yes."

That's been done before.

David goes to the bar.

Mac is at the bar, in his usual place, propping it up along with the other usual props. The old lags who'll die in this godforsaken place.

David wants to avoid Mac. He looks angrily away as if his anger will be immediately appeased by the service of the bar-boy who will let him jump the queue. This ploy often works but tonight Mac has caught the boy's eye first and by some strange hand signalling with which they are both familiar he lets it be known that he will buy a drink for David.

David is hemmed in by the crowd. He cannot move and knows he cannot forever pretend he cannot hear Mac shouting his name. It will look odd if he does not turn around soon.

Not that Mac does not like David personally. Only, he doesn't like the type: youngsters who think they know it all after a few months in the country. He is inclined not to like David but he is willing to give the young man the benefit of the doubt, aware, starkly at times, of his own shortcomings. Mac is, after all, comfortable enough in his own skin to be fairly tolerant and kindly towards someone who is not. He has no strong affections but equally no one has ever inspired in him a deep antagonism. Nonetheless, he expects humanity in general to do its worst.

"David," he calls, "here. I've got you a drink. Join me."

David pushes through the crowd: "I must get back to ..."

"Yes, yes of course but you can spare an old man a few minutes, surely. You can take something back to your lady wife with love from me. How is the lovely Mrs um, um, Mrs ... your wife?"

"She's fine."

David is impatient; he is looking elsewhere; he wants to go back to Sally. Yes! He actually wants to get back to Sally. The safety and familiarity of his wife whose unchanging act effectively tells him that it's all OK.

But Mac is determined to hold him for a while. Did he not watch the three of them in the first place? He knows Harry, after all. He has known him, in one way or another, for over ten years. He would like to know what has been going on. He will chaff Harry later and thereby learn more.

He will remind David of Harry.

"How did you enjoy your trip to Harry's place?"

David remembers.

"It was beautiful."

"Yes, but it can be a bit dull."

"I don't think so."

"No? So what did you do?"

David remembers. He does not reply.

"I wonder sometimes what Harry gets up to but he likes the place. He's that type. They make quite good planters. People like him."

"...Yes."

"Did you meet his man? ... Odd couple. But they make a pair. Don't they?" Mac watches David who seems to be miles away. He is amused.

"What?"

"I think he's happy in his way."

"Who?"

"Who else?"

"Harry?"

"Yes."

"He showed us the place. We sat around, talked, ate food ... I went for a swim with him."

"Oh yes, you did. It's a nice place for that."

"... I must go back to Sally."

"Who?"

"... My wife."

"Yes, do. Give her my ... compliments."

"I will. Thanks for the drink."

David returns to Mrs Pryce-Williams empty-handed but no one notices because someone else has brought the drinks. There's a lot of talking and laughing and drinking. Now it is David's turn to be quiet but no one notices this either because they are too busy being happy. Someone looks at him; he returns a tight-lipped smile as if to say yes I am quite happy being here with you all and I am a little drunk which is why I am not talking. I am after all is said and done David Pryce-Williams, Estates Manager for Haldan and Cruikshank ever so clever and likely to go far because I am such a clever chap, and that is my wife talking ever so seriously making a serious point about a pair of ladies' shorts she will never wear again and they're hardly Clara's style so maybe they can be used to wash the floor. Her legs are too white and, and, and lacking in definition. I'd rather touch those long brown hairy legs that turn so suddenly white and strong at the buttocks. He wants to say fuck you all but he grins at the man who is talking to him and says nothing at all. Whoops, David was drunk last night but I think his little lady wife got him home, although she was a bit past it herself. Yes, a good night. The Pryce-Williamses, such a devoted couple. He'll go far. And all that shit.

"You're in a Brown Study, old chap. What you thinking about?"

"Oh nothing, Bob. Have another drink? Whisky was it?"

"Thanks David. You need cheering up. Your wife's a gem. One in a million."

"Yes."

David goes back to the bar. Fuck that old wreck Mac he can shout as much as he likes. He can go to hell. Fuck him in oriental languages. I've got my M.A. in Oriental Languages and the History of something or other. What's he got? The clap. Herpes, I bet. You never get rid of that.

"Gi'me a whisky." He stops the bar-boy, leaning across the bar to grab his arm. "Gi'me a kiss." The bar-boy looks back at him smiling a nice, happy smile; gives him a whisky, he's heard it before. You can do what you like when you're drunk in the club so long as you maintain the peace. "No one cares a fuckeddy duckeddy do da dey, do dey, do they?" He laughs at his own joke because the bar-boy has gone to listen to others.

He looks towards his wife. She's gone! No, there she is leaning across the table talking ever so seriously with a frown and her jaw sticking out and her face is white with red blotches under the hot lights and she is sweating and her reddish brown-blonde hair that will be grey one day is a mess and the other woman with black hair and another white face and too much eye make-up which is a bit smudged is agreeing ever so seriously as well.

"Gi'me gin-tonic."

A charming smile, and a gin and tonic appear. Did he pay or was it put on the slate? He is, after all is said and done, David Pryce-Williams, Estates Manager for Haldan and Cruikshank ever so clever and all that baloney and he ought to be known by now.

He takes the gin and tonic to his lady wife the beautiful and charming old cow. He'd rather lay an egg and he laughs again at his own joke. She ignores him anyway, talking hard about what ever fucking nonsense she's got to talk about, which is alright, so he goes for a pee in the garden and drives off on the road out of town towards where he remembers is the road to Harry's plantation. I know he's only the bum manager. He's a bum altogether and I am … Someone who can appreciate an early piece of Brahms chamber music. I could tell him a thing or two about Schubert if I wanted. He had the clap too.

[][][]

It is not difficult driving at night because there is only one road, but because it is dark it seems longer and he wonders if he is on the right track. Yes that's alright. His headlights pick up a couple of recognisable huts beside the road he remembers from last time. A good thing he did the driving because you can never fix the way in your mind if you don't.

He keeps going. He hums a tune which turns into that bit of Sibelius which is not really a tune but he doesn't have a big stock of tunes he can hum. He watches the tunnel of light ahead of him that goes on and on, the insects slapping dead against the windscreen: lots of them, so he has to put on the wipers to clear the mess. Gosh have I got enough fuel? Phew, nearly half a tank. That's OK. He thinks of Sally, he thinks of Harry in the water, he keeps going.

He comes to the stony ground which is the riverbed. It's a stony plain at this time of the year before the rains have come. They will come any day now he has been told. Harry said it last week. Couldn't cross this way then. You'd have to know what you're doing and you don't have a clue. He's lost in this stony place and stops in a pool of silent light with the night roaring all around. No, it's OK because he just has to follow the tracks. Starts the engine and, accelerating too quickly, skids on the round river stones. Moves a little and then sticks on a bigger rock. Stuck, fuck it, sweats. Now I've done it. What to do? Looks at his watch. 1.30! In the morning, for Christ's sake. Reverses, slowly and carefully disengages from the rock with a bump. Gets out, moves the rock. Looks at stars. Wow, I am but a small thing in the universe. Returns to car and continues journey.

It's quite easy, really, just following the tracks. The bent trunks of palm trees flick past. His headlights illuminate the grubby white bungalow. He turns off the engine before he turns off the lights so that he sits there for a moment or two unreal in the din of the night. Innocent looking and calm, dead calm after the hectic, hot activity of the club which makes him want to puke in remembrance. He belches anyway before turning off the lights and slumping asleep over the steering wheel.

[][][]

A tapping at the window. It's Harry, leaning against the car door, naked, apparently. He shouts through the shut window.
"What's the matter?"
"Uh?"
"What you doing here?"
David is not sure for a second.
"What do you think?"
Harry stands back and folds his arms.
David can no longer see his face but the naked torso is illuminated by the half reflection of the lights on the bungalow. He looks up into the dark. He shouts.
"I've come to see you."

The torso moves back a little.

David is stone-cold sober and wide awake now. He winds down the window and switches off the lights. Immediately he feels intimate with Harry in the night that presses down on them. It does not matter what Harry thinks: it's only the two of us. He feels excited, dizzy almost, knowing something will happen. He recognises and welcomes what he felt just before they stripped for swimming. It is not lust but the recognition of his youth, the flowering of which he almost missed. Without Harry, he thinks, the budding flower of my youth would have dropped off dead before it opened. It's a sentimental thought but he thinks it all the same and for this reason sees Harry as his Christ and as the most beautiful thing he has ever seen. More so because he is sure that a part of Harry welcomes him. Unlike the doctor's son, there is nothing in Harry that he can corrupt; this time around it is he who is the innocent. Harry, he thinks, is worthy of my, of my adoration. Adoration is what he feels because it is not love. It is romantic infatuation which bathes Harry in very rose-tinted light.

David does not even consider Wanei enough to dismiss him. It would, in any event, be a disservice to himself, David Pryce-Williams etc., to have Wanei on a sufficiently equal footing as to be a rival. Might as well have Sally in opposition.

And true to his form, David sorts out the ideas crowding in on him, so that he is at the centre, directing the action. At any rate, that is what he thinks, but he is in a sufficiently sober frame of mind by now – above and beyond, as it were, the churning, dizzy excitement – to realise that he might have put himself in a foolish position, his flight from the club to Harry seen as an act of emotional irresponsibility, even. Nonetheless, here, he sort of reasons, he undoubtedly is, and here he undoubtedly wants to be. He is not going to be foolish but to take even one step back, to admit weakness in any way, would give all the appearance of foolishness; he is not going to have that. He will deal with the consequences as they arise. David Pryce-Williams, you know, he's not queer; he'll just fuck anything that moves.

He wants to move now but also he would like Harry to open the door for him. He wants Harry to bring him out. He wants

Harry to be, to be Harry as he first felt him in the club when Harry took hold of his hand and held it, seeming to weigh the worth of him. Weighing him against some sort of standard that was valuable to him and finding him OK. That's what he wanted but at the same time he was determined to remain in charge. Stubbornly so, if necessary. He must remain David Pryce-Williams; to lose one single inch would be to lose everything and be at the other's mercy. And as he thinks this he sees Sally in his mind's eye, as a drooping, pathetic, lost figure. He wonders how she would have got home. He feels pity for her, seeing her lonely in the world without him. Is it the spark of love? He must, he oddly thinks, stay strong for her sake.

"I've come to see you."

"What?"

"I've come to see you. I love you." David is amazed – again – by what he says. Amazed he can say it at the same time knowing quite well he doesn't mean it. It is the first time he has used the phrase. It is the one thing he has never said to Sally and she has never asked him to say it. It was always understood. It was part of the undeclared contract that it would not be said. For the first time, here in front of Harry, he sees himself squarely as a liar. Not as the liar that he is in his social essence but as a compassionately lying player in this particular drama. The idea, of consciously lying, makes him feel strong and in control. He wants to laugh.

But the laugh comes from the dark other. It is a laugh of disbelief, although Harry knows what David means.

"You had better come in." He does not open the car door for David but moves away into the house.

David sees the wrapper move into the veranda and disappear. He sits a little longer in the car. But he is hungry and his body reacts strongly to the thought of Harry. He gets out and follows.

[][][]

Harry sits alone in the naked room. It has just enough things made of plain timber to serve its purpose as dining room, office, library and occasional sitting room. It is no more than the largest of the three boxes into which the interior of the house is divided. The essence of the house is the wide veranda that encloses the three sides. Without the veranda, it is a shack.

Harry is waiting for David. The room has a back door from which he could escape. It leads down a few steps to the lean-to where Wanei keeps the pots and pans and things, where Wanei had prepared the meal with Sally six days before. A window – square hole cut in timber wall – stares out of the veranda-less back of the house onto a space one might call the back garden or back yard: anyway, a piece of the plantation taken into the service of the house. A clothesline runs from one palm trunk to another. Here, during the day, chickens scratch and a goat is tethered. Protected by a bit of scrub beyond is Wanei's decent little timber house surrounded by a vegetable garden. Oddly, Wanei has more privacy than does Harry himself, although Harry invades it when he wants.

Moonlight enters through the back window. It illuminates an empty wooden armchair opposite where Harry is, a suggestion of sprawling, spare limbs, draped over another wooden armchair. He is looking out of the front door at the slender trunks of the palms streaked by the moonlight. He hears David walk up onto the veranda but does not move.

David pushes open the flimsy front door and looks around the room, eventually fixing his eyes on Harry.

"Sit down."

The flimsy door slams shut, which makes David jump but not Harry; he would be surprised if it did not slam.

Harry grins then stifles a yawn.

David sits in the chair opposite the window. The moonlight touches him with silver. Despite the ugly Hawaiian shirt and white club trousers, he looks beautiful: younger than he is, with a sort of tough, unspoilt innocence; pale and angelic even. The flower has bloomed for Harry, who sees it.

"Sally?"
"Fuck Sally."
"She knows you're here?"
"Of course not."

"How ...?"

"I walked out the club and drove here. She doesn't know I've come."

"But ..."

"I said fuck her." David feels disloyal as he says this, and for a second he knows he is acting. But what else can he say? Stay in control. He cannot see Harry's face, only the curve of the man's lower chest and stomach. He wants to get on his knees but that would be unseemly. Stay in control. "I suppose she got herself home. Someone will have taken her. I could telephone her. You got a telephone?" He asks, sarcastically.

Neither of them moves. There is hypocrisy all around but mostly Harry's. He knows what David wants and he knows that David will get what he wants eventually, but he lets David make all the moves, insuring himself for later. He can say David made it happen. But one might say he gave himself to David as an act of generosity. Eventually he says:

"Well, here you are."

"Here I am."

And Harry watches, calmly; coldly, you might say. He is not, after all, the hungry one; he has other options. He is all David has. The bastard is playing a deliberate game. All the same, they are both titillated. But one might say Harry is generously giving David a run for his money.

"We'll sort things out in the morning."

"What things?"

"Things."

"The morning can look after itself."

"It will."

The roaring night holds the two men together in the same defined space of the crude and tidy sitting room. David in the moonlight: Harry in the dark. They might have been cast irrevocably together on a desert island.

"Do you want anything ... else? Apart from me, that is?"

"No thanks."

"Sure?"

"No." I said no. Do you think I wouldn't ask, wouldn't demand, if I wanted a drink or something? I am, after all, David Pryce-Williams. For Christ's sake, you little perv.

"I'll go back to bed then. You can sleep where you slept before. The things are ready. Just feel at home." He says generously.

David watches Harry cross the room in front of him. Watches him touched with the moonlight for a moment. Harry's gold in contrast to his own silver. Tarnished gold all the same, the body less pure looking: and patchy in colour and hair; a piebald horse of a man, he thinks, and not well groomed either, or well fed. A bachelor man alright, spare and bony, his ribs showing the signs of no wife to ensure regular meals. His hair needs cutting. But he wants him. He wants to grab him by that hair and pull him to the floor, the wrapper falling off to expose the naked man within his power. He wants to see Harry humiliated beneath him, aware of his inferiority. He realises the violence within himself, forgotten since the long-haired student whose dog-like, cringing acceptance of him would make him so cross that he would abuse him verbally: you ought to build up your muscles a little; you're a weed. Why can't you sit up straight instead of slouching at the table? A gentleman would never sit like that. At least wash your hair if you don't want to cut it; that's why you've so much acne. And in the end he would say, you don't mind me saying these things do you? I'm only saying them as a friend. The grateful, humiliated boy would say it's alright.

Now he feels the same for Harry: hating him and wanting him all at the same time. As he does, it occurs to him that he has never felt like this about Sally. With Sally he simply acts the way he thinks David Pryce-Williams would act, allowing his young body to do the rest. The simple idea is to warm Sally up and then fuck her in a considerate sort of way ensuring she has an orgasm. It seems to work and gets things done quickly. His mind does not get involved. He cannot imagine himself murdering Sally whereas murdering Harry seems entirely within reality. Funny.

He hears Harry's bed creak as he lays himself on it, and imagines him watching the moonlight slice through the living room. He stands and stretches his arms upwards, as if he worships the moon. The process drags his shirt up, and with one easy movement he pulls it up over his head. The muscles of his back arch a little, his hair is ruffled. His smooth-skinned, chunky torso has a well-fed appearance, its unsullied whiteness, tragic.

If Harry is watching, he would see the young man in profile stretched out to the moon.

David takes a deep breath as if he realises that this is how he feels at the peak of his prime before he dives over the edge. He undresses completely, leaving the clothes on the chair before going into his room to lie on top of the bed on his back. The position, no doubt, is the same as Harry's. The thoughts? Who knows.

[][][]

Opening his eyes to the solid, dark and now moonless silence, Harry is aware of David standing in the doorway. He waits until he feels the weight on top of him. The whole weight of David pressing him down. Feel the weight and test the validity of me now you little shit. All the same, David wants Harry to weigh him and find him not wanting. He wants Harry to appreciate his worth as to what he is just now at this precise point in his life, in the night, in Harry's bedroom, in the bungalow, on the plantation, twenty miles south of Port Markham, in New Sudan, about as far from fucking England as you can get.

Is not David offering his youth? As Harry feels David and hears him breathing in his ear, smelling the salty newness of the man, of the young man in his prime, he puts his arms around David as an act not of passion but of affection. David feels a surge of gratitude and this is how it is between them: affection and gratitude. There are almost tears, and this time there is plenty of time; the morning can look after itself.

Essentially, however, Harry, who will give nothing of himself to the younger man, is amused. He allows David to play with his body until he is exhausted.

"It's alright, it's alright. Sleep now, sleep."

8 Falling Over a Precipice

So in the bright morning, David sits, just as the week before, waiting for his coffee. He is dressed in his Hawaiian shirt – blue-and-white pattern of palm trees – and a worn-out, red wrapper of Harry's. The difference is that his ankles are crossed on the chair opposite, upon which Sally had once sat. Also, he is not acting cross, he is cross. He is cross because Harry had kicked him out of bed hissing don't let Wanei see you here. Get up fuck you I'll bring you a coffee outside. What the fuck did it matter if Wanei saw the two of them in bed? Who was Wanei?

The incident has disrupted David's romance but it has not brought him anywhere near reality. Wanei and everyone else would have to lump it. He was going to stay here as Harry's lover. He would drive into Markham every day. And Sally? Well, she'd just have to lump it too. Did she think he was going to give up his life just as he had found it? He saw himself going to the club with Harry rather than with Sally. The rebel, defying convention. Remarkable man, David Pryce-Williams; doesn't care two hoots; I admire his guts. He's just a randy bastard; he'll fuck anything that moves. No, not at all queer; bisexual you know. Like Mick Jagger. Just wants to experience everything life has to offer.

David could not resist the fantasy of the moment. What did it matter? He'd give up his job if necessary. He could help Harry run the plantation. Sally could go back to England. Good ... Good thing they hadn't had children yet. She could start again with someone else. He saw her with a single suitcase at the airport. Pathetic and defeated. But last night was electric: flesh on flesh as he had never realised it before. That's what he wanted every night for the rest of his life. How could he manage without it? This is happiness. Forever and ever. Amen!

Enter Harry, pushing open the door with his shoulder. Green work shirt with epaulettes and pockets; worn out, like the wrapper David is wearing, but well pressed. Khaki shorts which look as if they had been passed down by an older brother. Carries boots in one hand, the other carefully holding two mugs of coffee. He drops the boots on the floor.

"Here's your coffee old man. Shift your feet."

He gives David a mug and sits opposite, clutching his own. He has said nothing to Wanei yet, the two of them ignoring each other in the tiny kitchen. He wants to be kind to his guest and put him at his ease. He can manage one guest and is unlikely to throw the coconut this time.

"Sorry to chuck you out like that. Wanei, you know."

"It's OK," says David, wanting to be and therefore being immediately mollified. He reaches across and puts a hand on Harry's knee. Harry crosses his legs, squeezes the hand with his own and puts it back. David, wanting to be and therefore being warmed by this, not seeing the false smile on Harry's face: "Let's go for a swim."

Harry looks at his watch.

"I've got to work old man."

"OK, later." David smiles, thinking: tomorrow I'll go out with him.

"Yes," and then almost whispers, "before you go."

David looks out to the sea and to the clear horizon. In an hour or so it will be impossible to see where the sea stops and the sky begins. That is, until the storm clouds gather.

Harry is busy putting on his socks and boots.

"Look, I'll be back in an hour or so but you don't have to wait for breakfast. Just ask Wanei to fry you an egg and, and there's some bread. If you can wait there'll be rice." He looks up at David and then quickly back at his boots so that he does not have to catch the other's eye.

But David is focused on something out to sea.

"I expect you'll want to be off fairly soon."

"I'm not going back."

"You're OK to drive?"

"I'm not going back."

Although he heard what David said, Harry pretended that doing up his boots absorbed all his attention. He was not worried because in the end he would get rid of David. But it was a nuisance all the same.

"What did you say?" He seemed to be talking to his feet.

"I said I'm not going back."

"Don't be silly, man, Sally'll be out of her mind. You can't just disappear like that."

"Fuck Sally. I've told you already, I'm staying here. With you." David stares at Harry until Harry has to look up at him from his boots. He fails not to catch the look of horror on Harry's face before it transforms into laughter.

Harry wants to say No, that's your job not mine but instead he says.

"Don't be crazy. You've got to get home."

"I'm not crazy. I'm staying here with you. I love you." He is as calm and as cool as a cucumber. His heart thumps hard as he hears himself tell the lie but he is determined to do what he likes. Despite the evidence, he does not for one second consider the possibility that Harry, the flirt, does not want him. The same determination – stubbornness, almost – which makes him good at his job.

Harry's reaction? One part of him, what Mac calls the emotionally unstable part, wants to run away, to avoid the issue until someone else sorts it out. Probably Wanei, who would do something hostile to David if he was left alone with him. The other, the more calculating part of Harry, wants to laugh at David's declaration of love. But he is also flattered that David – a good-looking man, no doubt about it, who'd be successful in the gay bars of King's Cross or Manila – is focusing his attention upon him. He does not delude himself for one minute that David is in love with him because he recognises in David a little of himself: a romantic with a degree of self-centredness which will always restrict his ability to fall unconditionally in love with anyone, apart from himself, that is.

Sitting there, then, putting on his boots and having these ideas, Harry is, in fact, nowhere near the point of running away. Had circumstances allowed, he would have gone back to bed with David: he was something of a sexual opportunist, after all. But, at this point of the morning, with things to do, his practical frame of mind is to the foremost, abetted by the additional fact that David's ideas are entirely untenable given his job, his wife and the whole David Pryce-Williams-ness of his existence.

So Harry plays for time.

"Mmmm, I see. Well look, you just sit here and relax while I see to some things. I'll be back later."

"Alright." David watches Harry striding between the coconut palms. At one point Harry turns around and waves playfully. David waves back and then goes down to the beach. He will swim on his own. He walks into the sea fully clothed.

[][][]

Harry takes a roundabout route to the back of the house. Ducking the washing line, he goes to the kitchen where he finds Wanei.

"Let's go to your house." They disappear into a sort of shrubbery that defends the vegetable garden and Wanei's space.

The relationship between the two men is not unusual. Superficially it is unequal but it has endured precisely because, over the years, a sort of equality has developed. At the public level it is a fairly common master-servant relationship where a sort of mutual dependency and a certain mutual fondness have evolved. The master has the economic advantage and neither party would ever be able to draw the line between affection and better the devil you know etc. But each defends the other in terms of possessiveness: don't ever insult my house-boy; that is my unique prerogative. Similarly, never castigate my boss or my master; only I have the privilege to define him as an exploiting bastard. That sort of thing.

Thus Harry and Wanei; but there is more because when there are no guests they sleep together, thus creating an intimacy that transcends superficial differences. There is also an element of mutual respect – even gratitude – because the relationship has allowed each man to feel he has fulfilled himself and defined what he thinks he is in the other. All the same, they can act, this odd couple: they play games as much as do David and Sally. They play at 'you be the master and I'll be the slave'. This, especially during the day, when Wanei is working as house-boy, regardless of the presence of visitors. But games are not played when Harry goes to Wanei's little house: a sort of comfortable shed crowded with bed, chair, and a table upon which Wanei's few possessions disintegrate.

But the relationship is also dangerous, precisely because it is between two men; both selfish, sexually opportunistic and emotionally careless. A relationship between two equal charges; explosive, therefore, by its very nature. A sort of conflict between lovers but an alliance also, which can deal ruthlessly with anyone who thinks he can butt into their little world. Therefore, they gang up against David.

Wanei defines Harry as a weakling. He defines David and Sally as a single predatory beast exploiting Harry's weakness. Harry's weakness makes Wanei angry but the David-Sally beast only annoys, because he knows he will beat it in the end. He thought he had beaten it. Beaten it last weekend with the act which had started out as an act of violence, but which had transformed into something else. Dumbfounding him in the process, at any rate for the time during which he had worked on the meal with the woman, who had, as something temporarily separated from the beast, appealed to him: not in a particularly prolonged or thoughtful way, but as a sort of flash in the dark; something he might think about later, with affection, with the sort of affection you might feel for a stray kitten. All the same, he thought he had dealt with it, and here it was all over again.

Wanei's room is dark, the window shuttered. Having been allowed in, Harry lies down on the bed, his arms behind his head. He looks up at the ceiling ignoring the one-eyed anger of the other who sits on a chair, resting his bare feet on the bed.

Tell him to go, more or less says Wanei. I can't do that. Why not? He'd refuse, I have to look after him. Why? Because, because I have to. Because he is your white brother? No! Why then? Because he is another Englishman and he might be ill. Then he should be ill with his wife, not with us. We will put him in the car and drive him home. What if he refuses? We will get the boys to tie him up and carry him back, like a pig. We cannot do that. Why not? Because he is a friend. He is not, you have not known him long enough: it is because he is your white brother. Can I let him die? Let him die. Alright, it is because he is my white brother, damn you. Tell him to go back to his wife. I have done that, he will not go. Tell him again, you are supposed to be the boss here. If you will not tell him, I will tell him. Are you afraid of your brother? No, I will do it. Go now. I will. Will you make the breakfast? Yes.

They have given David a way out. If he does not take it, they are, therefore, absolved of the responsibility.

[][][]

Harry finds David back in his chair reading one of his books:

They had reached this unexpected development much too rapidly, much too crudely, unexpected because on her way to Pavlovsk, Nastasya Filippovna still dreamed of achieving something, though, of course, she expected things to turn out badly rather than well; Aglaya, on the other hand, was absolutely carried away instantaneously by her emotion, just as though she were falling over a precipice, and she could not believe her own eyes, and was decidedly at a loss for the first moment. Whether she was a woman who had read too much poetry, as Radomsky had suggested, or simply mad, as the prince was convinced, this woman, at any rate – though her behaviour was sometimes arrogant and cynical – was really far more shy, tender, and trustful than one might have supposed her to be. It is true, there was a great deal that was bookish, romantic, self-centred, and fantastic, but there was also a great deal too that was strong and profound in her ... The prince understood that; and there was a look of great suffering in his face. Aglaya noticed it, and trembled with hatred.

The Idiot, by Fyodor Dostoyevsky.

Blue-and-white Hawaiian shirt spread on grass to dry. David wears only the wrapper. To Harry he looks brooding and beautiful. Fleetingly, Harry wonders what it would be like to live with the man. The arrogant, self-deluded, simple man, who, for a brief moment, when his youth is beginning to fade, wants to challenge the universe.

"How's it going?" He says.

"'s'OK." David looks up, but Harry is looking out to sea, leaning on the veranda rail, beyond the shirt.

"You had your swim?"

"Yes."

"Breakfast'll be ready soon."

"Thanks." And indeed, David sounds profoundly grateful, so that Harry feels, feels not affection, but sympathy for the guy who is, after all, a suffering brother, of sorts.

What Harry wants to do is to discuss David's feelings with him in an objective, detached, reasonable, man-to-man, sort of way, avoiding emotion, encouraging David to explain his homosexual feelings without embarrassment. He would like, in turn, to explain that sexual attraction is not to be confused with love. He wants to apologise for having led David on. But, but he feels he would thus be encouraging the man to reflect too much. Also, there is a look of grim determination on David's face which makes him feel that reasoned argument would be a waste of time.

David certainly looks as if he is determined to go through with the whole thing; the whole drama of falling in love with a man. He is not going to backtrack; not only because his pride will not let him, but also because he cannot go back; he cannot go back to being David Pryce-Williams, heterosexual husband of Sally Pryce-Williams. If he fails, he will have to move on to being David Pryce-Williams, failed homosexual husband of Sally Pryce-Williams. He will have to live his life with a sense of failure. His idea of himself will have been shaken to its foundations. Not a bad thing, some might say, Mac amongst them.

The affair will have to end brutally and in tears. Then David will be able to lie to himself in order to restore David Pryce-Williams again, defiantly facing the world. He is defiant now.

"What's so funny?"

"Nothing," replies Harry, wanting to laugh but also wanting to help.

"Me, I suppose."

"No, David, definitely not you. The rest of the world perhaps." Whoops, stop it Harry, you're getting too close. That dark other half is watching. "Listen," Harry gently removes David's weighty, worthwhile, innocent-looking, big, sea-washed, clean young feet from the chair upon which he will sit. "Listen," he puts the feet onto the floor as if he values them, almost as if he is in a position of supplication; worship, even. "Listen," he sits down, elbows on knees, and looks at David who looks back, apparently amused. "Listen, you have to hear me out."

"Would I not?" laughs David.

Harry wants David to understand that he cares, albeit that he does not love. At any rate, he wants David to think well of him. But, gosh, must be careful; mustn't care too much, or, at any rate, seem to care. Must break the affectionate bond. Can't go on being a Wellington boot. This is a serious business. Got to get rid of him. So he says.

"Look David, are you feeling OK?"

"Why not?" David laughs straight at Harry. "Never felt better. I know what I'm doing. I'm not having a nervous breakdown, if that's what you think."

"Are you sure?"

"That I know what I'm doing?"

"That you're not having a nervous breakdown?"

David stares out to sea, ignoring what is obviously a fatuous piece of nonsense. He is smiling.

Harry looks at David's profile. Despite its slightly babyish features it has a sort of solid Roman nobility. The pale skin has been given a blush by the sun which is also bleaching the hair.

"Alright then," he says, "but just tell me what you're going to do."

"I said, I'm going to stay here."

"Why?"

"I told you."

"But even if I believed you loved me, I don't love you. You know that."

Smiling to the coconut palms and the sea beyond, David is unperturbed.

"I'll make you. You slept with me, you responded and you ate me. And you'll do it again given half the chance; you know you will."

"I won't."

" ...You're a liar then," and David begins to laugh.

"You're mad."

"Maybe I am." David looks at Harry until Harry has to look away. Catch that eye and ... Well God knows what might happen.

"But, what about Sally?" Harry manages to sound as if he is concerned, although his greater concern is for himself.

"I've already said, fuck her."

"You don't mean that. She'll be worrying herself silly. We owe it to her as ... as ... as a friend to at least tell her you're safe. What's she going to do if you haven't turned up by Monday morning? She's got to be told."

"Go tell her then."

"Tell her what?"

"For God's sake. Tell her I'm staying here."

"But, David, you're not. You can't."

"Who says?"

"I say."

David laughs a little more and then looks out to sea again smiling. He is confident or rather he seems to be. He is not so sure but he must keep on this course. He must maintain David Pryce-Williams at all costs.

"So," says Harry, "I don't have a say in the matter?"

Nothing but the smile.

"Do I?"

"Think about it. Are you going to kick me out?"

That is indeed the problem. If David was a neighbour, living close by, Harry knew that he'd probably want to sleep with him. In his wildest dream did he not think it might be nice if there was a sort of mutual threesome amongst the three of them? Could he honestly say that in certain circumstances he would not swap Wanei for David or, as he had already done, cheat on Wanei? Cheat on them both for that matter. Well, yes, he had cheated, and that idea of himself as a cheat makes him blush. It is not how he wants himself to be and yet if the opportunity did arise again, if David did come to him in the night, he is pretty sure he would not throw him out.

David is right, and they are a couple of cheating shits, Harry the worse because he already has what he needs. David, at any rate, can be excused inasmuch as Sally is not, is never likely to be, a man.

Harry thought of Wanei. He thought of their years together and he thought of what they had both given up. Wanei having given up the most, laying himself open not only to the taunts of being a 'man-meri' – a man-woman – but also to the charge, which he could never wholly refute to his own internal satisfaction, that he had sold himself out to the white man for some sort of economic advantage. He blushed again. You can't have everything in life and he had a lot already. It was a commonplace idea but it would do for the time being; it would have to. So he tried another tack.

"OK, well one way or another Sally'll have to know and it seems I'll be the one to tell her."

"So what are you going to tell her?"

"I'll tell her you've had a nervous breakdown."

"Say it, then. Say what you like. But you can tell her as well, if you want – I couldn't care a fuck – that I don't want to see her again and I'm staying here."

"OK, I'll tell her that but, in that case, David, I'll explain the truth, the whole truth."

"And what's that?"

"I'll tell her everything."

"I bet you don't. You'll want to cover up your own tracks. You've a good idea of yourself haven't you? You won't want to mess that up."

Fact was, Harry was as capable of acting out his idea of himself as was David. One of these ideas was that he was an honest man; honest to himself and honest to the social world in which he lived. If anyone had asked Harry if he was a queer, he would have said yes he was and he would have taken the consequences. But no one ever had asked him. So he says.

"Yes, you're right. I don't really want Sally to know that I encouraged you to cheat on her."

David snorts a laugh.

"But I'd feel better if I came clean. She already knows I'm gay."

Another snort.

"And come to think of it, whatever I tell her, she's only human."

"Indeed! And what does that mean?"

"It means she'll interpret the facts in a way that best suits her own needs. She will, David, just like we are. Either I'll be to blame or you'll be. Or she'll agree that you've had a sort of nervous breakdown and..."

"And what?"

"Never mind."

"I don't mind. You can tell her what you like. See if I care." He has an almost overwhelming desire to fight Harry there and then. He wants to smash him. But he does nothing and the feeling quietly subsides.

Harry sighs, not for himself, but for David

"David, please listen to me. The whole thing's impossible. Apart from anything else it's impractical. You can't just stay here. You're on a work permit which means you have to work. Your company'll soon come looking for you if no one else does. The word'll get out."

"No Harry, I've worked all that out. I'll get Mac to give me a job. I could run a plantation as well as anybody. Probably better than you. It isn't agricultural skills that count in the end." He wasn't far wrong, and Mac was short of a good man.

"Oh yes, and then what? You think I'll have anything to do with you? I'll tell you to go to hell. I'm not going to be responsible for you." Then he adds, with an unpleasant laugh: "But watch out."

"You don't have to be responsible but you wait and see. I'll just press my case, a little. I'll press it just by being around. You're the one better watch out."

Harry laughs unpleasantly again. He looks at David with a sort of pity mixed with admiration. He looks at David properly for the last time. From now on David is a thing to be got rid of. As good as dead, is David. The game is over. We have played our parts, we have discussed the subject like civilised men, across a dinner table, perhaps in one of those civilised houses you find in southwest London. We have acted our parts, actually with honesty, because we knew we were lying. Lies are the basis of civility. Harry knows it, Mrs Grant knows it, and Sally, thanks to David, is beginning to know it. Doesn't make them any better – the thief in the night and the assassin know it – but it helps them see through some of the shit. And Harry knows what he is doing with a most pure and a most deliberate clarity of thought. Had he not wanted, at first, to extricate himself from a difficult situation without hurting or at any rate upsetting the other people concerned? Who ought not, all the same, damn them, to have come down to the plantation in the first place. Better to have stopped at home and read a book, a dry and as dusty as old bones book. What a more emotionally honest Harry would have said to David was: go for God's sake go. It's not safe here. There's a swamp at the back full of crocodiles. Watch out. But he said nothing. Because having done his civil duty, he reverted back to being the Harry he was before he met David and Sally, the pagan, pre-Roman, British Harry. The naked Harry in the bush. The Harry, at any rate, who related to Wanei. An animal, an elemental thing part of the roaring, moonless, tropical night thick with its motionless heat. An idea that howls at the universe. Not something that would sit down to dinner in southwest London but something that would rather tear out your warm heart with its teeth. Or, at any rate, strangle you and throw you into the swamp.

9   Where We Exterminate Each Other

Sally is not drunk, definitely not, but she is certainly in a state of alcohol-induced detachment. She is aware of what she is doing, aware that it is a bit silly but determined to do it all the same. As if she is reading a book about herself. But is that really me, or only a vague approximation of me? I don't want to be like that at all.

The club is not empty but it seems to be. The lights full on so the boys can clear up. They are excessively polite wishing you to hell and out the way. Haven't you got a bed to go to? Smell of cigarette smoke and spilt beer, the room looks tawdry, and cheap. Very cheap in the bright light and the boys working around you ever so polite they think you are part of the cheapness. We will open the windows any minute to let in the air and the night, which will, in a couple of hours, give way to the dreaded dawn when, if you are still here, we'll sit and stare until you go home, damn you. Go home, sleep until the glorious dawn, when the sun will blast at your eyes and make your head ache. Serve you right.

Sally smiles at the table upon which her elbows rest. She is tousled as if just out of bed rather than ready for it, cheap looking, her face blotchy and tired out, just as David had seen her before he left. Seriously, though, she says, as if as sober as a ... as a ... whatever it is, she stares up at the other similar, only dark to her own fairness, woman who has gone home hours and hours and hours ago. She is waiting for David to take her home. What else can I do? I have not the faintest, foggiest idea. What does one do when one's husband has, apparently, forgotten one? As Mrs Grant might have thought of saying in a moment of histrionic insanity but would not have actually said it, not in a million years. I would have caught myself in time, Sally, this will not do. Where on earth has David got to we had better walk home it's not far. I will not let the grass grow under my feet although you may stay there until it is up to your chin.

This, Sally sitting all alone in the club a bit drunk and all washed out, is, as it happens, the lowest Sally will ever fall.

[][][]

Mac has not moved from the bar. He takes little shots of something and smokes cigarettes one after the other holding them in his brown fingers so that his lungs are spared most of the tar. Thus he does not need to go for a pee. He stares in exactly the opposite direction of Sally. He has been looking at the bar-boy all evening and now sees only the rows of bottles on the shelves behind. He cannot understand – he says this to himself, actually understanding very well – why the stupid woman cannot walk home, it's not far and it is quite safe. By being there, now between him and the door, she has insisted herself upon him. Damn the woman, he seems to think, but actually he is sometimes a compassionate and sentimental old fool in shining armour up on his white charger willing to do battle for any old maid, Sally included. Harry as well, if need be. David he supposes, also, as things are likely to work out and blimey why people get themselves into these complicated personal arrangements thank God I never married.

"Mrs Pryce-Williams?"

"Oh, hello," she says as brightly as she can.

"I didn't expect to see you here so late."

"Oh, we'll be going soon," she says a little less brightly.

Mac sits where the dark woman had sat before, so that Sally has to look in another direction. She looks towards the door into the gents' toilet and says.

"Can you please just check if David's in there? He's been gone rather long. I wonder if he's ill. That mousaka did taste a bit funny."

"It did but he's not in there. He's gone to see Harry."

"How odd."

But what is odd is that she is not a bit surprised.

"It was a spur of the moment thing," she adds, apparently pulling herself together.

Mac is surprised that she is taking it so calmly. She must be pretty drunk. No wonder she hasn't walked home. He wonders also where the drinks have come from because she hasn't and wouldn't have come up to the bar. She had not but she had drunk on an empty stomach not really fancying the mousaka. I just had a sausage roll with some HP sauce, some silly idiot brought back all the way from England. A teeny weenie bit of the HP sauce had dropped onto her peasant's skirt but you wouldn't notice it. Luckily it missed the white blouse.

"I'll take you home."

"Thanks."

She gets up, waves to someone and sways but he does not help her. He is, after all, the one who is supposed to be the old soak. Nonetheless, she stumbles on the steps of the veranda in her high heels so that he has to grab her arm and finding no way of letting go steers her to his car. It is interesting the way she lets him do it but ignores him at the same time. She is not being rude and he realises she is embarrassed. Not embarrassed at being drunk but at being abandoned by her husband. He rather hopes he is wrong and that they find David back at home, sprawled in an armchair dead drunk having forgotten his wife. Then they would have acted through the charade of his selfish male selfishness and told the joke against themselves for years afterwards about the time he forgot his wife. The Man Who Mistook His Wife for a Sausage Roll, ha ha ha.

He unlocks the car door and pushes Sally into the passenger seat. Another jolt of compassion, he feels sorry for this woman who is, after all, no sillier than himself and just a child really in an unfamiliar environment where everyone else seems to be in the know and grown-up but actually, not at all.

He drives very slowly through the empty night streets, which are so like the millions of empty night streets of his life, but he no longer feels sorry for himself.

He would like to go back home straight away but he cannot leave her so suddenly. The Pryce-Williams' house is too bright. He wants to turn off some of the lights. He feels awkward.

Because there are no shadows it looks like a house where dangerous things could happen. It makes Mac think of knives and blood and cheap Hollywood suspense movies that are depressing.

She is nervous, the coffee cup rattles on the saucer. Don't want him to think I've drunk too much. I am in control of the situation and of course I'm not a bit upset or surprised that David has gone down to see Harry. He said that was what he was going to do. Of course he did. We discussed it. He was, he was going to do some early morning fishing with Harry. It's a thing that men do. Don't want women around. Ernest Hemmingway and all that. In which case I had better be Mrs Grant.

Thus, Sally pulls herself together and actually does look a little less cheap and silly.

"Here's your coffee."

She is now standing in front of him, and he is sitting down, so he has to look up her nose.

"I've put in milk and sugar." She implies that it is Mac who needs the help. Saving the sweet old drunk. "Would you like something to eat?" Mrs Grant would have insisted, with the Rich Tea or Digestives on a little bone-china tea plate, which matched the teacup and saucer. Not a full set but it's amazing what you can do with remnants.

"No thanks. Sit down."

She sits a little away from him so that they do not have to look straight at each other.

She has washed her face and looks more like Mrs Grant by the minute. Mac is impressed. These English women. But he is perfectly aware she is putting on a supreme act.

The thing is that he will go along with whatever she says, however implausible it sounds. The fact of him sitting there, apparently relaxed – he is as good an actor as any Mrs Grant – reassures her that he will swallow anything she says. They are in on the conspiracy together. Is it indeed that Mac is the father she has never had? Sally the daughter? And all that baloney. Maybe something more. The idea flits through both their minds and does them no harm. It draws them together.

"Yes, he said he was going early morning fishing with Harry and it's just like my husband to go off like that."

Mac makes no answer, waiting for her to continue.

"He came back to get his kit and change. He said he'd come back to the club but just like him." Not at all like him. "He'll forget his head one of these days." The last thing he'd do. "So kind of you to bring me back."

"Not at all." Not at all Mrs Grant, glad to have been of service. "Will you be alright on your own?"

"Oh yes, Clara and Sam – the gardener – are here. I'll be fine." I'm a strong English lady, the very backbone of the empire. It's us keeps everything going, not you silly men, but we play the game of pretending you do.

You do indeed.

"I'll be going then."

"Call me Sally."

"Sally. But I tell you what." He wants to do something for her. He wants, all of a sudden, to serve this woman, whom he feels drawn to.

"What?"

"I've got to go down and see Harry tomorrow, why don't you come with me and we can all come back together?"

"Oh no, but it's kind. You go on your own," she insists, "I'm sure you'd rather. But dear Mr, Mr Mac ... "

"Do call me Mac."

"Mac, I'd be so grateful if you'd get him back here as early as possible. You must, then, join us for dinner."

"I will."

"Goodnight then."

"All the same, Mrs ... Sally, I'll just check on Clara, and I think it'd be a good thing if Sam sleeps on the veranda. He's a good boy."

"Thank you ... Mac." Now be off and do what you have to do for me.

He is surprised and rather impressed that she does not flirt or suggest anything intimate. They do not do the usual social kissing act. Sally is becoming Mrs Grant, and it is a good thing.

It is what she will need to be, if she is going to cope with Wanei and all that.

[][][]

Mac arrives at about eleven just as Harry and David have finished the late breakfast. They are sitting on the veranda and Wanei is clearing away. Everyone looks rather cross. There is a rumble of thunder out at sea but the clouds are not yet visible. He stops his utility truck beside David's expensive-looking four-wheel drive. The place is rather crowded, although Harry's own vehicle is down in the workshop being serviced. Mac realises that he has never been here at a weekend before. Were it not for David he would feel he was intruding on Harry's precious privacy. They watch him approach in their own ways. Harry gets up and welcomes him warmly. David shifts in his chair as if embarrassed. Wanei, hands full, watches above Harry as if relieved to see an ally.

Wanei, as it happens, is right: because, amongst the other things that come with having knocked about a bit, what drives Mac is a desire – not a burning desire but an insistent itch, as it were – to have everything neat and tidy and everyone acting in a way that does not ruffle too many feathers and that allows the surface of things to remain fairly calm. A pond surface, Mac might have said, had he been given to metaphor, which could perhaps reflect the sky above but should not indicate the turbulence below. Not too much, at any rate; the odd bubble, an emission of marsh gas, was alright in Mac's book because it comes up, expresses itself and is quickly gone, unnoticed if you happened to have been looking in another direction. Harry living with Wanei was fine. David having a fling with Harry was fine. Anybody having a fling with anybody was fine but no need, no need at all, to make a fuss about it. No need for anyone to get on their high horse about it. It was high horses caused all the problems. Humanity, after all, had infinite variety is what Mac said, and there was nothing new under the sun, nothing at all. And he was, was Mac, he was, he is, a good man. His attitude did not mean walking on the other side of the road, while he might, nonetheless, have turned the other cheek. No, not making a fuss etc., in Mac's scheme of things, did not mean accepting things that were essentially, fundamentally wrong. Mac, although the phrase would never have occurred to him, thirsted for justice. He could not tolerate, for instance, any form of racism; hated the attitude; loathed the very idea of it; had worked to break the club of the habit. He could not stand such a thing. It was the one thing that made him really cross.

[][][]

A digression, if you like, because the thing that has made Mac into the Mac we know reflects one of the worst episodes in human history. The human comedy being played out by these pretty worthless spoilt expatriate babies who live in and around Port Markham – a fairly irrelevant place to most of the inhabitants of New Sudan, let alone the rest of humanity – is not even a speck of dust in the universe of human suffering by comparison to what Mac experienced in his youth.

Mac is, despite his name, an Englishman. His Scottish father, as a boy, had migrated, with his family, to Leeds or Bradford or Sheffield, at the beginning of the twentieth century; he was a book-keeper; a good one in the Edinburgh tradition with a sense of honesty that is, is quite un-English in a way, thus marking him out as a Scot of the old school; he was well read and rather dull. Mac's mother, herself born in Leeds or Bradford or Sheffield, but of local farming stock, was a quiet woman who kept a good house and who lived to look after her men; she, also, was well read but not half so dull as her husband. Mac was the only son.

Mac grew up in a comfortable and secure home; he did not have to struggle in the slums. He left school just before the outbreak of world war two and began to study mechanical engineering at Sheffield University. This kept him out of the war for a year or two but he was called up in 1942. He did not go overseas until 1943. He was in Italy at the beginning of 1945, experiencing such fierce fighting that he was considered fortunate not to have been killed. Otherwise, not so: better, he often thought, to have died in the mountains, remembered by proud parents as a brave, handsome boy who had been no trouble to them and who had died for a good cause. No such luck.

By a series of, of accidents, but perhaps it was divinely predestined, Mac found himself with a detachment of British soldiers who liberated, if that is the word, one of the Nazi extermination camps: it might have been any: Treblinka, Sobibor (Did he come across Sally's father who would have been only a year or two older?), Belzec, Auschwitz or any of the other places where we exterminate each other for what reason, in the name of God, we will never have an answer. It is not what Mac saw that affected him so much, it was his understanding of the applied organisation and mass social support behind this, this, this experiment in social engineering, one might say (kill 'em all and make sure you do it), that numbed his youthful spirit. At first, it seemed to him that the cold, calculated inhumanity of the thing was what was wrong but after a number of days on the site, a combination of two things began to eat into his soul: the first was the realisation that it had not been, it was not, an inhuman activity but a fundamentally very human activity. It was – this pre-meditated and well-thought-out mass murder – it was, he concluded – and later experience did not alter his view – the very essence of human society.

The second thing that ate into the young man's soul was the fact of his rapid acceptance of what had happened as something that was, in the end, acceptable. He was not the only one – he might have been an American boy, a French boy – but all of them found themselves increasingly unsurprised by the horrors to which they were daily exposed; emotionally, they became detached from the survivors, to the extent, even, of resenting them. How thereafter, to deal with what was the truth about humanity? Humanity that was not Mac's goodly Mum and Dad but the organisation of death camps. What if Mac's grandfather had taken his family to Hamburg or Stettin or Berlin instead of Leeds or Bradford or Sheffield? Maybe Mac's father then would have been the one collecting the statistics of the people who were to be and who were gassed each day, helping to ensure that the quotas would be met. Maybe Mac, as a boy soldier, would have gone to Warsaw to keep order in the ghetto to guarantee sufficient numbers for transportation to the camps each month. Each man doing his job, doing his duty. I was just obeying orders; the usual excuse.

That the whole operation – the organised extermination of ordinary European civilians – was largely carried out, made to happen, made to succeed by essentially ordinary and in other respects – what damn respects are there for God's sake? – in other respects, other ordinary European civilians, was something Mac could not get his young head around. The idea went around and around in his mind until he was nearly mad. He could not lose himself in drinking and enforced joviality like his comrades. He could not do it. He may always have had the tendency, as an only child, but it was at this time that he earned his reputation for being a loner. A Loner: not disliked but left alone by the others. Leave him alone; he's happier on his own; prefers his own company. That sort of thing.

Back home in Leeds or Bradford or Sheffield Mac felt no better. He saw on the moors outside the city the same camps; he saw the ghetto inside. He could not talk to his parents, who grieved for the son they had lost every bit as much as if he had died in Italy, but they did not know why.

And just as Mac's parents had been well read so Mac himself had been fond of music, especially the German masters: Bach, Haydn, Mozart and Beethoven. He had loved them and had considered their creations the supreme climax of European culture; the one special thing that justified European civilisation for all its brutality. Before studying engineering he had even, briefly, considered a career in music: he played the piano passably and the French Horn very well; he was a useful chorister with a reliable baritone voice. However, after his continental experience – which is how he described it to himself – this music was worthless and ugly in his ears. The supreme creation of European culture was, he had learnt, the efficiently run death camp. The efficiency of mechanical engineering revolted him also. Had not engineering been the tool that had translated ideology into the efficient industrial infrastructure of the death camps? But he had to do something and in the end he followed his father – never less than a perfect model – training as a book-keeper, stubbornly refusing to raise himself to the status of a chartered accountant. He did not want to be that good at it. But he was the perfect student; he became the perfect employee: abstract company figures and books, his life. He became an avid reader but avoided most of the literature of the twentieth century.

But he hated Europe and everything it stood for. He fled to Australia, which was easy in those days what with the £5 passage. Australia wanted lots of good, white blood in those days. If the thing, whatever it was, had not been got right on European soil then maybe it would work out on the other side of the planet. His Mum and Dad believed he would find a nice girl out there and get himself together, so they were happy to see him go; they could lose themselves in their reading and ignorance of the world.

Yes, indeed, with the benefit of hindsight and forgetting that he was still young, Australia, Australia of the 1950s, was bound to be as bad as Europe, even if it was richer and better fed. The determined hedonism of the place astonished Mac. He could not see the point of it. It was the same old European pattern repeating itself. The same old prejudices and ignorance only instead of Jews and Gypsies it was the aboriginal inhabitants and anyone who did not look nicely and comfortably white. The idea of Australia revolted him.

He fled again, this time to New Sudan. You cannot run away, it is in the mind and all that, but Mac was young then and he had not worked it out in that way. He had not understood that he could have fled to the refuge of the New Sudan of the mind, just as easily in Leeds or Bradford or Sheffield. He did not have to go round the world in order to do it. But having got to New Sudan, he stayed; it accepted him and he was as happy as a Mac can be, given the circumstances. His view of humanity did not change. Why should it? Nothing that went on in the years of his life could persuade him that the Central European death camps of the 1940s were anything other than the human norm. It was only the Teutonic efficiency that broke the general rule. The

British or the French or the Italians would not have done such a good job.

[][][]

So ... so ... so here is Mac. Not the flippant type, although he might have seemed it on the surface. On the surface of the pond.

This Mac knows Harry who is a bit like a son to him. He has the right, given his experience, to view Harry as a sort of wayward son. He would not say he knows Wanei – that inscrutable one-eyed beggar is a wonderfully shadowy mystery to him – but he feels he knows Wanei and Harry as a sort of functional, and at times dysfunctional, animal, which forces itself into his consciousness from time to time. Is he envious of this animal? No, not envious, he could not begrudge that fleeting, dangerous happiness, or, rather, significance. The significance of living closely with someone else, with all its ups and downs. But he wished, sometimes, when he considered Harry and Wanei, that he too might have had some sort of experience of a spiritual, or whatever it was, intimacy. Something that brought contact. Not a family, God help me, but a unique knowledge of another sympathetic human being built up over time. Anyway, can't have everything in life. Thank God for the small things and stop moaning, you stupid man, he tells himself.

And what did this Mac think of David? He does not know him much, and, at the club, had given him no more than the benefit of the doubt. Of all the players in this little drama, he thinks David would have made the most likely death-camp officer: a loyal Nazi – in the German circumstances of the day – who would, Mac was sure, have satisfied himself, in moral terms, that what he was doing was alright. David would have done an efficient job and he would have gone home each night to be a good husband and father. The primary thing for David would have been that he must be one of the men at the top, running things – what was being run, beside the point – he would have to be in the know, one of us and all that shit nonsense. In the right circumstances David would have been one of the self-serving part of humanity who goes along with all of whatever it is, keeping their head down if required but nonetheless doing what has to be done for the sake of a peaceful life, for the sake of the children, for the sake of my pension, etc. No reason, all the same, to dislike the man, who was no more dislikeable than most of humanity, himself included. Still, the basic idea did predispose Mac to be less sympathetic towards David than towards the others.

The idea of what he ought to do came to him the minute he saw the three men on the veranda and was well defined by the time he shook Harry's hand. As he took it, looking eye to eye, with Wanei up behind, he thought that David, lounging there while his wife, while his wife, while his wife fretted, was a rude, ill-mannered oaf. It was outrageous that he had dragged her out to New Sudan in the first place, out to the back of beyond, merely for his own embellishment and, as it happened, for his necessary convenience because H and C – unlike his own lot – preferred its Port Markham expatriate staff to be married. It was outrageous that he should be here with Harry now. Outrageous that Harry should be so calm and matter of fact himself.

Mac smiles at Harry, winks at Wanei and ignores David.

"Well this is a nice little party. How is my friend?"

Wanei smiles; he recognises a fellow conspirator.

Mac pushes past, clumsily climbs the three steps up to the veranda and is angry. He is not only angry with David for being the ill-mannered oaf but also he is angry with Harry and even, a little, with Wanei. Yes, I've got their little game; their prancing, mincing little game as if they are lords of the universe, as if they are the sole planets spinning around the sun, the rest of us, incidental dust. Shove them all into a concentration camp somewhere in Poland and they'd feel incidentally dusty, themselves. I know what's going on.

Fuck 'em, but he smiles, a wise Mac smile. Oh shit, Jesus you all make me cross.

David with your stubborn determination to be what you think you are, what you think you ought to be. For God's sake just be, and leave it at that.

Harry, you, you precious, self-centred prick. None of this would be happening if you weren't forever thinking of your precious self; forever defending your space; scrambling up the grubby moral high ground only to rush down again having seen the view, your precious emotions being so bloody important as if anyone else cares tuppence. This is your fault; you playing Lord Snooty making the stupid Pryce-Williams people your pals, picking them up as something with which you can play. You condescending bastard, you think you're better than they are but you're not. You're not because you actually do know a little bit better, having waded through the shit already. You know where you are but they have not the foggiest idea.

And Wanei! What the hell are you up to? You silent, dark, devious, one-eyed little creep. Nothing in the open for you. You're a man of shadows; all in the shadows, your life. You watch and watch and watch; you work it all out and then you pounce and devour, just at the right moment and when it suits you. You cannibal!

Oh look at you all! You make me sick. And look at me. I'm no better. What am I but shit myself? What the hell am I doing here? Scrambled up the moral high ground myself. Prospero I am; the great, deluded manipulator. I create my own monsters – myself and Harry and David – only to have them turn on me and serve me right. Oh fuck it all. Why don't I leave everyone to rot?

 Get to it man if you're going to.
 So gentlemen. What's up?
 Wanei gathers the detritus of breakfast and flees.

Mac sits in the chair vacated by Harry who is sitting at the top of the steps, his body twisted around to look at Mac, a stupid grin on his face.

David, chin in hand, is gazing out towards the beach like a sulky boy. Hmm, Beautiful Woman today, no doubt. Beautiful, but what's he got to sulk about?

 So gentlemen. What's up?
 You want a cup of coffee Mac?
 Thank you.
 Wanei! Coffee!

They wait for the coffee. This wastes more time as the sun climbs up to be a whitish impression of light somewhere that is not very well defined. It's getting hot. They are all sweating. Drops of sweat catch in the small folds of David's thick, youthful stomach.

So gentlemen. What's up?

Help yourself.

Hungry Mac?

No.

So gentlemen. What's up?

Phew it's hot today.

Sea, sky a single washed-out bleakness. The palm fronds crackle – or seem to – hanging dejectedly. A vulture of some sort has come out from the rubbish tips of Port Markham. Maybe it can find some pickings at Harry's place.

Phew, it is hot.

It's got to rain; there was thunder earlier.

So gentlemen. What's up?

Phew, it is hot.

So gentlemen. What's up?

Be so kind, gentlemen, as to answer me. You owe me, if not all of us, some sort of explanation. Surely? Actually, Harry, I am not going to allow you to use this place as a sort of, sort of homosexual brothel. You and Wanei do what you like. That, your relationship, is the accepted state of things and we, and we tolerate it in the spirit, in the spirit, in the spirit of the age. I assume you're not corrupting the other labourers? The men. Not I trust like some Empress Catherine, Catherine the Great, who, I am told, used to take her pick of the palace guard every night. They were changed regularly and selected on the basis of their height and strength. Big, strong, Russian boys. Wonderful to imagine that it was the great Empress herself – a German woman, from, from Anhalt, I believe – who spread the pox amongst the soldiers, who then went on to give it to the Russian population at large. The pox, spreading out like ripples on the surface of the pond from the beautiful St Petersburg palaces to the whole of Russia and probably into Finland and Poland as well. This larger-than-life woman, in her expensive gowns, a bag full of the pox that she bestowed on the population as a gift; eighteenth-century germ warfare. No, I doubt you do that, Harry. Even the depraved Harry wouldn't do that. Wanei wouldn't stand for it for a start. He'd have slit your throat by now in his devious, dark fashion. But don't, don't, do you hear me, don't entice silly young men like this David fellow with the rivulets of sweat running down his chest and gathering in the gentle folds of his sat-down beautiful young belly. This stupid young man with nothing between his ears and nothing better to do than abandon his wife in order to play silly buggers with the likes of you, Harry.

And Harry, while I'm at it, did not I, myself, encourage the escapade? Muddling, messing and stirring up things? Planting the idea in fertile ground as it were?

Do you understand me?

Thunder! Did you hear it? I'm sure the rains are coming.

Do you understand me?

You will come back with me young man and apologise to your wife. You will come back with me immediately if I have to drag you by the hair. Do you understand me?

This coffee's shit. I'm sure Wanei puts salt in it. I'm so sorry. It's awful. Powder'd be better. Trouble is it goes off so quickly down here. S'no good trying to keep it fresh. I ought to grow my own but it's not the best place; too near the sea.

Do you understand me?

So Mac, what brings you out here on a Saturday?

... So Mac, what brings you out here on a Saturday?

I had to take Sally home last night.

Did you?

Harry looks in the same direction as David.

As far as she is concerned, David has disappeared. I said I thought he might be out here. But how should I know? I wanted to put her mind at rest.

Harry looks in the same direction as David.

He just left her in the club. I took the poor girl home. She was distraught.

Did you know that? Harry?

Harry?

He's here now. There he is. In front of me. I can see him sitting there watching, watching something.

What is his excuse for being here, Harry?

Come on Harry. I know you.

I know you.

I don't know him. I don't know what he is like.

But I know you, Harry. Don't I?

Don't I?

You two here alone last night, Harry?

Oh, Harry, you bad boy.

You been up to your tricks again?

How did you get him to come?

How did it work out this time?

You've interfered between man and wife, Harry.

And what does Wanei think?

He knows every damned thing.

He watches you like a hawk.

You asked him here as if it doesn't matter to anyone else what happens. Other people's lives, Harry. You shouldn't do it. Don't go messing with them; I've told you before.

I didn't.

Didn't what?

I didn't.

Didn't what?

Ask him.

You sure?

I am.

I don't know if I believe you Harry. You know, you know, you know, you can be a good liar when you want to be.

Ask him.

No, you'll do.

So what happened?

He came on his own.

Why? Mac is looking at the back of Harry's neck that is beginning to be weather-beaten and aged by the years in the sun. But Harry, I do not know him. This man we call David. I know you, though. Do I not? Well never mind, I will ask Wanei. He'll tell me the truth, because he won't spare you if he thinks you deserve it.

No need to ask him.

Why should this man David come here? Has he had a nervous breakdown?

It is, after all, Wanei's business. Is it not? And thinking of Wanei, or rather of Wanei's relationship to the whole thing, Mac laughs. It's all so funny. It's funny that anyone should take any of this, of this nothing as something. The coffee's awful. He puts down the mug. No doubt Wanei did put salt in it and will blame the taste on the staleness of what he has to work with. He knows Harry likes decent coffee. He can hear Wanei laughing back there in the dark; the one eye on its own somewhere in the dark, laughing.

You've got to see the joke.

I can.

He said he loved me.

No?

Yes!

That man whom we call David, that man who calls himself David Pryce-Williams, Estates Manager of the ever-so-fine, upstanding and decorous Haldan and Cruikshank, that man who is the husband of Mrs Pryce-Williams, our Sally, said he, said he loved you?

He did. It's funny, isn't it?

It's damned funny.

Wait 'til I tell them that at the club. Did he sit on your knee and look up into your eyes?

Darling, I love you.

I love you.

Do you love me?

Say you love me.

Say you love me just a little bit.

Say you love me just a teeny, weenie, itsy, bitsy little bit.

Say you love your little, wittle David.

Did he say all that?

Not quite.

But nearly?

Well ...
It's funny.
It's a joke.
One man talking to another like that.
I'm not sure if I'm disgusted or amused.
Do you love him?
Harry laughs. I love my dog.
There is laughter from inside the house.
I'm going.
OK.
Mac gets up.
Come on.
David follows him to the car.
Where are your clothes?
Inside.
Harry, get 'em will you.

Harry gets them. He throws them as a bundle to Mac who catches them with an amused exaggeration of a rugby catch. Very manly of the pair of them. Wanei watches from inside the house. He holds the salt tin. Hard to see if he is laughing or what, but his teeth are white in the dark. Mac is right.

10   The Suppliant Hand

Mac and David get into the car.

David is ... he is ... crushed I suppose is the word and defeated. Humiliated. Embarrassed a little as he thinks how Mac and Harry may discuss it later. In fact, they will never mention it again.

Later, David will feel only that he is a bit of a fool and later still he will have successfully persuaded himself that it was all a joke in which he played a positive and significant role. They really are chumps all of them and I don't know why I ever took them seriously. I am wasted in this place. Yes Darling, you are.

As the car disappears beyond the coconut palms there is another rumble of thunder. Wanei rushes out of the house in order to hit Harry. They fight viciously but Wanei gets the better of the match because he wants to draw blood. They stop when they are exhausted. Harry goes down to the sea to bathe. Wanei goes back to the house to tidy the place, restoring it to its usual Spartan and empty regularity. He has to purge it of the David man before he has his bath. He will have a shit and then he will have his bath in the rain that is coming. He will stand behind the house naked in the rain in order to wash his body clean. While he is cleaning the room, he breaks the spine of a book as he does the job and tears out a page.

But the contrary process of destruction was far more convincing, once perfected. So his skull saw, as the green lights drifted in the night. The lovely fireworks showed him the hand that had just fallen at his feet, thrown there. The fingers of the lost hand were curled in its last act. It lay there like a tendril that had been torn off some vine, and dropped when the motive, if ever there was one, had been forgotten. So the living skull of the green soldier looked at the suppliant hand. He was waiting in the darkness for an order. Which did not come. But would, he hoped. He was standing there. He was the last man on earth, to whom the hand had begun to beckon. Then the order came through the greeny, drifting darkness, and his sweat ran again. He kicked aside the soft hand-thing. What else could he do?

The Tree of Man, by Patrick White

This is what Wanei read before he used the paper in the latrine. In his mind's eye he was himself inside the skull and the hand that he saw was the hand of Harry.

Wanei does all this out of love for Harry whom he thinks is tied too much to books and music.

[][][]

That it?

Not quite.

We are here, standing, for a moment, on the veranda; the one that makes Harry's shack more of a respectable bungalow by wrapping itself around three of the sides. We look through the exhausted coconut palms, over and across the dirty-looking and broken raised reef towards the beach. The tide is out; the waves, therefore, are insignificant; Harry, more so, splashing around in the warm, sticky water.

The horizon is a sharp line. The yellow, late afternoon light squeezed by storm clouds; the darker band, low in the hot, dusty sky.

At last, Harry decides he has had enough. He thinks he will rinse off the salt and lie down. After all, he did not have much sleep last night. He walks back to the house. At the same moment, Mac and David reach the river. They drive across the great desolate plain of stones over which the heavy car wheels tend to skid. Somewhere, in it all, the river runs but it can be, and often is, anywhere, disappearing beneath the stones altogether sometimes, in this parched time of the year when the sky can be dark with dust. As they approach the farther, Port Markham, side – this grown-up man who has seen the death camps and the big, dumb boy who has seen nothing – the first big dumb drops of rain hit the hot metal roof of the car. Thus, they notice the dreary, hot heaviness of the afternoon as approaching rain. They are satisfied inside the metal box of the car that is high up on tough black rubber tyres. They are satisfied that they are safe, that they are cut off a little from the hard world around them and that they are going home.

They are not happy yet but yes, they are satisfied. David is not, as he might be in a more melodramatic tale, suffering. He is a little numbed and slow, as one might be who is now recovering, the body and mind readjusting, pushing the past into ... the past. Like an invalid, he is happy for Mac to make the decisions for him. This adds to his satisfaction because, as we know, his attachment to Harry was, and maybe still is, based on lust and an intellectual decision that he has a right to gratify that lust. There was/is no communication between the David-ness of David and the Harry-ness of Harry; had there been, Mac might have left well alone and let things work themselves out, but as it was he could not tolerate David's posturing and Harry's manipulation. So David is satisfied to allow Mac to make the decisions for him. The little embarrassment – for that is all it was/is; there is no shame – the little embarrassment that was so devastating to David at the time, is ebbing away, rushing fast as it scrambles around the rocks, leaving the beach clean and unmarked. Remarkably unmarked and prepared for new footprints.

The drops fall more quickly, now thrashing the car as a unified, animal attack upon it, outraged, it seems that the raw, energetic elements should be so defied by two bits of utter insignificance inside a metal box.

All the same, they are unrepentant, accepting the rain as another gift. The vehicle pulls up out of the riverbed just before the dust becomes mud. Windscreen wipers going like mad they are alone and perfectly silent with each other, isolated together from the angry, thrashing, impotent rain outside. Their satisfaction is turning to happiness; that state of being where things look good. In his mind, David is humming a little tune that comes to him; it is a bit from the Brahms quartet. Mac is thinking how good it is to have rain. He is looking forward to being on his own later in the evening reading a book with the rain outside. No need to toddle down to the club; quite enough excitement for one day.

Back at the plantation, Harry is in a similar sort of mood. Now he is on his own, the restlessness has gone. He is lying on his back in the dark house that is best in the rain when there is a reason for being in it. The torrent hammers on the roof. One might say it is deafening but it is only a background roar to the well-known dripping from the broken gutter outside the little bedroom window. What always makes Harry wonder, is the pressure of all that water being emptied onto the thirsty earth. It pushes the air through the house so that the flimsy doorway curtains flap out as far as they can be tugged and it draws in the wonderful smell of the wet earth that seems to breathe out in relief.

And what satisfies Harry most of all is the idea that all this rain is cutting him off from the rest of the world. It is especially cutting him off from Port Markham and from the tiresomeness of the Pryce-Williamses. He is satisfied with his lonesomeness; satisfied also that it is not complete for out there, somewhere, is Wanei.

[][][]

Wanei appears on the patch of grass between the two shacks we call houses. Having put his little red plastic soap box down on the ground beside his feet, he stands looking up into the sky. He holds his arms close to his sides, his hands clenched. The rain presses his light clothes to his skin so that we can see beneath; dark patches through the white cloth. He might be shivering but he stands immobile for a while. He begins to remove his clothes, placing them on the washing line beside him. It is already heavy with the sheets he has hung out in the morning. He strips to his briefs, stands a while longer and removes them also so that he is stark naked.

He is a black figure in the shivering grey water, as if he is something special in the universe. He points his arms upwards as if he would swim to the surface.

Crouching quickly to the ground he opens the little plastic box and gets out a piece of white soap. He rubs himself rapidly from head to foot. White lather covers him and is as immediately washed off his head and down his body as a rapidly disappearing garment of fragile white frothiness that is a white puddle around his big feet, leaving him shining, his skin resistant to the rain in its waxy cleanliness.

And Harry sleeps. A little later, Wanei will join him and they will sleep together in the dark. The river is in full flood now and has completely cut them off. They are – what do you say? – they are as happy as it is possible to be.

Their clothes hang together on the line to be washed by the rain. In the morning, they will be bleached dry by the sun.

I remember and remember that weather after the first rains that year. It was wonderful in my memory. Cool misty mornings burnt up by the sun in a deep blue sky that filled up with towering, towering cumulus clouds that strained and strained in the heat to collapse in the cooling rain that cut us off again until morning.

[][][]

Mac's truck turns ever so carefully into the drenched garden, pressing through the angry storm which surrounds the house. Two hunched figures duck rain, leap steps onto veranda. Massive, corrupted, branch of spreading flame tree hits ground, flowers turn to shreds orange petals spread around in bits. Lies there, innocent-like, on the sodden lawn as if it had not tried to kill them.

Sally is calmly reading a book in the sitting room. Above the storm she hears them hit the veranda floor. She is as calm as can be, this woman. She is wonderful in her calmness.

The front door opens. David stands behind Mac waiting to be invited into his own house. Had he not deserted it? And her? Tentatively he offers himself.

"Hello."

She does not reply but puts the book down with what Mac sees as deliberate elegance. She is dressed carefully, as a wife – or even widowed matron, Mrs Grant on the march – ought to be dressed. From now on she will impress upon her husband – and upon any other interested party – a subdued elegance which will soon cost no effort at all: wide skirt of some light but ample material of washed-out royal blue and a high-collared blouse. Her hair, as if rinsed in lemon juice, is up, emphasising cheekbones and ears. Aristocratic she looks or at any rate it is the Polish genes coming through.

"Hello Mac," she cheerfully replies, "thank you ..." Thank you for bringing back this reprobate. I'll deal with it from now on, if you don't mind.

"Hello Sally," replies Mac, with only a little less cheer. I have done as you asked or, should I say, ordered me to do. I am, when all is said and done, only a man, the function of whom is to serve, without question, a woman, a gentlewoman, like Mrs Grant, of whom I have heard but never met, and who will not tolerate any sloppiness in a husband or in any other man.

Sally smiles at what is, after all, her due, and dismisses him.

"Tea?" If you dare.

"No thanks Sally, I'll be off, your baby is safe and sound." I no longer associate you with the girl who was drunk at the club. I admire the woman I now see before me and I know that the invitation to dinner was no more than a social turn of phrase and not meant to be taken seriously.

"Goodbye Sally." I think I may have fallen in love.

"Goodbye Mac." You old ... character you, my mother would have appreciated you. She holds his hand a little and then she pushes him off: be gone for now, you've done your bit.

She turns on David.

"Oh, Darling, you are wet. Go and change this minute. Have a hot shower and then we'll have some tea." Don't say a word. Do it. Thus, on these conditions, he may enter the house. She has got him now and it is the best thing for him. He knows where he stands, the battle lines have been drawn but he faces the up slope with the sun in his eyes. Mrs Grant is already shaking her fists in triumph but Sally will be Mrs Pryce-Williams on her own from now on. She knows where she stands, one foot already on the beast she has defeated. "There's plenty of hot water." Go.

Sally walks out onto the veranda. Mac has gone, leaving muddy tyre marks on the green, spongy lawn where puddles are forming. The rain is a steady downpour, hard and impersonal, but within it, space and colour, shapes, are unambiguously defined. The very opposite of the bleached, vague uncertainty of the dusty weather which has been broken. She folds her arms so that they rise and fall with her breathing.

There is a new determination in her expression, and despite the healthy glow of her skin, her face is losing its childish lack of definition. Next time she goes to the club she will know what to do. She will not look anxiously for acquaintances to recognise her: she will take a seat – a good one – sit in it, and they will come to her. She will, in time, slim down and become truly elegant. David will not need to worry about her fat legs, his will be the issue. In ten years' time, their friends will wonder why on earth she married him.

Sally watches the thunderous rain, seeing Wanei in it, stretching his arms up to heaven. But it is only Sam the gardener, who is already clearing away the branch which had hit the lawn with such wasted energy only minutes earlier. He enjoys the rain. He will do anything for Missus William. He strips down to his briefs after Sally has gone back inside. Would have done it for her eyes had he thought more quickly, the strapping lad.

Sally does not want Clara tonight. I know about your tricks but I don't mind: I'd do the same in your shoes. I'll cook tonight, thank you, I'll enjoy it windows wide open to catch the cool night air. I'll muddle things and watch out for your consternation on Monday morning, struggling to regain control. But Clara is not confused rather she respects Sally for the trick. She recognises a sister in the struggle to bring David, and all the others, to heel.

[][][]

"Hello Darling, you look nice and clean. Sit down I'll get you a drink." She serves her Lord and Master. She sits on his knee but she does not insist. She is gentle, she is chaste, she is as elegant as the wife of a David P-W ought to be. She is what he wants and so she is what he gets. He wants nothing more from her. He does not want to engage her mind about Sibelius or early Brahms because he does not want to know her in that intellectual way. Her intellect, her intelligence, would frighten him. He wants to believe that women do not think in that way. Harry is the one with whom he had wanted to engage intellectually, because he thinks he would have dominated Harry intellectually, as well as physically. But Harry is not only in the dustbin but also he is welcome to be there the little shit who thought rather too much of himself I taught him the lesson he deserved.

Therefore, the real David, the David who wanted Harry and who wanted to listen to an early Brahms string quartet disappears quite quickly as the façade he consciously builds himself eats away at the man inside like some skin-thickening disease until there is nothing left. He is only one of those great towering, Italianate, stucco-covered structures in South Kensington, built in the middle of the nineteenth century, very tall and hell being a servant running up and down the stairs all day carrying coal, hot water and food on trays.

Sally helps maintain the façade, inasmuch as she applies the fresh paint and keeps the roof rainproof, but David is the engineer and there is a time, while they are still in New Sudan and Harry down the coast and Wanei nothing to do with them, when David could have kicked her scaffolding for six and let the paint peel and the rain come in. But he doesn't.

And why, to get back to the main subject, the change in Sally, noticeable when she stood on the veranda that rain-drenched Saturday, late afternoon become night? It is as much a biological change as it is caused by David's rejection of her at that critical time. She is pregnant. She does not know properly but her body has reacted to Wanei stepping manfully into the breach: gastrulation will begin any minute now. A new life begins.

PART TWO

11   The London Books

"David," she called as he was leaving the house.

He said nothing but she knew he was waiting in the hall, impatient, for further orders. He did not mind doing the shopping, he enjoyed it but he preferred to think he was not being sent out on an errand.

"Will you take the box to Oxfam, please, Darling? On the way." She had made it up especially. It was full of all the discarded books.

He did not mean to slam the door as he went out but the glass shook as it closed behind him. On the way he looked in the box to check she hasn't chucked out any of my stuff. It was mostly paperbacks. Things the children had grown out of and some other rubbish how they get into the house in the first place I'd like to know. But there was a book of short stories I might like to read on the tube sometimes. He slipped it into his pocket.

> A month passed. Women conceal their feelings better than men and a stranger visiting them would never have guessed that Doris was in any way troubled. But in Guy the strain was obvious; his round, good natured face was drawn, and in his eyes was a harassed look. He watched Doris. She was gay and chaffed him as she used to do; they played tennis together; they chatted about one thing and another. But it was evident that she was merely playing a part...
>
> *The Force of Circumstances*, W Somerset Maugham

But David had no feelings to conceal, he could only manage his life thereafter by throwing himself so thoroughly into the part, that he became the part. The player died. Not difficult in England, in London, in that up-and-coming suburb that had been the epitome of middle-class dreariness only a generation before. Now it was the place to be if you were young and making it. Good restaurants and the City handy on the tube. Sally sussed out the house and got it cheap from an old couple who had married into it and had not caught up with the times. Needed a lot doing to it and she did it; stripped the deal woodwork, ripped out years of ghastly DIY and painted the walls hard, bright colours. Her mother was impressed and gave her some good props. I'll sell the house and get a little flat nearby no Mummy hang on we'll visit you they didn't.

Life came easy because the script had been written by the colour supplements of the Sunday papers. Such clever people the Pryce-Williamses. Nice children too and so good of them to take in that child from New Sudan. Left on the doorstep. In a cardboard beer carton. Can you imagine! The father was some drunken logger apparently. Got a local girl into trouble or something like that. Sally was silent on the subject, waving away the comments about her philanthropy just as her mother would have done. She would not have minded telling lies on her own behalf but she was not going to tell lies about her son: he had a father of whom he would be proud one day.

So Wanei planted an English boy. It gave the P-Ws credit they did not deserve but Sally knew they were no better than all the others who devoured the riches of the earth. She got David to be a good London man who would get quite keen on his garden and who liked to hear a good concert from time to time although Sibelius Five was off the menu, for some reason all Sibelius for a while. Brahms more the thing. Sends a shiver down my spine he says upon his return alone because all that loud male stuff makes my head ache. She began to like quieter things, did Sally, in her thirties. Chopin to start with. The minute the boy was born she got herself pregnant again, and again two girls, Sonia and Alice, because of the books they were reading, which was odd because Sonia does not get a good deal. Sisters for Harry they had called him. Appropriate, for different reasons, although in her head he was Tuei. If Wanei had one then surely, this one had two. She adored him as his father's son. The girls could manage without her adoration being English girls they had Daddy if need be.

So to begin with it was all babies and paint stripping and scene painting. No wonder David focused on his work, listened to Brahms symphonies, began to read the novels of C P Snow, having done the Forsyte Saga and War and Peace. He wondered less and less about the woman he had married, who was giving him the setting for the life he wanted. They did not discuss much except for the books they both read sometimes but in the mid-afternoons, when she was alone, she would listen to a Chopin Ballade and think.

And watch. When she was not alone, Sally watched the people playing their parts in the set she had designed. She watched the David character who had been brought back to her to be taken in hand. Not once did she bother to wonder what went on inside his head, so determined was she to take him at face value. It is what he wants, she would have said, had anyone asked, and it's what he'll get. She listened to what he said only because it informed her about the set of people around them. Once or twice she wanted to challenge him, or just insist on the opposite, but mostly silent subversion was, she found, the best way of doing things. David admired Margaret Thatcher: don't you Darling she's sorting out the place. Yes, she's a woman: Sally voted the other way despite them being no better. Later, after the return and when she really did settle down she began to dislike Wagner because, it seemed, David liked it but she listened carefully enough so that she could define her dislike. The five songs touched her like magic and she began to think only an evil mind could produce such compelling, visionary beauty. The cataclysmic end of it all would be set to glorious music but in the end it was Brahms for her as well because she was not really eschatological. Dying embers more like and the later love songs for the clarinet player. They made her think of Harry back in New Sudan. No doubt the best part of David had found something there but it had been Harry who had destroyed that particular hollow man. She had reconstructed him and stuffed him again but more or less upon the same lines, headpiece filled with straw and all that. David was not worth it in himself, she had known that, but there was the baby and she needed some sort of angel, or sucker.

[][][]

Once she had settled down, she began to read Jane Austen. Again, she might have said, because she had read Pride and Prejudice in the days of Mr Prynne but, honestly, I'm reading her for the first time, only no one was listening.

> '...Did you not hear me ask him about the slave trade last night?'
> 'I did – and was in hope the question would be followed up by others. It would have pleased your uncle to be required of farther.'
> 'And I longed to do it – but there was such a dead silence! And while my cousins were sitting by without speaking a word, or seeming at all interested in the subject, I thought it would appear as if I wanted to set myself off at their expense, by shewing a curiosity and pleasure...'
> *Mansfield Park*, Jane Austen

Eventually, Mrs Grant visited. She took young Harry's room. He slept on the sofa. So sweet of you to have taken him in like that. The same way of looking at me as you had as a child of course he's learnt it from you. Harry looked at her as if he might follow her lead if only she would lead him somewhere. He watched his mother in the same way. He followed his gran up the stairs to his room. She said she liked to be called Granny so the girls took to calling her Gran, giggling and the real Mrs Grant, Miss Grant had they known, did not object, remembering her own gran in the house near Plumstead Common. They stopped on the half landing and she looked into the little boy's eyes seeing Sally, and herself. Really, she exclaimed to the world in general, you really are blond for a ... And she became interested in the architecture of the house. She knew about such things and could tell you stories about domestic buildings. Houses were, after all, as she had once discussed with David, only the stage sets in which we act out our lives, Wimpole Hall only a bigger version of the bay-windowed semi to which I have descended. She approved of their London house which was better than it might have been it was such a depressing suburb in my youth. So she turned away from the little boy with the questioning eyes whom she could not yet define talking to him like an adult, on the half landing: and I'm sure this door was a window once which is why the stairs and the hall are so dark.

"You see there," she said, pointing through the door from the half landing into the tiny sliver of a dining room, "They pushed out another room above the kitchen, quite early I should have thought because otherwise it would have been a bathroom with a lavatory. I should imagine, Harry, because the master of the house made this room for himself to get away from all his children." Her laugh was real. "So jolly to live in that room overlooking the garden. But, of course, it made the stairway darker."

The dining room was a narrow mezzanine projection that had been shoved out above the kitchen in about 1860. A tall thin window squinted at the little flagged yard with its old fig tree and patch of garden beyond. Mrs Grant had got it more or less right. The house was very early railway yellow brick, embedded, a little after, in London red. The plane trees on one side of the street planted to commemorate the accession – rather than the coronation, fortunately – of Edward VII. Mrs Grant approved of all this. She approved of the way in which Sally had set out to do things; the way she had taken control of the loud and bossy David of whose play-acting she had once approved. Now she despised him. She acted, nonetheless, the perfect mother-in-law wanting to strangle him every time he called her Mother in that patronising way his own mother would have wanted to be called by her first name.

And thus, admiring her daughter, dismissing her son-in-law, Mrs Grant liked the little boy called Harry and would have grown to love him given the chance. She was only a snob in material things and only then because she would have preferred the white-washed cell to anything superfluous. She began to learn about herself as she grew older. She was an intelligent woman which was why she was a good actor and knew the difference.

[][][]

The room was crowded with a few people who believed the dining table had come from somewhere more grand. It was battered and almost as old as the house. You could extend it by a sort of screw mechanism and put in an extra leaf. Sally had got it in a house clearance at Kingston. No one else wanted the hideous old thing and they had a devil of a time getting it up the stairs we'll never get it down again without chopping it up the children can do their homework on it when the time comes it'll go with the house as long as the house stands. Sally liked the idea. She sat by the door so she could go down to the kitchen or up to the children. Once installed, guests could not move out of the little room rich with red walls and huge gilt mirror reflecting soft flickering lights. You felt it a privilege to be here with the charming Pryce-Williamses and Sally's mother so nice and obviously, you know, a county type and all that ... crap. The guests were indeed a little cowed by the Pryce-Williamses, en masse, as it were, as if the P-Ws were, actually, the all-knowing major-domo, steward to some altogether higher and yet to be introduced being of towering importance. The P-Ws, it seemed, knew what to do, from the little abstract painting on the wall opposite the mirror to David's total knowledge of what wines to drink and when. In this respect you did what David did, respected his views on Margaret Thatcher and the City, and you did not wear a tie but rather an expensive open-necked shirt in brave pink or royal blue, the women almost in evening dress. The P-Ws set the tone for the street and single-handedly appeared to have raised property prices. They were, as it happened, the first of their type in the street.

"What do you think, Sally? Sally?"

"Sorry, I was miles away." She looks blankly at the boy-man opposite who does something for the BBC but who is, in essence, my father the MP. She always and always forgets his name although she fancies him a little and wonders what he would be like if he had been a labourer like his great-grandfather, broken and bent or fine looking despite his small frame. Why does he try to suppress the nice Midlands accent? It's about all he has. He looks up to David and will end up with that hard London accent that is aggressive with nothing to back it up but a knowledge of wines and my father the ex-MP.

"The war?"

"I don't know. I don't care. You can't call it a life or death thing for us here in London although she's doing it for us."

"I don't think we're defending western civilisation," says Mrs Grant not expecting an answer.

"Pure Clausewitzian," booms David with not a hint of the South Wales accent you'd have noticed in his unreformed youth. He has read it and all the commentaries. Not that he thinks about war. It is a response that comes without thinking because he has read the book: Clausewitz, Freud, Adam Smith, Jane Austen. A sort of automatic reaction; he no longer does it to impress, although BBC boy is.

"Swift and decisive is it? David, Dear. The pre-conditioned war machine swinging into action?" The Polish influence. He had talked when he was a little drunk, and she had not appreciated the depth of her own intelligence at the time. It's how Sally got this table. Mrs Grant sounded as if she was backing David, but she was actually trying to open a weak point in his front, through which Sally could pour her forces. David drank too much. She sipped a single glass for an hour.

Sally laughs and starts to get up.

Politics by other means.

"Yes, Mummy, in either event it ought to be the masses rising up on both sides. British coal miners and Argentine ..." She had no idea if they had coal in Argentina. "Cowboys. Let's have coffee in here. Anyone want the loo?" Musical chairs to get out they ought to have a pot beneath the table, Georgian fashion, the ladies holding on. Or did they? "Boys downstairs," she orders, "girls up. Mummy, please show them the way."

She waits for them to get back before she brings the coffee to block them in. No one can wander over to the bookshelves or change the music she has already put on. When it is finished she will select what comes next or allow the silence to suggest they go. She and her mother will say nothing. No liqueurs in any event to needlessly prolong the evening. David will offer brandy to the desperate, he can reach it from the little sideboard behind. But she will not touch it. Those days are over, her face getting less smudged as the youthful flesh falls away revealing for those who notice, Slav blood. But it is her mother's definition.

"There we are!" she gaily announces, demanding their attention which is drawn to the tray of coffee things she has dropped on the table with a crash. Attention please and she gets it and holds it as she goes through the ritual of making it the proper way like David showed me didn't you Darling when we were first married. But she makes it quietly and privately so that while watching – Mrs BBC who is called Helen, a little horsey thing with big hips, sweating under her make-up, makes mental note get one like it at Peter Jones – they listen to the music. Brahms clarinet trio. Sally likes the sad finality of it, wistful nostalgia makes her, makes her think of that other Friday night of Harry, David and Wanei. Let the boys do what they like, I want this man my dark shadow because he does not mess around. I am easy to get and he impossible to hold. I wouldn't have wanted to tame that one but I've got his son and her heart melts at the image of the sleeping boy on the sofa downstairs who is hearing the music even if he does not listen. How is it I can think of Wanei without regret and yet love the total man as if he holds the key to my heart?

[][][]

She smiles back at her mother who knows David never was her daughter's man. The father of the boy down there was my daughter's man and I am proud to have a daughter who has taken a lover, once, who turned her into this remarkable woman who has made my whole life real and worthwhile so that I am better off than the Duchess of Devonshire. I could get a little bedsit in South Ken and be more happy and walk in the gardens every afternoon taking my tea in the Orangery. But I like my little house and the garden, one more summer at least, please. She hears the music also but does not listen. One doesn't need to recognise it to feel it and anyway I'm a visual person. I see ghosts. Yes Gran? Yes Harry, the maid would lug coal and hot water up these stairs. I don't think this house had an inside loo until after the war. What war, Gran? When your granny was a girl they sent me to live beside Plumstead Common and my mummy died in the blitz which we could see from up there: the docks burning and burning. What's the blitz, Gran? Like fireworks only better. I saw the whole city ablaze. It was beautiful. Better than the Crystal Palace in 1936. Like fireworks, Gran? Cross my heart and hope to die.

Sally is not miles away. She has heard the question someone has asked her.

"David, the brandy? You'll have some won't you?" She smiles at the boy who is no more than Helen's husband now, much more than he is the son of an MP or something in the BBC. "Do have some. He's a grown-up boy, isn't he, Helen? David, don't be mean, they're walking home. It's only down the road. Give him as much as he can take. I love your house. Mummy'd love to see what you've done." She wants them gone.

Helen blushes with pleasure. She'll be fat one day and very upset about the school playing fields being sold for housing. As if other people are supposed to live in tents. Sally looks good: black silk blouse, hair cut short and ear studs that are tiny Antwerp diamonds. Her mother, similar in high-collared electric blue and choker, looks quite young in the candlelight.

There is another couple – much more real – who fill the table. Mr and Mrs Willis. He started life as a surveyor for the old LCC.

"The area was a bit rough when we moved in," he says, "there were blacks." He doesn't notice his faux pas or Mrs Grant's momentary frown because he is only saying what it was like. His wife, in a Chanel-style jacket, pats his arm and he takes her hand because he always does. He puts it to his lips because he always does that as well. He wants to give his love to his wife of twenty-five years and he is used to her. David watches the exhibition thinking he will do it to Sally one of these days in front of a suitable audience. Perhaps in front of the children. Not in front of your mother-in-law, David, she would scream with laughter. Mrs Willis is a severe-looking woman. There is thin leather piping on the shoulders of the jacket. She looks like the dependable type but you never can tell. She might have bitten her husband back.

"What?" says Mrs Willis.

"More coffee?" Is Sally's reply.

"Sally's in space," says David, proud that this woman who controls the table is seen to be his wife.

"I was listening to the music. What did you say?"

Mrs Willis repeats the question.

"What did you think of New Sudan?" She is a woman whom you would call handsome. The jacket really is Chanel, got at an auction soon after President Kennedy was shot dead. Tonight she wears it above black slacks and black patent leather pumps. Her brooch is a little Scotty dog her husband gave her for a wedding anniversary, gold with two little black, jet eyes. It looks good on the fine tweed. The children have left home but her second son plays an electric guitar in a band and sometimes comes home with his washing. He would recognise the Brahms: the great abstract composer, Mum, you should hear the double concerto. So she did and understood what he meant. I know Schönberg admired him but to be honest – she was, to a fault – I prefer Rachmaninov's second symphony. Oh Mum that stuff. Yes that stuff calms me down you can put it in the machine yourself. She was so in love with her son it hurt her.

Oh … Sally was about to say it was wonderful we had the time of our lives we were young. Brahms is crying for his youth. But she cannot lie to this woman as she would have lied to Mrs BBC who would have blushed and said it sounded romantic although she had never once in her life noticed the London sunsets you can see coming out of West Brompton station on the District Line. The polluted air does it, not God.

"God?" Mrs Willis laughs good-naturedly. She wants to know how this Sally reacted. Married to a stuffed shirt. How can she bear to touch him with that layer of fat which is so self-satisfied and unclean seeming? Her husband was lean, if not mean and would come to life in her hands. Yes, I do love him but it wasn't always like that. I have grown in love with my husband as a part of my family. He hasn't changed one little bit since I married him. I always knew he'd be bald. I have grown up. "Is God in New Sudan?"

Sally has heard this. She stops listening to the music.

"He is more likely to be than here. In London." She thinks of Wanei and she thinks of Harry and Wanei. She laughs for the woman whom she likes.

"What do you mean? I know God is not in London but why is he in New Sudan?"

"Oh, I don't know that He is but He is more likely to be."

The others are listening but have receded into the darkness beyond the two women. David is wondering what this strange woman, his wife, will say next. He does not think of Harry at all. Mrs Grant is remembering the little girl, Sally, and thinking: From whence this wisdom? She stands alone at the back of the stage.

Sally wants to throw off the question because it is almost a luxury to think about New Sudan, to watch herself moving around in those days. Too selfish, Mummy would say.

But the other woman insists.

"Why?"

Sally cannot get inside herself but can only watch herself. Even to the bump-bump in Harry's lean-to shack which was – is, she supposes – the kitchen. Was there an oil cloth on the table? There ought to have been. That is until the whole dark essence of the man envelopes her and enters her as if it is the most natural thing in the world and she was made for the act, that act alone. She thinks of the boy down there on the sofa and she wants to fly to him now.

"Well, I can hardly have imagined it. Can I?"

"God?"

"Yes."

"Why?"

Again she watches herself and herself with David in the house and garden with Clara, and then with Harry on the plantation in the sun-bleached bungalow.

"I wonder if he arranged it all?"

"God?"

"Oh, no! I was thinking of a man we knew out there." And she thinks, if he was nothing else, Harry was a catalyst, of sorts.

David assumes she is thinking of the reprobate, Mac, whom up until that moment he had forgotten. Forgotten, also, he was the man who safely delivered him into the hands of the woman, Sally, who at this moment wanted Mrs Willis to understand what she meant.

"I mean that the way we live here depends, I suppose, on electricity. Or something like it. If the lights go out we'd be helpless. We'd all die very quickly." She thought of the uselessness of the three men around her. But she was sure she'd manage somehow with her mother and Mrs Willis who'd be a chieftainess. She imagined the three of them living wild on Putney Heath. They'd keep Mrs BBC fat and then kill her for meat in the winter. Wanei'd be good at that. Young Harry, too, perhaps would inherit the cannibalistic skills. "Out there we, we Londoners with our four-wheel-drive cars and our cooler boxes, are silly children. To them we're just a cloud that covers the sun for a while. It'll pass. And the sun will shine again. When the lights go out they'll get on with their lives as if we'd never been. Is that God? To whom we are irrelevant?"

"We Londoners, at any rate," says Mrs Willis, perfectly satisfied with the answer, "who rule the world with our money." She fingers the little gold dog.

"Yes, in New Sudan, even London is nothing. They wouldn't even bother eating us."

The music stops.

David wakes up and briefly remembers Harry and the weekend.

"The lotus eaters if you ask me, ought to be made to do a decent day's work." Sees himself sweating in the Tube, and forgets.

Mr BBC grins, takes his wife's hand.

Mr Willis squeezes his wife's knee.

Mrs Grant moves as if to rise so that David must get up but then sits down again.

Sally guards the door. They are all her creatures. Did she put something in the coffee?

"So sweet of you to come," she says and releases them. Into the night. They have not talked much but the communication between the three older women has been substantial. As if Mrs

Willis has connected the mother and the daughter. Mrs Grant does, thereby, let her daughter go.

[][][]

And by the way, this Mrs Willis was real by virtue of the fact that she had always been comfortable with herself. This was partly her good fortune. She had been born into an ordinary world that was acceptable to her. The psychologists would say it was because her parents loved her without having to try. They were classified as poor but there was no striving for what they could not get. She always remembered winter Saturday afternoons in the particular warm security of their kitchen-living room, sitting at the big table beside the window that looked out into the yard. Their life happened around that table and she would rush outside into the turmoil of struggling South London all around just so that she could return and savour the safe certainty of life around the table. Her father dealt in coal in a very small way but he was a keen socialist and supporter of the Soviet Union until the non-aggression pact with Hitler. His favourite writer was Robert Louis Stevenson. In the evenings her father would read out loud to them sitting around the table in the semi-dark. Dickens also, and when she trained to be a teacher, English Lit. was what she wanted to teach most of all. She brilliantly inspired composition although she could not work out a plot herself. She had not the mind that could contrive things. Her mother was musical and played Mozart on an old upright piano, tinny and mechanical sounding but the magic worked through.

12   The Londoners

Mrs Grant did not meet Mrs Willis again but was relieved her daughter had such a neighbour. Deciding, in the end, not to make another trip to London, she was thankful for Mrs Willis being there and if they want me they can come up here, I have two spare bedrooms. The student days were over and if I'm short I'll sell the house and get a nice ground-floor room with French windows opening onto a garden. It never came to that: a year or two later she died sitting in her wing-back armchair watching the dying winter light while listening to the afternoon play but thinking of the visit of her grandson whose own idea it had been to visit his gran up there. He also liked the flat countryside that stretched out beyond the recreation ground at the back. And the big sky above. She looked at the abandoned apples on the lawn, remembering the ones they had picked up together off the damp autumn grass. Mostly rotten but with the healthy fermented smell somewhere between gin and eau de cologne. Like my life, she thought and the innocent boy had seemed to answer, hmm, making a big show of breathing in the still afternoon air, I love the smell, Gran, it smells of you. The bright, intoxicating joy of that memory had over-taxed her heart. She was ready.

Sally also dreamed, of Mrs Willis, of her asking thoughtful questions that demanded thoughtful answers or, at any rate, consideration. And in her dreams she was her mother watching and approving of everything so that waking, Sally understood her mother's struggle: her mother had climbed mountains and crossed deserts, not only so she could drink her evening coffee from the little Royal Worcester coffee cup but also so that Sally herself should sit comfortably in her London house watching her children who included young Harry, her Tuei. It was not enough in the end, or anything like it, but it was a good beginning. Better than waiting for something she could not imagine.

[][][]

The girls did not matter. They were Daddy's girls. Not that Daddy had much to do with it. The two of them, Sonia and Alice, drawn together in a conspiracy of giggles, had decided they would be Daddy's girls. It was an attack on his indifference. They sensed his monumental pointlessness, his grand façade behind which there was something, but only the essential framework. Once, in Kensington Gardens, they had walked around the Albert Memorial. They were studying the statue in order to find evidence of Albert's thing when all the fantastic fabric above and around him came into view. The ridiculously ornate structure was falling apart in those days. Daddy, they cried out together. Thus they understood their father but their mother was different, you couldn't get around her in the same way. You could go round and round her and still not know her or get a picture of her in your head like the Albert Memorial. The love they had for her was almost hatred. Life would have been easier with her out of the way. The little girls were close. Eventually, they split up and as adults barely spoke to each other. Natural with honest people. Why should we love our family?

Alice, the younger by fifteen months, was, nonetheless, the leader; the calculating one. If murder was to be done, Alice would have planned it. She was a nihilist by nature. One of those slim, pale girls whose hair hung flat upon her head. Neat and quiet as tough and determined as old boots. She mostly ignored her mother, which would have infuriated some women but suited Sally, she keeps her room tidy and does her homework. What more could I ask?

Sonia, by apparent contrast, was a round, colourful girl with masses of curly blonde-red hair, more naturally inclined to be a Daddy's girl. She was entirely under her sister's thumb so that the conquest of Daddy was a strategic thing directed by Alice. Leave Harry to Sal, as Alice disrespectfully referred to their mother; he's a ladies' man, look how he sucks up to Gran. But like her mother, Sonia was in love with her brother Harry. She got to be in love with a lot of men before she learnt some sense. There was a time when she would have eaten him.

David, nonetheless, detached himself, listening to the Brahms Second Piano Concerto on Sunday mornings while he read the papers and drank his coffee; Daddy's thing and the girls would deliberately intrude, as Sally had done earlier, to get at him.

Sally was thus left alone to cook lunch, which she enjoyed. The kitchen was perfect because there was room for only one operative. Mrs Grant had made useful suggestions: it's a galley, Darling, work with it. The back door gave out to a tiny sunken yard into which the window also looked. You walked up out of it into the garden by three steps upon which Harry would sit, chatting to his mother through the window, playing games. Or else he hung around the door into the hall, up another three steps, carpeted, and upon which he might sit guarding his mother from the others.

The childish order of the school classified you, and Harry was classified as black despite his being as much white as he was black. So from an early age he understood where he stood. He was popular because he was bright and loving but otherwise he might have been a freak.

[][][]

Sunday lunch was a ritual Sally was determined to keep. Some people, London people, had already taken to going to restaurants but the Pryce-Williamses stick to tradition such nice people. And that little boy.

"Mum?"

"Yes, Darling?"

He is just thirteen years old.

"Who am I?"

She puts down the baking tray but she does not take off her oven gloves

"You are Harry Pryce-Williams. Who else would you be?"

"No, Mum, where did I come from?"

She begins to pick up the tray again. She is not ready for this although she had expected it to come one day

"From the cabbage patch."

His silence is reproachful but it gives her time to collect her thoughts, which do not amount to much. Although she has never lied, either to the world in general or to herself, she has let the world think what it liked, which amounted to an untruth, she supposed. She wonders if he has asked his gran.

The boy grows restless, plays with his shoes. He wants to know today

"I'll ask Dad."

Who might have said you have nothing to do with me. But David was a good father. He worked at it, and never did he consider Harry as anything other than his son. It was his one good point.

"No, Sweetheart, Harry, listen. You are my baby. Really, you are, right from the beginning."

"Honest, hope to die? I came out of you?"

"Of course. You're my baby. My first baby."

"So... Dad?"

"Is not your real father ... I mean your biological father but you know he loves you as his son. His only son."

"Yeah ... I know." They had played father and son often enough. Learning to kick a ball, to throw it. The boy was affectionate and he understood the game. To have made David admit the charade would have spoilt things. "And Gran?"

"My Mummy, my mother, so she's as much your gran as she can be. And anyway, Harry, you have a real relationship with her. You can understand that. You're a big boy now. It wouldn't matter if she wasn't your gran but she is."

The picture was taking shape in his head but it was only a single line. He wanted to ask another question.

Sally could see it coming and she would not avoid it when it came. So she got in first.

"And, you know, Harry?"

"Yes, Mum?"

"I didn't know my father, your grandfather on my side, either."

"Did he die?"

"He might have. I don't know. He might still be alive for all I know. He was Polish. After the war there were lots of people moving around. He …"

"Was he Gran's boyfriend?"

The idea made her laugh. She had never thought of him like that. She had never thought of him at all because it had always been herself and Mummy. Until David came along. Now she was having to think and all she could think of was the whole of Poland and tragic Warsaw and a tall old-fashioned-looking cavalry officer who was dark. Maybe that's why I like Chopin? How funny never to have thought of it. And I don't want to think about it because I don't care, I am what I am. She thought of the boy's father. Not of the naughty Wanei but of the idea, of the warm darkness that had, she knew with delight, that had made her a woman in a way David could never, in a million years, have done. Poor thing. Yes, he was Gran's boyfriend. But he was more than that. Or something quite different.

"They loved each other a lot and I am the result."

"Did you ever want to know him?"

"I have never thought about it, to be honest."

The boy seemed to be disappointed. He looked at the floor. Red plastic tiles with grains of black in them.

Sally knelt down to put the tray in the oven. One hour and twenty minutes. She thought he might be crying. Her stomach contracted. She wanted to hug him and bury her face in his smelly boy's hair. She turned the clock.

"There! Now we'll peel the potatoes." Beethoven's seventh flowed out of an open door; the simple theme of the slow movement that always made her think of Peter and the Wolf. The door was shut and the music dropped into the background but it still went on in her head. Your father was not my boyfriend. Nothing so trivial.

"He was more than that," she said with emphasis, more to herself than to Harry. How on earth to explain it all to a thirteen-year-old.

"Was he before Dad?"

Oh, God, it would be so easy to lie.

"No. It was in New Sudan."

"I know that." He was defiant but not angry. He seemed to ask: Do you think I'm an idiot?

"Your father took me out there."

"No, Mum."

"No, Mum, what?"

"You met my father there." He emphasised the 'My'. He was proud of the fact.

"Yes, I did. You are quite right."

"Who was he?"

The house-boy. Was she going to say that? No.

"He lived with a friend of ours. We were all friends. That's why it happened."

"What?"

"You, Darling." The idea came to her: "You came out of that friendship. Out of New Sudan. Daddy and I were both glad. We saw you, we see you as a gift from New Sudan. A gift from God. Are you glad?" She watched him. She didn't want him to think they were all sleeping around like hippies. "I've only known two men in my whole life: Daddy and ... and ... and your father." Suddenly the picture of Mr Prynne came into her head and she blushed.

He grinned Wanei's grin, which was for all sorts of reasons wonderful to see.

"Yes."

13   At a Hotel

After another lunch, a year or two later, early September, she decided they would go to Kensington Gardens. They took the top deck of the bus, grabbing the front seats as soon as they were available. It was a family thing they did together. Even David enjoyed it, finding it easy to join in the game of spotting the sights, including those that were part of a children's world he did not understand. Sally sat behind. She did not join in this time but occasionally glanced at her children as if she was included.

The bus conductor downstairs was a black man, with long sideburns going grey. You looked over the top of my head when I entered. I wanted your kind brown eyes to see me. Her smile was ready but it was wasted, disappearing as her mind drifted towards the tops of the redbrick houses on the Fulham Road, a pair of grubby curtains waving at her.

The bus stopped at the bottom of Exhibition Road.

"Come on," says David, "this is where we get off." The girls push him ahead.

"Mum," demands Harry. He would have grabbed her hand, had it been available.

"I'm coming," but she watches them disappear down the stairs until they are out on the street below. "I'll catch you up," she says to the empty deck.

Finally descending the stairs, she looks down upon the greying hair of the bus conductor. It looks like a tightly woven rug, a little worn and threadbare. She clenches her hand and is standing beside him, beneath him she feels. I'll stay, I'll stay with you on your bus, she wants to say, I'll be upstairs waiting until … until we get to Hammersmith Broadway where we'll have tea holding hands, looking at each other across a white tablecloth. I'll see into you through your kind brown eyes as the world around us grows quiet. Afterwards, I'll walk home through the quiet backstreets under the sea sky to knock on my own front door. Mum where have you been, we were worried? Am I not here now? And, therefore, so are you. But she is on the pavement beside the Science Museum surrounded by the Sunday afternoon families. Sonia and Alice are way ahead dragging a willing David, Harry hanging behind. She is not with them, she is a little girl looking at Mr Prynne's socks.

And not once did they look around for her. Not until they reached the crossing opposite the Albert Memorial, the traffic roaring. Then, Harry was the one who held back, turning away from the others to watch out for her.

He frowned into the afternoon sun, unable to see her in the crowd. Thus, she was able to look at him as she might have looked at a stranger, at any young man whose budding manliness she found attractive. But she saw not the young man or adolescent boy, rather it was Wanei who stood on the pavement in the hot afternoon. The same slight muscular frame: an elegant savage amongst the over-fed and pampered Londoners, who ineffectively pressed in on his toughness, oblivious of the magical beauty, her vision. For an eternal moment, she watched Wanei, knowing at the same time it was not him but their son. Her heart beat so fast, she felt it with her hand, soothing it. Am I going to faint? I ought to sit down. There was nowhere to sit. Then, at last, he saw her. He frowned, smiled, closed one eye. All at the same time he was Wanei and her son, the big boy and the small boy. She was a silly, ignorant girl, then and now. Her heart burst with joy, she laughed and found herself crying, the tears pouring down her face. Harry ran towards her pushing the stupid, clumsy people aside.

"Mum, Mum, what's the matter? Mum it's alright." He put his arm around her protectively.

This was not Wanei. Wanei had been aggressive at first: she remembered the one-eyed frown of the cannibal. He had been resentful of the intrusion. He had frightened her as an incomprehensible threat until the very moment she had felt the spasm of anger, when she had walked out on David, demanding of Wanei, the slave, hot water for her bath. Please, Wanei, can you prepare the fish? While I have my bath. We'll cook the meal together, which they had done as a conspiracy against the others. They were deliberately naughty children, giggling and nudging each other bump-bump until it had happened as it had been destined to happen for, oh, thousands of years and in the very process she had thought this is what I was made for. A little of his aggression had returned but the very moment she might have been frightened he had been tender and she had been enveloped in a warm darkness which had flooded through her. It might have been love.

And here was young Harry, Tuei, now, wanting to be tender also, the clumsy boy acting the man, wanting to protect her. He was not Wanei standing in the busy London street with his arm awkwardly around her. He was emphatically and uniquely himself, who had been nonetheless created by a moment of mutual tenderness that had been, was still, as real, as tough as a sparkling diamond.

So now she must act, she must act her little part for him so as not to deflate his little male ego, despite being again every inch Sally Pryce-Williams, totally in command of herself, no less Mrs Grant to the soles of her boots. I could knock down the Albert Memorial. And more real than the Albert Memorial smashed to smithereens at her feet – the idea came to her like the sunshine breaking through purple, bruised clouds – he is not Wanei, he is my son, our son and as I look at him now, that is what I see. I don't see Wanei he is as much me as his father, he is all of us. Love is what this is and she smiled.

That's better but he was uncertain, now she was his mother again smiling her smile. He wanted to take charge of the situation but he did not know how to do it. In his mind's eye he saw David – Dad – using his hands to guide his mother in some direction until she resisted a little and quite clearly turning to face him began to laugh in his face, but seeing the pain turned away, allowing herself to be pushed forward again. Then he saw his dad but not my father leading them all somewhere, a little procession of a family obedient until his mother peels off leading them somewhere else, his father pressing on ignorant for a while of his loneliness. But then, realising his isolation and foolishness, a small frown appears on his face as if he is trying to see something in the dark. That, the young man recognised, not for the first time, is also pain. He smiled for David who had taught him how to catch a ball, and throw it, and kick it.

His mother beamed back at him. He was proud of her in some ways. He was proud of the way she dressed and acted most of the time. He was glad he had a mum who fell into the category of she's not bad looking your mum.

"There," she said, as if it was settled, "let's sit down somewhere. I could die for a cup of tea."

He looked around hopelessly. How to get her a cup of tea? How does it work?

They are standing outside a hotel. It is on a corner: an old-fashioned place, once a rather grand private house but too big and cumbersome for family purposes, probably from the moment it had been built. Ahead, towards the high street packed with buses and other traffic, the monolithic pile that had ruined the view from everywhere.

"That's no good," she said, without explanation.

"What?"

But she ignored him.

"We could go in here, Darling." She glanced up at the big bay window in which a couple of old ladies and a furious looking old gent were having some sort of tea around a small, high table. She took his hand so that they walked together around the corner, up the steps under a quite grand portico, and through an impressive front door, which was already open. They were met by a suave, good-looking man in an expensive dark-blue suit. He seemed to have put his fingers together and bowed but, actually, he had not. Sally felt she had walked onto the set of an Agatha Christie film. It was quite well done: "This'll do."

Harry wanted to drop her hand and bolt.

"Mum," he breathed through clenched teeth but he held on so tight it hurt her. I am an escaped lunatic whom he is holding on to for dear life or else ... she is likely to run at the wall and career around the room smashing things, watch out or my mum'll be on the ceiling next and I'll never get her down.

The man was black. He looked very black in the dim hall way so that his white shirt shone bright. Apparently as a concession to the hot September afternoon, he did not wear a tie. Neither did he smile

"Madam?"

So she ignored the supercilious bastard, but his eyes were nonetheless kind, like the other's. Instead, she studied the light-fitting above. It was a brass cage with little dirty windows. Really, isn't it time you got that cleaned? Want me to get up and do it for you? I could if my big brave son would let me go.

"Mum?" Harry was desperate.

"I think I need to sit down, Darling." He released her hand. "Can you do that for me? I feel ill," she lied very convincingly, even managing to sway a little.

Harry panicked.

"Tea. She needs tea," he shouted, forgetting to shut his mouth as he watched for her on the ceiling.

"Yes sir, of course." The man smiled a beautiful smile at Harry and then looked at Sally in a way that showed he was concerned, but whether for himself, for the inmates, or for the new ones, Sally could not tell. "Follow me." His voice was smooth and registered low. You had to listen to what he said. We're really a private hotel for properly certified and tamed lunatics but you're most welcome if you're sure she'll behave herself. I promise, I promise, girl guide's honour.

Sally pushed Harry ahead and obediently followed, realising, too late, that she should have gone directly behind the blue suit which was stretched just a little across confident shoulders. But the important thing was, Harry had taken charge, getting his daft old mum sorted out, it was quite easy, this is how you got cups of tea in public places, you asked someone and things happened. No, she wanted to add, you, my son, made them happen, but she felt, nonetheless, she had been taken in hand.

[][][]

Two floors up.

A room: once a bedroom of some significance with a view over the park at a time when the nights were quiet and you could hear the wind in the trees.

A woman, a little older than Mrs Grant. She stood by the window. She'd been watching two people on the pavement below.

"They weren't quite having an argument, I don't think, but he looked as if he was holding her back for a while and she was either laughing or crying. I couldn't tell."

A younger woman, mannish, in trousers, was packing things carefully into a suitcase.

"Perhaps they're lovers."

"Oh, I don't think so?"

"Why not?"

"Because he was coloured."

"What do you mean?" The other woman stood, hands on hips, frowning humorously at her friend. It was their connection: the younger, wiser woman guiding the older, who was afraid of the world and who therefore clung on to the manners of a remembered, regretted, childhood when things were certain, only they had not been, and she knew it. She was a kind old lady:

"I mean, it is unlikely. Am I old-fashioned? You remember the man from Botswana who wanted to marry a secretary or something. There was such a fuss."

"That was thirty years ago and being old-fashioned's no excuse. It's a bad idea that silly, ignorant people used to have."

A deep blush spread girlishly across her friend's face.

"You know what I mean. I mean ... I mean, what about Mr Pierce?"

"What about Mr Pierce, indeed," said the younger woman. "If I had a daughter, and she brought him home, I'd be pleased. He's a good man."

"But Mary, really! He'd be about twenty years older than any daughter of yours. That's much too big a gap."

"Exactly, Mavis, you're quite right. I was thinking of myself." And as she said it, she remembered the enigmatic conversation about New Sudan she had had with Sally Pryce-Williams at the dinner party.

"But if he came home with your daughter you'd only object to his age, not his colour. Would you? And I'm afraid I might." Mavis was brutally honest with herself. "I'm getting old."

"Nonsense. And since neither of us has daughters it's rather beside the point. Do you remember that film, *Guess Who's Coming to Dinner*?"

"Oh yes. Sydney Poitier. Beautiful man."

"Yes, but I hated the film."

"Why? Goodness gracious Mary, that's what you're talking about."

"No it isn't. Just the opposite. The girl's parents could only accept him as a son-in-law because he was someone very important. A surgeon or secretary general of the United Nations or something like that. It was really unpleasant, they wouldn't have accepted him if he'd been an electrician."

"No, they wouldn't, because ... It was Katherine Hepburn, wasn't it?"

"Yes and Spencer Tracy."

"And she was a frightful snob in real life, I read somewhere."

"She was."

"And she was a snob in the film. Easy part for her to play, I should think."

"So? Mavis, dear? You wanted to say?"

"I wanted to say, Mary, they wouldn't have accepted him because he was an electrician, not because he was black."

Mary walked over to Mavis and hugged her.

"You're right, Mavis, as ever." She looked into the street below. "Anyway, I can't see them."

Mavis seemed to have lost interest.

"No, they've gone now. I saw them walk away, hand in hand." She sighed dramatically: "The last little drama I'll see from this window." She disentangled herself from her friend, and turned to look out the window again.

Mary went back to the suitcase.

"Well Mavis, the other room is quieter and if you want to stay in London, you can't have everything, on your income. There, that's finished." She put down the lid with an efficient snap. "And I've always thought this room too big, and noisy: you'll be much snugger upstairs."

"You're right. As ever, Mary, and thank you ever so much for helping me. And now we'll have tea. I've told them, begged them actually, to save the table in the window, and Mr Pierce promised."

[][][]

They were seated on a low chintzy sofa in a lounge which also contained a tea table or two. The room, Mrs Grant would have noted, had once been the main dining room. An enormous mahogany sideboard the size of a battleship remained from the old days to prove the fact, as did a great spotted mirror in a gilded frame hanging above the cold alabaster fireplace which, itself, looked like the memory, a copy of something – a tomb perhaps – seen in Florence in the 1880s. Other things had been swept down into the room by the deluge. A more harassed, a less systematic, Mrs Grant had put it all together. Fact is we've had some fairly well-placed guests over the years, or rather guests who were once well placed, over the years which had begun to go bad about 1963: Lady This, Sir Whatsisname That, ex-colonials in heaps, the man who invented the D-bomb and that fellow who wore a flowing chiffon scarf in the 1940s, in addition to one or two actresses whose names used to be on the tips of our tongues. They all brought something: those Victorian water colours of Shanklin beach, the fine Chippendale chair in the hall, detective novels by the bucketful, and that hideous standard lamp in the corner which nonetheless sheds a useful light on autumn evenings.

It meant nothing to Harry. He had no learnt knowledge of all this ancient junk, despite his grandmother's comments about the dining room door at home. Later in his life he would have a memory of the way things were on that afternoon. A memory of a room, the details of which would evade him every time he tried to focus. Not so the people in it. He remembered them as immortals to his dying day. They were a part of his life, not as incidental figures in the landscape or as types in some literary construction, but as the very essence of themselves, as their naked souls, brought out by his own declared predicament. His mouth hung open. He looked gormless as boys of that age do.

"Doesn't it remind you of Granny?" she patted one of the chintzy cabbage roses beside her.

He closed his mouth.

"Yes a bit, but ..."

Mr Pierce appeared with the tea things on a tray, which he put on the low table, squatting down to do so. He looked as if he was doing something very deliberate and important, some complicated process, the mechanisms of which only he was capable of doing.

Sally looked down onto the top of his head where the hair was also thinning like a worn patch in a rug. She wanted to touch the polished skin beneath, to feel the perfect beauty of his head but he shot up, suddenly, through the hole in his hair, and stood back to look at them. He did not smile but he shone brightly with narrow eyes, which had, clearly, seen a lot and done a lot of smiling. Sally was warmed by their gaze, enjoying the fact that they were transferring some knowledge of her to his brain. But he spoke to Harry.

"I trust it is all to your satisfaction, sir." He looked down upon them sitting low on the sofa, beaming with his own satisfaction, waiting, as if his words were the well-rehearsed line of a play, the cue for a significant piece of action. Sally felt she was a member of the audience being encouraged to participate by the man who was directing things. Pretend you are this young man's mother so that you know all about the unusual but not entirely improbable or wildly extravagant circumstances of his birth. Mr Pierce seemed to wink at her as if to say I know what's going on in your head. She rather hoped he did. She would have entrusted him with her soul just then. By chance, also, the declining September sun shone directly through the large bay window opposite to where they sat. The light glanced off the old mirror above the fireplace making a golden square of light on the old-gold wallpaper above the sideboard. A reflective, nostalgic, autumnal light, which was, nonetheless, warm and illuminating, brightening the room and the people in it. The man who was Mr Pierce no longer looked black but rather bronze and glowing; Sally's blondeness, a glittering confusion of rich metallic colours; Harry, raw sugar.

Then, having adjusted themselves to the idea of being in the room, it is flooded with light which fills and fills it having no place to escape. It rushes through the windows with such force, it is blinding. There is light and nothing else. One would expect the fragile things to shatter but they do not although another hairline crack appears in the bone china teacup which has sat on the mantle-piece for as long as anyone can remember. The tea table, set in the window, becomes a black silhouette, a small potted fern sitting in the middle, a cardboard cut-out, the activity within a shadow play. The street beyond, kept at a distance by the small front garden and the fact that the room is raised above ground level, is suggested only by noises heard faintly through the bright silence of the room: a police siren is as suddenly lost in the density of buildings as it is heard; a burst of laughing conversation, a ghetto blaster blasts louder and louder, passes and is gone despite Stevie Wonder still reassuring us he only called to say he loved us. He may well have done: there was love in the room that afternoon, full to overflowing and plenty to spare.

A kindly, concerned smile glows on Mr Pierce's face as he watches the young man who might have been his own son. He presses his hands together as if he is squeezing something into a shape between them. Blood pumps into the muscles of his arms which are strong from doing things around the hotel. He relaxes, unable to contain the love he feels for the boy and his mother whom he would like to take into his arms and squeeze also. And yet he is no less than the Mr Pierce who is the joy of Mavis's life. When he goes out, she misses him with an ache in her heart. When she takes herself out, she thinks of returning to the place where he is. She is exactly thirty years older but my feelings are not those of a mother because he is, of course, black.

Mr Pierce was born in Lagos. He came to London as a small boy but he knew who he was. His mother deserted him by inconsiderately dying. So he was stranded in England which he treated as something a little distant from him and inferior to Africa, but he was by nature a kindly man and good to the natives whom he eventually described as wayward. He never did become entirely English, despite the efforts of one or two younger Mrs Grants. He owns the hotel business and its goodwill, which is considerable, but he does not own the building, which is on a lease that will soon run out.

"Thanks," says Harry, and Mr Pierce, satisfied, leaves them with the tea things and a plate of digestive biscuits. It's all we can run to, his back suggests, but there may be more, later. He does not look as if he would normally wear a jacket. Sally thinks his powerful buttocks ought more to be on show and is glad he does not wear a tie.

The china, Sally notices also as having something to do with the man: it is good. She likes that the plates do not match the cups and saucers. The worn silver-plated teaspoons have GNR stamped on them.

Mr Pierce reappears carrying more things on a tea tray. He ignores Harry and his mother because they are guests, entitled to their privacy. He walks over to the table in the bright bay window where he also becomes a black silhouette, part of the shadow play. He does his work deliberately but without any fuss. He takes his job seriously, not because his guests pay him but because he loves them, and because he loves them, they do not always pay what his services are worth, and sometimes they do not pay at all if they are pressed. Cheques have been torn up for angry old men who don't know where the money goes these days and things weren't at all like this in my day and I don't like the way this country's going if you ask me, which nobody ever does. Except, perhaps, Mr Pierce, because he likes you. But if Mr Pierce does not like you, you can't get in for love or money: try The Harrington round the corner. If you insist, you might get one night but I'm sorry it's booked tomorrow and we're re-decorating the whole floor next week pots of paint appear, as if by magic. Mr P likes what are called Edwardian colours. Certain long-term guests who have come to learn that Mr Pierce is attractive, have sometimes been done the favour of finding him in bed with them, although any sexual activity involved lacks that certain emotion which would otherwise suggest he is doing rather more than his job. It is rather a relief that the young man does not get above himself. The young man in question being over forty and the pleasant lines in his face show it. Nonetheless, he looks like a boy to me. Some residents have left him money in their wills but he is not mercenary: when his lease runs out he will either set up a similar establishment north of the park or decamp altogether to some place like Scarborough. Certain guests will go with him: they have no other refuge.

[][][]

His task complete, Mr Pierce leaves the bay window, ceasing, in the process, to be a shadow. He stands in the centre of the room looking very real indeed, more solid and reassuring than the massive sideboard which has stood there for a hundred years. Mr Pierce's view of the room is what gives it its substance; without his reality, it would only mock the faded gentility of its guests whose hearts would, therefore, break. He looks at Sally. He coughs. She lifts up her head and gives him the most winning of smiles, looking at him for a few seconds before turning her head to look at her son who is stuffing biscuits into his mouth. So Mr Pierce turns his attention also to Harry.

"I trust everything is in order, Sir?"

Harry is intent upon the biscuits.

So Mr Pierce repeats.

"Sir?" With not a trace of irony.

Harry, amused but uncertain at the same time, swallows the last of the biscuits. He looks at his mother who appears to be engrossed in a magazine, *Country Life* 1964.

"I um..." he says.

"Shall I bring you some sandwiches? And perhaps some more tea for your ...?" Mr Pierce is determined to bring this young man out and, as Sir Whatshisname That would say, up to scratch or perhaps, the mark.

Harry makes up his mind to be connected. He is, suddenly, Man of Action, still a boy.

"My mum, yes please, and ..."

"Yes?"

"Is there a loo?"

"Follow me."

Harry follows but so swiftly does Mr Pierce leave, that Harry is left alone in the middle of the room, centre stage as it were, and Sally, with a catch in my throat, saw a young man, quite unknown to me, who was, apparently, my son. No longer the small compact child I could hold in my arms and press into any shape I wanted, but a big, sprawling thing who, of course, now insists on locking the bathroom door and has done so for quite a long time.

What Sally sees, in fact, is a fairly normal teenager of the day dressed in well-fitting jeans, good walking-type boots and a T-shirt hanging out. He is a little better and broader built than average but no taller. He is fine boned with long slender fingers. Dark skinned, he looks as if he would be fine velvet to the touch. His curly hair is not close cropped so that his head looks heavy and substantial. His features might be called crude were it not for the high cheekbones which mark him as his father's son all right, giving him the same cheeky expression offset by deep eyes that seem to brood. But what will attract women to him in a few years' time is the way he walks. It is not an arrogant gait at all. No strutting like a cock as if he owns the ground but rather each step he makes takes the floor in a measured, deliberate, solid way. He is one of those people who make this world revolve beneath their feet. For the time being, however, he still has, a bit, the shuffling stagger of a boy growing fast. At the door he trips over so that he seems to be thrown out of the room into the unknown beyond. His mother laughs. Men, says Mrs Grant, will fall over at times.

[][][]

Left alone in the room, Sally drops the magazine and stares at the bright light of the window. She thinks of Wanei of whom her gangling son has again reminded her, and a song her mother used to sing comes into her mind. She sings it in a sweet, slightly broken voice which is nonetheless perfectly in key:

"And when I told them how beautiful you were, they didn't believe me, they didn't believe me." She cannot remember the next line but the picture of Wanei remains as if he is stepping out of the bright light, his shadow becoming as real as Mr Pierce himself. The room throbs with silent memories that pack it so tightly the silence is terrific and Sally thinks she has gone deaf.

A muffled conversation outside the door suggests actors who have fluffed an entrance. A muddle of some sort, which sorts itself out into Mavis who enters and makes directly for the table in the window. As a woman who has had to work for her living she instinctively knows what is her due although she would have given it up willingly enough had it been occupied. More shadow play in the window, she sits down and places her cardboard handbag on the table then takes it off and places it beside her feet. She moves the potted fern cut-out further back.

"Here we are," she says gaily to the room, "I knew Mr Pierce would look after us. You see, Mary, what did I tell you?" Only then does she realise her friend is not with her: "Mary?" She looks around for the lost item finally catching sight of Sally at whom she stares rather stupidly until she very obviously pulls herself together, as she has been told by the director a thousand times, dotty old lady, well bred but of limited means. "I'm so sorry, I didn't see you there. How do you do? I live here."

"That's all right." Sally sits back in the sofa ready to have a conversation.

"I seem to have lost my friend," continues Mavis, "we bumped into the most charming young man in the hall. I think she must be talking to him. I wonder if he's Mr Pierce's son, although he's never spoken about children. A relative, perhaps?" She asks the question as if Sally is bound to know.

"My son."

"Oh! That explains it. And why not? So unusual to meet someone so young here. Yes, I saw you from my window. I was wondering."

Sally is laughing because she feels happy.

"We came in because I wasn't feeling very well. It was his idea."

"Yes, it would be. His father ..." But she says no more, aware that she has said too much already because Mr Pierce is such a nice man and why shouldn't he be married to such a pretty white woman. Maybe they met as students. "I was a teacher, so I know young people."

"Sorry?"

"I said I was a teacher. Domestic science, so mostly girls, but more and more boys want to do it these days. They make better cooks anyway. Don't you think?"

"Yes." But Sally is thinking of Wanei and the billycan bubbling over with rice, spitting into the fire.

Mavis does not reply. She is miles away as well but she turns around to sit on the side of the chair so that she is facing Sally. They look at each other in the accumulated silence. Anyone else present, an audience perhaps, would feel terribly embarrassed wondering if they have forgotten their lines. But the two women are quite relaxed.

They turn their heads towards the door through which, on cue, Mrs Willis enters. Mavis immediately turns back to the table as if Sally had never existed.

"Mary," she calls, "here I am. You see, I got the window table."

Mrs Willis walks straight across the room and sits opposite Mavis, upon whom she is focused. She settles herself so that Sally – as alert as a terrier dog – sees her dark profile and the movement of her hands against the bright light of the window. Mrs Willis says with emphasis.

"This is fun. I like to look out of a window." She looks out the window to prove the fact, and then back at Mavis.

Mavis replies in an exaggerated plaintive tone.

"So do I, I shall miss it."

Mrs Willis laughs.

"Oh Mavis, really, it's a good room, high up, so you have a view of the sky. And it's much quieter. Think of Jean-Claude in his basement with only people's legs to look at."

"Yes, you're right. I must stop feeling sorry for myself but …"

"…You wanted to stay on here, and it's all for the right reasons but it's an expensive part. Jean-Claude had to go way up north even to get his basement and he loves London as much as you. You're lucky."

"Yes Mary, you're right. I'm just being silly. I know I'm really very fortunate."

Mrs Willis does not rub it in. She knows she is lucky too to have Mr Willis and the house in Fulham. Instead, she quotes the title of the book: "*And A Room of One's Own* … is a great thing."

Thus does Virginia Woolf put a stop to the conversation, and they both turn to look out at the street.

[][][]

Mr Pierce enters again, with more things on a tray, making just enough noise to catch the attention of the two women in the window. He is followed by Harry, who carries a plate of sandwiches.

Harry stands in the middle of the room immediately becoming the centre of attention, although he is oblivious of the fact, intent only upon the sandwiches. He puts the top sandwich to one side and opens the one below, suspiciously as if its contents were meant to poison him. He steals a look at Mr Pierce, who is setting more out for Mavis and Mrs Willis, and pokes a finger into the sandwich, noticing, as he does so, the two women. He glares at them so that they slowly look away from him and up at Mr Pierce as if to say your son, the charmer. Then they look back out the window. Harry is not at all disconcerted by their antics, sensing that they are somehow connected to Mr Pierce to whom he has also taken a liking.

"Ugh," he says, "egg mayonnaise." He puts the top back onto the sandwich, which he puts to one side along with its discredited partner. He then proceeds to inspect the next.

Sally wonders how clean his hands are.

"Harry, Darling, do come and sit down. I like egg mayonnaise if you don't, and I'm starving."

"Coming Mum," and, remembering his duty as protector, he moves swiftly to sit beside her. He looks at Mr Pierce whom he wishes was sitting on the other side of his mother so that they would be a family, publicly stating the fact. At that moment, he hates David for not being black, and he does not care if he ever sees his sisters again.

[][][]

During the little drama, the sunlight has shifted so that the accident of buildings which allowed it into the room, to strike the mirror, now obscures it. The room is comparatively dim as Harry moves back to his mother. Without the blinding light, the figures in the window resume their usual shape, their lumps, bumps and details. Mr Pierce is blacker, Mrs Willis's blouse looks like a man's shirt, the flowers on Mavis's little short-sleeved cotton jacket are as clear as ever. Her hair looks very silver against Mrs Willis's jet black bob.

The characters are closer.

Mrs Willis recognises Sally.

"Sally! I am so sorry, I didn't expect to see you here." Of all places, she suggests. She is pleased and shows more affection to her friend than she has ever done before.

Sally is pleased also.

"My son brought me. To tea." To meet his father perhaps or to begin the journey towards his father, or towards an idea of him, at any rate.

Mrs Willis has not considered Harry before as something distinct from the other children in the street who have flowed through her house over the years of her own children growing up. She has not considered him in relation to Sally.

"What a good-looking boy," she says without thinking. "I am pleased." She thinks of her own hulking boys who would also have stuck their dirty fingers into the sandwiches and wish to protect their mother. She hears a bit of the Rachmaninov symphony, remembering the strength with which she loves her own boys, remembering their first haircuts as little boys, when the backs of their necks looked so new and vulnerable she wanted to hug them for her own sake and would have died for them. She wants to hug Harry now, for the same reason and the idea occurs surely he is no less related to me than he is to Sally Pryce-Williams.

She is wrong, and sensing it, Sally wants to get things straight immediately but does not know how to do it. And, anyway is it any of my business? Is it not Harry's, alone? So she says nothing, only smiling at Mavis so that Mrs Willis remembers she also has not introduced her friend.

"Mavis my ..."

But Mavis cuts her short, sailing straight onto the rocks.

"Such a handsome boy, just like his father." She looks at the fine figure of a man who is Mr Pierce. "And I can see his mother too in his expression. Isn't it odd? You look at some children and you can see both parents, at the same time, but you can never quite see where the one ends and the other begins."

Mrs Willis wants to stop the chatter. This is what comes of not knowing the truth, she reasons, being a reasonable woman. She is cross with Mavis, but only a little because, in a way, Mavis's tactlessness is a sort of truth: she says what she thinks. But Mrs Willis is very cross with Sally because she wants Sally to be real: she feels like grabbing her and saying: out with it, girl, let's get to the bottom of this. How can I know you if you are telling me lies? How can you know me or anyone properly if you don't know yourself? This bothers Mrs Willis: public lies are bad enough because they distort the image of the world but secret lies are worse because they damage the liar, eating away at the essential person within.

Mrs Willis is only half right because Sally had not lied to herself since the moment David shrugged her off that time, and she has no intention of lying now. She had only seemed enigmatic at the dinner party because, while she had wanted to be honest with Mrs Willis, it was hardly the occasion on which to ... to spill the beans, what with David being around and all that. With the others, the truth did not matter, they would take it or leave it, except of course, for her mother, who had already taken it and welcomed it.

So Sally welcomes Mavis's chatter. It is much more to the point than it seems. So she says.

"Exactly, he is very like his father." She turns to look at her son. "But I think it is difficult for a parent to see themselves in their children, unless there is some very obvious trait like red hair or sticking-out ears."

Harry touches his ears.

No, Darling, neither were your father's, she thinks, they were sweet little things, almost unformed and they seem to have been pointed, but in my mind's eye. But seeing Mrs Willis smiling a smile of real pleasure, she states to the assembly at large.

"Yes he really is mine. I am his mother and you know it, don't you Harry?"

"Yes Mum," and he feels like saying 'So what's the big deal?' Instead he says, with an equal lack of grace. "But I want to meet my Dad." He looks at Mr Pierce: "Don't I?"

[][][]

Mr Pierce barely looks at Harry in reply so that Mavis, who is wonderfully unaware she has dropped a brick, dives in.

"Is he alive?"

To which Sally answers.

"I'm sure he is. He can't have been much older than me." And that, she thinks, is rather letting the cat out of the bag. It sounds like a one-night stand. I might have been drunk only, that time, I wasn't. The other time was different. I had failed and I knew it. I nearly fell down the steps but Mac held my arm. Or perhaps, I held his? She blushes and they notice and think it is for another reason: "I was such a child, I thought I knew it all but I knew nothing." She looks at Mr Pierce who has sat down in an armchair and is looking at his large hands, fingertips touching, as if he is thinking, only he is not. So she looks at Mavis who is watching her, and speaks to them all.

"But it was absolutely the most significant thing in my life." She wants to add: I promise, girl guide's honour, I'm a good girl, not sure if she would rather sit on Mr Pierce's knee or Mrs Willis's, or just prattle on at Mavis who would ignore most things except the important ones. "And this great lout beside me is my son! How on earth did it happen?"

So the whole thing is out and no one in the hotel sees it as a great, momentous statement. She might as well have said it is raining. They would not have doubted her word. Mrs Willis thinks: I got it wrong, no one said he was an adopted foundling they just assumed it because the reality was just a bit more complicated but I'm glad he is not the son of David Pryce-Williams because that would be difficult and the lies would be like discarded paper upon the floor in great thick wads. She was ashamed of disliking David Pryce-Williams because, as Mavis would tell her, he was only as God made him. But the idea of David Pryce-Williams as Harry's father would have made Harry wrong in a way she did not quite understand. A mother must be in the picture if only to put her son's dirty clothes into the washing machine and to listen to Schönberg because he had told her to. If only Mr Pierce was the young man's father, that would be a good thing but it was unlikely although it would do for a start. Mrs Willis did not organise people to do things but you tended to follow in her wake if you were not careful. Mr Willis was a case in point: one assumed he had changed his name upon the marriage although he was by no means under her thumb, rather he brought his love to her along with his bald head and large ears saying take these and do what you want. So she did not say Yes, he ought to know his father, because that was for Mr Pierce to say, if anyone was going to say it. But of course, whatever anyone did say, the idea of Harry seeing his father would never be allowed to rest because Mavis would wave it and wave it around like mad.

Mr Pierce, who had not told these people to try The Harrington next door, began to have additional, unexpected, thoughts about the people he had, somehow, expected. If we three went walking in the park now or if we three sat together in this room and had tea together the others would think you were my son, and I would be glad. And if they insisted upon me stating my honest opinion just now, I would say: yes, if I had a son, who is honest like this boy is, I would want him to want to know me.

[][][]

By this time, Mrs Willis had explained to Sally why she was there and about her relationship to Mavis who was an old friend. Mavis had explained that Mrs Willis, whom she called Mary, was in fact one of the pillars of her life. Mary had just said nonsense, when Mr Pierce spoke as if he had been talking all along and had only paused in order to allow these women to break in and tie up a few minor points. He spoke slowly and so quietly that even had he not spoken such obvious sense, they would have had to listen to him very carefully indeed. His voice, which came from the depths of his large and considerable chest, was warm and seductive. Thus Mavis allowed herself to daydream about what might have happened had she met such a man when she was a young woman: he might have been one of those GIs, and she would have learnt that there were such things as worthy men, and she might have been thinking about her own children rather than those of other people. Mrs Willis thought, as she listened, how she would like her sons to meet this man in a way that was not contrived. She wanted Mr Pierce to like her sons in the same way as he liked this boy here. She could not take her eyes off his face, wanting to get close to it and feel his breath. Sally listened, barely thinking at all, assuming, nonetheless, that what he said was directed at her, especially. Only later, thinking of him and going over the consequences of what he had said, did she realise he had been speaking mostly to Harry, bringing him out and considering him, even though he had not said very much. People do not say much, outside of books. Even if they chatter away, like Mavis.

So Mrs Willis had said nonsense and Mr Pierce finally said to Sally.

"But what does the young man say about it?" He leaned forward raising his eyebrows at Harry. "What have you got to say for yourself?" Then he fell back into the chair, which he owned, and apparently closed his eyes as if the answer did not interest him, or else he knew it already. Nonetheless, he put up his hand to stop Mavis filling the gap. It might also have been the signal for Harry to have his say.

Harry raised his eyes from the plate. He frowned at Mr Pierce with reproach because Mr Pierce was teasing him and because he had fallen in love with Mr Pierce with whom he would discuss all his dreams if only they were alone. So he detached himself from his mother and answered angrily.

"I told you, I want to see my Dad." Which is what they had expected.

"So why not see him?" said Mr Pierce, and he thought: Would I not want to know a son like you who would make sense of the time I spent with that woman, there, your mother?

"I don't know where he is," growled Harry, and added contradictorily. "He's in New Sudan."

"So go to New Sudan."

And Mrs Grant thought: I am breathless with the audacity of the man, whom she would have liked more and more, his certainty not unlike what was left of the Polish officer.

"You are more likely," went on Mr Pierce, "to find him there than here, and if you don't, at least you'll have a better idea of what he is." And, therefore, surely, he implied, of what you are. Mr Pierce thought of the dark, populated warmth of Lagos, the rain pouring into the narrow street jammed with traffic and a busy market struggling with the mud. In the room a lamp burned as if it was night. It was dark enough. The children stayed inside to enjoy their snug home, which was what their mother had intended.

Harry's mouth began to drop but he closed it and gulped down the last sandwich. He turned his whole body towards his mother.

"Mum?" I brought you here, did I not? Now I want you to leave. I will stay with the man here, who appears to know the answers better than you, and who may as well be my father.

To which she replied.

"I don't know," meaning to add: Why is it necessary now all of a sudden? But getting only as far as, "Why ...?"

"Because," said Mavis, filling the vacant space with her teacher's voice, "he must go. It is his duty."

His duty? The deceased Mrs Grant gasped, losing her breath altogether but delighted all the same by the turn of events.

"To die for his country?" Sally responded, amused and a bit cross at the same time.

"Of course not." Mavis was indignant. "I don't mean that, do I?" She appealed to Mr Pierce. "You know what I mean. Explain."

"No, you don't mean that," said Mr Pierce, and stopped.

"What does she mean, then?" Sally glanced at Mavis, laughing, so that the older woman was reassured. But Sally had to frown at them because this was, after all, a serious matter. Isn't it? The fundamental formation of my son's soul is at stake, it seems.

Well then, Mr Pierce might have said, and he undoubtedly thought it, she means what she says, and he said, in a rather solemn way

"It is Harry's duty to find his father."

Sally felt she should no longer be amused. Did not the man appreciate the ... the ... the whatever it was? The practical problems involved? She was cross, but unaware that Mr Pierce was intensely concerned for Harry and for Harry's mother and for the father in New Sudan, a country he would have to look up in the atlas. She was unaware, also, that her son had fallen in love with the whole idea of Mr Pierce, just as she had fallen in love with his confident hands, his thinning hair and his smiling eyes. But she was aware, acutely, that she was in a situation out of which she could not walk. Harry was, in this place, in this hotel, in the very centre of his adolescent life. Much depended upon what might happen. She understood that, and understanding it she thought of Mr Prynne's warm socks and the bump bump with Wanei in the old lean-to kitchen, which was, Mrs Grant pointed out, barely an apology for a scullery, or even a garden shed. So, confused, she burst out angrily.

"That's easy enough for you to say, just go to New Sudan, but it's not like going to ... going to France. Is it?" She looked at Mrs Willis as something solid that would reassure her but Mrs Willis only smiled back with her eyes so that Sally smiled also as if the whole thing was indeed a great joke and not so serious after all.

"I don't suppose it is," said Mr Pierce, "I've not been there." He thought of Lagos. Its dark, lamplit nights; the muddy water; the heat; the desperation and the laughter. He would have told them to go there too if it had provided the answer. He would have taken Harry, himself.

This vague response made Sally feel she ought to be cross again.

"So why is it Harry's duty? Tell me. Why isn't it his father's duty?"

Mrs Grant sucked in a breath, raised her eyebrows, looked down her nose: Really, Sally, don't act the fool.

Mr Pierce opened his eyes wide, looked at Sally and then at Mavis so that Mavis began to explain.

"Because ..."

But Sally had heard her mother's words, and cut her off.

"I know, I know. You're right, you're all right."

Mr Pierce smiled at her, she smiled back at his hands before glancing at his eyes, which were wide open and so full of warm, brown love that she wanted to go to him. Instead she looked at Harry who was mesmerised also by Mr Pierce. Thus she understood the love that connected the two men. Happily, she looked at Mavis.

"But you can tell me."

So Mavis told her, and Sally was surprised she had forgotten so much, and because Mavis's chatter contained a sort of wisdom, it filled Mr Pierce's heavier thoughts with light, making the darkening room brighter as if someone had switched on the lights, or polished the mirror. The gist of what Mavis had said was: because Harry's father does not know he has a son, ending up with:

"It stands, surely, from all you've said, to reason."

[][][]

So Sally looked at her son who was still watching Mr Pierce who was breathing heavily.

"It does. You're right," she said. It was the first time she had thought of it. She had not thought of sharing Harry with the man whom she felt she knew intimately but knew not at all, the man who was the servant and God knows what else of the other Harry who was also the godfather in absentia. She had a frightening vision of one of the club servants, faded and defeated in his lap-lap and old shirt being ordered around by a drunken ... someone or other. She might have shuddered only she did not: her faith remained rock solid.

Mr Pierce spoke out of his sleep.

"Even if he knew, does he know where you are?"

"No."

Mavis said.

"Has he any idea?"

"None at all. He might think we were in Australia." Of which, Sally added to herself, he has no idea either. No one does.

"And ..." said Mr Pierce, leaving the sentence to Mavis to complete.

"... Even if he did and if he thought it was his duty, which I never meant at all, how do you expect him to get here? I imagine he's poor and you're rich. Rich enough to afford a couple of air fares."

"Yes, of course," said Sally abruptly, as if accusing Mavis, "we have everything and he has nothing," adding, as an appeasement. "But what did you mean, then?"

"You know what she meant," said Mr Pierce roughly, surprising them to attention, "if you don't face the idea and seek it out, you'll regret your failure all your lives. Seek it out, for God's sake." He was wide awake now, and sitting up. "Seek it out and fail if you have to, but make the effort. Do it, because no one else can do it for you, you must find it in your own way. And when you do, Harry will be on his own and then he will be ready."

Having made the speech, Mr Pierce relapsed into sleep again, head tilted back so that his bristled chin stuck out at them, as a challenge, his hands resting on his stomach. Having thrown off his jacket, his white shirt was brilliant, denying his own failure from which he had learnt bitter lessons.

Sally knew he was right; the idea of going back to New Sudan was exciting but for Harry it would define his life: she looked at him for a response.

But Harry was looking at Mr Pierce, having moved to the other end of the sofa.

"Harry?"

"Yes, Mum, I hear," he said crossly. "He is my real Dad, isn't he? This man you're thinking of."

"Of course."

"So why can't I see him?"

"You can but ..." Fulham housewife, Mrs Pryce-Williams, living in a tastefully renovated mid-Victorian terraced house, appealed to a fellow Fulham housewife, Mrs Willis, living in an equally tasteful but less ruthlessly renovated late-Victorian terraced house: "It's not easy. Is it?"

But got no support. "I don't see why not. You just ... go. You'd go via Australia, I suppose."

"Yes."

"And that's not expensive these days. Is it?"

"No."

"And then you'd know where to go on from there?"

"Yes."

Harry moved back towards her, Mr Pierce smiled like the Cheshire Cat and Mavis said:

"Bravo."

[][][]

So it is settled. Sally is cornered by her friends. As it is already September, the earliest option is the next summer holidays, ten months away. Useful timing because by then Harry will be sixteen and a bigger sixteen than he might otherwise have been, having taken up Mr Pierce's offer of a weekend job in the hotel. He takes it because he wants to assert his independence to himself, and because the idea of his father is beginning to be like Mr Pierce.

It keeps Sally up to the mark, because the existence of Mr Pierce in Harry's life, and therefore in her life also, makes the trip to New Sudan a given fact that cannot be avoided.

Mavis does her bit also, encouraging Harry whenever she sees him, which is most weekends. When he was putting up the Christmas decorations – some of the aged things falling apart in his clumsy and amused but sometimes delicately dexterous fingers – she said:

"Six months to go, Harry. Aren't you excited?"

"Yes," he lied, as he imagined the given fact of finding Mr Pierce in the jungle.

And Mavis thought: I hope he won't be disappointed when he finds out his father has many wives and dozens of children. But she did not know that Wanei ate people.

14   A Great Wave

The boy, who is becoming a man, lives his life thoughtlessly. But he lives it, apparently, without disturbing the pattern of the household his mother has fashioned around him. A delicate cage out of which he might break, destructively and brutally, but from which he escapes by gently opening a door that has no catch. So he returns noiselessly, this boy who is not wilfully destructive although his bike scratches the paint and he leaves mud upon the hall carpet.

She makes them sit down for breakfast in the dining room. Therefore, she carries the things up the night before on a tray, after they have gone to bed. Then she sits awhile, sometimes reading, but more often listening to Chopin or Scriabin or late Brahms, very quietly, thinking of her children dreaming their dreams. There is a pop-up toaster which stays on top of the sideboard manufacturing an endless supply of crumbs that are collected on a small papier-mâché tray her mother gave them one Christmas. In the mornings, it is Sally's habit to watch the children without comment so that they forget her and act themselves.

The idea of breakfast without his sisters would astonish Harry who nonetheless treats them as if they are no more than the toaster on the sideboard, manufacturing an endless supply of chatter. This attitude infuriates the calculating Alice but makes the adoring Sonia giggle because she cannot quite believe the solid mass of aloof masculinity and life force is her very own brother.

He stretches across Alice to get the Marmite.

"It's rude to stretch," she says, trying to block him with her thin arm encased in tight red wool from which protrudes a spiteful bony wrist, pale and freckled. "It's bad manners."

He ignores her, grabbing at what he wants.

She furiously stares at her mother whom she hates for not telling Harry to ask nicely.

"You should say please. Then I would have passed it."

"What?" says Harry, incredulously mumbling through food, the fact of her existence having forced its way upon him. He stares at her as if she is entirely pointless.

"It's also rude," she adds primly, "to talk with your mouth full, Gran ... Granny," she minces with a slow glance at her mother, "wouldn't like it, you ill-mannered young man."

Harry shifts himself upon the chair and farts loudly. As he does so, he looks at his sister contorting his mouth to express the F sounds and then obviously changes his mind because she is not worth the effort.

Alice is red with anger and frustration. She knows her mother will not intervene or take sides. If Sally is appealed to, she is most likely to get up and leave the room without a word. Then Harry would laugh out loud, pointing at Alice, who would want to cry, only her pride would not let her.

Harry was not a bully. He did none of this in a mean, calculating way. It was only an expression of the exuberant life with which he was filled. But Alice had to be kept down. When the time came, he was the kindest of them all.

Sonia is racked with giggles. Hand across mouth, pressing down on chair, torn between an embarrassed loyalty to her sister and what she owes to her big bad brother who only the night before had given her all his Roald Dahl books. But she hates Harry for teasing Alice because she is in love with him. Suddenly she wants to cry and she looks at her mother who smiles at her and winks so it is alright.

Harry gets up. If his mother had not been there, he would have farted again, or belched.

"Bye Mum." He waits.

Eventually she says.

"Aren't you going to say goodbye to your sisters?"

He looks at Alice who returns his stare.

"No."

Sonia giggles and Alice inspects her split ends.

"Alright."

So Harry makes a lot of noise in the process of going.

They hear the front door slam and know that more paint has been scratched in the hall where he keeps his bike. Each woman is impressed with the self-possession of the young man who has just left them, the room vibrating from his energy. They are painfully aware of his absence, as if he has just gone to the trenches. Sally had wanted to hug him, hug them all, hold them safe for ever. She thinks: this is a play. But am I in it or am I watching it? She talks to both her daughters but especially to Alice, to placate her.

"Let's go shopping, we'll buy some clothes in Kensington High Street." It was Saturday.

Alice says alright and Sonia is relieved.

[][][]

Harry cycles along the backstreets of the London he knows to the hotel which contains the people who are part of his life. His life at this moment is especially his because it does not contain his family and because he believes he has chosen it. The world of the hotel exists because he believes in it. He has an idea that when he leaves the hotel, in the dark winter evenings, the interior of the building and the people within remain in suspended animation until he returns. The fact that things change position while he is away is because they have changed position in his imagination. The fact of a table moving from an upstairs room to the lounge, overnight, even scratching paint on the way, is an act of creation in Harry's mind, scratched paint included. So thought Harry, without thinking much. Had Mavis died in the night, as she was to do on another night, he would have felt a twinge of guilt wondering why.

Thus from his point of view, Harry owned the hotel. Had he not walked in with his mother, the hotel would not exist. Therefore, he allowed his family more freedom than he did the inhabitants of the hotel, because he had decided, for the duration, to detach himself from his family, as opposed to determinedly attaching himself to the inhabitants of the hotel. He told the family, the Fulham family, nothing. Sally had more sense than to ask, David was hurt or thought he ought to be, blaming his wife, and Alice pretended not to care. Sonia was the one who loved him all the more for the mystery; her Harry was out in the world killing dragons; he wore her scarf on his arm.

[][][]

"Go away and do something," he had said to the doting Harry soon after it had been understood that Harry would work at the hotel on Saturdays to earn five pounds. So the boy had picked up Mr Pierce's shoes, which sat side by side, warm and empty, in the small, dark room that was Mr Pierce's office. Harry had taken them away as a piece of Mr Pierce and he had cleaned them as a personal service. Not very well but he had done it as an act of worship. Later, he'd gone back to the little room, which seemed to be behind the stairs, when they were not going down to the basement kitchen; the little room which had once contained a new-fangled telephone – drat the thing. He had quietly replaced the shoes, glancing up at Mr Pierce snoozing behind his desk. Then he'd crept out to the hall to sit on the chair and wait. For things to happen. Mr Pierce he would serve, as he served no one else, not even his mother. Particularly not his mother. Not in that way: he'd protect her in a proprietorial way but not as a servant.

No one was employed to take care of the hall, the entrance to the hotel. There was no reception counter, such a contrivance would have taken up valuable space. The room was set out to suggest a place for sitting rather than as the narrow entrance generally associated with such houses. Where Harry sat, looking into the street through a narrow window beside the front door, was dark with panelling, circa 1910, the darker recesses of the room suggesting a deceptive spaciousness. At certain times in winter, the afternoon sun would glance through the window, throwing a square of gold onto the dark wall opposite, warming the room with a sort of optimism. The front door itself allowed in only a dim suggestion of light, obscured as it was by the pillared portico and coloured glass, circa 1880. There was a small, leather-topped table with two drawers, Maples 1912, and the chair someone had left behind, Chippendale style and just as well made. Here sat Mr Pierce sometimes, to receive guests, or to watch the square of golden light shift and fade or to read a book by the light of an Edwardian-style desk lamp he had picked up cheap in Shepherds Bush. In one of the drawers of the desk was the guest book, the contents of which Mr Pierce would change according to his mood. In the other lay one of the detective novels from the bucket: *The Tiger in the Smoke*, price 1/6d. Any noise drifting irreverently into the room, off the street, down the stairs, up from the basement or through the large mahogany door to the lounge with its one or two tea tables, was absorbed by the silent solidity with which the hotel greeted its guests, just as any attack upon Mr. Pierce was absorbed by the large black reality of his body, turning it into something good and acceptable.

Potential guests wandered in. Couples would look around and retreat, for some reason they found the place ... too quiet: they were not ready to be absorbed. Families rushed past barely registering the hotel's existence because we want a family room, cheap please, sorry you won't get it here. The odds and sods were the ones who drifted in. Or rather, were the ones washed up, obscurities, they once packed the theatre or had OBEs to prove their existence ... to themselves. Sometimes they would not do but mostly they would begin to understand themselves as they hung around the empty hall for exactly the right amount of time or else beat a hasty retreat suddenly afraid, even terrified, for some remembered reason. Because behind the desk there was Mr Pierce the whites of his eyes apparent in the dark, his strong white teeth startling you: Can I eat you? Or else he would switch on the Edwardian-style lamp to inform you we're full, try 'The Harrington' down the road. But you only had to think briefly, almost sub-consciously, this is my sort of place and there were an infinite number of rooms one of which was waiting for you.

The man's dark outline pushed open the door. He stood in front of Harry. He was not young, he wore a smart suit, he fancied himself. He looked at Harry, the scent of expensive after-shave lotion unable to disguise the odour of corruption. He looked Harry up and down, his mouth framing a thin smile.

"I want a quiet room please. Private." Harry looked at the man's shoes well polished military style.

"We're full." The man looked around the empty space, at the evening shadows. He was amazed.

"You can't be, it's November." Harry said nothing, began to pick his nose then changed his mind. "I'll pay cash, now." The man began to feel for his wallet. He had a trim figure for a man of his age but it could not disguise the air of ... decay. Harry laughed

"Try 'The Harrington', down the road." The man blushed.

"Thank you." He was gone. Harry continued to read the book he had taken out of the drawer.

> He was a man who must have been a pretty boy, yet his face could never have been pleasant to look at. Its ruin lay in something quite peculiar, not in an expression only but something integral to the very structure. The man looked like a design for tragedy. Grief and torture and the furies were all naked, and the eye was repelled even while it was attracted. He looked exactly what he was, unsafe.

The Tiger in the Smoke, by Margery Allingham. Chapter 10, The Long Spoon.

Harry enforced his presence upon Mr Pierce who, nonetheless, found he could neither resist nor absorb him. But the badly polished shoes left marks on his socks. He noticed this when he undressed that night. He said nothing about it. In time Harry's skill improved.

And Harry had his own idea of the hotel. Those dark places in the shadows of the hall were recesses in the walls where suits of armour stood or they were entrances to infinitely mysterious passages leading to wherever he chose. They were real not because he made up fantastic stories in his head, like his sister Sonia, but because the essential centre of him understood them to be a real part of his life and therefore they pointed to an infinite range of possibilities. It was later in his life he saw – in his mind's eye – the nature of the room, objectively, consciously. But had he returned to the space which was the interior of the hotel he would have said no, this is not the place, the interior surfaces are too flat, I will find the hotel elsewhere.

[][][]

Harry's hotel included only two real people. All the others were freaks. One of the real people, a sort of North Pole, was Mr Pierce, to whom Harry was drawn and who seemed to silently direct him or, at any rate, to confirm his direction. The other, the South Pole as it were, was Mavis. Mavis insisted because in Harry she recognised someone, something, the actuality of which proved her own existence.

The corridor on the top floor of the hotel was the narrowest. Accommodation up here is important, so much having been wasted on show on the floors below.

Mornings, early, Mavis, floor-length dressing gown of quilted satin, wine red, silver hair brushed, eyes clear, she sparkles, walks gently to the bathroom. The bathroom is small and black and white and chipped enamel 1950s vintage but it is hers, spotlessly clean, she has the key hung on a piece of silk ribbon. It lives in the ample pocket of the wine-red dressing gown, dry-cleaned once a year for a week when I am bereft of its comfort. Thus she is there. In the corridor she wills Harry to be there also. Therefore he is. He carries for her, at no extra charge, her morning tea, with which she eats two digestive biscuits from a tin decorated with pictures of the homes of the English monarchs, including those in Scotland. Also, she eats a piece of fruit, in season, nothing imported, if Mavis can manage it she struggles with a hard Cox's Orange Pippin in midwinter, oh for a hothouse peach. There's a shop at the South Kensington Tube Station where she buys them, near the Polish Café where she meets her friends. I like the Pyrex cups in which they serve their milky coffee.

Each of them, Mavis and Harry, is alone in the corridor until the moment of near collision, English breakfast tea cascading down wine-red satin, sugar to be brushed out of pile of worn indistinctly coloured carpet, milk sloshing around tea tray like a winter sea. But disaster is narrowly avoided every time. Harry is not a clumsy boy although his mind is miles away from where it ought to be and he is lost for words which, in any event, are unnecessary. She is the kindest woman alive, I would have carried the tea stain on my dressing gown as a gentle memory of gentle times. Thus each, in fact, creates the other thinking fast: she is not at all like my gran but he is one of those boys to whom I would teach the gentle art of cookery, he would cook his father, Mr Pierce, but I don't think he'd eat him, he'd prepare him a decent breakfast not like those foreign girls in the basement who come, and go, in winter. She had more ideas than Harry because she had lived longer.

"My goodness, Harry, you nearly had us on the floor then."

The boy laughs, not knowing if he can open his mouth or not, so he says.

"I've brought your tea."

"Put it in my room, I'll be back in a second, please."

The small room looks untidy although it is not, particularly. It has a view of the back of another house similar yellow brick, black with old soot, grey slate, batches of chimneys, the pointing crumbling, and the sky: a big slab of sky filled with morning light and Harry's heart beats with joy, he knows not why so he stands with tray in hands, she takes it from him.

Thus, he sits on the chair uninvited while she makes the bed in the corner and arranges cushions so that the room is no longer a bedroom but a room in which one lives and I would rather be here and have it than the whole of Buckingham Palace with all those rooms going to waste. I imagine she lives in a sort of apartment embedded within. Harry had never thought of it like that, thinking of his gran's bedroom, which by the time he knew it was precisely that in which one spent the hours of darkness, the curtains opened a little to catch the dawn rolling across the flat fields behind. I feel I've missed the whole day if I don't see it coming, she was that type of hard-working woman with not enough to do in the end except remember the smell of autumn apples on the flat plains of Pomerania, which she had been told about.

Mavis opened the curtains very wide as if to fully illuminate the young man who sat in the armchair. She sat herself on the bed to look at him, the tea-tray safely grounded upon a small wicker-bottomed chair I bought for ten shillings years ago in a junk shop somewhere in Westbourne Park. Most of the stuff in the room is her own. New curtains, I worked it out with Mr Pierce, a month's rent in lieu you can keep them when I've gone I said and where're you planning to go he laughed, this is your home.

"You see the lining Harry?"

He did.

"You need thick curtains in London to keep out the restless night."

He looked back at her considering this new idea. All his nights had been London nights. He knew not the dark.

"Or else I would not sleep. How do you do it?"

"What?"

"Sleep."

He laughed his breathy laugh, which was real yet embarrassed because there was nothing to say except.

"I sleep." He might have added, What else would I do? But she was not his contemporary so he looked at the floor, scrolls and cabbage roses, because it was ideas filled his head, not the restless London night.

"Your shoulders are getting big," she said.

He felt his shoulders inside himself. He connected them to his whole body, which was too big for the chair so that he grew and grew before her eyes. His head broke through the ceiling, smashing the Victorian plaster and lath, splintering the rafters of Russian pine and bits of an old wooden ship that had carried tea from Calcutta to the East India Dock and Welsh slates clattered down into the street so that with the amazed eyes of a giant, Harry looked around at all the London morning from Crouch Hill to Sydenham and Putney Heath beyond. He would have taken the whole of London in his hand only at that moment he did not want it. Looking was enough.

"It's carrying all those things with Mr Pierce. I saw you moving the table downstairs." Not only that, but also the press-ups, the pull-ups and a thing called a bull-bar which Sally had hidden because you shouldn't use it until your body is fully grown or almost, but I do have a handsome son. The girls at his school watched him and he knew it, the strapping lad. The headmaster had said as if butter wouldn't melt in his mouth but there was a part of Harry in which butter indeed would not melt and the headmaster conceded he was a good boy who wouldn't hurt a fly purposely despite there being a chunk of his teenage brain missing.

So Harry sat there with Mavis in the room which was not untidy when you looked at it but which seemed to be because Mavis was like that while his gran was, one had to admit the fact, more calculating, more … ruthless. Mavis was different inasmuch as she was impulsive but nothing that she did was without reason. Harry liked her without knowing precisely that he did. He felt easy with her because she was easy and did not press things. She merely suggested them. And set his ideas racing. Harry responded to the woman without the complications of carnal desire. Mavis was older than his grandmother had been. Mr Pierce had given her insight into the way men's minds appeared to work. Men like Mr Pierce, like Wanei and, as it happened, like Harry, both of them.

"So have you settled on a date?" Her eyes fixed on his.

"For what?" His thoughts raced to the party to which he had been invited near Ealing. He was not sure how he would get home. It was a long walk.

"For New Sudan?" She suggested the idea, as if it might be somewhere else.

Harry almost asked her why but the idea of Mr Pierce asleep in his office filled his head. So the idea of New Sudan evaded him. New Sudan was his father. New Sudan was the hotel. There was nothing to say so he said nothing and would have liked to have picked his nose.

"You must ask your mother …" Mavis felt she had said too much.

But he answered her.

"Yes."

So that, on another Saturday, in similar circumstances, she renewed her attack.

"Did you ask her?"

"Yes."

She dared not push it further but he continued:

"She said she would tell Dad."

And that was that for a while or so Mavis thought, thinking also it's not for me to interfere. But she knew it was. I wish I knew his grandmother, of whom Mary had told her, beautiful as a woman of that age can be who has lived her life to the end which is sweet not bitter, and the thought of her makes me happy.

"Have you discussed it with your grandmother?"

"No, she's dead," which was a fact as was the memory of the old woman who smelt of apples, who was actually as alive as she had ever been to her grandchildren. It was the perfume, I suppose. As Harry got older he sometimes confused her with Mavis who said:

"I'm sorry," thinking of her own mortality.

And Harry might have said thanks, only he was not sorry and he didn't know why, exactly. Grandmothers die, it's a thing they do for you, Mr Pierce would have said.

So it became settled in Harry's mind that he was to go to New Sudan to see his father because he wanted to say a date had been fixed and hear the approval in Mr Pierce's voice: your father will be happy to see you. Because such a son as you would make any father proud. You would make me proud. Although Harry was quite an ordinary boy who would misbehave as well as the next boy, but he was not the type who would deliberately hurt a fly and he was blessed with love on all sides.

[][][]

So a great wave of salty water built up in the hotel and it rolled westwards and crashed upon a small but rather comfortable house in Fulham opening all sorts of wounds that would take time to heal, if they ever did.

15 A Well Kept Lawn

It was the book Sally decided to read for the duration because she had read it before and because it settled her. Wilkie Collins made life seem to be a rounded and conclusive sort of adventure, where everything worked out for the best in comfortable circumstances. David saw it lying around, before she had started it, and began to read it himself. There was no point in squabbling over a paper-back book.

> The ugly women have a bad time in this world; let's hope it will be made up to them in another. You have got a nice garden here, and a well kept lawn. See for yourself how much better the flowers look with grass about them instead of gravel.
> *The Moonstone*

David looks up the minute Sally enters the room.

"Do you have a bad time of it then?"

"What? Darling?" She lies because he is not her darling. Only one darling in her life. It is a term she otherwise reserves for children, her own and others, and then only when she is preoccupied with something else. Her darling had bumped into her in the warm dark kitchen – a sort of lean-to at the back of the bungalow, really – and then greedily eaten a billycan full of hot, salty rice with his hands to satisfy his lust – for vengeance, maybe – the deed done. He who, at the time of eating – tearing apart the half-raw, charred fish with his fingers – had thought of the man whom they called David, thinking he ought to eat him as well. Stab him in the dark, chop up his body and throw those bits he could not eat into the salty water. Teeth flash in the dark and snap shut. Anyway, she cares nothing for what David thinks but you can't go halfway round the world without making arrangements of some sort. He had shrugged her off before, and would have strangled her given half a chance but he can act the good London husband, fucking her when he's a bit drunk and cooking pseudo-peasant Italian food made from things in boxes and tins you buy from Sainsbury's in the New Kings Road. The cheese is like plastic. He thinks of her fat thighs again. They are thinner now with patches of tiny varicose veins, which remind him more of Stilton cheese.

So she says.

"What you reading?" She knew what it was. She might have sat on the arm of the chair, and ruffled his hair like any good London wife of the class of people who live in old Victorian houses they have renovated and filled with stuff from Habitat. Instead, she moves away from him to straighten a black-framed photograph on the wall. It happens to be a black-and-white study of a stark naked New Sudanese Highlander who looks out at them with a sort of dismissal – I am no more concerned about my nudity than if I was standing in a field of English cows. Had he known they were watching, he would have despised them, thoroughly.

David replies as if embarrassed.

"Something." Shut up and go away. You know what I'm reading: we could discuss the merits of the plot; if we wanted to communicate.

She might have sat on his knee. She might have taken the book from him, looked at the title and raised her eyebrows a little as if she'd caught him reading *Little Women*, or, as she once had, watching *Mary Poppins* on a video. Instead she sits on the sofa opposite the well-designed Belling gas fire above which hangs a painting got from the Nicholas Treadwell Gallery in Chiltern Street, to fill the space on the wall. They are what you call well-read people. They read the reviews in the relevant sections of the Sunday papers.

He puts the book down, there is no Sibelius symphony this time. Nothing like it. But he has to say something

"It's about ..." What he wants to do is to get up, go out on his own and get drunk in a bar he has walked past in the Brompton Road but dares not enter.

He pulls himself together, or rather tells himself he has done so.

"It's about this very valuable diamond that gets stolen and everyone in the house thinks they know who stole it and is trying to cover up for him so it's not the diamond that matters – although it's the most valuable diamond in the world – it's their feelings for one another which count. A sort of secondary attribute of the diamond. I suppose."

She is barely listening.

"I see."

"It's called *The Moonstone*."

"I know. It was one of Mummy's favourite books. She said it relaxed her more than any other she knew."

Your mother was a calculating bitch.

"She was a discerning woman, your mother."

"She ..."

"Could sort out the wheat from the chaff or rather she recognised what was ..."

"Worth having."

And what was not. They could talk away like this by the hour as if it was something they both understood or rather had a common concern about. It avoided arguments and nearly convinced them, and certainly convinced the people around them, that they were the Pryce-Williamses, a couple united, taking on the world around them and winning a piece of it, indeed like the house in Fulham. Trouble was, there was not much they had in common and as their marriage ... As it went on, he noticed she had less interest in interior decoration. So that was another subject closed to them.

And this time also, he saw that she was on an even more distant planet than usual, staring at the dripping tap or the lighted candle or whatever it was she saw in the painting hanging above the Belling gas fire. But she was not seeing it with her eyes, not even focused. If I stop talking, he thought, will she notice? She did not but she might have been acting. The second thought occurred to him – it had never occurred to him before – that she's acting the whole thing even stumbling down the steps that time so the drunken old degenerate could catch her, but it was me he caught, in the end. I'll keep my mouth shut and see what happens. She can fuck off, I wish she would. For a whole weekend. And take the children. There are times when her very presence in the house annoys me. I can understand why some men murder their wives.

At times, work, just the idea of it, was a relief to David Pryce-Williams. He wanted to be always in the well-maintained Edwardian office block in the narrow street near the Tower, on the top floor, in the boardroom, where they had talked of having a woman on the board but the idea was never settled and the nearest a woman ever got to it was Mrs Tillingham whom they sometimes called Sylvia, although she had been baptised Harriet, who organised the rather lavish lunches they had and she did it very well, but it's alright Sylvia we can serve ourselves. I reckon we can manage to open a bottle of that rather fine stuff you got and let it breathe. You can come back and clear away later. When we've finished.

Sometimes they kill their children as well, and then they hang themselves which seems a pretty desperate thing to do.

But you have to say something acceptable so he says.

"I'm surprised she didn't leave anything to Harry. She seemed to be especially fond of him." So am I, he thought, picturing the little boy who would never throw the ball back but came running to him, holding it tight and then solemnly presenting it to him. It worried him that he seemed to like the boy better than the girls, even though Harry was more like Sally than they were.

When Sally saw David looking at her, as if he was trying to work her out, she smiled at him, seeing the solid boy whose body she had, for a brief moment, wanted to explore. She was on the point of going over to him, but she stopped herself, doubting her motive. Instead, she settled back onto the sofa, never taking her eyes off his until he smiled back and relaxed also. It was how they used to be, in the Earls Court days, before New Sudan. When the other had been all they had expected from life. When each had asked himself in his own way: Is this it then? And back had flown the answer: Yes, it is, so far. Sufficient for London but not for New Sudan. So she talked to him.

"I'm not surprised, at all. Why should she single out Harry and hurt everyone else?"

He wanted to say: she hurt me by making you financially independent. But as the words formed he knew it was not that. There had not been so much money after all. Had Mrs Grant lived a little longer, she would have had to sell the house. So he began to act the ideal husband, finding another idea, therefore, much easier

"Yes, you're right and I'm glad she put it all in your hands."

The right things had been done, from the moment Mrs Grant had decided to die in her house, sitting in the wing-backed armchair, gazing at one of the Victorian watercolours, listening to the afternoon play, knowing Sally would do the right thing for herself and for the family. At the time, David had approved: jolly good idea. He was pleased to have the Victorian watercolours for his office. The best pieces of furniture had come down to London and after everything else had been sorted out there was not much left – houses up there fetching nothing like they would in London, for all the town's smug academic affluence. Sally divided the proceeds of the sale into four parts: three for the education of each child and one part for herself. Jolly good idea, David had said at the time, you can buy me a nice present for Christmas. The ideal husband meant it, the little wife would fritter her part away on clothes, it's what women do.

And was I not pleased to have some of the china and some of the jewellery, some of which I am wearing now? A delicate golden bracelet like woven silk that feels smooth on my wrist. You can have the carriage clock for Christmas. He took it to the office also, where it looked well on the green leather of his desk as something apparently insignificant which nonetheless wore away his life.

So Mrs Grant's money – some of which had been paid her by David's father, as David's rent in the good old student days – would pay for Sally to take Harry out to New Sudan to find Harry's father.

"Yes, Darling, but I'm sure you'd have done the same thing."

"Done what?"

"Put it towards their education?"

"Yes." He puffs himself out, begins to get up and then thinks better of it. I think I can afford their school fees, quickly working out in his head what they were actually costing him, and deflating a little when he realises they will need Mrs Grant's money one day. "But they're not at boarding schools, and Harry's School costs nothing. Why would I need her money?"

"Well university then. They won't get a grant like you did. You clever man."

But at the time, he had wished his father had been richer.

"My parents won't leave anything like she did." Will their lives, therefore, have been of less consequence? "Houses in South Wales are worthless. They ought to have moved nearer Cardiff years ago instead of staying ... in that dump."

Sally had rather liked them when she met them at the wedding,

"I admire their determination not to get involved in London. They're not so, I can't think of the word, they're not so ... so canny as Mummy was." They never needed to be but don't think like that. You silly boy! I nearly loved you once. "They live the way they want," and they value ideas more than things, which can't be bad. They formed a solid partnership of intelligent shared convictions which, unfortunately, forgot about you, although you can't say they didn't do their duty. You can, after all, appreciate a Brahms symphony, in a way that might get you to Mahler, or even Bruckner, when you're older, and you've read War & Peace, which is why Sonia got her name.

But yes, my mother was of more consequence, because she lived her life as a work of art. She created her life for herself. She did not live it according to a political formula like they did. "They'd be appalled by the material life we live here in London." They'd be ashamed of you if they knew how you lived. "They wanted you to be a Marxist and to go around banning the bomb." They've probably forgotten you already. Did we have a son? There used to be a boy around. The idea of one, somewhere.

He thinks she is laughing at his parents. So he laughs too, sitting firmly on the perch off which she could so easily knock him

"I don't want to ban it. It guarantees world peace, World Peace, Sally, because, you see ..."

"David?"

"Yes?" He expects her to take the opposite view, as her mother would have done, from simple contrariness. He winces.

So she says kindly.

"Shall I put on a tape?"

"What?" He is surprised by her gentleness.

"Some music."

"If you like."

She picks something at random but she sees it is the Schubert piano sonata, 960. It will make David feel he, also, ought to be intellectual and stimulating, and magnanimous. He will, therefore, be confident in the part he has to play: Mr P-W, husband, of Sally: I can tell you, she'd never have done it without my backing.

[][][]

"Harry," she stated definitively, as if it was a chapter heading.

"What about him?" Is there something I have not noticed? Is there some trouble? Is he taking drugs? Or mixing with the wrong sort? He seems to be alright. I am proud of my relationship with the boy who is the best thing I have for a son. The girls get more and more annoying each day. I hope you can manage them when the time comes.

"He's beginning to ask about his father."

"I see. So it's time for me to get out of the picture, is it?" David looks at her blankly. Do I need help? I think not. Not me. Do you feel sorry for me? Although, to be honest – honesty being an emotion of which I am capable in, in the heat of the moment – there is nothing to be sorry for.

You might have felt sorry for the shrug that time when I wanted your young body for what turned out to be the last time.

What are you talking about? What shrug? What time? He had a picture in his mind, for some reason, of flowers, struggling to grow amidst a waste of arid, dusty ground. Pink, delicate roses, torn and wilting. Dying for rain.

"Oh David! Come on. Of course not. However much he loves you, you are not his real father. And no one here pretends you are. We've been through all that. I am not going to feel guilty."

"You have no need to be. He'll get over it. He'll grow up. I'll explain it to him. He'll have to get used to the fact like the rest of us. He'll have to get used to the fact that his father ... barely exists."

To you, maybe, but not to himself or, she thought, looking at the picture, to me.

He looks at her. Why is she smiling? He has not the faintest idea what he is supposed to do. What do you want of me? You can have anything you like.

"But he's got us. He'll just have to grow out of it. Life's tough. He'll have to learn."

"Yes, he's got us, but he can't grow out of it, he can't leave the idea beside the road and move on because the idea of his father is part of him. If we resist it, he'll move away from us as the enemy. I don't want to lose him. His wanting to know is part of growing up, discovering who he is. He needs to know who he is. If we make a mystery of it he might imagine all sorts of wrong things. We should help him." She thinks of Mr Pierce.

"Then why don't you tell him?" He blurted it out before he knew it. "You weren't raped!"

No, but you rejected me.

"I told him he was a good man."

"We don't know that. What do you know about him? Do you remember how he threw us out of the room? Scowling at us like, like, like a savage. It was outrageous. He was just the house-boy."

"He was, he is, Harry's father," she answered calmly. "Half of their genes match. We all drank too much to know what we were doing. We were young. Finding our way." She didn't want to say I know him better than I know you.

"We were. We still are," he said, thinking of the bar in the Old Brompton Road, with a sudden, surprising jolt so that he smiled. "It might have been anybody."

So she replied to his smile.

"Yes. It might have been you."

"It might have been his godfather. Whatshisname, Henry?"

"Harry."

"Of course. Who has never bothered to contact his godson. Rotten type altogether. A bum."

"Perhaps he's dead."

"I hope so. I hope ..."

"David! Stop thinking like that."

"Well ... why didn't we call him David?"

"Because Harry meant something to us then. Don't you remember?"

"No I don't." I don't want to. I daren't ... "Haven't I been a good father?"

"Yes Darling, you've been brilliant. It hasn't been easy."

It's been easier than the girls. Until now, that is.

"And anyway," she continued, "one of the girls might have been a boy."

Wish they had.

"We agreed to save the name for that. And Darling, don't be a crosspatch, two Davids in the house would be awfully confusing. No one'd know who I was bossing around." She got up, went behind his chair and gave him a kiss on the top of his head which smelled nice and it's amazing how he's keeping his hair. He's just like a virgin.

"But the thing is, and you know it, he needs to find out for himself and with Mummy's money we could go out there this summer and he can see things for himself. Mrs Willis will look after the girls, she's offered to have them to stay with her or she'll come and stay here if you like."

"So you've discussed it with her."

"Yes."

"You women!"

"Yes."

"I don't understand you at all."

"You're a man."
So it was settled.

16   The Start of a Family

Huh! That's girl's stuff, had been Harry's response to his mother's suggestion he keep a diary of the journey. Nonetheless, in his mind's eye, he saw Sonia doing just that. She was sitting at the dining-room table, head bent low, one arm protecting the writing also hidden by her hair all the colours of the rainbow under the streaming sunlight. Which, he would have written, flooded the room from the garden outside, crossing out outside. Through the dining-room window he looks down onto flagstones and fig tree squeezed between London brick, Dad's neat little lawn, apple tree and shed. But beyond is not the garden wall and muddle of London houses, rather a rolling countryside of summer green giving to the blue yonder and the great sky in which anything might happen. Once upon a time there was a boy called Harry who lived in London with his mother and his ... But Harry could not read what she was writing, he would live the story instead, so he looked down into the sky seeing the insignificant pattern of streets and parks which was London disappearing.

"There's the Essex coast," says his mother, leaning across him and pointing as if he could not see it very well for himself. "It looks so flat, you'd think the sea'd cover it all at high tide." And so what? I could have had the whole of London if I'd wanted but the sky is what interests me. Harry trampled the Essex coast, waded across the channel, trod on France, spun the earth a couple of times beneath his feet and flew, as if swimming through the air, to where he wanted to go. Like his father that time.

[][][]

Her face had a scrubbed raw look. As if she had been crying for hours. Only she had not cried at all, despite wanting to feel someone's arm around her who would say it's alright. They were all staring at her except for Harry who stretched his fork across the table to spear another potato, while, it seemed, no one was looking. He put the whole thing into his mouth. It puffed out his cheeks so that he had difficulty chewing it. Alice would have made a face as if she was going to be sick but she was looking at her mother, ruthlessly. David had said something like: It's alright, sit down, not in front of the children, act your age, subdue your selfish feelings and think of me for a change, I do not want a scene. It's too hot for a Sunday lunch like this, let's take the pudding outside. Playing the sensible father.

"Alright." She sat down and let him lead them out. Again, Harry was the last. He looked round but not at her. Instead he grabbed another potato with his fingers and walked out. He might have been whistling. She waited until she heard them in the garden, David getting the chairs out of the shed.

"Alice, help me put these up." Apparently she did.

Dad, David, asked me to fetch the bowls from the dining room. She was sitting there, staring at nothing. Not like her at all but at the time it did not register. My mind was firmly fixed on New Sudan and for some reason I had a vision of us hacking through the jungle. I took one look at her, grabbed the bowls and a handful of spoons and left her to it. I suppose there were all sorts of tensions in the house but I didn't notice them. Not consciously. I know now, that things were breaking up but at the time it was just the adventure ahead I thought about. At least I think that was it. I can't honestly remember how I thought. But what I do remember was going back through the kitchen and finding Sonia sitting on the floor in front of the open fridge crying her eyes out. It made me feel awful and I didn't know at first what to do. Everyone else, Mum included, seemed quite able to look after themselves, pushing their lives ahead of them but Sonia was like a wounded bird, crushed by her life rather than in control of it. I didn't feel I was in control either, not at home, anyway, but that didn't bother me because I could go to the hotel. Any time I liked. I could walk out of the house and go there. Sonia was stuck.

"What's the matter?" said Harry to his sister who was sitting on the floor in front of the open fridge.

"I don't want to see us all like this." She cried in great big waves, pushing out each sob as if it would drive away the pain. "Why can't we go on like before? Why is Mummy so mean to Daddy. Why do you have to go away?" Her red, wet, blotchy face accused him of causing all her misery. "What's wrong with Mummy?"

Harry stared at her, swallowing the potato with an effort. He dumped the bowls on the table with a crash, the spoons rattling.

This was my little sister who was my biggest fan and I was deserting her just as she needed me. She was part of me and Mum, not of Dad and Alice but it never occurred to me that she might come with us. I was quite prepared to leave her to those two, who were so self-absorbed they'd walk all over her without noticing they were doing it.

"Come on, let's go upstairs." They kicked off their shoes. He took her hand and led her up to his bedroom, which she already treated as a refuge. She liked the smell of the place. She liked its rampant untidiness compared to the sterile neatness of the room she shared with Alice. Harry's room was at the top of the house. High, so you could not see into the garden. Some Saturdays you could hear the roar of the crowd from Stamford Bridge. She lay on the bed, gazed up at the ceiling and sniffed. She felt a lot better, having been recognised by her brother who for the past months had ignored her, as if the gift of the Roald Dahl books and the beginning of his job in the hotel had marked the end of something. Harry sat on the little swivel chair beside his desk and swung round towards her, putting his feet on the bed so that they touched hers.

"I'm not going for long. We'll be back after a few weeks. You've got the holidays."

"I know," she said, playing the self-possessed woman just like Mummy did it, "but that's the problem. If it was term-time I wouldn't miss you so much but what am I going to do? On my own?"

"What you usually do, with Alice." He had no idea what they usually did. Out of his sight they did not exist. Or rather, the animal which was His Sisters did not exist. Sonia on her own was something, he realised, which belonged to him. He stroked her leg with his foot.

She stared back at the ceiling, the tears were coming back.

"Listen, you can use this room whenever you like. You can sleep in it if you want."

But before she could answer the door burst open. It was Alice. She could not see her brother so she ignored him.

"What are you doing here?" she demanded. "You were supposed to bring the ice-cream. We were waiting." She said it accusingly. Then, more kindly: "Come on, Mum's washing up and Dad's locked the door on himself." Thus the muffled orchestral music from below registered itself as Dad's rejection of them. Alice wanted the reassurance of her sister's connivance against both the parents as a common enemy and therefore, defined as something known. She wanted her brother, as well, to help restore the normality, so she noticed him behind the door. "Come on," perversely changing tactics, "let's help." And they did help, just as they had done when they were smaller, invading, and getting in Sally's way at first but developing as a useful little team, washing, drying, putting away and clearing the table. Alice hoovered and then put back the dining chairs, just so.

[][][]

Things got back to normal, everyone playing the expected parts. The children, chattering and playing amongst themselves, appeared not to notice their mother's quiet detachment. One of the bowls she had picked up off the table broke in her hands. It was already cracked. She threw it into the bin without comment. By the time she was wiping down the sink they had gone upstairs. There was the noise of hoovering above, which died down to become the opening movement of Beethoven's first symphony. Then a clatter of feet up to the top floor where Sally knows they will play an innocuous board game like Ludo, the sitting room closed to them had they wanted to watch television.

She goes into the garden to put back the folding chairs, which have not been used. She returns them one by one to the shed because she has nothing better to do. Each time, she looks along the backs of the houses, across the narrow strips of gardens – roses, honeysuckle and clematis pouring over dividing fences and walls – she sees the fresh green of the Virginia Creeper that covers the back of the Willis house. It will be brilliantly coloured by the time she returns from New Sudan. She might have done some gardening but the garden is already as neat as it can be and anyway, it is David's territory: if she touched it now, there would be another reason for her husband to be angry with her. Her self-possession has left her, and her knowledge of herself accepts the emptiness of the vessel.

She sits on the bench, looking up at the sky, which has no colour in it: a blank London summer sky when the air has not moved all afternoon, the traffic packed on Putney Bridge. Wearily she gets up and returns to the house, through the kitchen, up the little staircase, past the stripped pine door, with the brass fittings, behind which throbs the restless opening of the Saint-Saëns organ concerto: another, better day, refreshing raindrops falling on the quivering leaves of the Willis Virginia Creeper. At the staircase she lets her hand feel the smooth mahogany handrail from which she had laboriously removed spots of paint and dirt, when she was carrying the first baby. At that moment she would rather hold on to it than go to New Sudan. On one richly carpeted stair, she picks up a book discarded by a child. In the bedroom, which overlooks the street, she lies down on the bed, tries to sleep, fails and reads the book.

Apparently, it does not hold her and thus, leaving it open on the bed, she gets up, goes to the window, looks into the street and makes up her mind. Thus she goes downstairs and, passing the sitting room door again, heard another bit of the Saint-Saëns organ concerto, the bit just before the last big organ climax. In the street, the sky is the same. The book lies abandoned on the bed.

All the furniture, the big table, the chairs, the sofa, the lamps, the little side tables, the cabinet with the bottles of beer in it, the ornaments, the electric fire, the carpet, everything was stuck upside down to the ceiling.

The Twits, by Roald Dahl.

[][][]

Our house is like thousands of others in that bit of Southwest London that was built up before the First World War. Except for one thing: the staircase, which is in the centre of the house between the front and back rooms. When you come in the front door, instead of seeing a staircase ahead of you, you see a passage, which leads straight through the house into the back garden, by way of a back door with a window in it. When Mrs Grant came to see us a few years ago, she said it was quite a common arrangement in the Midlands. She said too many people blocked the view with a downstairs lavatory. I agree, it was the thing I liked best about the house when I saw it for the first time. You open the front door and there, seen clearly, despite all the usual clutter is the garden, not as an immediate thing but there, as a promise, inviting you into the house. A few months after we moved in, we planted a pear tree in the middle of the lawn in the line of view. When you open the front door it's like an old friend down there, welcoming you home. Derek has put up more shelves for his wine and for my jam, and for old pots of paint, coats and scarves and hats have multiplied like rabbits, there are the bicycles the boys have left behind and it's the only place for the tumble-drier but you can still see clear to the pear tree which has grown to a respectable size. I love it. The kitchen light lights it up at night. I was lying in a reclining chair under the pear tree when I heard the doorbell.

Get that she shouted at her husband who was doing something useful to the back of the house, half hidden under the Virginia Creeper. It is Sally Pryce-Williams who is greeted by the bald man, Derek, husband of Mary, Willis. He invites her to come through the house into the garden knowing she will want to see his wife, who may have invited her for tea, he wouldn't know. He wears shorts, his legs are hairy and his paint-bespattered T-shirt carries the slogan 'Fulham FC', but he is a kind man who kindly hands Sally over to his wife, who, as it happens, had not invited her, albeit a visit is not unexpected. For years now, the Willises have been willing to do things for Sally although Derek is as likely to remark I don't think we ought to impose uninvited, to which Mary is just as likely to reply nonsense if it needs doing we'll do it. Derek brought out a chair for Sally and then went in to make the tea and bring out the biscuit tin, the cake having been eaten up the previous afternoon by visiting offspring with an entourage of similarly hungry young people. I'll get on with what I was doing, if you don't mind, he says and leaves them.

What impressed me, because she had always seemed the most self-possessed of women, was that she had been crying. She poured out her story, sitting on the edge of the chair like one of those girls who have had a bad experience of life and who expect it to treat them badly. And having poured it out it didn't seem to be such a great big thing after all. She said as much, admitting she'd got upset over nothing. She said I suppose I'm a bit tensed up about going halfway around the world. I thought more like halfway back through your life, but I said and it's a wound, perhaps, which you're reopening although it's just as likely to be nothing so dramatic. Or something like that. I can't exactly remember.

What had happened was that David, whom I cannot say I knew well, although he was her husband and we had all lived in the same street for years, had got at her at lunch, apparently, or so she imagined, for leaving him and the family to gallivant around the world, for reasons which were entirely selfish. I asked her if that was what he actually said, to which she replied not really, but he kept asking questions.

Like what? I could see she was searching her mind and I wondered if it was not so much lunch itself but because she was feeling guilty. Some women think like that. They think anything they do, which they really want to do, is selfish and therefore bad. But I thought Sally'd got over all that. Eventually she said, like all the things I thought we'd been through. Like how were the girls going to get their lunch and what about the laundry? She might have said some more, I can't remember, but it made me cross and I asked her, did you not explain that he would have breakfast with Sonia and Alice before going to work and that they would do the washing up and then I was to call around about nine-thirty to see everything was alright and discuss lunch and perhaps take them shopping? Isn't that what we've agreed? And didn't you tell me that both Sonia and Alice said they'd quite like to do the housework for a few weeks and be paid something for doing it, especially as I would be on hand, very much on hand, if required?

Sally said yes, I was right and that David had said it was a good idea for them to assume some responsibility at their age. So what, I said, has David, your husband, got to complain about? To which she replied that he wasn't complaining only he was asking her to explain the laundry in front of the children at lunch time.

So I said why the hell can't he work that out for himself, and she looked as if she was going to cry again. I distinctly remember her saying that she thought they were turning into the sort of Southwest London, Fulham family she didn't want them to be, which was rich coming from someone who'd spent quite a long time trying to be just that. And this is the result, I wanted to say. Instead I said something like "Can he not use the washing machine? I thought he'd be rather good at that sort of thing where you pre-set it and just press a button so that what is expected to happen, happens." I was attacking the man for her sake. I wanted to make her laugh because I wanted her to get on top of all the nonsense and not have him sitting on top of her just because he had the advantage. But she didn't laugh, she only said that David asked so politely to begin with that he'd caught her unawares. Or, I thought, at a weak moment, the bastard.

I asked her if she felt guilty. She admitted it, but I wasn't going to let her feel sorry for herself, because that gets you nowhere. I told her she had nothing to feel guilty about because for a start she was doing it for the boy. It was something that had to be done, actually, whether she liked it or not. More to the point, whether David liked it or not. Then I began to feel a bit sorry for David, who couldn't help, after all, being stupid, and I tried to explain this to Sally. I don't know if I had the right to do it but I did. I told her that it was nonsense to feel guilty but because she was, she was imagining that David was getting at her, which even if he was, he wasn't doing consciously. She looked at me in a thoughtful way, which was not pathetic, and said nothing. So I said, he's afraid of taking responsibility for Sonia and Alice and therefore, he may be subconsciously wanting to punish you. But what I didn't say was who wouldn't be afraid of taking responsibility for Alice who would not be incapable of telephoning social services and saying her mother had abandoned her children to go on holiday. I'm glad I didn't say it because, as I discovered later, Alice was only sensitive and of all those Pryce-Williamses the one in most need of a secure and serene family life.

Sally then said maybe she did feel just a little bit guilty, to which I replied that how she felt was her problem but because David wanted her to feel bad didn't mean she had to. Harry needed to find out about his father and she had the right to come to terms with that part of her life. She agreed with me. She nodded her head and said yes, so I thought it was alright but then she asked me if I didn't think David was rather wonderful. I was amazed. Why? I said and then she went on about the wonderfulness of a man taking on a child who was not his own and who actually proved his wife's infidelity, showing the world that he was a something. She couldn't find the word so I supplied it: a cuckold, I said, and any man who thinks like that, these days, is far from wonderful. It would mean he was saying to the world look what this woman has done to me. It would mean he wanted to humiliate you. And anyway, I asked her, was he not entirely in control of things at that time? Could he not have divorced you when he knew you were carrying another man's baby? In which case I'm sure your mother would have taken you in and welcomed you both. I think that's what I said. It's what I thought, and anyway it made her laugh, and she said yes, her mother would have done that.

Then she said the one thing that made me really think. She said that what had happened in New Sudan, what had made Harry, had also made her more like her mother. It made her take charge of her life for the very reason that David had had nothing to do with it and, more significantly, I thought, because she hadn't wanted him to have anything to do with it. Had David wanted to divorce her, she wouldn't have minded, she would have managed alright on her own but – and here I distinctly remember her smiling in a way which was quite natural and didn't look at all guilty – but, she said, to be honest, I didn't want him to. I wanted his money to support us. She said she was quite prepared to do what it took and he wasn't a monster, just a man. By which time we were both laughing and I knew it would work out but it was obvious that David must have done something fundamental which had hurt her but which had made her strong. Although I wasn't absolutely sure at that time and I felt I ought to give him the benefit of the doubt. She would have told me everything had I pressed her but I didn't think it was the right time. She had better go to New Sudan first.

"But all the same," said Sally, brightly, "I do feel bad about leaving the girls."

"Well don't. Don't be silly. You're only saying that because you think it ought to be said. Honestly, do you really feel bad?"

"Not at all."

"Good. Well done! Let him live up to the image of a modern husband able to manage his daughters for a few weeks while his wife goes away on business. If he can't cope they can come here. I'll make it like a holiday for them. They can sleep in the boys' rooms. Have one each if they want."

She took me at my word because that's what she wanted me to do for her. Good for you, was what I thought at the time and I still think it.

17   And the End of Another

Back in her own hallway, Sally aims for the handrail and seems to caress, for a minute, the polished mahogany. But she turns towards the sitting room and flings open the door, which slams against the sofa. She puts her hand to her mouth as if to stifle a laugh. She might have caught David doing something he shouldn't, but he is standing at the music centre, absorbed in selecting another piece of music. If it's the kids wanting the TV I'll go out to the garden. Had it been only one of them he would have felt obliged to keep it company – Alice would have insisted – but the whole mob could look after itself.

Sally says to the back of his head.

"David, I want to talk to you."

"Of course," he says, turning his head, "what do you want?" The tone of his voice insists he is a reasonable man, willing to put aside something more important in order to deal with her little problem. Whatever it is, but, indeed, I do regret my response to your little scene at lunchtime because I would have liked to have been a more loving husband, in front of the children. But I am not going to be the one apologising because you're the one who is inclined to be hysterical. All the same, if she says sorry, I'll tell her it's alright and I'll even offer to make the tea. "Why don't you lie down? You look tired. Did you go out?"

"For a walk."

And there she stands as if I'm the one in the wrong. Am I the one fleeing the family home?

"Won't you sit down?" For all the world as if he's about to interview her. As if she is a stranger in her own house, and to make the point he returns to his own chair beside the empty fireplace. But I don't want to treat her as if she is someone of whom I have to approve. I want to treat her as if she is my wife in all the ways that the term implies to the world at large. We used to do a good sort of double act but it doesn't seem to work now. I feel I am on my own. Perhaps I always was.

She has, by now, sat down. She crosses her legs, and folds her arms, then unfolds them, laying her hands flat on the seat, each side of her, apparently ready to get up at any moment.

Why the fuck does she look at me as if I'm an idiot. Honestly, I'm fed up with the whole thing. I wish she'd get going to New Sudan and stay there. Then I could breathe.

"David?"

"Yes, Darling?"

"I think we should go away tonight."

"Where? What do you mean?" He knows exactly what she means. Alright, get your things and I'll run you to the airport now but you'll have a long wait, about 48 hours. And you can sleep on the floor, for all I care.

She ignores him, anyway.

"We'll go to the hotel."

Who is going? What hotel? What is she talking about? I don't know any hotels. But I do. It is the hotel where Harry works at weekends. The boy whom I treat as my son but who is becoming less so by the minute.

"The one where Harry works. You know it."

I've never been there, so it doesn't exist.

"Why?"

"Because we're all on edge."

On the edge of what? A volcano? Speak for yourself. I'm not. It was you lost control at lunchtime and upset the children. He looks at her blankly, wondering what to say that will break the silence.

"Why that hotel?"

And why not, he assumed she would answer, instead she said.

"Because we know it and it's on the way. Harry will feel happiest there."

"Not here? Not at home?" Once you have taken him away, he will not come back. Then, where will be this home in London we have built up? Starting it with the idea of him. Had there not been a Harry, would we have started it at all? Would we have bothered to go on with ... whatever it is? He does not want to think about what their life had been.

"What difference does it make? If we go a bit earlier?" She leans forward as if inviting him to come over and kiss her. "We're going anyway. A few hours won't make any difference and I don't think I can ..." She stops herself.

"Will it not unsettle the girls?" I've got work tomorrow, I don't want my evening disturbed. But he saw himself making them their tea, watching TV with them – we could put on a video and eat ice-cream – and putting them into bed saying it's alright I am here despite your mother going away. David the good father. Not a bad man even if he did sometimes only go through the motions.

More than they have been? She looks at him blankly.

"Alright then," but please go without a fuss. "Do you mind a taxi?"

"Not at all." She looks relieved.

And as if on cue, the door flies open again and there stands Harry. He looks at his mother and then across the room at David. He smiles at him: "Dad?"

"Yes?"

"Can I borrow the binoculars?"

"Of course," and with a rush of love which surprises him, "you can have them."

"Thanks, Dad." Harry walks over and kisses David and then looks at his mother who smiles back at him. She says.

"Harry, Darling, we're going to leave this afternoon, in an hour or so. Can you be ready? I've packed your things. Just put in anything else you think you'll need but not too much. Can you do that?"

"Yes," he looks incredulous, "but why are we going now? I thought it was Tuesday. I've promised Sonia ..." He stops in mid-sentence, not wishing to divulge a secret.

David watches his wife. The smile has frozen on her face. She is, he is sure, helpless and he begins to feel sorry for her. Another emotion which surprises him. He wants to get rid of her but he does not want to hurt her.

"It's an early flight, Harry, on Tuesday, therefore, we want to avoid a rush in the morning." He says it as if stating a formula for living. He does not want anyone to be hurt, including himself: "You can see how the girls ... your sisters are ... on edge." Searching for words, he has to use Sally's. "Your Mum's right, it's better to go today so that, so that ..." He wants to say, So that we do not have to repeat what happened at lunchtime and I am dreading us all getting together again for another meal which will end in tears. Instead he says: "So that we can all relax."

"What's the big deal?" Harry wants, all of a sudden, to fight David. He looks at his mother for support.

But David has got up and is now standing between them. With his eyes fixed on Harry whom he sees as loutish and threatening. He sits next to Sally and takes her hand. When she tries to speak he squeezes it, quite hard: shut up I'll deal with this. Is it not what you want? Now he is angry and the emotion confuses him because as he feels angry, he realises the love he has for Harry and the love he once had for the boy's mother, when Harry was small and helpless, when he was grateful for Sally's ... for Sally's what? For the motherhood she naturally gave to the child who was, in some strange way, his responsibility. I did not create the boy but I feel I was somehow responsible for him.

David remembers the old Harry; he remembers what he felt in the water; he remembers the other one but only as a black, threatening, presence; he remembers that old drunkard – whatever his name was – coming to fetch me back. He blushes with shame, there in front of Sally and her son, the young Harry, who came out of it all.

So he squeezes Sally's hand again but gently: I love you in my way and just as I am understanding something of my love, which involves you and the boy there so that you may as well have it because where else can I spend it and I want you to have it, you are going. So what am I supposed to think? What am I supposed to feel? What, on earth, am I supposed to do? I feel I have recognised the beauty of the sky, which has been above me all my life, only at the point of my death. I have missed all the there-ness of it.

He looks at Sally, and then at Harry. Both of them are oblivious to his feelings, despite the rush of blood to his face. Do you realise what you two are doing? You are going to the other side of the earth, there to find a man who is the father of you, Harry, and the man who, who did something to your mother, who made her, made her whole, like I don't seem to have been able to do. Where does it all leave me? You can stay there in New Sudan and never come back, if this man asks you, appeals to you, this whoever he is, this dark thing who is so powerful, who is, apparently, the very centre and foundation of your lives. And we've never, ever, discussed it. All we've talked about is the practicality of your absence, which might, for all I know, be forever.

So where does that leave the girls? Their mother and brother gone! And you say, you say, you say, you young selfish bugger, just like I was, you say what's the big deal? Well, maybe it isn't a big deal but you might at least understand that it might be a big deal. But I love you like a son, there is nothing wrong with my love, and as a father. ... No, as your dad with a small 'd', I'd have to say go find that man who planted the seed which is now you because, demonstrably, it is not me. He, as I remember, is as black as a moonless night and look as hard as I can, I cannot make out a single detail of him or of what he is. Except that I know he is, he is your father, a dark and, no doubt, warm and desirable darkness. Go and find him but for God's sake go now so I can get on with being the David Pryce-Williams I suppose I have always wanted to be.

But what he actually says is.

"Your Mum's right. Sonia and Alice are not happy and the sooner you both start your, your holiday the better. Go on!" He laughs, as if he means it. "Go get your stuff together. You're staying in your hotel." And he thought: if I took them I could see what it is like and take the girls with me. But he did not want to see it. It was a place, he imagined, where Harry did menial things like washing up amongst a transient population of migrants who spoke bad English or none at all. He imagined it a place without humanity. He wanted it to be like that so that home, this place in a street of houses, in Fulham, in southwest London, must be, forever, Harry's emotional anchor.

"OK, Dad." And he's gone forever, leaping the stairs to his room and Sonia still lying on his bed. The idea had been that they would sleep together that night and he had rushed down to ask Sally if they could.

So David says to Sally.

"Is that alright then?"

"Yes, thank you. I'd better get ready myself."

"Yes, I'll make some tea and call a taxi."

18   Via the Hotel

Harry shot upstairs as Superman, swift as a bullet, pulled out his bag from under the bed upon which the astonished Sonia lay and began to throw things on top of what his mother had already packed. Indispensable clothes, regardless of the climate in New Sudan, the prized aftershave lotion he used, although his beard was no more than childish down, and a wonderful book he had just got into called the *Colour of Magic*. Only at the door did he glance back at his sister who was watching him incredulously, and then accusingly as she caught his eye for a moment. He looked out the window, accidentally destroying the houses opposite with his laser-beam eyes, and thought: Why are girls so stupid, always wanting to make things difficult? It wasn't a big deal – Mum and Dad were quite cool about it – so why make it one? He wanted to feel sorry for Sonia but he was too excited about himself and for a moment he felt guilty.

"Bye," blowing her a sort of kiss with his lips, "I'll send you a postcard, give Alice a kiss for me," and he was gone. She could have followed him, she might have had tea with them but she stayed behind in Harry's smelly bedroom, only half aware of the commotion going on downstairs. Later Alice came up.

"I didn't go down either, I was writing my diary, but I'm glad Mummy's gone. Now we'll have Daddy to ourselves. Come on, he says we'll watch a video and you can choose it." She knew it would be Mary Poppins again but she was prepared to give Sonia anything she wanted. She hated her brother so much it had made her cry.

Harry had crushed the house behind him, carelessly flattening it with his heel as he left. Behind the taxi, the devastated street was a smoking ruin. No church bells, only the over-arching roar of a jet airliner turning out of Heathrow. Below it, Harry's footprints were clearly marked on the ravished districts of Fulham, West Brompton and South Kensington.

He had, apparently, gone to ground in Kensington Gardens, miraculously leaving the Albert Memorial unscathed beside the fleeing London traffic.

"My goodness," his mother said, "what have you got in your bag? It weighs a ton."

"I'll take it." He grabbed at it, throwing it up to the top of the hotel steps. He then went back manfully for hers, ignoring her as he did it. This was his place and if she must come then she must follow meekly behind.

Mr Pierce met them as if they were ordinary guests. He acted as if he had not met them before. He might even have said, try 'The Harrington' next door. Harry half hoped he would, then he could have sneaked back through the basement to find Mr Pierce's shoes and clean them. He wanted to be apart from his mother, he wished there was a huge gulf between them, across which he alone could fly. He wanted to be sitting where Mr Pierce was sitting, calling his mother what he wanted, Mum or Madam or Mrs Pryce-Williams. Then he could perhaps say try 'The Harrington' or zap her out of existence with one powerful glance.

His rightful place was the hotel. Yet he was not recognised and thus, he wanted to fight something no longer David, Dad, whom, now he had got out of the way of him, he could view with detached affection. Better now his mother or even Mr Pierce, only the latter, he reckoned, would be oblivious to any attack and might even laugh. With Alice he could have farted or picked his nose or scratched his arse – any of the things that maddened her – but with these two he had no chance and his impotence infuriated him. His only real choice was to turn heel and walk out into the street. But then what? I could walk all the way back to Fulham, to Dad and Alice and Sonia, all of whom I can fight and beat. I could refuse to talk to Mum if she follows me. And the idea he had the choice, a powerful choice, encouraged him and brought him back to the hotel which he loved so that he did not hate his mother and he began to feel sorry for her. He realised she had only met Mr Pierce the one time and what she was doing was booking a room which was very normal and Mr Pierce was playing his part as the detached hotel manager because otherwise he would have to ask: and what are you doing here, I thought you were going to New Sudan? And Sally, his mother, could have replied: none of your business perhaps I should try 'The Harrington'. It was years later I realised she wanted the reassurance of Mr Pierce as much as I did.

[][][]

"Hello Mr Pierce," says Sally, as if she has not a care in the world. "Can you let us have a double room with twin beds for a couple of nights, please?"

Mr Pierce, who has been standing, sits down behind the desk and takes the register out of the drawer. He opens it and scans down the lines with his finger. He has not yet looked at Sally as if he knows her. When he does look up, it is Harry at whom he glances. He almost winks at him but not quite. He says, to the world in general.

"You can have room 14, which has a double bed, and a shower."

"Oh, but we need a bed each."

"Who?" replies Mr Pierce, as if suggesting there must be no doubling-up in his hotel, or at any rate, no doubling-up in which he is not involved.

"Harry and I." She sounds astonished and as offended as if she had been born and brought up in South Kensington, about the time the house was built.

"Harry has his own room, at the top." It is Mr Pierce's turn to sound astonished, and he implies: You are not suggesting, are you, that he, your son, at his age, should share a room with a guest? That is entirely my prerogative, mine alone, being old enough and wise enough. "Harry," he commands, and he might well have said 'Boy', "take the bags upstairs, please. Then report back to me. Can you do that?"

"Yes, Sir."

Mr Pierce looks at Harry, incidentally ignoring Sally: the thing is, you can choose to remain a mother's boy or you can be your own man. And had Sally chosen to interrupt the thought, he would have added: because she is going to need a man to look after her in New Sudan, not a boy.

Sally says nothing. Mr Pierce watches Harry lug the bags upstairs and then hands the keys to Sally: Number 14. So that, at last, he looks into her eyes, holds them and smiles at her.

"Will that be all, Madam?"

"Could I have some supper?"

"In the lounge?"

"In the lounge. Toasted cheese will do."

"Fifteen minutes."

On his way up, Harry glimpses Mavis in the lounge, eating a sandwich. She waves at him as if she has been expecting him, but he cannot wave back because he has his hands full, so he gives her as big a smile as he can manage. Outside the beautifully painted door of Room 14, he puts down his mother's bags and waits for her to bring the key. He looks up the stairwell into the floors above, still thinking of Mavis. Therefore, does not hear his mother's approach across the thickly carpeted floor. She startles him.

"Thank you Darling." Opening the door and walking straight to the bay window, which has beautiful chintz curtains hanging to the floor. They were Mavis's choice. "What a lovely room. Look at that view. I can see the Albert Memorial." And because Harry says nothing. "Are you alright Harry? Is anything worrying you?" He smiles at her because he knows that is what she wants and he can honestly reply.

"No, Mum, I've got to go." He wants to find Mr Pierce.

Quietly closing the door behind him, Harry makes for the stairs to the floors above and finds himself following Mr Pierce, who stops at the first landing to drop Harry's bag at his feet. Harry drops also, to pick it up.

"Who cleaned your shoes?" he asks, accusingly.

"I did. But my shoes are irrelevant at this point in time. What you have to think about is taking the things out of this bag you don't need for New Sudan. It's the tropics. It'll be hot. You can wear shorts."

Harry feels anger well up inside him again. The whole world is against him.

"It's my stuff. I'll be carrying it."

In response to which, Mr Pierce turns around, continues up the stairs, and throws out, over his shoulder.

"I'll show you your room then."

Harry picks up the bag and follows the large, warm but now indifferent man, with whom he badly wants to be connected. As they rise up through the house he feels smaller and smaller, a lonely exposed thing in a threatening world from which there is no escape.

On the last half landing, the back wall slopes inwards to become the ceiling. It has a skylight in it, which is slightly ajar. Somehow, a sparrow has got into the house and is frantically trying get to out, hopelessly batting its wings against the pane. As Mr Pierce approaches, it presses itself against the glass, paralysed by fear, the little beating heart ready to explode. Seeing it, Mr Pierce stops so suddenly that Harry, focused upon his shrivelled-up self, bumps hard into him, dropping the bag. And because he is a couple of steps lower, his head nestles into the small of Mr Pierce's back. Steadying himself also, he puts his arms around Mr Pierce's waist, and so comfortable does he feel, within the warmth of Mr Pierce's body, that he stays there, waiting for something to happen.

But Mr Pierce is dealing with the terrified bird. Leaning forward so that Harry presses more heavily against him, he takes the little bird into his large safe hands and whispers the magic and endearing love words of his own Yoruba language to it, so that the little bird is calmed. He gently butts open the window with his head and releases it into the evening sky, of which, of course, it becomes an immediate part. Harry is so quiet and still that he might well have fallen asleep. Mr Pierce stands for a while taking in the night air as if it is he who needs reviving. He then takes hold of Harry's hands, holds them a moment as if they are as precious as the sparrow and moves forward so that Harry stumbles awake and at large in the manageable world again. He picks up the bag and without a word they continue to Harry's room, on the top floor.

Harry has not seen it before even though it has been waiting for him. He cannot even remember having seen the door, which, for all he knows, has mysteriously appeared in the wall. It is as beautifully painted, on the outside, as is his mother's.

The room beyond is perfect but strange. Bare but as warm as a living, naked body. Old, worn and empty but as clean as if it has been scrubbed and aired with the summer sunshine. It smells of pinewood and sun-bleached cotton sheets. Opposite the door is a large Edwardian wardrobe with curved edges. It is painted in a pale matt colour, like an undercoat. It looks like a separate piece of furniture but it is, in fact, an integral part of the room so that an old iron bedstead fits snugly into a sort of alcove made by the wardrobe and the wall beside it. On the other side of the wardrobe a narrow sash window looks out around a projection of the building over roof tops and into the sky. Beside it is a small, flat, black, clean, cast-iron fireplace, which has clearly not been used for years, and above which hangs a square looking-glass suggesting you can put your brush and comb, and anything else you like, on the mantle-shelf. The only other objects in the room are a small lady's chair in a corner, which happens to match the chair behind the desk in the lobby, and a large faded rug covering the centre of the wooden floor. On the distempered wall facing the end of the bed there is a mark and a nail showing that a picture no longer hangs here. The bed has been made up but the bed-clothes lie flat as if they have lain there for some time, waiting for someone to occupy them.

Mr Pierce drops the bag on the floor with a thump.

"You can put the things you don't want in the wardrobe. Then get down to the kitchen and make some beans on toast for yourself and your mother. If you're still hungry, you can boil an egg."

Harry replies.

"Yes sir." The door closes and seems to open again immediately as Mavis pokes her glittering head around it.

"You can use my bathroom, so you don't have to go downstairs." He takes the surprisingly cold key from her and places it on the mantelpiece. When he turns back, she has gone. The excess baggage goes into the wardrobe which is otherwise empty and smells of mothballs. Harry leaves the room noticing just a whiff of Mavis's perfume in the passage. He imagines her sweeping through it in her wine-red dressing gown.

[][][]

The idea of the hotel, being what it was, was to serve one main meal a day, at mid-day. A substantial and nutritious meal, which satisfied most of the inmates, enabling some to sleep through a good part of the afternoon and others to go on long walks, come sun or the lack of it, through the miles of London all around. Two cooks worked out a timetable between themselves: there was always breakfast and there was always lunch: no choice within the day – you had to eat what was put before you or starve – but a great variation between days. It might be shepherd's pie for lunch one day and rice with hot pepper stew the next. Vegetarians were advised to try 'The Harrington'. Mr Pierce had balanced things nicely by employing a Christian and a Muslim. The latter took his annual holidays during Ramadan and the former around Christmas although he was less fussy. Both tended towards the nominal and neither was excessively superstitious or neurotic. The arrangement worked. In an emergency a charming, mute Tamil of significant girth came over from 'The Harrington' for an hour or two. In the evenings, resident staff and even, on occasions, inmates who could be trusted – Mavis the Queen amongst them, in her day – did things with toast and cheese, and Tabasco and Worcestershire sauces. Or else it was sandwiches to ensure you did not starve to death.

But it is late and Harry finds the basement kitchen dark and empty. He works on a corner of the vast table. It has a Formica top with an abstract design, which Mavis had recognised as inspired by the Festival of Britain but which Harry sees as something from the Dark Ages. The words 'Use a Chopping Board' have been stencilled on the middle surface of the table. Harry has not noticed this before but he obeys the rule, cutting the cheese on the cheese-board and slicing the bread on the bread-board. He does the whole job carefully and lays the product on a tray with napkins and a bottle of sauce. The whole thing sits on the table, the food getting cold, as he washes up, wipes down and puts away. It is a remarkably efficient piece of food preparation, which until this evening he has never, ever, done before. He picks up the tray and walks to the door where he meets Mr Pierce who says.

"It's alright, I'll take it. You can go to bed. Please switch off the lights." It is an order, not a suggestion and only when he is about to switch off the lights does Harry realise he is hungry. He grabs a couple of apples from the fridge and fruitlessly searches, boy-like again, for some biscuits, before returning to his room. He does not see his mother or Mr Pierce and ascending through the house to the top floor, he feels he is leaving them far, far behind. The top of the house belongs to him. His mother will never know it.

His bedroom is lit by a single light bulb hanging from the middle of the ceiling. It ruthlessly exposes everything within its orbit but the room is, nonetheless, welcoming. Harry feels at home in it immediately and has no desire to explore what does not need exploring. His very presence in the room changes it. His bag in the centre of the floor is a significant addition. Mavis is somewhere nearby and the thought of her reminds Harry of the bathroom and of the need to have a bath. He takes off his clothes, places them neatly on the chair and walks, naked, to the bathroom. He is not surprised to find it scrupulously clean. Impersonal in its cleanliness it is, with no suggestion of Mavis except for its lack of dirt. The little frosted window, high up, is black and looks as if it would be cold to the touch. The lighting is not quite as ruthless as in the bedroom but it is ruthless enough and seeing himself in the stained mirror, screwed onto the wall with chrome-capped screws, above the sink, he sees only his acne and the dark smudge above his upper lip he wishes was stronger. He has acne on his shoulders as well, so he shakes his head and says out loud.

"This is not like Mavis's room. It feels dead." He thinks of his sister, Sonia, and the thought makes him feel sad. It is the sort of bathroom she will have when she grows up and I cannot change the fact. He thinks: I will send her a postcard from New Sudan. One for herself not half of one to Sonia-and-Alice.

On the cork-topped dirty clothes box beside the bath there is a clean white towel and a piece of hard green soap. Hot water splutters out of the tap, running more smoothly when he adds the cold. The room soon fills with steam. This obscures the mirror. Mavis would have had bath salts, the glass bottle standing on the cork. Harry wishes he had a radio and the sense of being himself, alone, in the room is suddenly so intense, that he rushes his ablutions, pulls out the plug and dries himself hard and fast with the rough clean towel. He scrubs hard at his acne. Only half dry, the towel around his waist, he bursts out, leaving the door open, the light on and the water still gurgling down the plughole as he would have done at home. In the corridor, however, he faces Mavis's door, and without thinking much about it, returns to the bathroom to clean it. He finds the cleaning materials, and does not do a bad job. He dries it all down with his towel, which he then returns to his body. It is the first time he has cleaned a bathroom in his life without having been nagged to do so. It is also a job done with love and therefore a gift remembered through time.

He cleans his teeth and returns to his bedroom, where he reverts to type, flinging the wet towel on the floor, partly covering his bag, before getting into bed. The sheets, which look as if they ought to be cold, are warm to his touch as if his own body has ignited them. Halfway down his feet touch a piece of paper, which he fetches up. It is a letter from Mavis, addressed *To Harry for You*. It reads as follows:

My Dear Harry, I am writing this just in case I don't see you again. I hope you find it and it is really to wish you bon voyage and a good time in New Sudan. It will be an exciting adventure for you. I think of you often, because knowing you and having our little chats has meant a great deal to me. Mr Pierce is such a nice man and he has been very good to me and I count him as one of my closest friends but there is something between us which makes it difficult to make a complete connection. Perhaps it is because he was not born here and is therefore not quite English. Perhaps it is because I am pre-war and he is post. There is something we cannot quite understand *about each other. But My Dear Harry as I have remembered my life as old people are apt to do I have often thought of you. I hope you don't mind me saying this. I never had a husband, or children or grandchildren and therefore in my old woman's fantasies you take the place of all those dreams and I do hope you will not be offended when I say this. But you are a big boy, Harry, and you are a <u>man</u>, which I recognised straight away. Go in search of your father and find your dreams but do not be surprised by what you find. Life is as full of the unexpected as it is full of the mundane. Accept what you get with gratitude because you cannot have everything you want or even desire. And, Harry, excuse an old woman's advice and nosiness but I can't help being interested in you, and I thank God for the gift of you.*

God bless you, from your friend,
Mavis. XXXXXX

He turns the paper over as if he might find something else on the back but there is nothing. He reads the letter again and frowns. Then he smiles, and frowns again because he has left the light on. He gets out of bed still clutching the letter and once out decides he wants to talk to Mavis. He wants to thank her for the letter and reassure her that he has read it and understands it. He pulls on his trousers and walks to her door, puts his ear to it and knocks very quietly. There is no reply so he tiptoes back, tripping in just the place where he once might have spilt her breakfast things only he hadn't. He crashes onto the floor, where he kneels silently for a while absolutely sure he must have woken up the whole house. Nothing but a deadly silence, the old bricks and the massive density of buildings insulating them all from the London racket all around. He crawls back to his room and to his bag through which he frantically searches for a pen and some paper. He finds an old ballpoint pen but no paper. In the end, he tears off the bottom of Mavis's letter, including some of her kisses. Upon it he writes, or rather scribbles: *Love from Harry, See you in September XXX.* He draws a heart with an arrow through it. He slips the message under her door and then carefully goes back to his room. He puts her letter into the wardrobe, switches off the light and then rushes into the bed kicking his feet to the bottom. The night glow of London pours in through the window but he is used to it and, holding himself, as he usually does, he falls asleep.

He hears her voice, Mavis, sitting on the little chair. She looks very grand in her dressing gown, which is more luxurious than usual, the great sweeps of it more like the ball-gown of a Dresden china figure, which Gran said Sally's father had actually rescued from the devastated city after the war. His loot, she called it. She allowed them to play with it. Her hair captured all the light in the room, transforming it into the silver which the moon would have poured in, had the bright London night allowed it. Do you like my tiara, Harry? After all these years of saving the coupons from the packets of tea I finally had enough to get it. I've been saving them since the war, most of my life but it's been worth it. Have you seen it before? Yes, he had, on the head of the Queen in the picture on the lid of Gran's biscuit tin. Then he knew it was not Mavis here, but Mavis somewhere else and working it out in his head he must have fallen asleep because when he woke up, dying for something to drink, she was gone. I'll see her in the morning and ask her what she was talking about, he thought but the next time he woke up it was bright daylight and someone was knocking on the door. It was Mr Pierce, who by the time Harry had woken up properly was standing beside the bed in an old pair of tracksuit bottoms and a T-shirt, stained and showing off his round tummy. He looked very large in the room and he smelt warm. "Ramos" – one of the cooks – "cannot make it and they" – 'The Harrington' – "won't let Sam" – the Tamil – "go until later this morning, so you'll have to help me and Doreen" – the early morning cleaner and occasional chamber-maid, although there was not much that was maidenly about her – "do the breakfasts. I've already taken Mavis her tea," he lied. So Harry spent all day running around for Mr Pierce, for which he was paid ten pounds, in US dollars, to take to New Sudan. In the evening, Sally took them all out to dinner at quite an expensive restaurant on the Gloucester Road because, she told Harry, Mr Pierce refuses to take anything for the room, he said I'm his guest and you're a worker. She treated

Harry as if he was someone she had met in the hotel who needed feeding and she allowed Mr Pierce to boss her around as if she liked it. It was opposite to the way she treated Dad, who, in similar circumstances, she tended to ignore or at best to appear as if she was acting the part of his wife. But Harry liked the way she responded to Mr Pierce and he liked the way the waiters assumed they were a family. They were late back and set off very early and before Harry thought of Mavis again they were in the plane to Hong Kong. He was glad he had slipped the note under her door, although, of course, it was never read.

[][][]

Hong Kong was night, a hotel room, television, a huge meal in a large restaurant full of noisy people and too much artificial light, and an early start to the airport through the dark which nonetheless had pieces of light in it. His mother knew exactly what to do, which impressed him, but she did not treat him as a child but as she would have a travelling companion whose fare she was paying. Nonetheless, he noticed that she was becoming nervous and less confident as they approached Port Markham. His own excitement was, therefore, tempered by his concern for her, and by his relief that she had stopped annoying him. Feeling that she was in some way dependent upon him, and knowing, also, that he could escape from her if he wanted, made him feel big. He felt bigger than the whole world, as if he might burst out of the aeroplane at any minute, stepping down into the incredibly blue sea below, scattered with a rash of islands around which he would wade, smiling down at the people looking up incredulously at him. He saw himself being met at the airport like a pop star and answering the reporters' questions, yes I've come to find my father and no doubt his father would see him on the television and come out to find him. He laughed out loud.

"Are you happy?" His mother was smiling at him but she did not look at all happy herself.

"Yes," and for the first time in the whole journey he felt really excited, the butterflies in his tummy almost painful. "Are you?"

"Oh yes." It sounded sarcastic. "I'm just wondering what we're going to find."

So he felt a sudden protective love for his mother who was sure to be like Mavis one day.

"Does it matter what we find? They don't really eat people."

PART THREE

19   To the Beach

By the time they reached their hotel room, Harry was used to the smallness, the quietness and the dustiness of Port Markham. Already he felt an affinity with the people he had seen from the window of the bashed-up old taxi: women selling fruit and vegetable things he did not recognise, sometimes pathetically small amounts; youths, hanging around in small groups watching the ground but glancing up at him as he passed by, you ought to be one of us. For these boys, in particular, he felt a sort of adolescent compassion: part of him was embarrassed, part wanted to be with them. Thus he resented his mother and turning to her, he studied the small lines on her face, the tiny veins on her nose, which was more defined, more bony than he remembered. She returned his stare, blank-faced. He was not sure if she would laugh or cry, so he took one of her clenched hands in his and opened it.

"Are you alright, Mum?"

"Yes, thanks, look at how some people have to live."

But the heap of shanties did not shock him because, already, they were an acceptable fact of life. Clothes hung on the dry, shrubby trees, a naked child squatted to shit beside the road, laughing at the world around it. These people, he thought, are Port Markham. In London, people were incidental to the buildings. Here it was the opposite: people made the place. I'd rather say I'm from Port Markham, than admit I'm from London.

But what did shock Harry was the hotel. It was Hong Kong again, only on a smaller scale, the bedroom something especially detached from the manifest life outside. The room had its own, separate, air-conditioned climate, chilly after the sweaty heat of the taxi. The view, across the bay, was the view of any beautiful tropical bay from any expensive hotel bedroom window, the swaying coconut palms and the lush vegetation thankfully mitigating the squalid human settlement, which would otherwise have offended the critical, aesthetic, Western eye.

They sit on their beds, facing each other, fagged out and depressed.

"But we can't afford to stay long in any event and I think we should save our money for the end of the trip when we might need it." Says his mother, so Harry feels a little less he has cheated the young men hanging around outside.

Sally watches her son go to the window, and then swings her legs up onto the bed, lies down and shuts her eyes. Her breathing becomes regular and the little frown on her forehead disappears.

Harry watches the people on the beach. They walk slowly and apparently aimlessly. He wants to leave the room in which his mother sleeps. He imagines himself in the view, out there, on the beach. He wants to be with the other aimless wanderers. He looks back at his mother, who is, he notices, as young as himself and, he will remember, later, as beautiful. Then, startling him, so that he laughs, she cries out in her sleep.

"We can't afford it." She looks at him for a moment, and subsides back into sleep. He thinks: then we should contact my father as soon as we can. Perhaps he is one of those people down there on the beach.

[][][]

Dinner, downstairs, each table isolated in the fluid night, through which, bare-chested, bare-footed, waiters pad, carrying the precious light as flakes of gold on oiled skin. They materialise from the darkness as something reassuringly solid. Each wears a necklace of sharp, curved, sharks' teeth, but it is their own which flash, as a trained smile: Sir? Madam? We are, apparently, the pride of New Sudanese manhood, here at your service. We are here to serve you, with detached willingness, but do not engage us with your flippant badinage, do not seduce us with your friendship. We are the conquered race in here. Out there, is another matter.

Harry felt ashamed as he gave his order. But the waiter ignored him, refusing to meet his eye. His mother did not even attempt to make a connection, adopting an icy detachment, staring at the menu and clipping her words.

Harry looked at the man's navel, which was large, and screwed tight like a rubber band. He sensed his own, wishing they were alone and not with his mother. Suddenly she answered her own question

"Because there's nothing to worry about." He thought: Am I worried? But she rushed forward, while at the same time appearing to concentrate on the menu: "We can afford it if we have to, it goes on the credit card, and it's only Granny's money, sitting there in the bank." Just for this purpose, she might have added, but didn't.

The waiter returned with an astonishing arrangement of fruit and hibiscus flowers. It embarrassed Harry. "Did I order this?" Apparently I did but I don't want him to think it's the sort of thing I would normally eat. He stared at it and wanted to get out but he was stuck with his mother who was looking at a concoction of sea shells with frozen amazement. He was about to laugh when she spoke.

"But it's not the money. It's the place that's wrong. Why put them in that ridiculous get-up? It humiliates everyone concerned. If it doesn't, it ought to." She started to eat as if it was just something that had to be got through. Watching her, Harry felt better and almost laughed as the waiter disappeared back into the dark, having played his part in the farce. He thought his mother looked beautiful with her wavy blonde hair and not trying to be young in the floral, print frock, which nonetheless made her look crisp and fresh. He was proud of her and it was how he remembered her, years later. My mother was brave, he told his own children one day. But after dinner, as they walked through the lobby he thought of his father, and with an idea of Mr Pierce in his head, he told her.

"I'm going for a walk."

He wanted to know what it would be like not to be Harry and to be with those other un-named ones who wandered about the beach. To his surprise, his mother did not object, saying only.

"Here, give me your wallet and wristwatch. There's no point inviting trouble." She smiled at him, in order, he assumed, to show she was not worried.

He gave her a brief and clumsy hug

"I'll just look at the beach, I won't be long, Mum, twenty minutes."

Outside, he pushed through the thick, warm air, amazed at the terrific din made by the night-time insects: we own the whole world and you are but an incidental thing in it. Even the endless crashing waves we subdue, in the night. The people on the beach walked in the wide spaces of their own thoughts. The light was the phosphorescence of the sea reflected on their warm, naked skin; flickering, broken fragments of light, ever shifting; insubstantial hints of light only, the primary source of illumination a mystery. And finding his own space, Harry felt the idea of himself so large, so unbearably forceful, that surely it must break upon all the other ideas, which the men on the beach had of themselves.

Thus he removed his shirt and tied it around his waist in order to be able to feel their ideas warm upon his own skin. And he felt that thus his awareness of himself must – must surely - mingle with that of the others. He wanted it so badly that he let his eyes meet others mere specks of light in the dark, and he wanted to say I love you because that is what he felt. He wanted to say I am here with you, and had they taken him and gently killed him for his wallet and his wristwatch, he would not have minded greatly because death at that moment was no less wonderful than life. So that when the other young men were beside him in the dark, touching his skin and testing its reality, and when he smelt the clean saltiness of their bodies and heard the soft caress of their voices, his heart leapt with joy and they understood him and loved him to death and would indeed have taken him to ensure he was theirs. They would have died for him and understanding this possibility of brotherhood as something good and better than all the riches in the world, Harry wanted it and wanting it, started his journey towards his father.

Man to man, you could say, so that he laughed out loud and saw the moon up there, the source of the primary light. Then, the boys tapped his warm skin with their warm hands and ran off, laughing, so that he gave chase but lost them, their laughter absorbed by the insect roar of the night.

Harry looked up at the stars – more, millions more, a storm of stars, than any London night he had seen. He had made the connection with the idea of his father who might have been one of those naughty boys who would have taken his wristwatch without any malice whatsoever. When he got back to the hotel, and he realised his shirt had gone, he laughed.

20 Mac (with respect to John Dos Pasos)

So this is what I am,
Or rather, what I have become,
Each step deliberately and thoughtfully taken
To where I am
Now, at this point in time.
This
Is
Me
And, I am astonished,
It should be so.
But it is.
It
Is
The fact,
I could bite off the reality of it,
The hard reality
Of the space,
Which is my room,
In which I have lived.
Fantastic,
Is it not?
Nothing between what was,
Then,
And what is,
Now.
No movement,
Only a series of real points in time:
The one where I am,
Obliterating all the others.

[][][]

Mac is an old man; no getting away from the fact. He will wake up in the room in which he has slept for thirty years, and think, even worry, about the future. But I have no future. I am an old man who will, one morning, be cold and unthinking in this bed, in this room. I, the man, Mac, will have come to an end. The hard fact will be ... Will be nothing. But, he will as often think, the hard fact now is that I am the man they call Mac, alive. I have today, which is as much my last day as was my new day a thousand days ago. Thus, with satisfaction, he recognizes the simplicity of My Life and the lack of encumbrance. He is up and out with as much agility as he had when he first understood his life belonged to him. But since when he has stripped away the non-essentials, layer by layer, until he is only the essential Mac, who has grown more distant from the others, who has not much to say for himself, and who has nothing and lives on less. A man, nonetheless, who will listen to your troubles and who will help you if he can. But, was he not the man we used to see around? Indeed, and come to think of it, I've not seen him for a day or two.

The ramshackle company for which Mac had controlled the finances, administered the cash and generally acted as the one solid thing about it, had long since off-loaded its assets in New Sudan. Including the plantation, down the coast, run by Harry Williams. These days Mac has little to do and just enough money with which to do it. He wants nothing more from life than what he needs to survive and he is more likely to give away money than to take it. So trustworthy is he understood to be, that he is often asked to take care of the smaller local businesses when their owners are concerned with some other crisis elsewhere. Trade stores, small plantations and the like.

But when Sally Pryce-Williams brought her son to New Sudan in search of the boy's father, Mac was at a particularly loose end.

Some evenings, however, when home was a dead end, he'd stay on the club veranda. The rattan armchairs were falling to bits and things were disappearing one by one but the familiar place reassured his sense of some sort of existence beyond himself. Soon, he would think, the birds will reclaim it for their own. You looked down towards the garden, heavily shaded with trees. What was once called a lawn is for part of the year so wet it more resembles a swamp from which frogs croak through the night and swarms of mosquitoes make sitting out impossible after dark. In the good old days the drains were maintained and DDT was sprayed. In the good old days there was no need for the wire fence between the garden and the golf course beyond. In the good old days livestock and night visitors did not wander into the club compound. In the good old days before independence there was no golf course. There was the airstrip. Sundays, the expats would sit on the veranda to meet the mail plane. Their mail was delivered in its own bag, distributed by the post-mistress herself, who had been, for a while, the Governor's niece, or something like that. He remembered a pretty, blonde girl, with a posh accent, who'd danced with him at a club party once.

What had not changed was the big view, which, thought Mac, will see me out. Between low hills, the flat plain ran towards the sea as if, any minute, the high tide would rush in and submerge it. When he was younger, Mac imagined that the very act of his watching was enough to bring the water up to the veranda steps, to his feet. But as he grew older, he found he did not assume such power, preferring to look at the incidental hills, with the extending town amongst trees on the one side, and the neat chequer-board of farms on the other. But better than looking, he liked best to feel the land beneath his feet and to meet the sea on its own terms, at the crumbling coral shoreline. This he had done countless times, the first, as a young man, who had strolled, aimlessly, alongside the airstrip, the sea and the sky above growing bigger until nothing but the sea and sky filled his mind to bursting. Then he was happy to be an insignificant but excited, living thing, that was not afraid. And as apparently insignificant, also, an incidental fragment of something almost inconsiderable, the cluster of volcanoes on the horizon, a whisper of cloud, or something like it, hanging about them. Insignificant-seeming, in the distance, but unavoidable across a crystal-calm sea, always impressing themselves, despite heavy cloud or delusional heat-haze. In fact, the volcanoes lay on the other side of the great bay; they made a peninsular of their own, silently threatening that part of the island which included Port Markham.

But what mattered the most to Mac was the greater sky over all of this, which would not only see him out but which would see out, also, the whole of Port Markham and New Sudan. I am happy to live beneath it, on the edge of this great bay which creates the towering cumulus clouds of midday, or the black wall of rain sweeping in from the sea so suddenly that if you happen to be in a small boat on the water, better abandon it and let the storm carry you home to the shore.

And so, today, when I watch the sea and the sky as one blank canvas of yellow light hard on my eyes, when I feel the dead weight of the afternoon, when the only hope of relief is the night to come, I am happy. I am happy, because I know that this dead, heavy weather is the prelude to better times when a great wall of glorious water will flood the lowland, driving me from this old colonial veranda where I sit, and which would like to trap me in the clubhouse, hammering on the roof, were I not able to laugh in its face, break open the door, take it at its word, and dare it on the hills, allowing it to thrash my body with all its might. The young man loved the wild rain on the hills; he would laugh into the raging sky. I can wade across the sea and take those volcanoes in my hands and drown them if I want to.

There was a young woman standing in front of him, holding on to the handrail, one foot on the steps as if asking permission to come up to him.

"Mac!" She said, with joy in her voice, apparently, and inexplicably relieved to see him.

[][][]

Mac knows he is not dreaming, but he does not recognise the woman who is, nonetheless, attractive in a wilted sort of way. She looks as if she is not used to the heat. A rumble of distant thunder, and he thinks: there'll be rain soon. Did she call my name? She's acting as if I know her. But I don't.

The woman, wearing a wide, floral-patterned skirt and flat, blue sandals, which match her smart T-shirt, is leaning back on the veranda rails by now, looking at him. She stands a little to one side, so that he still has the view, clear ahead of him, through the trees. She pushes back her damp, curly, blonde hair, and smiles.

"What a wonderful surprise," she says as if she is rehearsing a part. "I can't tell you how glad I am to see you." She screws up her eyes. "I can't believe it's really you."

Who else would it be? Sitting here at this time of day? The Emperor of China? Mac looks straight ahead but the sea and the sky are empty, giving no indication from where the little bit of thunder had come. He listens for more, then he looks at her and decides she is pretty. He sees the desperation of her smile, which makes him think he would like to help her. The idea passes through his mind – it is not a defined thought – that he would like to be the only white man to whom she can turn. He wants her to be alone and in need, in desperate need, of assistance in this place where she has washed up, and where only he, Mac, knows the ropes. If I know nothing else, for God's sake.

He begins to get up but she stops him, bending towards him and touching his shoulder affectionately.

"Don't get up. Do you mind if I sit down?"

"Of course not."

She sits in a chair pressed close to his.

"Do I know you?" says Mac. "You act as if I did."

She says nothing.

They watch the view ahead, together, until he is sure he wants to make a connection.

"They call me Mac."

"I know." She replies to the view. "But don't you know me?" She might have been hurt but it does not show. She touches the top of his hand, his liver-spotted hand, as if to say: There, surely you remember this woman, who is sitting beside you, who is touching you?

Mac fixes onto the view: don't think I'm suffering from dementia or anything like that. I've been here for forty years and

I've seen dozens of pretty young women like you. That postmistress, way back, for instance, whose hair, once as blonde and curly as yours, is likely to be as grey as mine by now. You were probably a little girl last time I saw you. Why would I remember you? Was your father a planter? Not many of them had children. They tended to be solitary people but one or two of the odder ones were married. You must be here for a reason, and it won't be for a holiday. But he said nothing. If I look at the view long enough, perhaps she'll go away, then I'll wish I'd said something more. I'll feel a pain in my heart when she's gone. She has reminded me that I miss certain people, who have been in my life.

"I'm Sally Pryce-Williams."

"Who?"

"Sally Pryce-Williams! Surely you ..."

The name meant nothing. How many names can you keep in your head? There was a time when everyone had a double-barrelled name or a title of some sort. After the war it was Major This and Group Captain That. They've all gone now, to live in suburban bungalows in Queensland. And I'm just Mac, which ought to be name enough for anyone.

"All the same," he said, "how long ago was it?"

She thought for a moment.

"Sixteen years. Sixteen years," she repeated, "I can't believe it. Half my life! Almost, anyway, I'll be forty any minute. An old woman."

Which made him laugh.

"Forty's nothing from this end. You look like a girl to me."

She waited for him to say more but as he didn't, she got up as if to go.

"Thank you, anyway."

She looked, suddenly, so defeated it broke his heart.

"Don't go. I want you to stay. What is it? Why are you here?"

She settled back, as if pulling herself together, trying not to cry.

"I came to find a room, two rooms at the club. The hotel's impossibly expensive."

"You want to stay here?" He was astonished.

"Yes, it used to be quite good."

He stared at her.

"Didn't it?"

"It wasn't bad but it was never that good and now it's a health hazard. I'm not sure the plumbing works anymore and you'll have to share your bed with cockroaches and anything else that decides to join you. You won't find sheets. Forget it, Mrs ... Sally." Because had she not called herself that?

She looked taken aback.

"I see. Well, we'll just have to manage the hotel, I suppose."

"You're here with your husband?" He was disappointed. But what did I expect, a woman like you wouldn't travel on her own.

"No, my son."

"I see." That's better. "So what ...?" The question hangs in the air and they sit in silence, again, apparently absorbed in the view. A definite rumble of thunder but he feels immobilised, unable to decide if he should make some sort of approach to this woman, who is called Sally. She hadn't denied it. But what would I do about the son, who might be an infant or some great sulking adolescent with whom I would not be able to deal? I'd lose my temper. Like I used to do with the man Harry, before. And why, for God's sake, has the idea of Harry suddenly come into my head? Why has she made me think of him, now, of all times, when I had put all that behind me? The man, Harry, who had been such a known, albeit explosive, quantity in my life. A problem child, as it were, whom I had willingly taken on, once upon a time.

Lovingly, as it happened, and thinking of Harry, Mac forgets the woman altogether.

She turns, leaning her whole body towards him. He feels the warmth of her and he wants to smell her but he daren't. She almost touches him again but changes her mind

"Mac, do you really not remember me?" He shakes his head. "I can't believe it. You were so important in our life, in my life, once, I've never forgotten you."

The idea pleases him. He takes a deep breath. The slight scent of soap and clean sweat makes him dizzy.

"I was so embarrassed when I saw you sitting here, because I had always thought we'd fundamentally disturbed your life, that time. I blush when I think of it. I was such a silly, empty-headed noodle." She is cross with herself.

What is she talking about? He wanted to interrupt her but she raced on, desperate, it seemed, to keep going now she had started.

"You helped me so much, you helped us both. I'll never forget you, 'til I die. You were wonderful, much more wonderful," she smiled at him, insisting on his eyes, "obviously, than you know ... It was such a big thing in my life." She sits back with a gasp: "You must have thought me absolutely worthless."

What can I say? I find you attractive now. I want you to stay with me forever. I'm glad you are on your own, with your son who cannot be old enough to be of much help. I want to help you, but then, in that time before, whenever it was, you were nothing to me. You were such a small factor in my life that I have forgotten you. And I am astonished, although I ought not to be, that I, Mac, had such an impact on your life, on anybody's life, once. One ought to be more careful. We charge around in our lives bumping into other people and making a mess, or even, just as thoughtlessly, perhaps, doing some good. He stared back at the view but he was not sure if it was thunder he heard or the resonance of an unsettling idea. I'd like to say I'm sorry I forgot you. But he kept silent.

For a moment, she looks at the view with him, decides to get up again and then changes her mind. She turns to him:

"Are you alright?"

Mac does not answer.

"Anyway, how is Harry Williams?"

"What?" He is stunned. Had she been reading his thoughts? A small jolt ran through his body as if he had been hit, hard, on some vital part of his head, irrevocably damaged. He wanted to say more but he was stuck.

She ran on regardless, unaware of the devastating blow she had struck.

"Do you think I could find him? Is he still on the plantation? It's a long time ago. I'd really like to see him." She prattled on. And on: "When I saw you just now, I thought it was divine providence, because I knew you'd know where he was."

I know that, but he did not look at her although he saw her clearly in his mind's eye: the girl who had become a woman before his very eyes. He remembered her alright and he wanted, suddenly, to laugh with relief. The memory of her and of that time flooded back so that the pain subsided. He thought of her triumph and he laughed out loud.

"Yes I remember you, Sally." And I'm glad to say I have remembered you, I'm glad to have you here beside me because one thing is certain: that man who is your husband, whatever his name is, is nothing – I can wipe him off the map. Mac forgot he was old.

Sally said.

"Sixteen years is a long time."

It's nothing to me and my God I remember it all now but I don't want to remember the man Harry because the memory of him, in whom I took a fatherly interest, is painful. He had a self-destruct button, that boy – always a boy to me – a button with which he could not resist playing. He was one of those boys, those men, who could not lie down in the sun and read a book, he had always to be on the move, doing something, messing around with something.

"He would bump into the furniture."

"The furniture?"

"He was always bumping into it. People too," and unaccountably, apparently, Mac thought of Wanei. "Harry, Harry Williams, and I remember, now. You were friends. All of you. You made a little trio for a while, and no one else was allowed inside. It was a funny little episode if I remember but what was the name of the other one? I can't even remember what he looks like."

"You must have hated us."

"I did not. If I had, I would have remembered you."

"Despised us then."

"I might have done had I thought I was better than you. I might have despised the pair of you, you and ... and ... and him, but I didn't despise you. In the end, I rather admired you. I was indifferent to you, if I was anything, and I'm not proud of being that. We have no right to be indifferent to anyone who comes near us." He thought of what he had seen as a young man in war-shattered Germany. "Or rather, I was interested in you, for about a week: the time you asked me to fetch your ... Fetch him back from Harry's place. I was angry, but not with you, I was angry with Harry and that boy of his."

"Wanei."

"Yes. You seem to have remembered the most insignificant details."

She did not answer.

"But please don't think you disturbed my life, although I appreciate that the whole thing was, is, important to you. For me, it was one of a whole lot of things to do with Harry Williams, which did ... which did affect my life, but which did not disturb it. I am sure people with families go through a lot more. They get attached, for a start."

"Sometimes," she said vacantly. Then: "I suppose it's a sort of vanity to think that I, that we, could have had any, any ... any meaning."

"Well you see I'd already been here over twenty years when you arrived and I'd known Harry for over ten of those years. I'd watched him grow from being a raw boy to being, to being what he was when you met him." She was no longer strange to him.

"A big boy."

"Yes." Mac laughed. "He was a big boy, the nearest thing I ever had to a son."

"So he's gone?"

"Oh, yes, he's gone alright." But before she could ask any more questions he pressed on: "And you weren't here long. Were you?"

"Barely a year."

"Exactly, and we only met in the club a few times. I didn't like either of you, at first. You represented, in my head, a

London company coming over here and treading all over our cherished ideas. Big capitalism and all that. The sort of expatriates who generally come up here are running away from the big world, they like things to stay small and manageable and safe, so we didn't like you. You were not safe. And then just as I'd got to know you – and I still disliked your ..."

"David," she supplied.

"You disappeared and I never heard of you again. I'm sorry. Until you appeared today, you had not taken up much of my life. I was bound to forget you, or push you to the back of my mind."

"Of course. And we did rather fancy ourselves."

But it was not them in particular Mac had not fancied. He did not fancy humankind in general, including himself. He only fancied people once he had learnt about their redeeming features. If they had any. Neither was he the type to encourage intimacy. Certainly not the type to encourage a heart to heart. She thinks I know everything, he thought, I won't disillusion her. If she wants to spill out everything, I'll let her and maybe I can do something for her. If she tells me nothing, I'll let it go and leave it at that. I'll forget her all over again.

Just when he thought she would get up and leave him she said, with an effort.

"But it all went wrong when we decided we could help Harry Williams."

"There's nothing worse than deciding you ought to interfere in other people's lives. Particularly when you don't know them."

"I know, it's very arrogant and it got us into a mess. A big mess."

"Not so big." He smiled at her, wanting to hold her eyes but afraid to. "We sorted that out. Didn't we? And I never blamed anyone more than I blamed Harry himself." He looked at her: "You must forget it, it was a small thing, in the end." He wanted to tell her more but there was no point so he added, rather lamely: "Really a very small thing, believe me." And he looked back out to sea.

"Yes, it was a small thing; in the whole universe. But there was more to it than you know. That's why I'm here."

She was beginning to spill it out, but he would not push her. He said nothing. Let her think I didn't hear, if she wants.

"I had a baby."

You couldn't ignore that.

"Your son? The one you mentioned?"

"Yes."

"Is having a child the sign of a repaired marriage then?" And he thought: I've said too much but you'd think producing a child, after that stupid, pompous ass of a young husband of hers had run away, would be more likely to avoid the issue than face it. Ought not the parents to get to know each other first before embarking upon children?

"I don't think that's got anything to do with it." She was not defensive, she was presenting her case, and beginning to do it quite well: "A woman will marry a man because she thinks, or instinctively knows, he is the right father for her children. I didn't love David when I married him but I knew he would be a financial success and at the very worst he'd play at being the dutiful husband and the good father. He's lived up to my expectations." She laughed: "And that's the first time I've admitted it. You haven't changed, Mac."

His turn to laugh because he was impressed with her and liked her even more: "I'm sure you're right. What would an old bachelor like me know about such things?"

"As much as anybody and I'm sure you'd have made a good father too." Before he could deny the suggestion she added, apparently with a sense of relief: "Anyway, he's not David's son. That's why we're here."

"What?" And he thought: well, that is a turn up for the book.

"Harry, my son, wants to find his father."

He turned towards her so that his larger view became the overgrown garden towards the road: "Harry? I didn't think he had it in him. It confuses the issue a bit." He was astonished and not a little pleased. It would be like having a grandson.

"No," she laughed into his eyes, "Wanei. Wanei's his father."

[][][]

Momentarily, Mac was both disappointed and alarmed, his heart jumped.

"Oh my God. But listen. ..." He wanted to hold her. He calmed down.

"Yes?" She was still laughing. Her happiness made her blind to his consternation.

So he said, very calmly.

"Can you tell me what happened? But don't if you don't want to."

"I want to tell you." She told him of how she had been confused by David's responses to her that weekend, how she had played games, without knowing the rules, pretending she was in love with Harry Williams when she didn't even know what love was, and how she had let Wanei make love to her, almost as an act of self-destruction but at the precious moment it had been more than that. She told him everything and the more she told him the more she wanted to tell him, so that he understood her and he began to understand how she felt about Wanei and he began to understand how significant that weekend had been for her.

"Until that time," she said, "David was the only man I had known in that way, but that weekend I thought I was in love with the three of them because they were men, or rather because they were male and I was female. And I just had this feeling that I wanted all of them to make me a woman. It was a sort of yearning for something I didn't know. There was a man, a lodger, we had when I was a girl. He gave me the same feeling, just looking at his socks, which frightened me, and my mother sent him away. I thought I wanted David but he wasn't interested so when Wanei offered it, in the kitchen, I took it and I've never felt more happy than when I knew I was going to have a baby."

She paused, then.

"I think that's what I felt." And she thought: Is that what I said to Mary Willis? "Am I bad?" Let him be the judge, I don't care but he said

"Do you think you are?"

"No! It was good and I have, we have, a wonderful son. Something wonderful came out of it. I want you to meet him."

Mac smiled at her.

"I want to meet him. But I have to tell you something first."

"What?"

"I shouldn't say it." But he wanted to tell her. To tell her how he had felt that time.

"Say it. Please."

"I hated your husband that time. I wanted to humiliate him and make him suffer. I had him in my power and I know now that I could have got Wanei to kill him." He saw the arrogant young man in his mind's eye, sitting on Harry's veranda, the sweat running down his chest and catching in the folds of his stomach. "I still hate him." He looked at Sally and he wanted her to agree with him, to belittle the man, his memory, the whole essence of his existence.

She touched him again, took hold of his hand and held it so that he shivered with emotions he thought he had left behind years, decades, ago

"Don't, don't hate him Mac. He has been such a good father to Harry. He couldn't have done more for him. And not his own son: he hasn't had his own son, we've had two daughters."

Mac felt a little sick as she said this and thought well, it was a nice idea while it lasted. So this man, who is called David, does have a redeeming feature. I suppose he's grown up into a half-decent man, and from what she's said, she must love him. I should be glad for her but – and he almost said it aloud – I resent him all the more. I should have let Wanei kill him, it would have saved us all a lot of bother. He shook himself free and said.

"What a muddle."

"Not really. We've all got used to it and I'm proud of Harry."

"Harry? Why are you proud of him?"

"Harry, my son. We called him after ... after your Harry."

"Yes, of course," you told me something like that, and he thought: even now she doesn't know how bloody Harry messed around with them. I won't disillusion her.

So she rattled on, knocking his dreams for six.

"Because Harry was as much involved as anyone and at the time we had rather a soft spot for him. I still have, he's supposed to be the godfather. And it's a nice name."

"It is," he said. "Thank you."

"For what?"

"For remembering him. Because ... he's dead." He tried not to sound dramatic, but she did not seem surprised.

"Is he? I'm sorry. He would have been nearly fifty by now. What happened?"

"He was murdered."

"Murdered? How awful." She said the right things but did not sound as if she was particularly shocked. "By whom? How?"

"He was murdered by your son's father, Wanei."

21 Steppenwolf

There had been a time when Wanei could sit aside from himself and remember his life. It was the time when he could swim up through the water and easily reach the light. It was the time when he felt he was himself and when you might have said he was happy, although it was not a term he would have used.

It was not the time, which came later, when Wanei felt he was trapped inside himself, which was a dark place, where what light there was, he associated with pain.

But in the time of his happiness he would remember his life before, seeing it, from the outside, as something bathed in the silver moonlight of the present. The time which was, you could say, Wanei's formative years. They were hard times, mostly uncomfortable and often lonely and in which he had lost one of his eyes and thus acquired his name. But Wanei did not experience these times or remember them as bad times, they were what life was. The fact of life was the reality of life in which Wanei learned to struggle and, in the end, survive on his own terms. It was at the end of this time when Wanei met the white man, Harry Williams.

In the beginning he was tossed around by a warm and gentle sea, which, nonetheless, threw him up alone on the beach when it had had enough of him. His own theory is indeed that his mother drowned, most likely she drowned herself, taking the baby boy with her. But he, unwilling to accept his fate, was carried back to the beach. A thing washed up, half drowned, if not completely. A barely human thing not supposed to live. It was a moonless night. He awoke with a feeling of what we would call the anguish of loss. Nonetheless, he stood up and, obviously, went in search of his mother. He might have been sleep-walking. He walked into a stick of some sort projecting from a fisherman's hut at just the height of his childish eye. Pierced by a searing shard of nauseating light, which exploded inside his head, he lost control of his senses. The little body collapsed, an anarchical confusion of sensations: a strange smell of burning things unknown; small, sharp, pin-pricks of painful light; and the roar of the universe, which was, actually, the soul longing to escape. It twitched and trembled upon the ground as if its separate parts had fallen apart. Its head was paralysed, the one eye oozing blood upon the sand, the other staring blind. It shitted and pissed and vomited, in silence, in the dark, and then lay still.

In the half-light of early morning, the fisherman tipped out his night catch upon the thing. Thus he found it as he sorted and cleaned what he had caught. This is a strange thing I have found in the sea. He cleaned it up a little and, aware of the novel weight in his arms, eventually carried it to the mission station. Here, the strange white men, who covered up their bodies as if they were afraid of them, unaccountably took in those of the beachside who would otherwise have perished. I found it on the beach, the fisherman told them, which was the truth, but he did not add, some years ago. So the boy, who was, by this time, about nine years old, was taken into the mission where he would be held and trained, unless he decided to run away, in which case they would not stop him.

The mission was, like the fisherman, benevolently indifferent to its charges, but it fed and clothed them, and it was not, as an institution, wilfully cruel. Unless a boy showed an obvious aptitude in some useful field, he was allowed to find his own level. Where he made himself useful, he tended to stick: in the carpentry shop, in the kitchen, in the garden. It was, furthermore, the habit of the local European community to get its house-boys, its gardeners, its security staff from the mission. At his entry, so small and underdeveloped was Wanei, whom, for some reason, they called Stephen, that he was judged to be no more than six or seven years old.

The missionaries themselves were emotionally hard men far away from home, the massive, hot stretches of the South Pacific Ocean were not the well-defined man-made spaces of Europe, even its fringes. They struggled against homesickness. Christian brotherly love was easily seen as a necessary antidote to

Western materialism back home but out here, amongst a people essentially innocent and corrupted only by the great European ideal, it seemed not only irrelevant but also, somehow, to be part of what was wrong.

You see, Stephen, Brother Michael had tried to explain to Wanei about the time Wanei, the boy, was becoming the Wanei we would recognise as Harry Williams' house-boy, you see, if you apply the Christianity of Jesus Himself to New Sudan, it works. The meek shall inherit the earth and all that but because you are meek, because you are good and innocent, because you suffer and have short, brutal lives, in any event, then I have no doubt you will fly straight into the arms of a loving God, even though you eat one another from time to time. So what has our religion got to do with you? Nothing. Our sermons about hard work and thrift won't get you to heaven any faster. More likely hold you back. Better, you give us, the lost souls like me, a hand in simple goodness. He looked at Wanei, touched him on the shoulder and drew his hand back sharply as if it had been burned.

Yes, said Wanei, we do eat each other from time to time, but is that not a sort of love, in itself? I would not eat you if I did not love you. And Wanei knew that Brother Michael, with his pure white skin, his thick, black, shiny hair and the bones beginning to show through the flesh of his face, did sometimes want to eat him. Wanei liked the idea, an idea, nonetheless, which stopped his mouth. At first, Brother Michael would touch Wanei, and Wanei liked the sensation of Brother Michael's large, soft, white hands upon his skin, or the warm pressure of Brother Michael's hand upon his head, gently scratching his scalp. One time, Brother Michael tickled the inside of Wanei's ear so that Wanei's whole body shivered. He took the hand and bit the offending finger gently. He knew that Brother Michael wanted to touch him with his mouth like the kiss of Jesus on his disciples, but instead, Brother Michael walked away and would not look Wanei in the eye and Wanei was glad he only had one eye and therefore could not see everything. Afterwards, although Brother Michael was very good to Wanei and would laugh and tell him he must do the right thing and find a wife, nonetheless, he never again looked straight at Wanei or touched him. This made Wanei unhappy, as a boy growing up is unhappy when he finds he is alone.

Wanei became what is called a loner; the Steppenwolf type[2]. When the mission boys were given their food they would sit together on the grass in twos or threes with their billycans on their knees, picking at it and sharing. Eating of food together made them brothers, who would die for one another. But if another boy sat beside Wanei, he was ignored, not because Wanei did not want him but because Wanei could not give himself up to the other boy or get inside his head. He could not allow himself to be controlled in any way by the other boy; no part of himself could give way. Instead, he closed his eye and looked about the dark spaces inside his head. The only light he recognised was the narrow band dividing the black sea from the black sky. So the other boy would move away, sometimes hurt, sometimes defensively dismissive, wishing only to inflict a hurt himself but unable to find a weakness in Wanei's apparent self-sufficiency.

Wanei was, therefore, left alone and the more so as he grew up and grew strong with the work and food of the mission. His life had had a bad nutritional start so that at twelve years he looked more like nine or ten. At sixteen he looked like a healthy fourteen year old but at seventeen he was almost a man and looked it: small, compact, strong and black. His one eye made him look a little threatening if he looked hard at you, but his smile made you laugh it was so giving and you knew you could trust him to death in practical things. He was not a man who would ever maliciously steal or take something for pecuniary reasons but his emotions were an unknown quantity. They had not been tested. Wanei's legs were slightly bowed but the thickness of his thighs and the unusual strength of his short calves hid this defect.

The other boys discovered life as a gang on the beach but Wanei stayed alone and learnt his life from his own lonely experience, which was limited. It was as if there were no

---

[2] The book by Hermann Hesse.

transfer of ideas to Wanei, all his ideas came from within himself. Had Brother Michael not touched him then the idea of pleasure gained from physical contact with another would have been unknown, a gap in his knowledge; perhaps an idea of something missing, but nothing more. But Wanei had been touched, and he felt it still. He wanted to get close to Brother Michael but the more he tried the more he was evaded. Brother Michael wanted to hurt him and drive him away: stop following me like a shadow, boy, you're driving me mad.

But Brother Michael had his own dreams, of waiting for Wanei to grow up and running away with him. So he prayed to his own God, convincing himself he was doing the right thing, which, in a sense he was: interfering with a minor was a serious offence: the church might overlook it but the good Brother Michael's conscience would not. God's compassion apparently fell upon Brother Michael, but not upon Wanei, whose isolation increased. He felt, sometimes, he was shut up within himself.

The young man brooded. He had an idea he might kill Brother Michael, and eat him, because then he would be sure of him. It was only an idea, but it was real. Beyond the mission, Wanei had little idea of how society, what was then the colonial society of New Sudan, was regulated and controlled. Had he murdered Brother Michael and eaten him, he would have expected to have been dismissed from the mission, but an arrest, a trial and imprisonment would have been incomprehensible. A murder, in Wanei's idea of things, was merely a thing to be done, the inconveniences of the act to be minimized. But the idea of eating Brother Michael appealed to him in a more sensuous way, although, as I say, it was not yet a maddening, driving force in his life, it merely gathered dust in the cupboard.

Just past his eighteenth birthday, the small, well-made young man whom Wanei had become attracted the attention of one Mrs Wallace. She came seeking a house-boy. Brother Michael saw the chance of getting rid of temptation. He described Wanei in favourable terms: he's quiet and diligent; he gets on with his work, and although he has not shown any specific skill or pressed us to allow him to do a special job, I can assure you, Mrs Wallace – What a charming young man, although those innocent blue eyes don't fool me for a minute – he is just what you need.

"He does a good job in the kitchen, in the garden and ... around the place. He has learnt a little carpentry, he can mix cement, and he has a little elementary knowledge of electricity," Michael explained.

"He sounds a perfect little treasure."

"He is." I would like to keep him with me forever. He is a paragon. I love him with all my soul.

"Can I see him?"

"You may." Brother Michael called Wanei. Trying not to look at him, he explained the situation. "Stephen, Mrs Wallace is looking for a house-boy ..."

"I'll have him," Mrs Wallace broke in. Sold. The hammer hit the nail. "But, to be honest, a second house-boy. I have a first boy, Nicholas. But I need a second. I have to do a lot of entertaining." Fact was, Mrs Wallace was not a complete fool, she knew the day would come when Nicholas would have to go and, as she said to her husband, I need a standby. But this one looks fine. It was love at first sight. He looked so strong. Wanei was indeed strong: one of his jobs in the mission was to turn the generator, one of those large, slow, 25 KVA Listers that run and run for years but which require a strong arm to turn the starter handle. Wanei was proud of his muscles. Brother Michael was proud of them too. He had encouraged their development. He noticed Mrs Wallace's approving eye.

"So, Mr Stephen," she said, "would you like to work in our house? You'll have your own room and food, and I'll pay you a dollar a day."

Wanei's grin cemented the deal. He had caught Mrs Wallace, had he known it, hook, line and sinker. The sunken left eye socket, as she saw it, only enhanced his physical perfection elsewhere. The clothes she bought him consisted of small shorts, tight T-shirts and the cheap sandals everyone wore. He bought his first lap-lap with the help of Nicholas, who taught him to tie it in just such a way as would attract the attention of Mrs Wallace: tight around the buttocks and the knot at the front pushed just low enough to expose the top one or two pubic hairs.

Between them, Mrs Wallace and Nicholas corrupted Wanei, from the minute he announced I am Wanei. Stephen was gone forever.

[][][]

Mrs Wallace was the wife of an attaché to the American Embassy in Port Markham. She could not help being spoilt, assuming the whole world was there for her service and consumption, but within these constraints she was a helpful and even generous woman, materially and emotionally. She was a professional asset to her husband who was not much interested in anything other than his job. They had no children and she was reaching an age where she expected to have none. I don't mind she said to her friends I'll baby-sit yours, which she did, willingly, occasionally having another woman's children over the weekend. She would have made a good mum. Her husband did not signify, you're just a dry old stick, and they could play affection as well as the next couple.

Mrs Wallace had never been called beautiful, or pretty, but she was often called attractive and striking. Twice in her life artists had asked to paint her portrait: one hung above the Wallace fireplace in Bethesda, Maryland and the other, in a small art gallery in Portland, Oregon. Both pictures showed a strong-featured young woman with a noble if somewhat wistful aspect. Life is bound not to give me what I deserve, her expression seemed to say. Empress of Russia I will not be and that is my tragedy. She would have made a good model in the days when they had to stride down the catwalk dragging an expensive fur coat behind them. Sometimes, and especially if she put on too much make-up, she made you think of a handsome, fine-featured man, done up in drag.

Mrs Wallace could not take her eyes off Wanei. She likes you said Nicholas don't sell yourself cheap. She did not like Nicholas in the same way but she trusted him in the house. He padded around in bare feet. He was proud of his large, round tummy, and, as Mr Wallace once stated dryly and rather uncharacteristically, for he seemed not to notice the servants, he knows on which side his bread is buttered. I know, replied his wife, that's why I trust him he keeps the house as clean as I could do it myself. There is something womanly about him. Yes, thought her husband, he is as soft-looking and as calculating as any woman but there's nothing queer about him. He did not share these thoughts with his wife. At home, he wanted her to have anything she wanted. You might have thought Mr Wallace willed Wanei upon his wife. If that's what she wants, let her have it, I don't mind. But the fact was, Mr Wallace seemed not to notice Wanei at all. It was left to Nicholas to manipulate the new boy, and from the beginning, Nicholas liked having Wanei around because it improved his status as head-boy. Wanei soon learned what was required of him.

"Why does she look at me like that?"

"You are her servant."

"But she looks at me and looks at me until I look at her, and our eyes meet. Then she smiles. And I don't know what to do."

Nicholas smiles. "You know what women want?"

"What?"

So Nicholas explained to Wanei what women wanted because Wanei had no knowledge of them. He had not moved around the beach with the gangs of boys at night, so he did not know what they did with the older girls who taught them things.

"Have you not dreamed of women's breasts and wet yourself?"

"No." Wanei had only had ideas of the welcoming outstretched arms of Brother Michael but he could not explain his feelings to Nicholas.

They were sitting on the little veranda of the staff quarters, their voices lost in the roaring night, which provided only a scant, white, phosphorescent sort of light.

Nicholas said: "Do you not know yourself?"

Wanei was not sure what he meant.

"I'll show you. Come to my room." Nicholas sat on the edge of his little pallet bed and pulled off his lap-lap so that he was naked. "You see?" And he showed Wanei how he could stimulate himself to erection, playing with one of his nipples as he did so. "It's easy." Wanei was not shocked or even particularly fascinated but only mildly intrigued; Nicholas's action was just another thing people did. "You try it," so Wanei followed his example but without much success. "What are you thinking of?" said Nicholas dryly, "think of a woman, think of eating her mouth and touching her skin. Think of biting her."

All the same, nothing much happened so Wanei put back his lap-lap, which he wore when he was not working, and walked out into the night. He wanted to think of Brother Michael but he could not while he was with Nicholas.

Nicholas followed: "Don't worry, wait 'til she does something and don't be afraid."

Wanei laughed, he was not afraid, only interested, but he would like to have talked to Brother Michael about it.

[][][]

Mrs Wallace – sometimes she was called Bertha but she hated the name – wanted Wanei. She felt she was slowly burning up. Soon, she felt, she would be nothing but ashes. Her husband began to exasperate her and she could only breathe properly when he was out of the house. She was taller than Wanei, by a few inches, and of course older by a decade, nearly two. One half of her wanted to pick him up and sit him on her knee, undress him like a doll, the other wanted to go down on her knees before him and humiliate herself. She imagined him making love to her like a hungry impersonal animal, putting his warm, black hands around her neck. In the end, she was angry with him, believing he was teasing her with his indifference. She was aware that her impatient anger was a waste of emotion but nonetheless, it drove her, one afternoon, after her husband had returned to work, to pounce on Wanei. Afterwards, it was the word she considered most aptly described what she had done. It was one of those hot exhausted days, when you are sick of the sun and long for a day of grey mist and drizzle.

Mrs Wallace, Bertha, watched Wanei come towards her chair with the coffee. She was inside the house, the windows open to catch the breeze, the luscious garden shimmering beyond. As he stood beside her she stroked the back of his calf, as if absent-mindedly. She wanted to ask, in a civilized and adult manner: May I do this? She would have preferred his adult consent but her mouth was dry and words would not come. She felt the warmth of his body in her hand, the hint of fine hairs. For a moment, he seemed to stand frozen. She did not know what to do. She blushed and looked up, praying he would look at her. Thankfully, his one eye stared back at her and he grinned, as embarrassed, at that moment, as was she. But she read connivance, swallowed and moved her hand up the inside of Wanei's leg until it lay between his thighs. She caressed his small tight balls, still looking into his grinning face, which did not look away and which appeared to have relaxed into genuine enjoyment. Wanei wore no underpants – no one did – so she easily persuaded herself he had omitted to wear them for her sake. He must have been waiting for me to do this. The monster! She was right, in that respect.

What happened next? Asked Nicholas, that night, as he played with his nipple. Wanei calmly described how he had been undressed and played with and manoeuvred: she was moaning as if she was in pain, but I think she was happy. Did you like it? Wanei considered for a moment: I liked it when I stabbed her and I wanted to hurt her but after the saltwater came I did not feel like that. He could not define the combination of feelings of disgust and pity. He had badly wanted to run away and find Brother Michael.

Well done, said Nicholas, you're a man now. Listen to me, and he explained what Wanei should do next and what he could expect. And in this way, with Nicholas egging him on and with Mrs Wallace ready to do anything, Wanei came to resemble the devious little shit that Mac recognised about the time old Harry had, at any rate, not discouraged David's interest.

[][][]

Nicholas told Wanei to act, at all times, as if nothing had happened. Had he known the phrase, he would have said you must act as if butter would not melt in your mouth. Do not look at her, do not show the slightest facial expression which might suggest an intimacy and above all, do not touch her. Let her make all the moves and if she initiates anything, go along with it. This is not quite the way Nicholas expressed himself – they spoke the simple local pidgin – but it was the gist of the message.

"Is it because I am her servant?"

Nicholas laughed: "No, it is so that she will become your servant."

What happened was that Mrs Wallace began to give Wanei things: new clothes, a leather belt and a transistor radio. The latter emitted small, tinny voices, and a noise, which Nicholas said was music. Wanei put it on the table in his room and turned it up as loud as it would go because that was what you did. He heard the noise it made but it did not speak to him, so when the batteries ran down he did not replace them. He appreciated the silence, and he threw the dead thing into the shrubbery.

"Why doesn't she give me money instead of this rubbish?"

Nicholas laughed again.

"Wait, don't worry, it will come."

"What if I ask her?"

"Don't do that."

"Why not?"

"They don't like it. If I want a girl in the town, I pay her because she asks me to pay. If she asks too much we can talk about the price or I can find another girl. It's fair, but these people don't like you to ask for money like that."

"But I want money so that I can do what I like with it." Wanei thought of Mrs Wallace and of her hot, panting breath, with distaste. "What if I told her husband? What if I told him about what she makes me do?"

"He won't believe you."

Wanei was astonished.

"But I am not a liar."

"They think we are all liars. He will ask her and she will say you are pestering her. She might say you raped her."

"What is rape?"

Nicholas explained.

"But that is a lie. Why would she lie about me?"

"She would lie because she would not like to tell her husband the truth. She is supposed to only want the body of her husband."

Wanei thought about the body of Mr Wallace. It was dried-up and grey, like something dead. It was not robust like the body of Brother Michael. He understood why Mrs Wallace did not want the body of her husband. He looked down at his own body and he put the tip of his forefinger onto his navel and pressed hard until he felt his whole body through his finger. Yes, he thought, I like my body. I know that Brother Michael likes my body in the same way Mrs Wallace likes it but he is afraid of me.

And for the first time in his life, Wanei felt sad. He wanted Brother Michael to look at him and to touch him like Mrs Wallace looked at him and touched him. He felt that if he could connect with Brother Michael in that way, there was nothing he would not do for him. He would give him everything he had, he would lie at his feet, he would die for him. Wanei imagined Brother Michael being sad and he imagined himself comforting Brother Michael with his arms. And as Wanei thought this, his cock became very strong and he understood how it was that Nicholas could make himself strong just by thinking.

"Would Mr Wallace kill her if he knew?"

"You make me laugh," said Nicholas, but he did not laugh this time. You must understand these white people if you want to live a long life. Mr Wallace will always believe her lie, even if he knows she is lying.

Wanei said nothing.

"These white people are always lying. They lie so much that they believe their lies. Mr Wallace will lie to himself about his wife and he will believe his own lie. Why? I don't know why, but it seems that the truth hurts them."

Wanei frowned.

"If Mrs Wallace asks me if I like her, I say yes, I like you. But, always, I remember I am lying because if I forget, I would ..." He hesitated: "I would forget myself."

"And that is why they don't know themselves. They forget they're lying," said Nicholas.

"I don't understand."

"You don't have to but you have to know them. Just understand this: they can do what they like, but if you do something they do not like, they will tell lies about you. If she says you raped her, he will believe her, he will tell the police, the police will believe him and you will be in trouble. They will put you in the prison. If they want to kill you they will kill you."

"But I could kill them."

"But you would not get away with it. The law will not let you."

"What is the law?"

"The law is the thing the white people have made up to keep us as their servants. They will use it to trap you."

"I don't want to be in a trap. I will fight my way out. I will be like a wild animal." And, he thought, I would run back to Brother Michael.

Nicholas pulled him inside the room and sat beside him on the bed.

"Listen to me."

"Yes?" Wanei did as he was told.

"This is your life for now. Be patient. She will give you more things. But you have to understand that they like their things very much. If you get in between them and their things, you'll find you've got plenty of trouble. When you need another job, what counts on the paper are the words He Does Not Steal." Nicholas stressed each word.

"But I don't steal. Why should I? I have what I want."

Nicholas sighed: "I know, but they always think you steal things unless they know you do not. So it has to be put on the paper. What they call a reference. If it is not written down then they will assume you are a thief – a stilman."

"But why? What is wrong with us."

Nicholas looked at Wanei sadly.

"Because we are black."

Wanei looked at himself and saw that he was black: "Is that a reason for making me a thief?"

"No, but it is what they think."

"All of them?"

"All of them."

This is why Brother Michael does not want me, thought Wanei. He thinks I am a thief. Wanei looked at his feet resting on the ground which shifted beneath him.

[][][]

Nicholas assumed Wanei got some pleasure out of his association with Mrs Wallace. But Wanei was not so pleased: soon after the first bit of money came out of Mrs Wallace, he began to dread even the idea of contact with her. It was not worth the money, and he tried to avoid her by not letting her catch his eye. The tactic, however, made things worse. His apparent indifference, the increasing efficiency with which he did his job, and the fact that he never once indicated that there had ever been carnal relations between them, made her fall in love with him. Or rather she fell in love with an idea of him. She thought it was love. She invested in him a wisdom he did not possess. She put him upon a pedestal and worshipped him as a man who understood her and who was infinitely patient with her. An illusion, which she, nonetheless, believed with all her generous emotions. But the perverse truth, the game fate played with her, was that she had, indeed, experienced with Wanei a sexual response, quiet but memorably powerful, beyond anything she had experienced before. Wanei's apparent ardour and – a word she herself used after she had calmed down a bit – efficiency, was, she assumed, the result of his consideration for her. It was not, but ironically, later, when Wanei began to hate her, when he calculatingly wanted to hurt her body, he did indeed consider what he was doing, sometimes quite methodically controlling the angry passion he felt.

Thus, when Wanei refused to look at her, Mrs Wallace believed it was because of his tact and good sense. What a wonderful man, she would think, imagining herself stealing into his room in the night, where he would make room for her on his bed, look at her, smile at her and take her in his arms. It never came to that but so ardently did she think about it that in an odd sort of way, in her head, she believed it had happened. And believing it, she began to touch Wanei, lightly, as he passed by, as if to say: there, this confirms what we are to one another. She imagined his responses, the most insignificant gesture interpreted as a loving recognition when, in fact, he was trying to tear himself away. They were both mad.

One afternoon, watching him carefully, beautifully, wiping the glass-topped dining table, gracefully moving his whole body to do it, she could not stop herself. From behind, so that he was startled, she took him in her arms, holding him as tightly as she could. He turned on her, angry, before he could control himself, but her eyes were tight shut in ecstasy. She had lost her mind, interpreting his roughness as romantic passion. She enjoyed the pain he inflicted and enjoyed even more the memory of it so that more and more she could not stop herself going to him, sometimes twice, even three times, in a day. They said nothing to each other. There was no other communication between them.

Wanei dreaded her approaches. She was a hungry animal that wanted to eat him. His life in the house was unbearable. In retaliation, he did degrading things to her only to find her willingly degrading herself for him. She was working herself up into a state where she would have let Wanei kill her. But Wanei could no longer talk to Nicholas, whose idea was that a man was on top of a woman, it was a man's duty to maintain that position and anything less demeaned your manhood. In later years, in the times when he was able to think about his life rationally, Wanei was sufficiently sure of himself to be able to say fuck my manhood if that's what it means. For now, however, he was a boy and unsure of himself. He was not going to let Nicholas see his weakness. He tried not to lie to Nicholas by saying nothing but if Nicholas asked him questions then he was forced to lie. Yes, I'm fucking her and I like it. But the lies made him hate Mrs Wallace all the more because he did not want to lie about himself. Each conscious lie diminished him, ate away at his idea of himself. What he wanted to say to Nicholas was, I'm fucking her, it makes me feel sick and I want to kill her. And rapidly, the idea of wanting to kill Mrs Wallace was associated, in Wanei's mind, with the act of fucking her.

22   Sally Finds Her Man

Mac had told Sally they had better stay with him. He'd help them find Wanei. He knew where he was. Although wasn't it a wild-goose chase? What did the boy expect to find? But I suppose people want to know who their fathers are, even if they're murderers. I wonder what I'd feel if someone turned up claiming to be my offspring? That'd be a turn up for the book. Plenty of children in Port Markham have no idea who their father is. Young Harry doesn't look out of place. But how is Sally going to respond to the truth about the image she's carried in her head all these years? Wanei's not your straightforward sort of man. He's a murderer for a start and I'm not sure he isn't mad. Ought I to say something? After all, I've taken her on. In a way. But she might tell me to go to hell. It's none of my business.

"He's a nice young man," said Mac.

"Thank you," replied Sally.

"You don't treat him as a child, I've noticed."

Perhaps because I feel like one myself.

"Looks can be deceptive."

"They can but he's not as grown-up as he looks. Any more than I am," she laughed. "Didn't you see him at dinner? I was surprised he got through it." She thought of her daughters, with David, and then deliberately put them on one side.

"I didn't. I did. I don't know. What youngsters have I known in my life? Apart from myself." He remembered Poland. "I've only dealt with thoroughly grown-up people," he spat out, "the thoroughly corrupted ones. What do I know about innocence?" He thought of Harry Williams, and he put that aside. Better to live for the now.

Sally looked into the night. She wanted to touch him.

They were sitting on the veranda, after dinner. Harry had gone down to the beach. As Sally had noticed, and Mac had not, he had wanted to be a boy that night, not a man. During dinner he had been raw and shy, resisting attempts by his mother to bring him into the conversation. Mac had made no attempt. In any event, why patronise the boy? And now, he was glad he had the mother on her own. He was more relaxed. He wanted to create an understanding with her before he approached the boy and got to know him better. At least, a part of him wanted to. He was not sure what sort of understanding he wanted. He was a decent man. Another part of him felt bad for wishing to appropriate her for himself, taking her, or, at any rate, a part of her, away from her son. It's outrageous of me to think I want to be in a position to have any sort of understanding with her – beyond the practical – now, or later; or ever, for that matter. She's asked me for help and here am I, here am I having thoughts about which I ought to be ashamed. And if the boy was not around, somewhere, I'd be more pressing. I know I would. He inhibits me. It's a good thing. Shouldn't I get to know him before I get to know her?

He tried to think of other things but could not. I can't ask her what she thinks of me. She'd have the right to laugh in my face. He looked at her face, illuminated only by a contorted, distant light from somewhere in the house behind them. He put the bits together in his head. She's younger than me but we've had a lot of shared experience. New Sudan and all this – a picture of a club do in the old days flashed through his mind – for a start. But then there's the boy, so innocent, and he's the reason she's here. She could be my daughter, for God's sake. I'm old enough. I'm a selfish bastard. He groaned out loud, managing to convert it into a cough at the last moment.

"Is the room alright?"

"It's lovely." She did not look at him.

"That's stretching a point. It hasn't been used for years. I hope Simon's aired the sheets properly." Simon was the servant he'd had for years. His shadow.

"I love it. It's so simple. I wish I lived like this all the time."

Like what? But he didn't want to ask. Instead he said.

"It hasn't got any curtains. We could rig up a sheet of some sort."

"Oh no, that would spoil it. I want to see the stars."

"Yes, and the hills, and the sea and the sky. What more could you want?"

"Nothing," she said and then added after a pause, "if only I could be a part of it."

"What do you mean?"

"I mean I wouldn't just want to look at it. I'd want to live in it."

"How?" He wanted to challenge her. He wanted her to have to say she wanted to stay here with him. "Could you be a fisherman? Or one of those women who work themselves to death farming?" He was cross with her but she was not to be baited.

She laughed at him, at herself

"You're right, I could only be a part of it by being a tourist. But I'd still like to walk along those hills and come to the sea that way."

"You could go in a boat," and he thought: I'd take you out, if only you'd ask me. I don't like being in boats. The sea's too big, in all directions. I like to have my feet on the ground. Or I think I do. You could stay here with me. Then you could live in the view. And she might have answered: What? As your nurse? Dealing with your incontinence? No, he would have replied, Simon can do that if it comes to it but I'd like to go to bed with you. Not for the sex, not at my age, but I'd like to lie close to you and hear you breathe through the night. I'm mad. She's established here for the duration. And she has a right to call on my help because that's what I've unconditionally offered her. I have no right to ask for more. She'll be friendly and she'll show her gratitude by helping in the house and by disturbing my routine as little as possible but that's enough, she'll say, I owe you no more.

So there was silence between them. And a distance.

"Mac?"

"Yes?"

"It's very kind of you to do this."

"Do what?"

"Putting us up. Letting us disturb you."

"It's nothing. I want to do it. Please understand that. I'm not sure exactly what it is you want but I want to help you do it." There, he'd said it, and she was surprised.

"I'm not sure myself but we're here now and I want to do it for Harry. He wants to find his father."

"Is that a good thing?" There, he'd said that as well.

"Yes."

"Are you sure?"

"I am, because, because especially now we're here. If we went away without seeing him, then Harry, my Harry, would always wonder about his father, thinking of him here in New Sudan as ... as ... as something like ... he might see anywhere, on the road-side, begging, or some fat man behind a counter."

She was right, of course, and her confidence was infectious.

"He who dares, and all that."

"Yes. I didn't know my father, but my mother made no mystery about him. There were pictures and I knew who he'd been. He was someone I could respect and like because my mother told me, often... And I could see the love in her eyes when she spoke about him."

"Did you miss having a father?"

"How can you miss what you don't know? But perhaps I'm always looking for a father figure. Perhaps," she laughed, and was about to touch him but didn't, "perhaps you're my father figure. You're acting like one, humouring your silly little daughter."

Yes, I'll be your father, which emphatically precludes me from being your lover, or even your admirer. I don't want to be a dirty old man but here I am being one. He said:

"There's nothing silly about you and don't you go thinking you are. You might have been once but your father figure now is saying you are a very sensible and thoughtful girl and I'm proud of you."

"Thank you."

He was glad she didn't call him Daddy.

"But then why do you think Harry, your Harry, would miss having a father, if you didn't miss it?"

"He didn't miss it, having a father, that is. There was David, who has been wonderful."

"Yes," I'd forgotten him. There's always him. That young man with the sweat running down his young man's belly.

"But that's not the point. The thing is that Harry wants to know about his biological father, he wants to know about his genes, and there is so little I can tell him because I know so little myself. I could say he was a house-boy but I haven't, because …"

"It doesn't look very good admitting to your son that he is the result of a fling with one of the servants? Although," he added, afraid he had been too rude, "I'm sure it's not at all uncommon. Servants fulfilling a role their masters cannot." *Lady Chatterley's Lover*, he thought, but I'm hardly the Mellors type.

But she took him seriously.

"No, it doesn't look good. But not because I had a fling with a servant. It's because there's a lot more to Wanei than being a servant. Being called a servant does not do Wanei justice."

"It doesn't. There's nothing servile about that man. But does being called a murderer define him any better?"

"I don't know, but it could, and there's no getting away from the fact, which is rather less accidental than ending up as someone's servant. But from what you've told me there seems to have been a reason for it. An understandable reason. Wanei isn't a … What's the word?"

"A pathological murderer?"

"Yes. He doesn't sound like the type who'd murder just for the pleasure of it. Not as a disease: he'd have to have been driven to it."

"We all feel driven to it sometimes but we don't actually do it."

"But maybe it was the last straw and he was driven over the edge by Harry."

"Oh yes. Harry Williams got what he deserved and, come to think of it, men like that are, perhaps, more inclined to commit, what you might call, uncivilised acts."

"Men like what?"

"Homosexual men. No, I don't mean that. I mean men who have crossed the boundary, who have faced up to what they are and who have acted upon it. They haven't been pushed to the outside, they've taken the decision to be outsiders or at any rate see themselves as outsiders."

"So having taken that one extra step, whereas we might think about murder but not actually go the extra step and do it, they would?"

"Something like that. The character trait, the kink, if you like, is not being a murderer but being someone who is not afraid to take the extra step. And that, Sally, is why Wanei, your son's father, is, has to be assumed to be, dangerous. We'll have to tread carefully. I know him, and I'm not sure I'd trust him."

"Well, we are going to see him – once you've found him – and don't forget ... I knew him once upon a time, as well. In quite an intimate way. And I can tell you one thing."

"What's that?"

"He didn't rape me. He didn't coerce me into doing something I didn't want to do. It wasn't, and this sounds horribly crude, it wasn't because I was in the mood. It happened because I wanted some sort of revenge on the other two."

She was talking as if to herself, as if she had forgotten Mac, as if she was having an intimate conversation with her mother. He wanted to stop her because he thought she might feel embarrassed, later. But she looked at him as if to reassure herself that it was him, and no one else, to whom she was talking

"And having taken that step myself, and having experienced a little fear, what Wanei did was, was ... There's only one word for it, it was wonderful. It made me feel like a woman for the first time in my life and I could laugh at all you silly men and admit that I didn't love David at all and never would."

"So you took the extra step too! Just like him."

"I hadn't thought of that before."

"And would you say you loved Wanei?" He had to push her but she didn't seem at all disconcerted.

"In a way, yes. Not in a possessive way. I felt as if this was the one man on earth who had been made for me, and if our relationship was only to last those few hours, those few days, then it was perfect, and right and proper. So you can see why Harry, my Harry, our Harry, the Harry who came from Wanei and me, is so important. And why it is so important that he meets his father."

But what if he's not wonderful? It was a long time ago. What if you've built your whole life upon an illusion? Is it not better to keep it that way? But he said

"And I'll help you find him. I'm pretty sure I know where he is."

23 Mother of Exiles

About the same time as Sally and Mac are chatting on Mac's veranda, David is in a flat somewhere in the South Kensington part of London. He thinks it is the Brompton Road. He is not sure. He remembers climbing up a lot of stairs in one of those enormous Victorian houses that make up the district. Finally, they had got through a narrow passage into a remarkably large flat. It must run across the top of more than one house. A lot of white paint, is the first thing he thinks of when he wakes up to the bright morning light pouring through a window up above them. It is going to be a beautiful day.

He turned onto his back and looked at his watch. Ten to six. I'll have to take a pee soon. Too much beer last night. He had not felt so calm and contented in the morning for years and years. Not since, not since that time with whatever his name was in New Sudan. He remembered the beauty of that early morning, also, lying beside ... beside him.

And it is true, he had not thought about Harry Williams since they had left New Sudan. Had you asked him any time, any time in the last, say, ten years, he would have said, no, I regret nothing. I've done exactly what I wanted to do.

But now he remembers everything. I thought I'd sorted out my life then, on that morning: I'd stay with him, whoever he was, for ever. He frowns: So what did I do wrong?

It's not going to be so easy this time. There's the house for a start. It's worth a lot of money but I won't be able to get at any of it because they'll have to live somewhere. At least 'til the children grow up. But perhaps they should go out into the country or somewhere like ... like Esher. The schools'd be good for the girls. Harry'll be away to university soon enough.

I could get a little flat. A studio'll do. I could live a bit further out. It'd just mean sitting in the Tube a bit longer. Putney, or somewhere like that. And he thought about walking on the Heath at weekends, a beer in the pub – the Green Man – and home for a good read. On his own, for some reason, although the idea was to be free to ... to ... to be with someone else. Was that it?

Or, a good part of Brighton, near the Downs. They could have quite a large garden. Sally'd like that.

He looked at the white ceiling and the sloping walls. It was a strangely empty room. Clean. His mind was not working rationally but rather, as he relaxed, emotionally. He was able to be himself. Nothing, at that moment, would have upset him. He was not acting the Fulham father and husband. Fuck them, flashed, almost subliminally, through his head, from time to time.

Perhaps we could run away, I'll take what I can grab. There must be £10,000 in the bank. He turned his head to look at the turned in, curved back of the other, gently breathing. He imagined them living together, this, this, Wallace, Wallington, Wellington, Winston, Winston, that's it, this Winston and himself living in a vast, anonymous city, in a room, amongst others, with an un-made bed, the sheets rumpled and grubby, but warm, and in which they lay, or rather, in his mind's eye, looking down upon it, in which they had lain, together.

He turned his own body around to watch this Winston, whom he knew only as something beautiful and desirable. He fixed his eyes upon the back of the man's neck, a whole country of small lines he wanted to explore. He moved closer and sniffed the skin, gently touching it with the tip of his nose. Winston made a small noise from somewhere in his sleep so that David took him and caressed him and the half-sleeping man responded until they were both satisfied and slept again, David holding the other in his arms, sitting him on his lap, wanting to take the whole body into himself. For this divine moment, he thinks, I'd give anything.

The sun poured in through the window above them, it was getting hot, the traffic was loud below. David dashed out to take his pee. When he got back, Winston was up, a towel wrapped around his incredibly lean body. So lean, he seemed to be leaning forward, his shoulders too heavy.

"David, you want de bath first?" The voice was like treacle. It was how David always thought of the man, when he wanted him: the treacle, pouring, slow and smooth and thick out of the tin. "I'll make us some coffee, David."

Hearing his name spoken like that, like treacle, was wonderful to hear. He wanted to rip off the towel and play games but as he approached the other backed away showing his teeth in a grin.

"Not now, David, I have work to do. So do you."

"Fuck my work, Winston ..."

"Not Winston" – he stressed the Ton with great force – "not Wins-ton. Wis-dom. Wisdom, Wisdom, I have de Wisdom. Go get your bath. I tell you or I will beat you."

David obeyed. He masturbated before he washed. When he returned to the room, Wisdom was dressed in a smart, tight-fitting pin-striped suit. No tie. He was beautiful. Elegant, tough like wire.

"I have made you de coffee."

"Thanks." David approached, and again the other retreated, grinning, baring his teeth. Beautiful.

"See you, man."

"I'm not going. I'll hang around here today."

"I have things to do, man, you can't stay in de flat."

The voice like ... like ... like treacle. David wanted to go on his knees.

"Why not? Will you throw me out?" He wanted to be manhandled. "I'll stay in here."

Wisdom laughed.

"De others here too, man."

"I'll come with you."

"A honky like you? You bad battyboy man, dey'll eat you. Dey'll cut you with knives."

"I'm not afraid." He was not. He wanted it. I'd let this man, this warm man, cut me up. And eat me, if he wants. The idea of Wanei flashes through his head and is gone before he recognises it. He will remember it later.

"You want me to spank you?"

The idea was electric but he answered.

"You want me to spank you, bad boy?"
"Listen battyboy, I tell you what."
"What?"
"You be a good battyboy. I see you tonight in de ..." He mentioned the name of the bar where they had met the night before.
"Alright but ..."
And to stop his words, Wisdom kissed David on the lips and ran away, slamming the door behind him.

[][][]

"Daddy didn't come home last night."
Alice is not worried, but she wants to re-assure Sonia, so she lies.
"He telephoned."
"When? I didn't hear."
Since their mother had left, Sonia, as the older of the two sisters, thinks she ought to act the part, but she does not feel it. She lets Alice take the lead. She resents that they have been left on their own. First Mummy goes but at least we know where she is. Then Daddy disappears but she resents her mother more.
"This morning when you were in the bathroom." Alice is no less angry but she wants to protect Sonia more than she hates her parents.
They had taken their dinner out into the garden, sitting on the bench beside the tool shed, laying out the things between them. His had sat alone on the kitchen table, a salad. It had taken hours to prepare, cutting the vegetables into incredible shapes, the way Sally had taught them, and then setting it out in layers, with the home-made mayonnaise. Beside it, a pink ice-cream had collapsed into the dish, together with the sponge biscuit which had been stuck into it. The whole mess was enlivened by the dye from the hundreds and thousands, as if some colourful insect had died in it. They sat until it was dark, in their shorts and T-shirts, picking at their food. They did not mention their father so they did not talk much, but each felt

close to the other. When they went to bed they left the things outside and the French windows wide open.

Sonia pretends to ignore the explanation. She gets up and goes out into the garden. She knows Alice is lying but she does not want to admit it. Twenty-five years later, looking into a similar garden, from the small room into which her life has been squeezed, she remembers that morning as the time they began to grow apart. She thinks of it as mostly her fault but I couldn't help it. It was an emotional thing. Alice told the lies but I kept the secrets.

She wants to cry on her own but she does not because she is not sure what is upsetting her. But I couldn't care less if I never see Mummy and Daddy again. She sees a picture of her father lying in the road. He begins to sit up, looking around, bewildered and then falls back, blood pouring out of his mouth.

She feels sick and runs around the back of the tool shed to wretch but nothing happens and she feels better. She no longer wants to cry but she wants her brother badly, so she makes herself busy, clearing the dinner things from the bench, carrying them into the kitchen. But as she is about to clear away their father's uneaten meal, Alice stops her.

"I'll do that. I'm going to eat it for breakfast."

"Alright. Will you clear up?"

"Yes."

She turns her back on Alice but she knows she is watched. It annoys her, just a little, as it has not done before. She wants to make contact but she feels isolated and cut off from her sister, despite suddenly being overwhelmed by a hot wave of affection.

But Alice is determined to press herself upon something, and it still needs to be Sonia.

"I'm not going to do any more cooking. How much money have we got?"

Sonia is relieved by Alice's defiance but it does not stop her feeling she is floating away.

"I don't know. Look in the tin. It's on the table."

Alice opens the old tea caddy in which their father puts the money for them and sometimes a shopping list, before he leaves in the mornings. They stay in bed. It is the school holidays. She grabs some of the notes.

"I'm taking this, for myself. I am not going to do any more shopping for the house. Except I might buy some crisps. When the food runs out we can go to the fish and chip shop."

"Or the pizzeria," Sonia adds, so that Alice can see she is still with her. She giggles as an automatic reaction. "And when the money runs out we'll sell some of his things."

"Yes, David's things. I am not going to call him the other word any more. Do you agree?"

"Yes, I do." And Sonia felt a lot better. She wanted to kiss her sister, not meaning it affectionately but as the sealing of a pact. "What're you going to do?"

"I'm going out."

"Alright." No point in trying to stop her, and she did not want to know why.

Alice said: "What are you going to do?"

"I'm going to read," and she found that by positively, publicly, as it were, rejecting her parents, she thus felt that for the first time in years they were indeed her real mother and father.

[][][]

Upstairs, she tidied the room and then sat at the little desk, which her mother had painted blue. They had stencilled on flowers together. She took out her diary.

She carries the key on a slender golden chain around her neck so she has to bend over the book to unlock it.

As she began to write she heard the front door slam. Relieved, she took the diary downstairs and sat at the dining-room table, looking down into the garden.

I'll write this first, she thought, and then I'll do some housework but Alice is right, I'm not going to do any cooking either.

Dearest Harry – I miss you – I am waiting for you to come back. Daddy – she feels disloyal but uses the word, nonetheless

– did not come home last night. Alice is cross but I don't feel anything. If I never see him again I won't mind. He might have been run over but I don't think so because the police would have come here by now. They would have found the address in his wallet. Am I wicked? Alice pretends he phoned us but I know he didn't. If you look at Daddy in the eyes he always looks away. Sometimes I think he is not my father. Sometimes I wish he wasn't. Sometimes I wish I had no parents and no family. But I would still want to know <u>you</u>. Not as my brother but as my boy friend. Sometimes I wish you was my boy friend and I could talk to you like that.

But she dared not write what she really felt.

There was more she wanted to say but she closed the book, quickly opening it again and adding a long line of kisses. Then she shut it finally, bending over it to lock it.

[][][]

Mrs Willis put her table in the window where once there might have been a dressing table. Thus, while working, she can look up out into the street, her back towards the bed. The whole house is behind her.

She spends more time looking out the window than she does at her work, which is, most often, the reading of a book. The sort of book classed by some as difficult. She does it to expand and exercise her mind. She thinks it is as necessary to her as is the walk to Bishops Park and along the river. Sometimes further, across the bridge and up Putney Hill. Then, passing the Green Man, where once she had drunk half pints of bitter beer with Mr Willis in the early, childless, days of their marriage, she will stride across the heath towards Wimbledon Common, and begin to feel free of London.

Mrs Willis makes careful notes in a small, specific notebook with the idea that she will write a short essay about what she has read. Essays have been written: one on Roman Britain; another about Sheep Farming in Tudor England and the Birth of

Capitalism. In another age, about the time the house was built, perhaps a little earlier, these essays would have been considered worth publishing. Not today: Mrs Willis does not give enough weight to her references, she is not academic enough, her sentences are too short, her paragraphs, likewise.

The book will be something like *Dombey and Son*, or John Stuart Mill, *On Liberty*. Thomas Carlyle is waiting for the winter but Mrs Willis is not at her desk every day. Sometimes a week will pass, even longer, without it being used – Mr Willis would not dare go near – but the solid fact of its existence is what Mrs Willis thinks keeps her sane. This is not the case – she could live without it – but, it is true, she cannot use it when Mr Willis is in the room. Lying in bed, Sunday mornings, for instance. Fortunately, Mr Willis is an early riser. This morning, the minute he leaves the house – about eight o'clock – she rushes up the stairs, makes the bed, throws the old-fashioned counterpane over it, and pauses for breath. She surveys the room, and then, with equal vigour, pulls an armchair and an accompanying occasional table more into the centre of the room, setting them so that the sitter will have the light behind him and, a view of the door, which she shuts ever so quietly so as not to awaken the sleeper beyond. She resists the temptation to lock it – that way lies madness – and then goes to sit at her table, alone with myself at last.

She stares out the window. So like her own is the house opposite, she sometimes expects to see herself in it, staring back. Her breathing becomes more regular as she forgives Mr Willis his existence, even thinking fondly of him. Thus, she remembers, again, that one of their sons is encamped in the house for a few weeks. This makes her smile but before she has decided if it is Rob or Dan – the masculine names with which their friends designate them – her eyes have come across the small pile of books in front of her, and she is wondering which one to take up. As it happens, she might decide to take up nothing because the establishment of her space, the reclamation of the room as her own, has dissipated the urgency which drove her into it in the first place. She is not – this Mrs Willis – one of those people who feels guilt for not having commenced, let alone completed, a task she has set herself. There is no headmaster in the sky. Nonetheless, she does take up a book, and begins to read:

> The Sutherlanders who did remain in the Red River and Rainy Lake country were perhaps the best – Mathesons, MacBeths, Bannermans, Gunns and Mackeys. They faced the harsh lands with courage. They carried muskets in their hands as they walked behind their ploughs. They fought Métis and Cree to defend the Red River Colony, and they called their land Kildonan. It is still called Kildonan.
> *The Highland Clearances*, John Prebble.

[][][]

Mrs Willis is attached to the Highlanders driven from their homes. She inherited the attachment from her father, the South London radical, who was incensed by the idea of people being driven from the land by some bloody capitalist bastard who wants it all and leaves nothing for the rest of us. He was writing a paper for the Fabian Society at the time, about the European settlement of the Kenyan Highlands – but she agreed, finding it difficult, all the same, to get her head around the spreading circles of injustice. The Mackeys had fled to the Red River Valley. But what about the Cree they displaced? What happened to them?

She looks up, out into the sky, above the slate roofs of London, the chimney pots of Fulham, the television aerials of the houses opposite. She tries to imagine the Cree people, hopelessly fighting against the invaders, whose sense of an injustice done to them drives them to pass on the oppression. She imagines the lonely ploughman in the valley, dogged in his determination to make the land his own by ploughing it, by breaking it. It proves his existence: no ploughing, no land, no man. In her mind's eye, the log cabin beyond disappears. The prairie – or is it scattered trees and rocks? – reclaims the land. The man, despite his efforts, is forgotten.

Above this idea, like the sky above the television aerials, is the Cree warrior, on the hillside, mounted on his little piebald pony. He looks down upon the dispossession of his land, the wild-looking land which makes an abundance of sense to him, being made into something senseless. Mrs Willis sees also, the wide valley cut by a motorway, humming with the noise of useless traffic. In an epic Western, she thinks, the brave warrior would turn tail and, in a cloud of dust, gallop off into a glorious sunset to meet another fine day, elsewhere. But where is elsewhere? He is, in fact, destined to be of the subordinate race, his virility wasted, harried, hunted until bound and impotent, he is driven into the desert or to squat ignominiously on the edge of the so-called civilization which has rejected him. She sees him on the burnt edge of London, living off the waste, the washing drying on a winter hedgerow, dirty children playing beside the dangerous road. It's not fair she says to the sky, thinking, actually, of the landscape of her youth. Where can they, where can they breathe free? [3] A stupid, Euro-centric poem, if there ever was one thinks this woman in an upstairs room in Fulham on a Tuesday morning late in July. But she feels passionate enough for all that, while behind her, unappreciated in the moment of passion, in another part of the house, sleeps one of her sons, who breathes carelessly. It is he, nonetheless, who warms her passion.

She thinks of the other children who have grown up in the house. How many? In eighty years. Ninety years. I must find out exactly when the house was built. There was a time when the

---

[3] *The New Colossus*, **Emma Lazarus**
Not like the brazen giant of Greek fame,
With conquering limbs astride from land to land;
Here at our sea-washed, sunset gates shall stand
A mighty woman with a torch, whose flame
Is the imprisoned lightning, and her name
Mother of Exiles. From her beacon-hand
Glows world-wide welcome; her mild eyes command
The air-bridged harbour that twin cities frame.
 Keep, ancient lands, your storied pomp!' cries she
With silent lips. 'Give me your tired, your poor,
Your huddled masses yearning to breathe free,
The wretched refuse of your teeming shore.
Send these, the homeless, tempest-tossed to me,
I lift my lamp beside the golden door.'

house was not here, but now it is, as a well-established fact, pressing down upon the earth. When exactly were laid down the foundations of ... of ... of what? The sky, towards which she has been facing through all her thoughts, catches her specific attention again. Through cracks in it, the sun is now evident. She imagines the blinding reality of the brightness above London's silver roof.

A bedewed field, she writes, elm trees and a hawthorn hedge heavy with summer growth, children hurrying for the blackberries. Gypsy children, perhaps, in their wild youth and innocent of the rejection to come. Or perhaps they play on a fragment of wasteland amongst the gravel pits, brick fields and remnants of market gardens, where disconnected bits of buildings wait to be joined up, amongst them the one which is now inhabited by the Pryce-Williamses. An aged horse, struggling cabbages and a hoarding which says houses to let on this site, eighteen shillings a week? I must look that up too. What did a house cost in eighteen eighty whenever it was?

A gypsy camp then, a couple of old-fashioned, horse-drawn, caravans she remembers seeing in a book of old photographs, Victorian Surrey. An old crone sits by a smoky fire, remembering her father, the navvy who helped to build the railways pushing a wheelbarrow up the steep side of the Surbiton cutting, cutting through the gentle countryside of woods, gentlemen's seats and grateful cottages, the distant Thames a flash of silver in the trees seen from Ditton Hill. They moved on, she hopes, to the corner of an old orchard now buried beneath the Kingston Bypass.

And what about the children? The children who picked the blackberries? What happened to them? What happened to all the children who walked out of the front door of this house for the last time. Out into a hopeful morning like this one? To war, she thinks, seeing her own children, the Boer War, the Great War, the Second World War. She has a vision of front doors flying open and a flood of young men pouring into the street, all looking, somehow, like her sons. Laughing they are and patting one another on the back, playing games, sharing cigarettes. They are in khaki but they are gone. Left behind, only a memory of laughter, crushed, in the end, by the thump, thump, thump of marching boots, echoing in the empty street, through which the dusty wind blows. They are buried beneath ... beneath all sorts of things, and forgotten.

Mrs Willis is torn apart by her emotions: part of her cannot move, so drugged is she by her own sensational imagination; another part wants to rush into the back room where the boy sleeps and will probably sleep beyond lunchtime and into the best part of the day, given the chance. I am a useless woman. What do I do but stare out at the world? She wants to look at him, to be sure he is there. Instead, she looks down into the street, at her own front gate, past which a girl, not a child, not quite a woman, is passing. Her attitude is aggressive but her legs, exposed below shorts, are fragile, unable to carry the weight of her determination. She is in pain and she is alone, thinks Mrs Willis, and she is Alice Pryce-Williams. What on earth is she doing out this early in the summer holidays? Children, adolescents, don't get out of bed at this time unless they have to go to school or unless something is wrong.

Mrs Willis thinks of opening the window and shouting but it is too late. I must speak to her. Rob, Robby, she calls as she goes downstairs wondering where she has left her shoes, I'm going out for a minute. He does not hear. The book is discarded upon the table:

... and the evictions that continued to take place were small erosions as the small lairds aped their superiors, leased their land to sheepmen and took their gentility southward to the terraces of Edinburgh or the squares of London.

[][][]

"Alice. Alice, where are you going?"

Alice begins to walk faster, almost running. She is a wild animal that must not be frightened.

Mrs Willis stops and calls quietly: "Alice, Alice come and have some breakfast." So calmly, so lovingly, so like a caress, it is a wonder Alice hears at all. But she does.

She turns around wanting to make a spiteful face and to tell Mrs Willis to mind her own business. Instead, her expression dissolves. She wants to cry but she has learnt to control herself
"I've had breakfast ... thank you."
Mrs Willis imagines an unfinished bowl of cereal.
"Will you come and have some more?"
Alice wants to be persuaded.
"Alright."
So it is alright. They retrace their steps together, Alice surprised she wants to chat.

[][][]

The kitchen of the Willis house is a large room, which takes in what had once been the dining room. When Mr Willis knocked out the wall with an inexpert idea of structural engineering and the load-bearing nature of walls, the whole back of the house threatened to collapse. The back bedrooms were evacuated of small children, while professional builders, procured at enormous emergency expense, shored up the happy home. The final solution had been, still was, a steel girder of industrial proportions supported by steel uprights, no less industrially massive. These uprights were set into reinforced concrete dug down below the original foundations, disturbing, as it happened, medieval soil, evidence of past inhabitants who had rested for a while on the land, a tiny piece of charcoal, a fragment of pottery. A cosy Victorian backroom, narrow French windows, a bit of stained glass, cast-iron fireplace with Minton tiles, all gone. The loss regretted but not mentioned so as not to hurt your father. In their place, a sort of garage, stranded, the new concrete floor waiting for oil stains, and a debt ruling out any chance of completing the project, at any rate not in my lifetime but we've got the space in which ... to live. And they did: the sink remained together with the plumbing for the washing machine and various bits of furniture accumulated over the years to make a comfortable place for a family held together by love rather than by things. The industrial installations were eventually painted over, first with blood-red rust-resistant paint, then, some years later, with black, ideal, so the label on the tin said, for exterior wrought-ironwork. A variety of abstractions and graphic observations of life were posted on the walls, ranging from the infantile to the adolescent, and in the end, the profoundly wise. Che Guevara was a hero. From the kitchen end, the room looked large and somehow naked despite the clutter, suggesting years more of possibilities to be realised. On winters' nights it was brightly lit, throwing light out into the garden but today, on a summer's morning becoming bright, it is the garden that fills the room. Alice sits at the large table having not said a word. Mrs Willis is doing breakfast, frying things on a gas stove.

Alice had accepted the apparent disorder of the house with relief. She did not feel in the way as she sometimes did at home. She could have hung around all day, all week, and no one, she felt, would have minded. She was right. The only thing she was a little nervous about was the possibility of bumping into Mr Willis. She was not sure how she would deal with him, his bald head, his breath, which smelled of toothpaste, his sudden bursts of laughter, and his strangely young voice, which would say things like you'll be breaking hearts one of these days young lady, so that, actually, I felt older than him in my knowledge of the world and I had the idea of breaking plates rather than hearts. And the plates had names on them but looking at Mrs Willis, busy at the stove, not trying to make polite conversation at all, she decided she liked her. Her plate would remain intact but holding the one with Mummy written on it, she smashed it on the concrete floor, feeling only a little bit guilty as the silent fragments blew away like autumn leaves.

"Robby, Rob, Rob, breakfast," Mrs Willis calls up the stairs, apparently bringing to some sort of consciousness the sleeper in the smaller of the two back bedrooms. He is, as it happens, already half awake, enjoying the idea of a day ahead in which nothing had to be done but within which anything might happen, the place being, as he expressed it himself, the bosom of my darling family. He meant it, he would do things for his mother for the joy of doing them. That her sons were not slobs was a pleasure to Mrs Willis. She left them alone and never nagged.

Doing nothing was an honourable occupation in the Willis household based upon the assumption that your larger life was otherwise useful to mankind but Robby, who was Robby, indeed, in the bosom of his family for all his Rob-ness elsewhere, intended to spend some of the day gardening, which he liked as much as he liked music. The Willis garden, semi-wild, apple trees as old as the house, the pear tree planted by Mrs Willis in the early days, was mostly Robby's creature, lovingly tended by Mr Willis during his son's physical absence.

But doing nothing, and gardening, was to be an unlikely option on this day. The tone of Mrs Willis's voice from downstairs, loving and apparently undemanding though it was, suggested to Rob that he was needed and, if he really wanted to please his mother, although she was not likely to make a fuss, then he was needed now, now, if you wouldn't mind too much. Naturally, therefore, he bounced out of bed, stood up straight, touched his toes, hair, brown and youthful gold, brushing the floor, and stretched out his fine young body towards heaven, hands open to take and deal with whatever might come. See Mum, this is how I do it for you. No stroppy business. Two minutes and I'll be with you. Let me brush my teeth first.

So that she will not wonder if he is up and about, he puts on a tape, quite loud to announce his activity: organ music by Messiaen, which sounds wonderfully weird to his youthful ears, but not so much to his mother's despite her preference for Rachmaninov. When it stops, she will know he is on the way. The great thing about my mum, he had said, when he was more a teenager than a young man, is that she does not make a fuss. Neither, he added a few years later – his thought processes were protracted – is she tight-lipped about it.

Indeed, Mrs Willis was not one to make a fuss, but she was able to speak her mind; she would not keep her children, or even her husband, in emotional suspense. Where were you when I needed you, you bad boy, she said to all her beloved men.

The music stopped. And when Robby poured into the room he was so big that there was a rush of the air displaced. It rattled the plates on the dresser, it pushed at the back door, it escaped through the open window, shifting the leaves of the pear tree.

Alice felt herself sway in a warm breeze. She shifted also, on her chair, a little, as if to make way for, oh, a dozen careless young men ready to ignore her. She wanted to bite her nails but she didn't. They sat side by side. She liked the sleepy smell of him.

But he was wide awake interested in this stray my mother had found. He spoke to Alice, nonetheless, as if she had always been in the house: "Hello," absent-mindedly, as he helped himself to cereal. He knew the Pryce-Williams girls as other children in the street but not much better. He had watched them grow up and thought them aloof and snobbish at first until he understood their detachment as a studied indifference to the rough and dirty sex of which he had been, when younger, a prime example.

Alice, as an advanced ten or eleven year old had confided in Sonia, some years earlier, as if it was a secret of which she was half ashamed, half proud, I wouldn't want that dirty Robby Willis to touch me. He doesn't wash his hands when he's skinned a cat. She had a picture in her head of him doing something repulsive with his hands in a methodical way, biting his lip as he concentrated on a task which would make her look away but not walk away. Now, she looked at his hands and liked them. They were clean enough. Long and competent looking. As if they could do anything. His mind, she thought later, was the same: he had ideas which she found herself falling in with. Much later in her life she said I would have done something bad if he'd asked me. And in those days I could have done something very bad – killed an animal for the pleasure of it. But the Willises put me on the right track.

Robby, Rob he would have to be to the adolescent Alice, was like his mother: a large-boned sort of person but, unlike her, as a man, he had not complete control of his limbs. They would shoot out and damage small unimportant things and be forgiven, or else go in the wrong direction before they collected their thoughts. All the same, once settled, he could sit quietly enough, sprawled over a chair too small for him although he was not tall for a young man in those days in southwest London a little under six foot. He was as spare as a man of that age who could be energetic should be but, like his younger neighbour, Harry Pryce-Williams, he had what Sonia and Alice agreed were presentable shoulders. He cut his own hair, which, as a result, was thick, like his mother's but longer. Tie it back she would say, thinking he looked like Rasputin, only more fair, with the same kind eyes shining through the obsession. That's bourgeois, Mum. Which is what we are, she'd reply. That's why you're tall and had music lessons. There was a piano in the front room – that part of the house which had escaped Mr Willis's attentions – but Robby had preferred the violin and moved from there on to the guitar.

The essence of Rob was his music. No one denied it him. It was a fact of the Willis family. Alice looked unmusical, fragile, pale and hungry beside him. Without asking, Mrs Willis put bacon and eggs, orange juice and a pile of bread and butter in front of them. Then she left the room without a word.

Alice wanted to swing her legs, look out the window, and ignore the boy beside her, but she was fascinated by his hands, which were feeding him. She took a piece of bread and butter and slid it under a fried egg with the idea of offering it to him like she might feed an animal. Poking a lettuce leaf at the pet rabbit, for instance.

"Mummy says this is not healthy food," she said. She might as well use her mother against him.

"That's why you're so skinny. You wouldn't last a day in" – he searched for a word – "in the world."

"I would."

"Alright." He swigged orange juice.

She ate the fried egg very daintily, as if it was a great delicacy.

It amused him. These Pryce-Williamses, he thought. He said.

"Put some salt and vinegar on it."

She obeyed, wanting to be asked what she was doing in the house.

He said nothing, apparently absorbed in the process of eating an enormous quantity of food.

"What was that funny music?" Thinking, you are an even funnier boy I want to laugh at you but you don't look bad on this food.

Rob explained, telling her that Messiaen had been a prisoner of war and that he was fascinated by the sounds birds made.

"Messy who?"

He laughed.

She laughed, eating more food than she had eaten for days.

He watched her.

"You are like the *Turangalila Symphony*."

She pretended to ignore him having not the faintest idea what he was talking about. But she took in every sound he made, listening out for the noise of his eating.

Later in the morning, Mrs Willis heard music, the sound of which she was familiar but she did not know the name. What did she say, she wanted to ask, when her son burst in on her later, but she kept her mouth shut and accepted his explanation.

"There's trouble in that family. You'd better go home with her, I'll start the supper."

24 Groping After It

She forgot the luggage and the motor-cars, and the hurrying men who know so much and connect so little. She recaptured the sense of space, which is the basis of all earthly beauty, and, starting from Howard's End, she attempted to realize England. She failed - visions do not come when we try, though they may come through trying. But an unexpected love of the island awoke in her, connecting on this side with the joys of the flesh, on that with the inconceivable. Helen and her father had known this love, poor Leonard Bast was groping after it, but it had been hidden from Margaret till this afternoon. It had certainly come through the house and old Miss Avery. Through them: the notion of 'through' persisted; her mind trembled towards a conclusion which only the unwise have put into words. Then, veering back into warmth, it dwelt on ruddy bricks, flowering plum-trees, and all the tangible joys of, spring.

Howard's End, E M Forster.

Sonia was lying on the bed, reading, when they arrived. It was midday and Mrs Willis had the idea of getting lunch ready with the two of them. Then she would take them shopping. They could go to Hammersmith Broadway.

To her initial relief the house was clean and tidy. Much too clean and tidy she thought almost unconsciously, as Alice and Sonia showed her round. Typical of the Pryce-Williamses, who held themselves too tight, as if they might explode any minute. And do them good if they did, she said to Mr Willis later. Better now for those girls, than when life has got more complicated. They walk around with their feet bound up if you ask me.

"I won't go in there," she said, when they came to what Alice called the parents' room – the words might have been painted on the door. David Pryce-Williams can wallow in his own mess. She gently shut the door. She would have locked it had she been able; and thrown away the key.

[][][]

It is an expensive furniture store and they have agreed upon the general awfulness of everything. Each thing they look at makes the two girls giggle more. Mrs Willis is beginning to wonder if they are not becoming a bit hysterical. She sits down on a sofa, hoping she won't have to ask them to be quiet. Sonia detaches herself from Alice who is inspecting a sideboard which she will one day recognize as sub-Sheraton in style via turn-of-the-century Tottenham Court Road only a lot less robust. She sits beside Mrs Willis, who tries to think that she is not prettier than her sister.

"You should have seen Granny's house. It was just right."

"In what way?" Mrs Willis is interested, remembering the elegant woman at the dinner party.

Sonia thought hard, screwing up her eyes but seeing nothing specific.

"I don't know. It felt right. I can't remember. We've got some of the things at home."

Mrs Willis kept quiet, watching Alice who had moved on to a matching dining table and chairs, absorbed in her study of them.

"Mummy is different."

"Why?"

"In Granny's house I felt ..." She should have said she felt safe but it was not as if she associated her own home with danger. There was nothing frightening about the house in Fulham despite Alice saying there was a hidden room somewhere. But it was not the half-cellar below the stairs and there was no attic, the roof disappointingly flat when viewed from the road. Sometimes Sonia imagined herself living in the attic, which wasn't there, safe in her own little space, which no one else knew about and into which she had spirited some of her grandmother's things. She imagined herself creeping down to the kitchen unseen to get food, using the bathroom in the dead of night when the house was asleep. I'd grow old in my tiny room in the roof, like a little mouse, and they'd move out and someone else would move in. An elderly lady who played the piano. I'd watch her playing but she wouldn't know I was there.

Mrs Willis said nothing. Alice was fingering a collection of curtain samples, apparently outraged by their grotesque patterns. She looked over her shoulder, wrinkling her nose. She seemed to say, quite pleasantly, like a grown-up woman, plain colours are what is wanted but Mrs Willis was not sure if she had imagined it.

"At home, it's different, I don't so much." Sonia was referring to something said, Mrs Willis had not caught. The girl felt she was betraying her mother, picturing her struggling through the jungle in New Sudan, which she imagined as the inside of the dark laurel shrubbery of Bishops Park where they were not supposed to go but where they had once seen two of the gardeners – young, short, dark men dressed in loose denim overalls – holding hands, who had shouted at them to go away and they had run off giggling but afraid wanting to hold hands in the same way.

[][][]

Three women sitting in a row on a sofa, Sonia in the middle holding Alice's hand, because Alice had joined them.

"This furniture's not honest," Alice said but she could not think why she felt that way and wanted to ask Mrs Willis what she thought.

And as if she had read her thoughts Mrs Willis said.

"It's because that chair was made to look like a chair someone else made a long time ago and it's not even a good copy. If you sat on it, I'm sure it'd creak. The engineering's wrong. It's not beautiful."

"Does a chair have to be beautiful?"

"Of course."

"Why?"

"Because if it is well made as a useful chair it must be beautiful. It's a matter of good engineering ... and no unnecessary decoration."

"Does that make it beautiful?"

"That is beauty ... in a thing."

"What about a person?" And Alice nearly added, without knowing why, like Rob, who was what Mrs Willis was thinking about also. How he had poured into the room making the air move.

"That's ... another sort of beauty. Beauty in the eye."

"What do you mean?"

But Mrs Willis again said nothing. She thought of all the people who made up her life. Who were sort of thrown at her and whom somehow she had to catch. Like Mavis, now safely under the protection of Mr Pierce. Like these two who seemed to be under the protection of no one. And their father, the odd man, she thought, who protected him?

"What eye?"

"Of the beholder."

"The person who looks?"

"Yes."

"Makes the beauty?"

"Sort of, but the person who is being looked at has to be worthy of ..."

"Of what?"

"Of love."

"But I'm not beautiful."

As if she had said I am not worthy, which made Mrs Willis almost gasp with pain, with anger and amazement. What makes a child think like that? It was terrible. So she laughed and said.

"You are, you are."

"Why?" Alice asked quite objectively, content, it seemed, to be not beautiful.

"Because you are loved."

"Who by?"

And Mrs Willis did not say by your parents because she could not have faced the challenge to that statement had it come. So she said.

"By Sonia and by me, now that I know you."

Alice smiled.

"Is Mr Willis beautiful?"

"Of course he is. He's a darling."

Both girls giggled.

Mrs Willis laughed also.

"I promise you that in my eyes he is very beautiful and he makes me feel like the most beautiful woman in the world."

Sonia turned to look at Mrs Willis, and indeed did see that she was beautiful although you could not say she was pretty like Mummy. And I was glad that I thought of my mother just then as a pretty woman.

Alice looked at her knees, making up her mind that she would rub cream into them and would never wear stupid shorts again. She stole a look at Mrs Willis who reminded her of Rob. He had spread out an old tartan rug with a hole in it over the bumpy grass, suggesting they lie down to look at the sky through the leafy branches of the pear tree. He had said this is what I like to do. When she had followed his example he added.

"I think about my life."

"Do you?" She had answered him only because she assumed he expected it.

"Yes," he paused, "but mostly about what is going to happen, because ... what has happened has happened. Don't you?"

Alice had not thought about it, her life having been, as she did begin to think about it, quite a long one, mostly spent with Sonia. The rest of the family was not real. Sometimes she was sure she had been born somewhere else. She thought of Mummy and Daddy and Harry as one family and herself as something separate. Separate even from Sonia who was her best friend but not her sister. The family was not real and now it had disappeared altogether. She giggled.

"So my wish has come true."

"What wish?"

"The wish that it was just me and Sonia in the house and they've gone."

"Gone where?"

"I don't know," and she explained what had happened and about the fight between Mummy and Daddy before Mummy went away with Harry: "And now Daddy's gone. He didn't come home last night." But instead of crying, she said: "I hate them."

"Do you? That's rather a strong emotion." came his cool reply.

"Well I don't like them at the moment, although I like my brother." In her head, for a moment, Rob was Harry beside her. Then because Rob said nothing she tried to picture her parents but I saw them in separate rooms. "Don't you hate your parents?" She wanted to be reassured.

He laughed.

"No! They make me laugh sometimes. But", he added, because he knew she wanted reassurance. "People do hate their parents, I think it's the normal thing."

"Do they wish them dead?" She wanted to shock him.

But he wasn't shocked.

"I'm sure they do, sometimes." He thought of taking her hand and he did indeed move his leg minutely nearer hers. But he took it back.

"I do, often, and now Daddy's been run over and Mummy and Harry've died in an air crash. I think I must have willed them dead." She sniffed and thought, now I ought to burst into tears but I don't feel like it.

Rob laughed again but he managed to say.

"I don't think it works like that."

So having got used to talking a little bit about her feelings to Rob, Alice found she could continue talking to Mrs Willis as an extension of Rob. In fact, she was unusually chatty talking about the furniture around them but not mentioning her parents once. When the man came to ask them if he could help, it was Alice said no thank you we think all the furniture here is ugly and instead of being offended he said yes I agree I tried to get a job at Heals but they said I was too old. On the way out Sonia said I feel sorry for him, Mrs Willis said yes, it's a disgrace he's not much older than me. Alice said:

"Where's Heals?"

"It's in the Tottenham Court Road. We could go tomorrow if you want."

Both girls said Yes please.

They walked home, keeping to the side streets Mrs Willis knew well. I thought it better to go straight back to their house and face the facts, she said later to Mr Willis, trying to get it all straight in her head. I thought we'd better meet their father, or else decide what to do if he didn't appear.

They did not reach the house until nearly eight o'clock because they stopped in a café which Mrs Willis called the Greasy Spoon.

"No good being hungry and I'll have to apologise to your mother for feeding you so badly. Tomorrow we'll go to a vegetarian restaurant I know in Carnaby Street. It's near Heals."

"Mummy never allows us to have chips at home," said Alice.

Mrs Willis thought I bet she doesn't but she said.

"She's quite right. They give you spots."

"Alice doesn't get spots," said Sonia, "but I do."

And Mrs Willis did not say, looking at the pair of them, it's the pretty ones who get the spots when they're young. But looking at Alice she could see she how she might attract a protective, confident sort of man. She was delicate looking, her skin translucent. The robust sort of men like that.

25　The Voice of Kindness

David was not home.

"Come back with me," says Mrs Willis.

They resist the idea.

"But you can't stay on your own here, in London, I'll stay with you."

"We can," says Alice, "we've done it already."

"I think it's against the law, you're still minors. Your father could get into trouble. Do you want that?"

Sonia said, quite decidedly.

"No we don't." But she didn't look at her sister.

Alice thought why can't Rob come round but then thought she didn't want him when Sonia was around. Then she felt sorry for her sister and was glad she felt sorry. She wanted to hold her hand. I'd feel sorry if Sonia was run over. Then I would want to cry.

In the end Mrs Willis was firm.

"Either I stay here or you come with me." She was wondering how long she should wait before she reported David's disappearance to the police. They would think it odd if she waited too long.

"We'll come along with you," Alice said quickly. "Come on Sonia."

"Have you got overnight bags?"

"Yes."

"Pack what you want for tonight and tomorrow. We'll go to Heals in the morning."

So it was decided and they trooped around the house together to be sure it was properly locked up and everything turned off.

Just as they were going Sonia said.

"What about Daddy? I don't want him to come back to an empty house." Adding, as if defending herself: "He'll wonder where we've gone. I think I ought to stay." She dropped her case on the floor and stared at the others defiantly.

For the first time in her life, Alice was torn: Should she support her sister, the only person in the family to whom she was solidly attached, or go with Mrs Willis? At the time, standing in the hall, I was not thinking beyond Mrs Willis, who was a person I liked but who was nothing to me compared to the reality of Sonia who was, in those days, like my twin, my Siamese twin, but I was acutely undecided, I remember. I wanted somebody to decide for me and say you are doing the right thing. I badly wanted to go with Mrs Willis, who I was quite sure was leading me to where I wanted to go; somewhere exciting and new, away from the family, from the family house. Not because I was especially disenchanted with it but because, I think, I wanted to start my life on my terms. I wanted to choose with whom I wanted to be. I didn't want to be where my birth had put me. They knew too much about me and I hated them for it. I don't think it's an unusual feeling at that age. But Sonia was holding me back. I almost disliked her for it.

"Come on Sonia, Daddy can look after himself. I'll write a note." Alice ran to the little hall table where a notepad lay beside the telephone: 'Dear Daddy, we've gone to tea with Mrs Willis. We may stay the night. I hope you are alright from Alice'. Then she added Sonia, put three kisses and a little heart like they had done when they were smaller, pushing notes under their parents' bedroom door, where they lay forever, as far as I know. No one ever responded to them.

Sonia looked at Mrs Willis, who smiled and held out her hand. Sonia took it. Mrs Willis said.

"Don't look so worried. I'll pop back later and talk to your father." Damn the man she thought, picturing him, immediately, fumbling around in the dark and empty house, lost. So in the end she felt sorry for him.

[][][]

I had not a great deal of affection for them. Nonetheless, I played the good father and they were what I might call a part of, a fixture if you like, of the happy home. I was, I thought I was, content. I had what I'd always wanted. What I remembered out of New Sudan was something belonging to my youth. Times past and all that. But when Sally went back, taking Harry with her, I felt I had been left behind, cut off forever from that throbbing, hot, colourful place which will always be – as I remember it – twice as alive, if not more so, than this bit of South West London which is, at best, a muted sort of place, which is mostly grey and on a hot summer afternoon the most unbearable place on earth. I am put down in it and I want to be out there, not in this grave I have dug for myself. I would rather die of malaria there with that man holding my hand than be here which is nowhere knowing that if I never see those two girls again I will soon forget them, very soon, if only I have that Wisdom in my arms. He stares into the tumbler resisting the strong desire to dash it at the wall – a fashionable shade of tomato red – and run away.

As he is about to get up she touches him, just above the wrist, as if she has heard every word and is replying yes, I understand. He does not jump because he is not a bit surprised to find her there in the kitchen, this woman who has sat at our dining table and looked interesting. Who is she? Indeed, worthy from the visual point of view, if that is the way to express it. She is a friend of my wife's and I suppose, therefore, she knows where the girls are.

He pulls himself together. If she wants to damn me, let her. I'll make it easy.

"Would you like a drink? Let's go into the garden."

He gets up, pulling himself away from her. He switches on the lights, pours her a sherry, dry, for which she has not asked. It's a bottle we bought for Mrs Grant who'll never drink it now so it's been relegated to the kitchen. He pours a draught into his own glass; quite a lot but he is not drunk, nowhere near it, that will come later. Or it might not, if she can get through the façade of him. For now he is thinking quite straight but his head is full of ideas, one of which is the idea of packing a bag and running away. She can take the girls until Sally comes back I couldn't care a fuck. I'm director of quite a large and distinguished company in the City. I have a reputation for organising things and getting them done. I've been known to cut costs by thirty percent and get an enterprise into the black just by improving the administration. Some people would say it's not real management but it makes money and it's got us this house in Fulham and later, if things had gone on as they might have done, something large and very solid on the Putney side of West Hill, Wandsworth.

She follows him out of the back door, into the little yard and up a couple of steps into the garden, which does not have the overgrown and almost wild nature of her own; more a feeling of abandonment. She had expected to see bits of rubbish lying around, a broken push-chair on its side, one of the greenhouse panes broken, the smell of damp brickwork, but it was just an idea I had, there was nothing that an afternoon's gardening would not have put right. We sat on a bench beside the little shed, looking back at the house, from which shone the small light of a small window which must have once been that of a scullery. It was oddly near the ground, a cool storage place in the days before refrigerators. From above, the illuminated London night reflected back from a bank of brown-silver clouds, dirty, I wanted to wash my hair. I felt I was inside one of those great hangers near Bedford built for the airship things. We were trapped together in a great room and I was no longer angry with him. What could he do? His wife, the mother of Alice, gone, I was sorry for him.

I wanted to have a blazing row with someone and she would have done but she might have said damn you take your children back. I didn't know what sort of woman she was, then. I didn't know she was the sort who seemed to have lived before so that in this life they start out wise and are not bothered by all the petty things we think so important but which are, in fact, worthless. People like me have to start learning from the beginning. It's painful and we make a mess of it.

They understood each other, and indeed because he had forgotten how old he had become, thinking he was still the boy in New Sudan, he treated her as being older than him by a much wider margin than she was. I felt she was old enough to be my mother.

"Their mother will be back next month, then I will take a holiday on my own. I think I can manage them 'til then." But I'm lying and I know it because the truth is she will come back to someone else and the boy perhaps I will not see again. I cannot manage those children day after day. I don't know who they are: the one so quiet she is half a shadow, the other like a flash of lightening which might strike me dead.

"When did you last have a holiday?"

"Oh ... Christmas, New Year. The usual thing." He might just as well have said sixteen or seventeen years ago, when I was with that chap in New Sudan only they dragged me away. What difference would it have made if I'd stayed? The girls would not have been born. I might have worked it through, got it out of my system, only it doesn't work like that and anyway, come to think of it, he didn't want me. I'd forgotten that. It was the other he wanted, that dark, dark thing as densely black as a black hole, who seems to have got everything I wanted.

"I don't need holidays."

But she understood him. This house beautiful, the Tube, Parsons Green to Temple, wherever it was.

"Is that a life?"

"No!" He laughed. "I read about lives, about great lives in badly written books, which do not do them justice. Who wants to know about Oliver Cromwell if you don't know what it was like to be him? What did he feel like at six o'clock in the morning? What was more important? His piles or the subjugation of Ireland? For God's sake. Shakespeare could do it but there's only one of those every five hundred years. Have you read Richard the II?"

"I saw it once, years ago."

"He wasn't a bad king. Quite good in fact but very young. Eighteen or something at the beginning."

She thought of Rob.

"And everyone wanting war and he was a sensitive type. Drove him mad in the end and he did stupid, paranoid things. His beloved died when he was a young man. In the end they murdered him, starved him to death, or something, in Pontefract Castle. Imagine doing that to Edward Heath?"

She could not.

"Edward Heath would be older."

"Do you like music?"

"Yes." Again she thought of Rob.

"I love it. The bigger the better. Beethoven symphonies, the *Misa Solemnis*. Brahms I remember when I was a student. It was the gallery of the Albert Hall, lying on the floor. I'd never heard anything like it. Do you know the Sibelius Fifth?"

"Yes."

"Do you like it?"

"Not really."

"Why not?"

"It's too big. He wants to dominate you. Beethoven takes you along for all his grandeur and confidence but in the end ..." She stopped herself. She wanted him to talk but he said nothing so she continued. "It's only a description of our poor humanity. Music should be an inspiration but we make it a substitute for life."

"When I was with him I didn't hear the Sibelius Fifth, I didn't want it. I heard the blood pounding in my ears. I felt his body in my arms." He talked as if to himself. "In the city here ... we need music. Some music."

"Go on," she said.

"You look at these houses which are very ordinary houses we would not have been seen dead in eighty years ago and we think we're lucky to have one now."

"We are."

"But it's what they stand for. A house in Fulham, which used to be a despised suburb but which is now an extension of Chelsea, the Kings Road and all that ..." He wanted to say shit.

"But I like my house and I've sat in my window and I've looked at the moon above the roof tops and I've listened to Chopin on the radio and I haven't thought I wasn't living my life." She said it to help him, not to brag.

"My wife does that. But is it all there is?"

"Not at all. It's not the substance" – she thought of the ironing – "it's, it's sitting back and contemplating your, your soul. If you like."

"Yeah, it's not the substance alright. It's not what you want to think you've done with your life when you're dying. Written it, played it, danced to it not only listened to it."

She looked at him.

"You want to dance?"

"In a way, yes, I do."

"Then what's stopping you?" If he'd asked her she would have danced with him.

He waved his hand at the house

"All this." It was as if he had prepared a speech and decided not to say it. Why waste his breath telling people what they already know.

She said nothing.

He nonetheless answered her

"No, you're right. And you don't have to tell me it's the inside that counts. I know that. In the end it's me on my own. I can't blame them and all this. And if I was free I'd live the same way. I like my job. I'd have a house in Islington and it'd be done just so. I'd do it in the style of the year of The Congress of Vienna." And he added after a pause: "I've often thought about it."

"Don't you like people?"

"Not really." He leaned back and looked into the wicked, wounded, London sky. "I see people hugging their relatives, their family, even crying and I think it must be fake."

"Why?"

"Because how can people feel like that? We're in ourselves. We can't get out. It's the way we're made. We're amoebas. Only a bit more complicated and we collect Spode china or bet on the horses. There's no sense in it."

"Yet you respond to the music?"

"But if all the family were killed in some dreadful accident, I'd feel nothing. I wouldn't feel devastated. I'd go on. I'd feel free. I just wouldn't think of the kids when they were small."

"It's because you've never loved anyone. You've never loved anyone body and soul. And you've never been loved in return." She wondered what on earth his parents had been like and she felt sorry for him. But he's intelligent. He knows what's what. He must get himself out of this hole and Sally must take the consequences. I don't suppose she's helped things. She's certainly never loved him. She said,

"What do you want to do?"

To pack my bag and go to Winston, Wisdom, was what he wanted to say. But she wouldn't understand. She's a woman. She doesn't know how men feel. Especially about each other. So he sighed, afraid to be completely honest with this honest woman, who had begun to break through the façade which protected the man. Had he told her what he felt she would have knitted her brows and said that's a tough one but it has to be faced and dealt with head on.

In answer to his silence she said.

"When did you say Sally gets back?"

"Next month."

"Then you must have a break before then."

"I ought to wait."

"But you can't talk to your, to Sally in this state of mind. You must know what you want, before then." I mean, she might have added, you can't just not come home again without telling anybody. That's not responsible. "It's not fair to Alice and Sonia."

"But I can't just leave them either. I mustn't let them down again. It's not their fault."

"It's not their fault but you won't help them or anyone, or yourself if you don't get things clear in your own head. Take a week or ten days off. Go, go walking in Derbyshire or Northumberland. It'll be beautiful now with the heather coming on. Say it's a sudden business trip. It might well have been. Can't you take a few days off?"

"Oh yes! Haven't I done that already? I'm more or less my own boss." And as if to prove it he said: "Alright, I'll do it," and starting to play the decisive David Pryce-Williams again he began to feel better. "Are you sure you can look after the girls? Do you mind? I can let you have their keep."

"I'll give you the bill when you get back!"

"Thanks." He nearly hugged her. That night he finished the book he was reading, and had a good night's rest.

Can the transports of first love be calmed, checked, turned to a cold suspicion of the future by a grave quotation from a work on political economy? I ask – is it conceivable? Is it possible? Would it be right? With my feet on the very shores of the sea and about to embrace my blue-eyed dream, what could a good-natured warning as to spoiling one's life mean to my youthful passion? It was the most unexpected and the last, too, of the many warnings I had received. It sounded to me very bizarre – and, uttered as it was in the very presence of my enchantress, like the voice of folly, the voice of ignorance. But I was not so callous or so stupid as not to recognize there also the voice of kindness. And then the vagueness of the warning – because what can be the meaning of the phrase: to spoil one's life? – arrested one's attention by its air of wise profundity...

A Personal Record, Joseph Conrad.

26 But There is no Need to Hand it On

Harry Williams was not quite thirty when he first set eyes upon Wanei. He was unsure of himself and awkward insomuch as he thought of himself as a freak who blundered clumsily around in a sensitive human world which would be horrified if it knew the things that went on inside his head. Lie low and say nothing was his motto up to the point in his life when he had done a small thing successfully. This was sorting out a run-down copra plantation. He surprised himself and therefore, foolishly, assumed he could do anything. Up to that time he had, by his social detachment, only appeared to be arrogant. He was not. Rather he had a low opinion of himself. But after the copra plantation, a tiny bit of what you could call arrogance entered and corrupted his soul. It was not so much that he thought himself better than everyone else but rather that he thought the sort of people he met in the club not worth his attention. He took Wanei back to the plantation like a man who had bought a slave, whom he would treat kindly but whom he would, undoubtedly, own.

To the human world around him, Harry Williams was shy, easy going, even kindly, despite the apparent arrogance. Good looking in a lean, outdoor way. Women would look at him more than once but he noticed them not. Nonetheless, and as quite the opposite of Wanei's Brother Michael, Harry Williams was essentially an opportunist, albeit not the calculating kind. He took what came to him and made the best of it in the simple terms by which he wanted to live. He had not set out to become a planter but having ended up running a plantation which was, in his own words, at the back of beyond and in the middle of nowhere, he liked it and stuck to it, quite tenaciously. But he had had no burning desire to be what he had become – Conrad's desire, for instance, to be a seaman – because, essentially, he did not believe he existed. In his mind's eye he was a blank space and because of this he did not have a positive moral philosophy. He had, rather, an idea of himself, himself in the public realm that is, which kept him out of trouble, as a man who could be trusted to get a job done and as a man who did not take things without paying for them. These things included human things. He could never believe that anyone would want him for his own sake, for the pleasure of his company. What defined him to most of the world in which he insubstantially moved was his desire – easy going, at first, rather than passionate – to be alone. After all, as his nearest neighbour – about fourteen kilometres up the coast – had said of him in the Markham Club, I hardly know Harry whatshisname. What is he? I don't know. Give me another drink.

I got to know Bro Mike because, at that time, I wanted a friend who was as detached and dispassionate as I was. Someone who would not get too close. And true to expectations, Bro Mike, the name Harry gave him, as if making some sort of personal claim, kept his distance. A small distance but a distance which was always there, narrow but impossible to leap, as if, as if he sensed my ability to corrupt him. In the end Bro Mike put Wanei between us so it was Wanei I took, waiting for him to corrupt me.

The efficiency of Wanei as a house-boy impressed Harry. Within days he was better fed, tidier, cleaner and altogether better organised than he had ever been in his life. He bossed Wanei around but Wanei was an irresistible force, serving meals, for instance, when he thought it was fit for Harry to eat them. They ate the same food but Wanei ate his, as he also thought fit, in the lean-to shed at the back which was the kitchen. All along it was Wanei who maintained appearances. On arrival he refused the little box of a spare room offered by Harry, preferring to sleep on a mat on the living-room floor. He was happy and he soon built himself a little hut out the back which was as comfortable as anything Harry had to offer.

[][][]

So Harry Williams lies on his bed trying to hear Wanei breathe beyond the curtain. He is in an agony of youthful night-time desire yet afraid to call on the ignorant god he worships. One night, one of a series of moonlit nights, I stood over the beauty on the floor watching it bathed in silver. I felt like a shit, my watching of him enough in itself to corrupt him. I wanted the silver thing there in the shadows of the night, the warm breath, the cool hands, the sweat, the almost feral smell of the man which made me feel so dizzy I had to squat on the floor beside him. I imagined his eye green, wicked, fearful yet desirable. I wanted him to be as bad as myself.

But Wanei was innocent, and could have been good. He grew to love the strange tall man, his skin so startlingly white where the sun had not touched. The softness of that skin, his malleable, subtle yet awkward body that would suddenly be as still as death itself and seem to stop breathing. Had not Wanei also watched in the night? Stood at the door listening? At other times also. They watched one another and when the time came, contact was gentle with a gentleness which surprised them both.

[][][]

Two men, damaged by life – Who isn't? – lonely as are such men. Not the loneliness of a man in a strange city seeking the company of the bar or a bought woman but the loneliness of a soul lost in a universe which makes no sense because it has no reason. There is no God. If I am all there is in the universe – not created because there is no creation – and this universe is the only space in which I move, then I am not even damned because there is nothing to damn me. Therefore, the hand stretching out to find another is the act of creation. The gentle connection when it came was, nonetheless, like a thunderbolt, an electric shock, which shook them so profoundly in the first few minutes of knowledge that they were never the same again. It was too big, far too big even to talk about but they were tied together, these two, forever. Two men dynamite, as the boys became men, together, the one making the other a man in his own way, fighting well enough to draw blood at times, but neither could sleep properly without the other nearby. It was not madness that drove Wanei to kill Harry Williams: it was the inevitable outcome from the beginning. One of them would have killed the other. Only Mac understood the explosive nature of the relationship and that because he almost loved Harry like a son. When it happened he was shocked but not surprised and knowing Harry as he did, his reaction was, obviously, that Harry had asked for it. He never blamed Wanei. Rather he felt hopelessly sorry for the man he barely began to understand: Harry was bad enough but this one is beyond my comprehension.

[][][]

It is a cliché to say that people come together, there is a dynamic reaction, and they draw apart forever traumatised but ready for the next, or rather the continuing, interaction. We are all monsters, to which we give the name Uncle Fred, Mummy, the Tollingtons next door, me, you, all of us for God's sake, humanity, which does terrible things and wonderful things. Things which would not happen without our neuroses. Without them we would indeed be David's amoebas. We do what we do and we don't know why we do it; if we do, we don't want to think about it. Did I do that thing because I want you? Because I want to get back at you? At someone else?

Philip Larkin's famous poem says it all.[4] The kids have to inherit all this… This shit, this potential, this amazing thing

---

[4] **This Be The Verse by Philip Larkin**
They fuck you up, your mum and dad.
They may not mean to, but they do.
They fill you with the faults they had
And add some extra, just for you.

But they were fucked up in their turn
By fools in old-style hats and coats,
Who half the time were soppy-stern
And half at one another's throats.

Man hands on misery to man.

called the experience of life, or of being alive; they have to handle it and pass it on. And the key character at this point is Harry Pryce-Williams. The name is confusing but that is his name and Harry is the link, the one defining the other. Without Harry there would have been no Harry, in both directions. And this young Harry has come to meet his father, the apparently mad murderer and worse – who took revenge on David, apparently, by fucking – it is the only word which describes the act, at any rate its initiation – by fucking David's wife, one half of the David-Sally beast.

It had happened before. That time a boy, biologically a young man, whom Harry, old Harry, Williams that is, had picked up in Markham with the idea of making the plantation clerk. The boy was girlish and wise in the ways of getting what he needed and what he needed was a job and the sort of comfortable security his soul, you could say, craved. A boy he was, but emphatically not one of the boys. Life would treat him rough, if he was not careful, he would end up dead on the beach, possibly mutilated in some horrible way. Harry was to be his salvation, he was not going to ask for much and he intended to do his job properly. He would suffer the humiliation of his life under the protective eye of a master. He had hoped it would turn out this way. Only Harry Williams, damn him, would look at the boy the young man in a way which said I appreciate your budding good looks small and well built by the streets although you have not the precise compact energy or the stubborn black force of the other one his eye glowing green in the night. Wanei saw all this and his anger with Harry made him decide to kill the boy. The obvious answer to a problem. He might have thought he was saving Harry from the boy but that idea did not enter his head. What drove Wanei was the comforting idea that we two are destined for each other and all that, he might have said, in his own way: separate us and you might as well lobotomise me or block out the sun. Get between our natural connection, which is, as it were, ordained by the whole way the world is put

---

It deepens like a coastal shelf.
Get out as early as you can,
And don't have any kids yourself.

together, and you will get hurt. The boy, let us call him Elan, was not hurt because he caught the green eye in time, and ran for his life. Harry came across him a few years later, behind the counter of a trade store, somewhere. He had two little tufts of hair on each side of a shiny bald head above unremarkable ears. He looked ridiculous in his tight clothes and the way he wiggled his bottom made me feel ashamed.

The night Elan ran away, Harry came to Wanei's little house. Wanei made room for him on the narrow bed. Not a word was exchanged. They lay side by side. Apparently no connection but Wanei's anger was terrific for all that he could not think, specifically, why he was angry. It was the carelessness, the casualness of Harry's whatever you could call it, his dalliance with Elan, that made Wanei want to kill, to commit a bloody act that would explain his state of mind. Harry put his hand on Wanei's chest, felt the raging heart, and pulled back as if he had been burned. A good thing or else his hand would have been bitten through. A good thing Elan ran far away, all the way to Port Markham, or else he too would have been bitten through. More so, for they would have stalked him, in the end, together, and caught him. They would have done things to him and left him for dead if not mutilated as well, such was the madness of that thick, moonless, tropical night. Wanei would have led the game, appeasing his anger in the process, Harry following, able to justify the action to himself by the very cool and calculated last act, strangulation or something like it. The law of the jungle, the way these chaps do things is amazing. He had seen a dead man lying on the roadside early one morning, years ago, his chest ripped open, the heart removed and the other organs also, all placed neatly on one side.

In sleep, the two had come together and in the morning the Elan episode was, apparently, forgotten. But it had drawn them closer, like outlaws who made their own rules. Only just below the level of consciousness they were ready to act, to keep the unwanted world away from them. They did act, a little later and that particular young man, more calculating than Elan, more in the Wanei mould altogether, who had fleetingly caught Harry's eye, was lucky to escape with a bruised neck – he was not as strong as Wanei but his fear gave him the advantage. Fate, it seemed, was keeping them away from the crime but had you studied their faces, as did Mac, you would have caught, in some expression, an unguarded thought flying through the brain, the change. In Wanei, a tightening of the jaw muscles, which, relaxing, then seemed to masticate some thoughtful meal, his fists nonetheless clenched, loosening only as the idea passed, the eye, dead, staring. Harry would look no less dead, his expression blank for seconds at a time as if in some sort of catatonic fit. Where's 'e gone? Some wag would say in the club, 'e's in 'is own little world. Give 'im a nudge. But they did not dare. They were afraid of him. He's mad, that fellow, stark raving, if you ask me. He'll do something funny one of these days. I need another drink.

[][][]

David and Sally had landed right in the middle of all this, unaware, obviously, of the dangers, noticing only something that seemed merely picturesque. Wanei, sensing David and Sally as the single David-Sally beast had, metaphorically, you could say, stabbed Sally, and his hands did indeed play around her neck for a moment or two. But his feelings had changed so subtly as he did it, that at the time, he barely recognised the emotional crisis of the moment. That was to dawn upon him years later. Suffice to it say, that at the time a tiny bit of what you could call affection entered his corrupted soul. All the same, and perhaps even as a result of that affection, David's return the following weekend would have been fatal had not Mac taken him home. Thereafter, Harry and Wanei became a creature of the night. They fairly ignored each other during the hours of daylight, as if there was something between them they did not want to look at. The apparent relationship of plantation manager and house-boy was no longer a difficult act. Each did his job in the appropriate way, the early youthful affection, arising from delightful novelty, having given way to something that was as deeply bad as it was irresistible. Yet neither of them could have described what it was that drove them. On a beautiful day, clear, with high cumulous clouds and a sea breeze, life was perfect, the smiles on their faces genuine. But the night, the night, the twelve hours of the thick tropical night, made them different animals altogether. In the dark, these two understood each other perfectly and wanted each other with a hunger that made them like ravenous beasts, dangerous but happy, sometimes deliriously so, mentally unbalanced they were, with no doubts about each other or about themselves. We rule the world. They were a single charge of energy, their senses sharpened by the darkness through which they moved. They were nocturnal animals, hunting, heartless to anything that crossed their path, capable of trampling it to death like the devil-man will trample the righteous one to a bloody pulp. Only the high, frozen, full moon could stop them. Then they would calmly watch the black and silver world beyond themselves, humbled by the height of their emotions, and loving to those around them. At such times Mac had visited, drawn to them in the seasons of the full moon, because at those times, Harry and Wanei would pick you up and love you like a child. But the moon has its own dark phases and is often obscured by cloud. In these dark times, when the night is a solid, wicked thing which roars, then, naked, a part of it, like the sacrificial blood in the oily river, Harry Williams and Wanei prowled, as if, you might say, they were the very devil in his element. Try taking them away from it and they would have fought you. Try prising them apart, impossible. They were young men still. They would have killed. Or, Wanei would have done, Harry going along with him. The law of the jungle is justified... in the jungle. No second thoughts. The very last man to pass through – half wild himself, from the gutters of Port Markham – did not stand a chance. He ended up in the swamp at the back where the crocs ate his body. Then Wanei, the blood lust up and in a raving madness of desire, turned to Harry, beating him to a bloody mess first, the man, the mad man, actually laughing as he received the blows, one eye blinded by gushing blood. He tries to grasp his maddened lover, to hold him close, to calm him, to love him, to say I was only playing games my Darling. I love you. To which Wanei replies, I'll love with these warm loving hands around your neck. I too can play games. Your neck is strong but I am stronger. I love you as I loved Brother Michael and I worship you even more but my god must be good and you are not good enough. An idea is better than poor reality. I'll love you to death. And he did, without regret, because the loving had only just begun. Wanei then ate Harry Williams.

[][][]

He ate him a night or two after the new moon. Mac thought he would visit, anticipating the pleasure of sitting on the veranda with his friends, listening to the sea crash upon the shore, driving back home in the early morning restored. He found Wanei alone, looking a bit the worse for wear, his skin grey and in need of a shave to the degree that a small woolly beard had materialised, but otherwise not much more wild looking than usual. Bachelor boys living alone on a farm are often dishevelled. He was squatting outside the house beside a dead fire.

The very last thing I expected to see was a cannibal feast. I did not see it. I assumed a goat and Harry somewhere in the vicinity. They did it from time to time and drank beer. Sometimes inviting some of the workers to join them. They might well have been smoking marijuana, which would have accounted for Wanei's dissipated appearance. But as I approached I could see something was wrong because even for the devious little bastard I assumed Wanei to be, he looked up at me in a distinctly odd way. Not quite a challenge but defiant all the same. Get out, it seemed to say, if you know what's good for you, and if I hadn't known him, I would have got out. And he's drunk, I thought, but as I was about to walk past him, to get to the veranda where I had intended to wait for Harry, the smell hit me. It was like a wet towel in the face. A filthy towel that smelt like an open cesspit. I wanted to gag. Wanei smelt like sin. Not that healthy smell of stale sweat you get from people who work hard in the sun but as I say, he smelt of sin. Shit and piss and vomit, I could have managed but this was worse, worse than rotten meat. I stepped back as if I'd hit an invisible wall.

"What the fuck, what the hell have you been doing Wanei?"

"I've eaten him," he answered in the local pidgin.

And I knew, immediately, he had. He'd sat there for a couple of days, butchering – a skill he'd learned at the mission – cooking, or perhaps not cooking all of it, and eating Harry's body.

I didn't look, then, at the litter all around. And afterwards, when I did, it didn't look so bad. The clothes had been removed and I never did find the head, although I didn't look hard, I didn't want to find it. Away from the smell, I can tell you, I wasn't in the least shocked, or even, really, much surprised. I wanted to laugh. I had seen a lot worse.

"But you can't eat your master?"

Have I not done so?

Had Harry died in some other way, murdered by persons unknown, for money, or drowned while bathing, I would have been badly affected, but killed and eaten by Wanei in what was obviously an act of love, however … however final, was a comfort to me. My own love for Harry, if that is what it was, was transferred to Wanei. The last thing I wanted was for him to suffer from an unfeeling system.

"Run away. I'll help you. They'll never find you in the bush." And they wouldn't have done, they wouldn't have bothered to look for the kanaka who killed Harry Williams, who himself was not rated very highly.

But it wouldn't have worked. I wasn't thinking properly. Where would one such as Wanei run to? He had nowhere else to go. He was a non-person. The greater part of him was defined by his love for the man he had eaten. There wasn't much else to him I thought then, and honestly, my heart went out to him. Having eaten Harry, Harry was truly a part of him. If you must kill the one you love then eating them is surely the right and proper thing to do.

I suppose I perverted the course of justice, or whatever it's called, but I was sure, absolutely, that Wanei was not mad, despite appearances. No doubt there was something in his genes that predisposed him to eating human flesh. Cannibalism had been a part of their culture until we'd disabused them of the habit. I knew the authorities in Port Markham, some of whom were drinking buddies in the club. They would listen to me, especially if I pretended to be outraged by the conduct of a house-boy, murdering his master and stealing his things. Trouble was, apart from the books, Harry had nothing worth stealing and Wanei placed little value on the written word. He despised the white man's literature.

[][][]

Indeed I did. These superfluous pages of writing. What did they say to a man? Harry would devour them but they gave him no pleasure. He always frowned when he was reading. It did him no good. Reading is a disease, and an addiction, a substitute for life. When I ate him I felt I was eating all the words he had taken inside himself. That's why I vomited. You cannot digest words men write down. You cannot digest their vanity, their desire to be remembered. What is writing but a sickness? You must throw it out and be yourself, your elemental self, uncorrupted by knowledge.

Yes Wanei, indeed, but it passes the time and allows you to forget your troubles. Between that age when we get to know ourselves and understand the fearful transitory pointlessness of our lives, and that time when it is nearly over, what else, in the end, is there to do but read? Or else we would think about the sudden and accidental nature of our lives. Terrifying thoughts. Banish them with the written word but now I must sort out the mess you've created.

I knew Wanei was not mad. Most likely he was saner than the rest of us. But hearing the details of what he had done, the world would lock Wanei up in the madhouse – New Sudan had such places, where you were generally put in chains – for the rest of his life. I wasn't going to let that happen. Harry wouldn't have wanted it for a start. Better the world believed it was some sort of argument between men which had ended in tragedy. A lover's tiff which had gone over the edge, if you like. People might think that and snigger, but that was what it was, after all. They'd only be sniggering at the truth, if I know men, afraid of it. About Wanei, the worst thing they'd say was he'd sold his bum for the best price. Half the world sells its body to the other half, anyway. It's how things work.

We cleared up what bits of the body were left and threw them in the swamp. Wanei was nonetheless adamant about not letting me have the head. Otherwise, quite cooperative; the house-boy doing his usual job in the end.

"Let me do the talking and keep your mouth shut."

He did, very efficiently, so that his silence and his downcast rather dusty appearance gave the little magistrate's court an impression of remorse, which may have been true for all the words I did get out of him.

He got ten years, seven, with remission. New Sudan prisons in those days were humane places of refuge. You got out most days cutting grass and cleaning out drains around Port Markham. In his red lap-lap Wanei looked fine and people gave him food but he would not look them in the eye. Had he done so he might have disorientated their souls and given them bad dreams. His one eye was bloodshot and had a staring, fixed quality as if he saw and saw something forever there in front of him which he could not quite make out although he had a good idea of what it might be.

I visited him from time to time but I could get nothing out of him. He'd greet me with a smile of sorts and thank me for the things I'd brought him and I'd remark he looked well. At first I wanted to talk about what had happened. Who else could I talk to but Wanei himself? But he had nothing to say. The deed was the thing. Why, he'd have said if he'd said anything, talk about it? Wanei defined himself, I began to understand, by action, and when he wasn't doing something he observed the people around him. I bet he observed Harry to the last detail. Indeed, he read him like you and I, the less sane part of humanity, read a book. What went on in that dark place inside his head when nobody was around, God only knows.

27 I Dreamed I was Dancing (David)

I dreamed I was dancing with her and having given me that piece of advice she said nothing more but she held me firmly. Indeed, she must have been guiding me because it was a step I did not know. But with her holding me I could do it. And then I was dancing on my own and Winston was sitting on a chair across the darkening room watching me. A small smile played on his lips, like the one on Harry Williams' lips all those years ago, when I wanted to stay with him but he knew I damn well wasn't up to it.

I woke up alone in a little room in one of those hotels north of the Park Bayswater. It was £14 a night; no one could say I was wasting money. I cannot say I was happy but I felt more free than I had for twenty years. Certainly since I took the front bedroom in Mrs Grant's house. Before the stupid idea formed in my head that I could make Sally into the sort of wife I thought I wanted. When I thought I had the whole household under my thumb including that boy whose name I have forgotten and who was putty in my hands and who has probably had a better life than me as a doctor in Hartlepool or somewhere like that. Only I was too stupid to see that Mrs Grant was the captain of that particular ship. I was barely the cabin boy but I assumed I could take Sally and bully her into being what I wanted. And for a while I thought I had got what I wanted: good wife, good job, commanding position, of sorts, in the world I wanted to be in, and a good house on the horizon given the money I was making. New Sudan, they all said, did it for me. It did do it for me, it gave me the sight, the smell, the feel, the taste of another world just to be sure I'd never be happy with the one I'd got. And the bloody irony is, that Sally has been exactly the sort of wife I wanted and she's been absolutely bloody sure we've lived the life I wanted. She's done a faultless job within the contractual terms I set. So good that there have been times when I've thought I was happy, getting off the tube at Parson's Green, walking home through a neighbourhood which has got better and more valuable with every year we've lived in the house she found and got so cheap. So how is it I want to find fault with her? Not for her, her dalliance with that dark, dark force or whatever it was, out of which came our Harry whom I feel is no less mine than is Sonia and more so than Alice who might have come from China or from Mars for all the connection I feel with her. It is, I suppose, because none of it was what I wanted. I daren't blame myself.

Winston – alright Wisdom but he's Winston to me for all he's as wise as a cat – Winston was kind to me but I wish he'd been rough, roughed me up. Then I would have thought I was lucky to have got away from him, with my life. But his kindness, his gentleness, his wisdom, was worse than anything bad he might have said or done to me. He made me love him, or at any rate, want him all the more. He was, he is, lovable but he sent me away all the same. So I am not worthy of his love, just as I was, I am, not worthy of the love of Harry, before. I'm damned but he's an angel and he'll go straight to heaven into God's arms. So I ought not to be happy, but at this moment, the grey London dawn creeping into the room, I feel as calm and as reflective as ever. Man, he said, in that wide accent which I suppose is West Indian, Jamaican music to my ears now I listen out for it in the streets, Man, you an' me, we're too different. You live up there – he pointed to Putney or Muswell Hills – I live down here – he pointed a long elegant finger at the expensive carpet beneath his feet, toes widely spaced like his teeth nothing tight or closed-up about him. Anyways, he looked out of the window at the sky but he was listening to the noise of the street, you'd cramp my style. It'd be like living with me granny. He turned back and looked at me and then slapped me gently on the face. He let me love him one last time. I ate him wanting his whole body and a part of his soul as well but I couldn't get at him enough. His beautiful body, his tough gentle nature was too good for me. Call me, he said as I left. I did, last night, but someone else answered. It always will be, I know that.

A woman's voice, South Kensington type of accent or perhaps the affluent Surrey suburbs. White, I was sure of that. Perhaps she was his secretary. Arranges his diary.

There is no television in this cramped room, which is nonetheless clean, but there is a radio built into the headboard of the bed.

He switches it on and fiddles with the knob which wants to fall off. Eventually he picks up Radio Four and thus tunes into London and the political wrangling of Westminster. Swansea, Aberdeen and Droitwich do not exist in the world of the BBC. He sees, in his head, that part of Fulham in which he used to live. That little knot of streets is where they get their world view, or Hampstead – he pictures the view of London from Parliament Hill – if they can afford it, Highgate-Muswell Hill if they can't. Portland Place is slap in the middle and for some reason he sees a balloon rising above Regents Park, gaily painted with fashionable ladies in a basket suspended below. They are looking down onto a view of pale-green, water-coloured fields which will be covered with railway lines and packed with cheap houses any minute.

The man who is still young moves easily around inside the small room. He is a little on the heavy side – those city lunches – and his hair is not as thick as it was. His buttocks sag just a tiny bit although they invite a slap or two but you would say he was thick-set rather than fat and quite healthy from all that London walking. He has already lost a few pounds and will lose more over the next twelve months. His chin and his cheekbones will become noticeable. He will have quite a Nordic look about him, especially when his hair is cut short. Later that morning, as he moves around the little dining-room in the basement – bright light, cheap pine and everything comes from a packet except for the toast which pops up – he looks like an American tourist in his chequered shirt and his expensive jeans. He wears those moccasin style shoes that are not very waterproof but fashionable at that time in southwest London. He has decided to spend the day in the Victoria and Albert Museum. As he walks across Kensington Gardens – Lancaster Gate towards Gloucester Road – he thinks not of his children with whom he has walked the same spaces. Rather he is glad to be unencumbered with family. This is the life! He is, he discovers, as an idea lost but happily recovered, happy to be in his own company. Happier, he suddenly realises, his heart beating for joy, than he has felt since, since he cannot remember. Since he was a boy walking through the hot bracken on the hills behind the grubby town. He stops, looks up at the sky where scraps of cloud are being blown eastwards. He hears the leaves rustling in the fresh morning breeze. The hum of the traffic behind is nothing. Here I am, he thinks, alive and glad to be so, looking at the sky and looking forward to the day. He pictures himself walking down Putney Hill on a grey drizzling London morning, going for the tube which will be crowded with other commuters, those who have got on at Wimbledon, Wimbledon Park and Southfields having got the seats. I'd be happy doing that. Thus he continues forward and we lose him amongst the thoughts of the other morning walkers. He is not the man with the dog on a lead.

[][][]

When you are young and lean as is Wisdom you wear the close-fitting clothes and the cocky hat of the street. Indeed you strut the streets about Earls Court Road. The waisted shirt open to show your chest, the tight trousers to show off your crotch. The bulge, the bump, the packet, your living. The other young man walks towards you dressed from the Sunday supplement and pushing, for God's sake, a pushchair, with a baby in it. And you look at his face until you know he sees you. And you see his eyes appraise your body resting on your bulge which moves like an animal stirring. Poor fucking bastard he is in hell, inside the cage he has built for himself and the family he hates and who hate him only they don't understand their feelings and if he didn't come home one evening they would not miss him and over the years they have built up a false image of the man they had wanted as a husband, a father. The man who had dreamed once he was lying in bed with the smooth, young body of a black man. One of those naughty boys from the streets who die young from a bullet inside the police compound in the dead dark morning. But he awoke and searched around in the bed for the young man who was not there. Instead he touched his wife whose flesh was, at that moment, in the night, repulsive to him. So he thought his heart was broken and would never mend and he wanted to kill her God help the poor bastard. David escaped all that, just in time. But it didn't do him any good, either.

28   Wanei, and, at any rate, Sons

Surely Harry could have found his own way back. Somehow. Mac wishes he had stayed at home. He feels the sun on his back the minute he steps out of the truck. Since he last trod it, the path has been abandoned. The tall, prickly grass presses in on him annoyingly. He expects to find his path blocked. But he presses on, feeling, suddenly, that something has happened to which only he can attend. Hurry, hurry but despite his determination to push past the ruined bungalow, he stops dead in front of it as if it is a crouching tiger. He stares at the dead skeleton of the building, at a small tree pushing vigorously between naked joists towards rafters which no longer support a roof.

He watches the tree grow, the leaves unfolding one by one, each turning to face the sun. So he imagines his past, and with such a burning desire to have it back, his body heaving with the memories, that it hurts: Give It Back To Me So That I May Rebuild The House. He challenges the universe, and so the desiccated bush all around falls away, the ruined house puts on flesh and the view beyond opens to the endless sea and the great sky above. For a heartbreaking moment he thinks, I am young, I can do what I like, I have all the time in the world. But there, sitting on the steps, is the old Harry, like life itself, sly and manipulative. He looks up at Mac, screwing up his eyes in the sun: take me or leave me Mac but this is how I am. This is how life is. It eats you up. The sun lights up his young face which is nonetheless corrupted by the desire for corruption. Behind him in the shadows of the house is Wanei, the one eye glowing in the dark. How is it, thinks Mac, that this place, quiet under the sky, the wide sea an ever-forceful presence, should be so corrupted? He remembers the other young man, pompous, foolish, deluded and yet sturdy in his youthful prime despite the firm muscular body promising flab. What had made him want to throw up everything for the worthless life of a beach-bum? To be used and abused by Harry? Who was, of course, fascinating, and undoubtedly the cause of all this, this whatever it is, which is, nonetheless, not – and Mac shouted it out loud – bad. It Is Not Bad. Life, the life we had was a good thing. I won't damn you Harry, I love you, my son.

I'm mad, he thinks, and shakes his head, smiling, the ruin is a ruin, the heat of today beats upon his back, Harry is not there, sitting on the step, the insects scream and the sea thunders on the shore as it has always done, breaking down the memories, one by one. He laughs out loud: you're lucky, Harry, you never got old and you'll be here 'til Kingdom come but I'm still alive and I'll deal with the reality of whatever happens to me for a few more years. If I bump against the others in the process, so let it be.

"Wanei!" He shouts out. "Where are you, you bugger?"

[][][]

No reply, and he thinks: it's going to be a nuisance if he's eaten the boy. But in his mind's eye, Mac sees the Norman Rockwell picture of disconsolate father sitting on the railway platform beside bright-eyed son packed up and ready to go to summer camp... or to war. So he is surprised to find Wanei whistling happily as he does the housework around the little hut, a pot of rice boiling over the fire.

"Wanei! Why are you happy?"

"Boss?" Seeming to wink.

"Where's Harry? Your son? You haven't eaten him, have you?"

Wanei does not pat his tummy but gestures to the beach, and gets on with his work.

"We'll eat when you get back." I've been expecting you. I had been waiting for you to come and sort things out for me but to tell you the truth I don't need you now. I haven't felt so happy for years. Not since the time when Brother Michael was my friend but last night I came upon the house which was a finished product, solid, sound, resting on the ground firmly, challenging the earth. Like Harry's house in the old days but better: curtains at the windows like they had at the mission, and comfortable chairs, with cushions, on the veranda, and I found appealing the idea of sitting on one of those chairs looking out at the world. There would be someone else, whom I loved, sitting on one of the other chairs, and we would be talking, from the depths of our hearts, about what has to be done. And indeed, as I drew near, I felt I was walking towards the house as an act of definition, and the choice was mine. So that there arose out of one of the chairs, where he had been waiting for me, my son. How could I resist such an attraction? He opened his arms, and I took him in mine for a moment, hugging him tight. Then I let go, and it was his turn to move off into the world, while I kept the home warm for him. Oh, I feel so happy, which is why I am whistling now.

But by this time, Mac had moved on towards the beach, nonetheless infected by the happy whistling. This is not the Wanei I know or rather this is not the Wanei I had thought about. The eating of old Harry must indeed have been a joyous affair. And as he thinks thus, so he sees the young Harry seated on the sand beside the sea. He has his legs drawn up and he rests his head upon folded arms, looking out towards the horizon, Mac assumes, thoughtfully.

As it happens, Harry's mind is a blank but it is not resistant to ideas, so that Mac, watching, sees him grow larger: a wild boy, the sturdy legs, burned dark brown by the sun, nonetheless suggest an innocent blush, the arms are almost black and, as he draws closer, Mac sees that Harry's hair has grown, prodigiously, standing up in woolly tufts within which bits of grass are fixed. Indeed like his father's hair in the days Mac assumed him to be mad. A wild boy, who might spring up and run away if approached too suddenly. Mac imagines watchful, suspicious eyes, avoiding contact. An animal, perhaps dangerous. There is in Harry's blood, after all, the something that Mac can only understand as cannibalism.

Mac was afraid Harry would argue against the idea of returning to London to continue his education. Why, he might say, make good in a bad world? And is New Sudan not good? Is it not the reason I am here? I have run away from the world. Life on the beach is a struggle for survival, but even a short life, if vivid, is better than a London suburb.

"And who am I," Mac said out loud, "to persuade you otherwise?"

Which the boy assumed was no more than the ravings expected from one so monumentally old. He turned round and met Mac with an open smile. Here was a man who will not have secrets, who could not hold them even if he had. Here was a two-eyed Wanei who did not lurk in the shadows. If his father craved the night then his mother was a sunny day and it all showed in a happy laugh.

"Uncle Mac!"

Was he teasing? Well then, a good thing. I'll be your Uncle Mac if that's what you want, and easy to say, as he almost does, but you can't spend your life as a beach bum. But Harry beats him to it, pouring out his ideas in an attack of verbal incontinence: I can't live like this. You could say it's too good for the likes of me, a London boy, but that's not the point, I've seen the world, and I want to be a part of it before I reject it. Let it break me if I cannot break it, he suggests, which is all, Mac thought, the world is fit for. Any of this is better but the boys on the beach might as well be London boys. They're just as likely to take your shirt and love you at the same time.

[][][]

The picture – the manifestation of the idea – Mac had of Wanei, as he drove away with Harry, was of Wanei madly waving goodbye and, apparently, wildly happy, standing in the sun. Looking back through the car mirror, he saw that Wanei had already turned back towards the plantation. Is it us who have rejected him, or Wanei who has rejected us? Fact is, Mac, no one has been rejected, rather, much rather, the reverse.

I am not going to ask him if he had a good time. Better say nothing. As easy with him as with his mother. Neither are chatterboxes. His father has never had much to say for himself either. He's a thinker, if he's anything. And what on earth is he thinking now? Mac felt guilty. He did not know why. But is it not words, Mac, if not caresses – hardly appropriate at this time – which connect us? It might be said that those who mistrust words are afraid of making connections. Men of action and all that. Man may wish to be an island, but is that the point?

"It was fantastic."

"What was?"

"My Dad. We did nothing all day but swim and eat and sleep. At night-time we watched the fishermen go out. Then we walked along the beach." And, he might have added, swam and ate and slept. Bald, enthusiastic truthful statements, Harry made, assuming, as he had a right to assume, that Mac would understand. It would take all his life for Harry to fully understand the beauty of that time, to juxtapose it against life's more mundane realities. There was the soporific heat and the hypnotic rhythm of the sea, but, most of all, the moon. Each night more silver than before until it saturated the two men with its magic light, Wanei, in particular, glowing from within, the precise opposite of the light-devouring blackness which had, until now, been his essential characteristic. They had grown closer by the minute, creating, in their isolation, by the very lack of conscious desire or, for that matter, resistance, bonds that would bind regardless of time and distance, all the tighter, in fact, because of it. But Harry, living the moment, was unaware of all this, for now. He was concerned with the adventure, the endless holiday, his father had allowed him. No hurry, no rush to get the thing done. Take it or leave it, drop it even but let the events occur in their own time, if they occur at all. The two were never apart. No point in being apart. The point was, Harry would, in the end, get tired of a pointless existence. That had not been the original idea but it had developed in Wanei's head as he began to know his son and to build up a picture of Harry's life in London, a place not unlike Port Markham only colder and, for some reason, darker, in which people were like the Wallaces or like Mac, the mission being an unnecessary institution because everyone was accounted for, secure and happy in his place.

Endless was the one hard fact about the relationship between Wanei and his son, Harry. Being together on the beach could have gone on for a day, a week, for ever – which, in a sense, it did – but hanging around the beach, the beach was bound to prove a bore to the young man who had things to do, and who, in any event, had, unavoidably, the London temperament, which would have to be worked out on another beach less empty or seductively beautiful. Brighton or Southend, more like. Had Mac not appeared, the time must have come when Harry would say to his father I'm going back to London, and Wanei would say to his son you go. Left behind, Wanei might feel the pang of emptiness which proves love but it would pass to be filled up with what might be called the surety of love. I do not have to behold my true love.

"I'm glad," says Mac. He is. He is, beside the boy, radiantly happy. He wants to sing. "He's a good man your father."

"Yes," Harry replies enthusiastically.

And your mother too, he wants to add but does not because it would cause embarrassment in this men's world. He nonetheless continues to think of her, as the boy beside him recounts the story of which Mac takes small account.

"I think," he says, at last, interrupting Harry, "you should save all this for your mother, unless, that is, you want to repeat it." He laughs to show he is not serious but the boy is not offended. He is too happy for that, watching the dry bush pass by, which is part of the adventure, and thinking of his life ahead in which his father will be a defined figure. He is proud he has his father's blood, swelling, rushing, careering around the inside of his body he is drunk with the idea.

29   Sally

Because he is a different idea to each of them, Wanei stands between mother and son. And because Harry wants to be free and is old enough to be as free as he wants, this is no tragedy but rather in the nature of things.

Affection built on memories, there remains, and the affectionate habits of the years make for a useful language, in which there is no excuse for misunderstanding. Nonetheless, when Harry starts to talk of London, Sally is taken aback: there's no hurry, Darling. But there is: impossible for him to stay in New Sudan separate from his father. He must be on the beach or return to London: there is, Mum. I'm starting school again in a few weeks. Or something like that, because she had forgotten all about London or even why they had left in the first place. Her idea was that they would stay here now, because it was what she wanted. No reason, any longer, for the London end of things. That had all been a mistake: a place separate from Harry and herself. More so now Mac held her in his welcome embrace. All children want to go to London and New York but that doesn't mean they can. This is your home and you have to make the best of it. Don't lay it on me, not returning to London: it doesn't exist. She knew she sounded mad. It didn't need Harry to point the finger at his own head. I'm going to pack is what he said but did not add I have the return half of my ticket. There's Mr Pierce and Mavis for a start, the people I have chosen for myself. But he was only doing what anyone would do so she couldn't shout after him don't talk to your mother like that. The tears were pushing up from her stomach, and she wanted to run to Mac, to beg him not to let them take me away, but she swallowed hard, and sat down carefully upon the armchair, with the new thick foam cushions covered in the bright cushion covers she had made.

Thus she looked out towards the sea, which was disappearing under a purple, velvet sky, the first stars showing. It's all being sucked down the eternal plughole, she thought, with a snigger, but the emptiness left behind frightened her. Yes, Sally, you bad girl, you idiot, you naughty girl, you have your commitments. Go back and attend to them, your husband, David, your daughters. What would Mrs Willis say? Stay, for God's sake stay. The curtains in the front room, the afternoon sun will be bleaching the colour from them and David will not have drawn down the blinds, the Persian rug upstairs ruined. Alice leaving bits of food around to spite me. My house, I must save it, put the books straight upon the shelves from Jane Austen to Emile Zola, so much to read I haven't done Proust. I'll get Mrs Willis to send things out because I don't want to leave this man Mac, who is real because I cannot read him like a book. He is not a character. He has no bloody beginning, middle and end. If I go back to London it will never let me go and Mac will die of old age while I am away because if I leave this, none of it will exist.

"Mum, where are the binoculars?"

"The what?"

"Dad's binoculars."

What does he need them for? Cannot he see the world perfectly well without them? Might as well look through the wrong end for all the sense it makes. The idea! Of going back to all that, of having to explain all those things which now make up my life like a confession you abandoned your daughters you wicked, wicked thing but Mrs Willis understands. Does understanding a thing make it less bad?

"I've got them," she replies, I'll take them back to him along with my ... my contrition. There, "I've put them in my bag," alongside the books I haven't read. You wicked thing.

"Thanks Mum" And the young man whose height makes her wonder how he can pass through the door without banging his head leaves her to sort herself out.

[][][]

Sally sleeps on her own. She wants Mac to be apart from her restlessness, she wants only her own hands to caress her own smooth body, which is sticky with the annoying heat. She cannot shake off a recurring dream. I won't, she tells her mother, the two of them stranded in the neat modern flat, above the butcher's shop in Potters Bar, which sells sanitized, pink meat which comes from the hygienic abattoir in refrigerated lorries. I won't, and her mother says, over and over again, you don't have to although they ought to drive the animals down the green lanes from the Welsh Hills to London, and the man down below would be large and ruddy chopping the meat into chunks, raw and bloody, the splintered bones worth the gnawing after the soup. The large and ruddy man is grinning above his bloody apron, he is not the pink young man in the nylon coat who deliberately cuts into cubes the meat which has been, in fact, butchered by a machine in a factory in Park Royal. All you do is add an Oxo cube to give it man-appeal or I could let you have a packet of Walls sausages done up in cellophane. But he is nonetheless a strong young man, and he has Mr Prynne's hands so that there are Mr Prynne's large, warm feet coming out of their warm socks on the kitchen floor, mottled blue linoleum. Dark hairs and white, virginal skin but he had to go because, of course, it was mother who was tempted. Sally giggles in her sleep but there is blood on the apron which is her blood which she cannot flush down the lavatory. I was so ashamed. For some reason.

In the morning she is shiny damp and her bones ache but I'll be fine after a shower so Mac does not bother to worry and is no more willing to consider the consequences than is she. Yes, he replies, to Harry, tomorrow morning we will check your tickets to confirm which flight will take you to Hong Kong. Mac, the idiot, imagines their parting at Port Markham airport, the boy excited, Sally, apparently blonde and radiant, her eyes looking at something in the landscape. Look after your mother and good luck he says as he gives Harry a hundred dollars. Mac you shouldn't. Goodbye, kiss-kiss because one does and they're gone. He goes back to the house which is full of ghosts. And it is not as if Harry no longer cares for his mother, it is that he is a hundred feet tall and she as tiny as a field mouse.

They do the usual Sunday things but they might as well be old friends who have met for the day, let's do the same thing next year. Mac thinks of Sally only in terms of her absence. Sally thinks, increasingly, that she would like to lie down on her bed below the window with the view of the recreation ground, and sleep. I'll bring you some toast and you can listen to the radio, says her mother. About four o'clock just as Mac is suggesting they go for a swim, she is violently and painfully sick. Mac is hauled across the coals by the doctor at the mission hospital its Malaria you of all people should have known better, she's sixty per cent dehydrated she could have died. They put her on a drip, drug her, and leave her.

[][][]

At one stage, Sally shouted out that the bed was intolerably uncomfortable. There's something sticking into my back. It's killing me, and then, thank God, she was turned over by capable hands and the last thing she felt was a pin-prick in her left buttock.

She saw the grubby-white ceiling through the slowly rotating blades of the fan. She had just been lain on a crisp, white sheet. Another was being drawn up over her body just as she made up her mind to open her eyes properly. The stern features of a nonetheless kindly face smiled down at her. Sally thought: I don't know you from Adam, or rather Eve. Or do I? A smile was obviously expected in return so she gave one. It made her feel much better.

"Well done," said a voice, antipodean but familiar: "You've had a good sleep."

The nurse – it must be – wore a brief white coat which hugged her spare body suggesting beneath, clean nakedness. She stood up straight in order, it seemed, to have a good look at Sally, cool, calm and awake for a change. Brown arms folded, she was, Sally, decided, a no-nonsense athlete, an Amazon even, about to throw off her clothes and streak manfully across the plains. Her hair, for the time being held back, would be streaming in the cool breeze made by her own movements. In London, it would be cut in a short bob and she'd be wearing, of course, a man's shirt, reassuringly androgynous. Sally grinned at the shining black eyes of a bronzed god, or rather, goddess.

"I'm Madeleine. They call me Mad."

"Another one!"

"Indeed. I must go. I'll be back in a jiff. You rest." She was looking at the temperature chart.

When Sally opened her eyes, it was night. Mad was sitting beside the bed holding a paperback book bent back in one hand[5]. Her legs were crossed so that one knee pointed, accusingly, it seemed, at Sally, who said.

"What time is it?"

Mad put the book on the bed where the fan ruffled the pages.

"Eight o'clock, I'm off so I'm only attending to you." Her hands were large for a woman's but beautiful.

The hands that have handled me and re-arranged my body, thought Sally. I wish you'd handle me again but what she said was.

"What day is it?"

"Wednesday."

"So I've been here nearly two days. I must have fainted. What happened?"

"A week and two days, a lifetime, more like, cerebral malaria and you've been a lot of trouble," Mad laughed, "but it's all over now. You're past the worst."

"I'm sorry."

"Forgiven, forgotten, it never happened. My bruises are going down."

Sally wanted to ask more but the effort was too much. The book on the bed weighed a ton. She tried to reach it but the effort was too much. She closed her eyes for a second, and when she re-opened them there was an old man sitting beside her.

---

[5] *The Tiger in the Smoke* by Margery Allingham

"Where's Mad?" she said, but he only smiled and by the smile she knew it was Mac. She wanted to ask if he was alright but no sound came and she was not even sure if her mouth had moved. Well, she thought, he looks OK, so she forgot him.

It must have been the middle of the night it was so quiet. She felt a lot better but tired.

"If I shut my eyes I won't want to open them again," she managed to say to Mad.

"That'd be easier for me, I've had you on my hands for a long time. Just the two of us."

"But what was all the commotion last night?"

"Two nights ago. They tried to cut off the head of the patient in the next room." Mad laughed good-naturedly.

Sally felt a giggle coming up: "Why?"

"Oh, some family feud. But you were as good as gold. You weren't afraid at all. I was proud of you. You'll do well here."

Sally was overwhelmed with happiness. Then, as suddenly, bitterly disappointed, but not a bit ashamed.

"Oh, but I have to go home. I'd forgotten," and she tried to get up but as Mad looked at her she felt her energy, what little she had had, dissipate. She fell back on the bed, exhausted. "I have to take my son back to London," she whispered.

"Such a nice boy," said Mad, as if she was going to say it anyway. "They'll be in Hong Kong by now."

"Oh, so I've been left in New Sudan after all." She didn't mind at all. She felt like laughing although, she supposed, it was not a laughing matter. She felt that Mad was looking at her but the light was too bright to be sure.

"Something like it."

Wonderful what strangers will do for you in times of need. And if I'm dead, they'll not miss me, or care. They will a little but it won't last long. They have their lives to live. They're young, even David is not so old. They're all free to take what they want, and there will be times of radiant happiness, without you hanging on to them. My daughters, the one clever, the other beautiful. But I don't want to hang on to them. I don't even like them, much, ever since ... they ceased to need you, ever since they let go of the nipple. They are truly the blessed ones. But I have to prove I am not running away. From where? From what? It's my duty I owe it, I owe it to ... to whom? To what? To England. And Mad screamed with laughter. To a sheep station four hundred miles north of Adelaide. What would your mother have said? She'd have said, she'd have said ... Sally thought of the wedding. Her mother had been glad to get rid of the pair of them at the time. No more lodgers, and the bedsit idea had been Sally's, not her mother's. A cheap baby-sitter.

She put out her hand, wanting to make the connection. Mad took it, and together they raced across the grassy plains, naked and burnished gold by the sun. Summer in the Steppes of Central Asia. The book her father had never got around to writing. Music by Borodin.

[][][]

He had worked it out in his head like the plot for a novel, revelling in the swirl of ideas as he drank the free wine and listened to the loud music through the earphones. *Symphonic Variations* by César Franck. Clever, concert-hall stuff written for a large industrial orchestra for a semi-educated middle-class audience that liked a good tune, or two. No better than marching music, he thought later, when the tune came back, marching the young men off to die in the trenches. But here, he enjoyed the boom, boom, boom, as the ideas, the one now more fantastic than its predecessor careered around the empty spaces inside his head. The high, he knew, would be followed by the low, which would, this time, be short-lived and bearable in the knowledge of Sally being with him for the rest of his life. Indeed, I know, there will be little storms: she is, after all, a woman. But the fact was, the fact was, that when you were stuck in New Sudan, you were stuck. You could not run off anywhere. You had to work things out; together; and they would. He smiled at the passing air hostess who apparently ignored him but returned with another bottle of free wine. That old man will hardly be able to stagger off the plane but he's no trouble, and he's forgotten how old he looks as he makes passes at me. Bless him. Thank you, said Mac, all the same, and then forgot what he had wanted to say. Oh yes, My Dear. He was not, never had been, the type to pinch bottoms. Of course, she'll need persuading but that won't be difficult because she wants to be persuaded. All I have to do is put forward a coherent argument against which she'll have no defences. Am I not the erudite man of experience who, well into his sixties, is fit and wiry and attractive to a woman like that? Am I not the one, he marvelled, looking at the air hostess, who did not know what on earth he was talking about, who put the, the bloom back into her cheeks? She crept ... No, she had not crept, furtively, she had strolled, as bold as you like, because she knew what she wanted to do, into my room and casually, wilfully, stripped off whatever she'd been wearing and got into bed beside me, as if, as if we'd discussed it before and decided to do it while the boy was asleep. Carnal knowledge between consenting adults, and all that. You know what I mean, he had wanted to say to the air hostess but she had gone off to attend to some other old customer: smile, humour them and disarm them with your charm. Dis-charm them with your arm they used to say when they were training but if you slap a face on board it can cause an incident, and you'll lose your job. But it had been entirely unexpected. I had not thought about it not because I am a gentleman, or anything like that for God's sake, but because I assumed however much I adored her, I was, in her eyes, a repulsive old ruin. And yet she came. She snuggled up beside me and my disgusting old smells, and as I clasped her buttock in my hand all the old responses returned as fresh as when I was a boy.

They had not said a word at first and he had so badly wanted to take the emaciated little head in his hands. Neither could he kiss her forehead above which the hair had been cut she looked like a little boy. He had said.

"Could you eat something?"

"Not even for you, I'm afraid, just now."

"Then for the nurse. She'll be cross if I don't feed you. I'm terrified of her."

"Alright."

So she drank the thin salty soup which he had fed her spoon by tiny spoon but it made her feel sick so he gave her the salt and sugar water which they fed to the babies with diarrhoea. She drank it from a plastic mug sip by tiny sip. The effort had exhausted her.

"My head burns," she said and put up her hand to brush away the hair which was not there. "My hair," she whispered.

And he had laughed: "They had to cut it off. You look so cute, like Mia Farrow."

"But you're not a bit like André Previn," and the joke cracked the ice a little before she closed her eyes.

The house was as neat and tidy as it had been before. The chairs lined up along the back of the veranda as if nothing had happened. Only it had because there were the new colourful cushion covers she had made. She's escaped, was my first thought, but then with relief I realized she must still be up at the hospital. They wouldn't have let her come home alone. I was ecstatically happy, walking on air, you could say, as I went out to find her. There is always a wise, grey-haired American doctor at these mission hospitals in the South Pacific. I had known a succession of them. This one – he was bound to be – was younger than me but I still assumed his superior knowledge of the way things worked, or, at any rate, happened. I wanted to cry like a boy and hear him say you'll get over it, there're plenty more fish in the sea these English women are not worth it in the end, I can tell you. All form and no original ideas he hadn't liked Sally, or any woman for that matter. But he'd more likely say you old fool you're the one who should've died. What's the good of you? He could not have been more than sixty. I hated him but he smiled kindly and said: you missed her by minutes. Do you want to have a look? I said yes. So I did. She looked like a little boy. Like Mia Farrow, I thought, with her hair cut off, and it made me laugh, and I did feel she was laughing with me, so I felt alright, not so much sad as empty of my life. I knew my own time had come also, whether I waited ten days or ten years.

I packed her things in the suitcase which I put under the bed of the room she had used. Then I took it out again and put it on top of the bed. If you look at it you can see the view out of the window as well. I have not been in the room since. Within a week Simon had made the whole house as if she had never been, indeed a machine in which to live. And die.

[][][]

Nonetheless, the family in London could not brush off the death of the woman who had stood for mother, for wife, so easily. It was less ... sanguine, was the word David eventually used, when he explained what he thought she would like to hear, to Mary Willis, who, nonetheless seemed strangely absent. He knew he was lying. She knew also. She didn't blame him. She didn't blame him for feeling a sense of release. He said as much to himself at the corner of the Earls Court and Old Brompton roads: I can do what I like. As if he had not been able to before! But acting, in his London way, he had meant to ask Mrs Willis for her advice: no really, Mary, please tell me what to do. He wanted her, his wife's friend, to think well of him. He wanted her to like what he presented to her even though that he knew she saw right through him. He knew also, he was only the incidental father of the children Sally had left behind but wanting to be seen to do the right thing, he did, indeed, do it. He did what a woman like Mary Willis, but not Mary Willis herself, might have advised: keep the house going until they get used to their mother not being in it but get rid of it as soon as they don't need it. A house without a mother, a guiding spirit, the real Mrs Willis would have said, is a useless thing full of ghosts, to which Sonia, for one, might succumb. What the real Mrs Willis thought, but did not say, was that David ought to leave London for his own good, and don't end up in David Pryce-Williams' perfect house in Islington. And, she thought, getting used to life without Sally is something we have to do. She might, after all, be doing no more than staying out there for a year which is what Mac had thought of, and then see if duty calls because if they can do without you for a year they can do without you forever. So they had to do without her as it happened, with the benefit of not being able to say she's abandoned us. David, the official David, member of the board David, did resent the loss of the official Mrs P-W but the glimpse of a Jojo or Winston at the bottom end of the Earls Court Road soon put that idea out of his head.

David had said to Mrs Willis: join us for the meal. He needed her. She had said: no I can't come, I'm busy. You must deal with this on your own. Afterwards, if you come to me I am bound to help you. He did not talk to her ever again, not even at the wedding.

30   Alice

Before, she would have ignored her father, or said No to his face, knowing she could get the better of him by challenging his dignity, by hurting him in front of the others. Her mother, on the other hand, could not be so easily contained, or defined. Her mother would demand their attention, insist upon her position at the centre of things. Not by her sudden outbursts of bad temper. You could laugh at those. They had laughed, when smaller, uncontrollably, despite, because of, their embarrassment, having accepted the magnificent gesture of the broken plate. But the tears that followed. Then, cold and white, rigid with anger herself, all she could do was walk out on her mother and go to her room, defeated. Then she hated, actually made herself hate, all of them in equal measures: her father's distant helplessness, her mother's stupid histrionics, her brother's careless snigger. But beyond her deliberate hatred of them all as a single hateful thing which damned her to tears of frustration because she knew she ceased to exist for the hateful three of them, the moment she left the room, beyond all that, what she fled from was the downcast, the defeated attitude of Sonia whose suffering and compassion was the most unbearable thing of all. Sonia used to say, when she was very little – later she could only express it by looking down into her plate, her face burning – Why can't we all be happy? Her mother snapping back at once: because it's not the human condition and never will be. Then why can't we all love each other like Jesus says? As if you could turn it on like a tap! Oh, go love a cow, I screamed at her. Love is one thing but expressing it is another. I loved my mother but I wish I'd had the courage to slap her face, and make her look at us. I'd slam my bedroom door, all the same, so they'd know where I was, and Sonia'd follow me a bit later with little knockings on the abused door. Go away, I'd mumble just loud enough for her to hear, I don't want you. It was Sonia I loved the most so it was her I wanted to hurt the most. Who else was worth spending my love on? In those days? And she'd go away but I knew she'd return – again, and humbly again if necessary – I've brought you some pudding, until I let her in because I was hungry. Mummy's alright meaning they'd started to wash up as if nothing had happened, and we'd plot some horrible revenge against Daddy like cutting up his favourite tie.

Now, it was different, My Mother, thinks Alice, is no longer here to attract our attention. I have My Father at my mercy but, and here she forms the words in her head like a quotation, I have no desire to have him so. It made her feel free, no longer oppressed by her family.

She looks at her father who is messing around at the cooker, squatting on the floor apparently unable to work out how he should remove the large Pyrex dish from the oven. He is using a tea towel instead of the oven gloves so it is bound to slip out of his hands to smash on the floor a mess of meat, pasta, tomatoes and broken glass. A fitting memorial to the woman whose name is never mentioned.

Sarah, Susie, Sally, was it? Because the woman they called Mummy, my wife, Darling, for God's sake because she was not a dear thing too bossy by half is an idea from the past as relevant to them as, as the Glorious Revolution. They are not efficient yet but this ill-matched, ill-assorted, crew, as it were – which does not work very well together but will nonetheless muddle through – feels, each one of them, released, the breath of freedom one felt on the first day of the long school holidays here was your real life out of which you could bite large hunks at will or else, save it for later the choice is yours. They each felt it with a greatly suppressed emotion which might explode at any moment, probably as infectious laughter and David would be able to say Yes, that is how it is, I read it in a book, you do not have to be ashamed of being alive. But they remain silent and Alice watches her father, surprised to see he is a young man because he is no longer the man in her life. He has lost weight but he is a bit pathetic, dressed in fashionable London clothes bleached cotton twill trousers and a pale blue cotton shirt, because his hair is thinning from a little pink patch on the top of his head which she would like to touch and say I'm sorry.

"Here, Dad, I'll do that, you lay the table," which he does, ordering the others to obey which they do because this is the last meal they will eat together as the family they used to be with her at the centre.

He said: "I loved your mother." It was true. "I can see that now but I resented her because I wanted to live with someone else."

But they were not listening.

[][][]

As Mrs Willis said, yes, it's what people leave behind that haunts you, things, reminders, which make you regret what you did or did not do. In that respect you haunt yourself with your imagination. David had asked her to go through Sally's things in the bedroom. I want to go in there and find she's gone. I'll do the bathroom myself, it won't take five minutes. The rest of the house is either common property or the children's rooms, and they can do what they like. They're old enough aren't they? Oh yes, but I don't know about you. You are nonetheless old enough to find your way out.

Sonia and Alice had joined Mrs Willis without being asked. They had enjoyed taking the things they wanted and had not been in the least offended when she had refused the things they offered her. When they finally go, she thought, I wouldn't mind the big table in the dining room but it'll never get through the door, and one day I'll sit at it with some other people, not unlike the Pryce-Williamses. In the drawer of Sally's bedside table she found a collection of Somerset Maugham short stories. A bookmark marked a story Sally must have been reading. I'll take this if you don't mind. But they were not listening.

At the weekend David took a load of plastic bags to the Oxfam shop on Fulham Broadway. He burnt all the papers in the garden, making a quick hot fire that would not worry the neighbours. It was easier, in fact, that she hadn't left a will. He scrupulously put all her money into Unit Trusts for the children.

In the end, the only problem was Sonia. It took him a while to get rid of her.

31   And Sonia

Dear girl – it was how he saw her, and it had taken great courage to say it – I only want to help you. All the same, it sounded silly to them both, as if he was some aged Uncle Arly[6]. Don't call me girl. She frowned, the lines between her eyes concentrated, as if she was looking for herself in a dark place. My hair's going grey. He could not see it although, indeed, her hair was a mess. She pushed her fingers through the unruly curls. Pan-scrubber! She smiled at her own literary joke, then clasped her hands together on her lap, squeezing her fingers white. Bad girl. Idiot. Control yourself.

"Go away."

"I can't do that. Someone has to stay with you."

"For God's sake why? Have you appointed yourself as my ... my ... my jailor? Sorry." She nearly reached out to him but her fingers would not let go.

"Because we're both ..." Mad was not the word he wanted. They were not, in the literal sense, inmates of Bedlam or exhibits of the Imperial War Museum. "We're both maladjusted." Then he added, because she had screwed up her eyes as if he had said something maddeningly stupid: "To this world. To this bad world."

"Oddballs? Weirdos? Freaks?"

"If you like, but if you really want me to go, I will."

---

[6] O! My aged Uncle Arly!
Sitting on heap of Barley
Thro' the silent hours of night,
Close beside a leafy thicket:
On his nose there was a Cricket,
In his hat a Railway-Ticket;
(But his shoes were far too tight.)
Etc
Edward Lear

She said nothing, staring at him as if he was something from her own imagination which she had just realized did not exist.

"I'll be in the next room then." He moved to get up. "You can call me."

But she wanted him to be real. He was the type she liked: small, weak looking, his ears and nose too big. He wore glasses and he had a short-sighted stoop. He might have been an entomologist. Perhaps he worked in the Natural History Museum, naming things. He walks the streets because he is afraid to buy a bike and he is an expert on the domestic architecture of London. He met Sir John Summerson at Sir John Soane's Museum in Lincoln's Inn Fields when he was a boy, a teenager, spotty. I bet, she thought, he reads books by the bucketful. But they don't help him and one day he will write a book but not the sort likely to get published. He is, in fact, a realist. He calls himself a scientist: he observes things and draws conclusions. He has a sort of wisdom drawn from books. Secondary data he calls it drawn from E E Cummings and Joanna Trollope. He is the last person to tell her she should not have done it.

"Just bang on the wall." He got up.

"Don't go."

And once they started talking, she did not stop. I must be boring you to death. No, I'll use it in my novel. When she was inclined to stop, he'd prod her with another question which was quite impertinent but essential and to the point. There is no point in beating about the bush he said later when he wanted to lie on the bed with her. No I can see that, she said, feeling more sane than she had for years, you're a mass of contradictions. No more than you.

"You see, as I see it, dear woman with the greying hair ..." He stopped. "Do you mind me saying this? Analysing your family?"

"That family," she corrected, "I don't own them, they might be anybody's. Are you embarrassed?"

"Not at all." He was only saying what he thought. Stating the facts behind the case, as he put it, to which she had not got to listen if she didn't want. "Send me away if you want."

"I don't want."

He was sitting, now, in the only armchair because she was allowed to lie on the bed legs up, shoes removed by his own hands.

"I think it's alright now," he said, "I'll keep you talking. I won't let you fall asleep." But he had, nonetheless, an Arab, a Semitic, look about him. Put him in the sun for a while and he would have burnt as brown as Harry. Let him run around awhile in it and he would become strong and confident.

"I'm hardly likely, the amount of coffee you've poured down me. I'm more likely to walk on the ceiling." She no longer felt like a bad girl. Not even particularly silly, with him there. He made her want to talk. You were stripping me stark naked. You'd have been a priest a hundred years ago.

"You see," he was saying, as he massaged her foot, "you had no one, not just in the end but almost from the beginning. No one wants the third child in England if they've got a girl and a boy. Janet and John, John and Mary."

"But..."

"Yes?"

"I wasn't the third child. I was in the middle. So much for your psychology," which she immediately wished she had not said. She no longer wanted to deflate his ideas. I wanted you to stay beside me. You made me feel safe and I wanted us to start out with honesty this time.

I wanted you to strip me naked. But he wasn't deflated.

"Well you act as if you were, and you admit you let Alice take the lead. And then also your mother would've said she's the pretty one, she's got that, she'll be alright. Harry with his New Sudanese blood, Alice the awkward one, they're the ones who need my help. These are the ones I can mould and make of what I want. Over these ones I can express my power." He had been looking at the floor, but he stopped for a moment and looked up at her: "You were the lucky one. You escaped all that ..."

"Fucking up?"

"Yes."

"But so did they in the end."

"Yes, and New Sudan did that. It ate her up but she had all of you and that man ...?"

"Mac."

"Mac, and your father had his Wisdom and all the other ones, and his house off Essex Road."

"Which he values most of all."

"And Alice got her Rob and that whole blessed family."

"God bless them."

"And Harry has his father. And his art out there. And a string of female admirers if he's what you say he is."

"He's better than that."

"I'm sure he is. I see it in your eyes when you talk about him." He paused, squeezing her foot until it hurt. "When did you last see him?"

"I can't remember. Years ago I went round to that hotel. He had his studio there. He was very kind. He said I could visit him any time. I think he would have let me live there. There were plenty of empty rooms, only ..." She trailed off.

"Only what?" He looked at her on the bed. At a little girl dressed up in all the old clothes she had found in the trunk in the attic, decorated in all the jewellery she has found on her mother's dressing table. But she cannot understand why she is so sad, so she lies down and cries. Her face is swollen and red. She died in an upstairs bedroom in Royal Leamington Spa[7]. He thought of Newington Green Road for some reason, feeling depressed and beginning to understand why she had wanted to do it. In the silence, all the ideas about her began to settle down in his head. Page after close-written page of it until it weighed like lead and he knew that if you put a match to it, it would not burn, it was too dense and ungiving. Her life seemed no less real than his own: southwest London, north London. They would go

---

[7] **Death In Leamington**
She died in the upstairs bedroom
By the light of the ev'ning star
That shone through the plate glass window
From over Leamington Spa
Etc
John Betjeman

to Kensington Gardens by bus. We used to go to Alexandra Palace. Dragged up the hill on hot afternoons. I'll buy you an ice-cream at the top, Dad'd say, look at the view. They'd look at it, the rows of red-brick houses running across the flat valley floor and up the slope on the other side. That's terminal moraine, he'd say and they'd see a lake surrounded by birch trees under a wide sky, the shadows elongating, because one holiday he'd taken them to Sweden and they'd climbed a similar hill and indeed looked across a lake surrounded by birch trees to a low ridge on the other side, brown and naked in the summer heat, rising out of a cushion of dark green, black almost, pine trees: see Mount View Road running along the top? There's Grandma's house with a view over the dusty city. They had seen it, vividly, and remembered it. One summer Dad went off on his own and never came back. It's that dratted ecologist from Uppsala, his mother said. He's taken up with her. I knew he would good riddance.

"Only what?"

She bit her lip. She felt ashamed every time she thought about it but she remembered she was not ashamed in front of him so that her face lost its flush and she looked at him.

"Only Mr Pierce put his foot down. He thought, he knew, I was bad." She interrupted the question on his lips: I did have bad thoughts. I can see that now."

He wasn't going to argue or ask what the thoughts were. He didn't suppose she didn't know her own mind. The lake was as real in North London as it was in Sweden. Just as easy to drown in as to swim across.

She swam on now regardless

"He had let Harry use the big front bedroom as his studio. He said it was too noisy for guests. He said the double glazing would cost a fortune. The ceiling of that room must have been twelve feet high and the window was a massive bay overlooking Kensington Gardens. The old sashes rattled like mad when the lorries went by at night. I'm sure all the noise influenced Harry's paintings at the time. They're manic like the music of whatshisname, Miles Davis."

"How did you know?"

"Know what?"

"That the lorries rattled the windows at night?"

"I used to sleep with him sometimes in the room. I was, I am in love with him. That's what Mr Pierce didn't like."

"What's wrong with loving your brother?" Who was this Mr Pierce? Some sort of judgmental god? A shadow over Harry's life? He did not like the idea of Mr Pierce.

"I didn't say I loved my brother, I said I was in love with him. I wanted to have sex with him. When I was a girl, my fantasy was that he was my husband. I created a world in my head where it was possible. I pretended my parents had been paid a large sum of money to take care of me. That was why they were so distant from me. They couldn't love me because I had not been their baby. I was close to Alice because I had to be. She protected me from my parents' evil intent. That's what I pretended. I thought it all out. Anyway, we shared a bedroom and I quite liked her. Right up until she met Rob Willis she included me in everything she did. I was her right-hand girl."

"But it doesn't make sense," he blurted out before he could stop himself.

"I didn't say it made sense. It's what I felt. It was the little world I made for myself when I wasn't happy. I don't think it's unusual."

"It's not. Go on."

"But all the time I was awfully in love with Harry, and he was always kind to me so I could pretend he loved me ... in that way, too." When Mummy lost it that time and threw the dinner on the floor and Daddy was so hard on her and we all knew we'd fall apart sooner or later, I just felt awful but Harry made me lie on his bed beside him until I was calm. And I was calm, the minute he was beside me. Very big and solid. I shall never forget it. He smelt ..." She smiled, the blush finally dying from her face. "He smelt like boys do, sweaty and not very clean. Really rather revolting but I liked it then and told myself he was my husband and I'd have to submit to him. It was about the time of my first period."

She looked up at the ceiling while he caressed her foot, moving his warm hand towards her ankle. He was calculating, surprised by his own audacity but she did not stop him.

"I was wicked."

"Hardly." He laughed. "You were not. You were not." He squeezed her hard, wanting to hurt her a bit.

"I was. I remember his breathing. He tended to breathe through his mouth as if his nose was blocked. He talks in a breathy sort of way. Whenever I hear a man talk like that I feel bad. I love it. I miss him."

"But it's odd."

"Oh yes, very."

"No, not in that way."

"In what way then?" She pushed her leg towards him, as if she was daring him, wanting to frighten him.

But he wasn't frightened and he wanted to say I can be as bad as you if that's what you call bad. He moved his hand to her calf. He had never touched a woman, another human being, like this, in his life. Flesh on flesh, as he had often thought about it. He wanted to explore her entire body in a kind and gentle way.

"I mean that Harry was more likely to have been, to have not been the child of your parents. Did you not say they pretended he was adopted?"

"Not quite. That's not fair to them. They merely left it to anyone who thought about it to, to draw their own conclusions. But he was definitely Mummy's baby, you see her broad forehead and the way he looks at things sometimes as if he can't work them out. But there is something, something, not mysterious but complicated, about his birth, his being brought into existence. Daddy always treated him as if he was responsible for his ..." She searched for the word. "For his creation. It's not because he loved Mummy. In fact I think he rather disliked her but it wasn't because she'd been unfaithful or anything like that."

"He would dislike her, wouldn't he? The way he is. She'd have been in the way."

"Oh no." She was emphatic and she wanted to defend the people who were, in the end, her parents. She would have sat up only she still felt a bit sick. "Oh no, I'm sure he loved her once, or at any rate valued her. She was just the sort of woman a man like Daddy, ambitious and a bit ruthless, self-centred, would have wanted. But in the end she outgrew him. She controlled him."

"Like she controlled you all."

"Yes, but he hated that, that control, more than he hated her. I think you can only control a woman – if you want her – by loving her and by making her your willing slave."

"And your father's heart was not in it."

"No. Or my mother's. She wasn't going to be enslaved by anyone. She'd rather have died."

"She did."

"Yes, but Daddy didn't kill her although I'm sure he did something which hurt her very much and which would have destroyed her if she hadn't made herself strong and independent. I don't know what it was and maybe it wasn't his fault but it was something that made her hard and brittle and…"

"Tempestuous?"

"A bit, but madly frustrated at times, and difficult. You could love her, but not like her. And, I suppose because, at bottom, we did love her, I suppose we wanted to hurt Daddy for her sake."

"Poor man."

"I don't know." She laughed. "Him and his silly house in Islington. I can't go there without wanting to break something. And that's another odd thing, when I think of it."

He said nothing.

"When I go there I feel awfully guilty. I feel I ought to do things for him."

"Why?"

"Because he's my father?"

"Did you choose him?"

"I might have."

He had not expected that answer

"Do you love him?"

"No!" She laughed again. "I break his things. I drop his old Spode or Delft or whatever it is. I put boiling water in his Ming dish. It cracked and the water ran out onto a table of inlaid yellow wood. He was very upset."

"It was an accident."

"Nothing's an accident, Daddy says. He said unravelling his Sibelius tapes when I was a little girl was no more an accident. Once he shut the door in my face and then opened it and said you'd better come in I can't stop you. He'd done something to his lips. They were fatter than they ought to be. They looked funny on his lean, lined face. He'd make a handsome old man but he wants to be young. He's still got most of his hair."

"Eighteenth-century man in a powdered wig and high heels. No soul."

"Yes, only he's early nineteenth. 1815 is his year. In view of the railways which would have spoilt his house in ..."

"Euston Square."

"Once, I'm sure, he'd put on make-up. It made me feel sorry for him."

"But he doesn't want your pity. No one wants that."

"No, it's a useless emotion. I felt like the Ming dish myself, all the same, just a hairline crack through which the water was pouring. When I was empty I didn't hate him or pity him. I felt nothing. The door is blue with black studs on it. Do you know the Sibelius Fifth?"

"No."

"I heard it live once. At a Prom. It's like Daddy's life. You don't know where it's going but it ends with something final and irrevocable, like the door slammed in your face. Before we were born. But he goes on living to a sort of script. I don't like that part of Islington. There's nowhere to walk except streets. It's the human condition. Not tragic, just pointless."

"What's new?"

"Nothing."

She giggled and nearly threw up.

"I ought to have a bath."

"I'll help you."

Afterwards, they talked and talked until it was dark when he cooked baked beans and made toast and tea. When he was lying naked beside her, face to face, he was surprised by the way his body responded. I didn't think it would be like this. But it is.

The End